MW01485739

DARKROOMS

DARKROOMS

A NOVEL

REBECCA
HANNIGAN

wm

WILLIAM MORROW

An Imprint of HarperCollins*Publishers*

Without limiting the exclusive rights of any author, contributor or the publisher of this publication, any unauthorized use of this publication to train generative artificial intelligence (AI) technologies is expressly prohibited. HarperCollins also exercise their rights under Article 4(3) of the Digital Single Market Directive 2019/790 and expressly reserve this publication from the text and data mining exception.

Lyrics on pages 45 and 338 taken from "Girls Just Want to Have Fun," songwriters: Cyndi Lauper/Robert Hazard

Lyrics © Sony/atv Tunes LLC, Emi Blackwood Music Inc., Beijing Zi Tiao Wang Luo Ji Shu Ltd.

This is a work of fiction. Names, characters, places, and incidents are products of the author's imagination or are used fictitiously and are not to be construed as real. Any resemblance to actual events, locales, organizations, or persons, living or dead, is entirely coincidental.

DARKROOMS. Copyright © 2026 by Rebecca Hannigan. All rights reserved. Printed in the United States of America. No part of this book may be used or reproduced in any manner whatsoever without written permission except in the case of brief quotations embodied in critical articles and reviews. For information, address HarperCollins Publishers, 195 Broadway, New York, NY 10007. In Europe, HarperCollins Publishers, Macken House, 39/40 Mayor Street Upper, Dublin 1, D01 C9W8, Ireland.

HarperCollins books may be purchased for educational, business, or sales promotional use. For information, please email the Special Markets Department at SPsales@harpercollins.com.

hc.com

FIRST EDITION

Designed by Nancy Singer

Library of Congress Cataloging-in-Publication Data has been applied for.

ISBN 978-0-06-341959-9

25 26 27 28 29 LBC 5 4 3 2 1

To James, for everything

PART 1

COMPOSE

Take your time with this bit. Get to know your subject. Wait for the right moment. You'll know it when you see it.

John Lyle,
*The Little Photographer:
A Kid's Guide to Perfect Pictures*

1

CAITLIN

London

Thursday, December 19, 2019

It was three days since Caitlin had slept, and today the shadows had arrived. She knew they were coming by the way the old coffee smell of the office took on a burnt, smoky tang. Like a bonfire had been set somewhere among the computer towers and monitors. Next, the feeling, like a film forming over her skin. The forewarning only served to allow dread to set in ahead of their appearance; these engulfing shadows that seeped in from the periphery. She had learned to live with them, to ignore the stab of alarm each provoked, but still she startled as the office manager's drinks trolley rattled out from the creeping darkness. It was the afternoon of the Christmas party, and Vector Point management were proud to offer the minimum refreshments of cheap beer and tepid pizza. Small comfort: she had only three hours left of her temp job here, which meant she was only four hours away from picking up a tranquilizer from Lola, her friend with a side business, and then maybe five hours from finally sleeping.

Closing her eyes, she laid her palms flat on the desk and took a deep, anchoring breath. If she could face the shadows, they might dissipate.

It's not real. There's nothing there. I am safe.

Her eyes snapped open—*now!*—as she whipped her head around in the direction of the shadows. It worked. The real world surfaced once more from the darkness, and Caitlin found herself staring wide-eyed at the office manager as she completed her rounds. The woman sped away, avoiding her gaze. Caitlin flushed. It was humiliating and frustrating to prove them all right about her and her weirdness.

Her colleagues, the "Vector Point rock stars going above and beyond for your team," had already shed their professional skins, top buttons open and mascara smeared onto cheeks. The temperature crept up, the air grew ever hotter, breath and body heat formed condensation that strained inside the windows.

And then there was the fat, ripe wallet tucked inside Mark's back left pocket. Almost as unignorable as his voice, floating above the tinny speaker sound of Wizzard wishing for Christmas every day.

Caitlin rolled her shoulders and massaged the back of her neck.

It's not real. There's nothing there. I am safe.

The shadows had been contained for now, but she still felt wrong, lost inside the too-big suit of her skin. She turned back to her monitor and the emails that awaited her.

ATTN: Lunch theft is CRIME. Delete.

Caitlin—handover today?? Delete.

Q4 data pull OVERDUE. Delete.

Reminder: valuables not to be left unattended. Delete.

If she could focus on just this one task, on deleting one email after another, she could bring herself all the way back. All she had to do was get through the afternoon. She could do it. She could keep the shadows—and the Hanging Woods—at bay.

"All I'm saying . . ." Mark paused for effect, the way he did, "is that Caitlin is pure filth; she is *gagging* for this."

Caitlin had joined the company on the same day as Mark. They had met for the first time in the lift up from the building's shared reception to the office, both of them nervous and smiling too much.

Guffaws from Mark's audience.

The laughter stung. Caitlin and Mark had sat next to one another for the full six months, both admin assistants. She had taught him how the database queries worked. They had brought each other tea on occasion. She had thought they were friends once.

"You'd want danger money to go near it"—the music cut out, and Mark's words boomed across the office—"but you know what they say about crazy girls."

It. Her.

Caitlin became aware of herself as only a body, an assemblage of parts, nothing more.

With red tinsel draped like a feather boa around his shoulders and the neck of a beer bottle held loosely in his fingers, Mark stood not two feet from where Caitlin sat and talked about her like this.

An awkward chuckle rose as someone hit replay on the playlist. Everyone had heard. No one said anything.

Caitlin could confront him. Then Mark would tell her to take a joke, or repeat his "compliments" to her face. Caitlin could call him out. Then Mark would twist her objection into something that proved they were right; she was psycho. Caitlin could just leave, slink out under the pretense of getting a new bottle from the small kitchen across the hall. Then Mark, and everyone else, would think they'd gotten to her. Mark could do anything. Caitlin could do nothing.

Two months ago, Mark had been taken into a meeting room and made permanent. Caitlin was the first person he told. She was next, he was sure. Caitlin didn't particularly like the job, but it would have been nice to be asked. Since then, Mark's voice was all she ever heard. Boasting, mostly, an occasional sympathetic wince as he told another colleague that he had been chosen over Caitlin. For the record, she'd have thrown herself out of the window before spending six more months either in this office or near him, but no one asked her opinion.

She stood up. She tipped her head back and drained her drink.

Fuck it, she thought. *Fuck this and fuck their handovers.* She strode past Mark toward the drinks trolley. One bottle of wine remained, three-quarters empty and poised over the glass of a distracted accounts girl. Caitlin took it from her hand. Facing the room, she downed the last of the wine straight from the bottle, then slammed it back on the trolley. At her desk, she put on her coat and collected her bag. She approached Mark's group. The pack of white-shirted, sneering male colleagues averted their eyes and sniggered at her behind their beers.

"Mark!" She waved him over to the aisle between the banks of desks. He unfolded himself and sauntered toward her. "It's my last day! I just wanted to say thanks so, so, so much for everything!"

Caitlin pulled him into a hug, then stumbled hard enough to knock him off balance. The men guffawed. They saw her as wasted already, too unaware to know she was the butt of the joke. Mark had been right about this one and they all knew it. *He* knew it. He glanced back at his audience, eyebrows waggling in comedic suggestion, long enough for her to tip that heaving wallet out of his pocket and up the wide sleeve of her coat.

"You coming tonight?" Mark asked, pushing her back into a standing position. He directed his question over her head, at his friends, but he held her by her ribs, fingers splayed underneath and around, just shy of actually touching her breasts. Caitlin numbed herself to the intrusion, as she always had. His wallet rested against her wrist, steadied by her fingertips.

"See you there!" she sang, and stumbled out of the office. The whole place erupted in laughter as soon as the door closed behind her.

She darted into the kitchen space and popped the tops off of all the remaining bottles of beer before dumping them to drain down the sink. *Enjoy your party now, dickheads.*

It wasn't enough. She cast about for something more, for some way to truly hurt them, but there was so little here that anyone could care about. She plugged the sink, dumped the tea bags and coffee filters on top of the mess of beer bottles and turned the tap on fully. The sink would overflow before anyone noticed. It was a tiny revenge, but it helped mollify her. She could leave now.

Before the lift doors closed behind her and carried her away forever, she offered a final middle finger to the office. The doors slid shut, and with that movement came the slithering darkness once more. It needed something real. It needed blood. Sleep would have to wait. Caitlin buried a scream in the crook of her arm.

2

DEEDEE

BANNAKILDUFF

THURSDAY, DECEMBER 19, 2019

Deedee should have been happy. The last two years of studying had all been leading here. To this squad room that smelled like bad coffee and someone's reheated fish curry and vibrated with the constant buzz and trill of mobile phones, landlines, and radios. Motion surrounded her, yet she had spent the last four hours reviewing four seconds of fuzzy CCTV footage. It had ended once again but she couldn't force herself to hit play.

"G'wan and make us a tea, would ya, Deedee?" Connor McPherson, known as Mac, swung on his chair and dropped his head backward to look at her. "Gasping for one over here after the morning I've had." Mac was small, with sharp, beady eyes and a weak chin. He carried himself with the kind of swagger that invited trouble and had the air of a man not likely to fight fair.

"Officer O'Halloran," Deedee corrected him. "And no." She stared straight ahead. Months of Mac's needling had left her brittle. He had even weaponized her nickname, Deedee, bestowed upon her by baby Roisin as she struggled to pronounce "Deirdre."

"Go on with yourself, what are ye even doing?" Mac ambled over to perch on the edge of her desk. "Every one of the rest of us has been out and about, maintaining law and order."

Chuckles from the other officers even as they shook their heads in gentle reproach. Nobody wanted to intervene and none of them would be on her side.

"I'm busier than you if you've got time to wander around chatting shite." Deedee was stung, and her tone missed the jovial we're-all-pals-here quality she was going for.

Still seated, Mac hooted. "I've made more arrests than you've cooked hot dinners. And that's saying something."

A real thigh-slapper, that one.

Deedee felt herself redden and hated herself for it. She wasn't ashamed of having worked in kitchens, yet when Mac spat it back at her, she wished she never had. She searched desperately for something to say, a barb to throw at him. In kitchens she had always been quick, witty. It was only here, where it most mattered, that she was struck dumb.

"Mac, you got that report ready for us?" Florian Carroll called over. "Only I've got to be out of here on time tonight."

Flo had been an old party friend of Deedee's from before either of them had ever dreamt of joining the guards. The memory of swapping pills on the dance floor while music thumped through her chest set butterflies fluttering in her stomach. She swallowed hard.

"Give us a minute, Carroll," Mac called back. His eyes were still on Deedee. "You heard the man, we're in a rush. The sooner you get a round of teas in, the sooner we can all get on."

"Mine's three sugars," one of Mac's cronies called across the room.

It was like a nightmare, the danger getting closer and closer while she was paralyzed. Frozen, she gaped back at Mac, unable to form a retort, unable to do anything.

Should she just do it? Maybe if she laughed while the kettle boiled, made a joke as the tea steeped, she could pretend it was fine. That she wasn't being humiliated.

"Come off it, Mac. I thought we were friends and you're sentencing me to overtime while you bicker? Shameful. Isn't it shameful, lads?" Florian addressed the room, charm beaming over them. "Here, are you not allowed to use the kettle, is that it? Need someone to teach you?"

The energy in the room shifted as one person sniggered, and then another. The tension broke and Mac chuckled, held his hands up in surrender.

"I could do with a master class, yeah." He spoke to Deedee again. "Next time."

He took his time getting up, strolling over to Florian's desk.

Deedee turned back to her computer. Her eyes were blurry—from too much time looking at the screen, of course. She focused on the portraits that lined the walls; every superintendent Bannakilduff had had since the nineteenth century. She recognized only the last few, the portraits taken by Colm Branagh. They had a different energy, something of the man captured in each. Colm was gifted behind the camera; he'd shot his last official portraits from his wheelchair even as the exertion left him exhausted for days afterward. Deedee swelled with pride at his skill, as though by dating his son, some of that talent was conferred to her.

Colm had taken the one of Mac's dad, retired in the early aughts, bristling with arrogance and violence. In his portrait of Doyle, their current superintendent, she saw a defiant hostility at odds with what she knew of her old family friend. Doyle had told her to apply; that here her energy and passion, her strong instinct for right and wrong, all of that would be an asset. It hadn't been yet.

She'd known being a guard wouldn't be all shoot-outs and high drama like in the films, but she also hadn't expected this much tedium or the kind of rubbish men like Mac would put her way. This was supposed to be a job that really mattered. Gardaí were supposed to be respected.

Worse, she was no closer to Roisin's case, to finally understanding what had happened to her sister. Her private investigation had brought her nowhere. When Roisin had finally been declared officially missing, a full and terrible day after Granny had reported it to the guards, the calls had flooded in. She was spotted everywhere from Cork city to Baja, Mexico. Each call sent Deedee's young heart soaring with hope for nothing—only for more crushing disappointment to follow.

She had attempted to follow up on these sightings, at least the ones not obviously by crackpots; calling around to people all over the world or requesting access to public records. She'd turned up nothing. She'd interviewed Summer Solstice Parade '99 participants, combing through the reportage at the time: more nothing.

In her imagination, there were paper files protected by a sleepy guard on the brink of retirement who'd be easily bought off with chocolate biscuits and a friendly chat. In reality, all files were digitized and password-protected, and there was no chance that Deedee had made anything like a friend. Her naivety could make her cringe herself inside out.

Rubbing her fists into her eyes, she took a gulp of water from the bottle on her desk. Her head was wrecked and the hangover wasn't helping. She'd taken the last of her ibuprofen an hour ago and it hadn't put so much as a dent in it. She couldn't keep drinking and going out like she had been when she'd been in the restaurant, not with morning shifts.

No point thinking about it. She couldn't go back to chef work after the way she'd quit Baroque. Which was unfair. The meal hadn't actually *hit* Councilor Niall Wilson, but it was the kind of incident that would always count against her. No one ever cared what led to her outbursts; how the young waitress had knuckled tears out of her eyes as she told Deedee that Councilor Wilson had slid his hand up her skirt. *As a joke, like,* she'd said.

The kind of joke Deedee was sick of.

She restarted the footage for the thousandth time, tapping her finger against the desk on the main beats.

An empty road, a row of houses to the right, a tiny slice of grass leading to a play park to the left. A dark-colored Ford Fiesta with the license plate 152-D-23190 glided into view at the top right side of the screen. *Tap.*

Both the driver and front passenger doors opened. Two large men with dark baseball caps exited the car. The driver's head was out of range of the camera. The passenger kept his head down, but the large black rose tattoo on his neck confirmed him as Jason O'Sullivan. Which meant the other was his brother, Kevin O'Sullivan. *Tap.*

These two were from the next town over, Kinafallia, and they were from a long line of people who wanted things but mostly things other people already had. Just the name made most folk around here purse their lips. You didn't need to know the particulars to know they'd done it, whatever it was.

In the background, at the top right of the screen, the legs and paws of a cocker spaniel puppy were visible as it passed by on the other side of the street. The CCTV footage drained the color, but by the lighter patches on her haunches and the limp in the hind leg, Deedee recognized the dog as Copper, a Romanian rescue pup. Sweet, but too playful for Frank, Deedee's old basset hound. No *tap.*

Some young lad had overdosed on tainted coke in the playground across from here. The papers were full of what a waste it was, his bright future no longer on the horizon and so on, but Deedee could read between the lines. He'd dropped out of college, barely passed his Leaving Cert in the first place, wasn't going anywhere. Depressed. Anxious. The type who knew all the excuses.

Jason O'Sullivan, with his tattooed neck, patted the top of the car as he waited for his brother to join him. Kevin, all steroid muscles under a hoodie much too small for him, passed under the camera. *Tap.*

Deedee paused the footage with both men in frame. Jason's hands were shoved into the pockets of his tracksuit bottoms. Kevin's were held loosely by his sides, one holding his phone, the other obviously empty. If there were drugs on their person, well, they could be any-where. She hit play once more.

The pair strode out of frame without a look back. They were gone. *Tap.*

"How's it going?" Superintendent Doyle appeared in front of her desk. He was tall, ever smiling, and ruddy-cheeked, and she desperately wanted to prove him right about her potential.

"Good. Good, yeah. There's definitely something there," she bluffed loudly, for the benefit of the room.

Doyle moved to look at the screen with her. "Play it again for me, would ya?"

"It's only a couple of seconds." Deedee scrambled to think of something smart to say. She'd barely passed her Leaving Cert herself—understandable, given her circumstances—and at times like this, when she knew they wanted an answer but she couldn't give it, she felt stupid and ashamed. She'd had a lot of these moments during training. It never got less excruciating.

"Reckon I've got the time to watch it again so."

Deedee hit play. She tried to gauge the superintendent's reaction without turning to stare at him as the video played.

"Well," he said. "Not a lot there."

"Not a lot," she agreed. She caught herself drumming her fingers on the desk and stilled her hands.

"We'd like a couple of witnesses really. Someone who could say they'd seen the brothers in the park with the kid."

"We door-knocked, but no one was talking."

She had, it was true, albeit perfunctorily, because no one around there was ever happy to talk to the guards.

"What's it saying to you then?" Doyle asked.

"The car is properly registered and up-to-date," Deedee stalled. Around them, the squad was quiet, waiting for the punch line. She could practically hear their ears straining to listen in. She thought of

Copper's silky spaniel ears. Copper would be a good witness. The gears turned once more, and—

"Sir, a cocker spaniel walks past, and it's Copper. I know her."

"You know the dog?"

"Well, I mean, there's a language barrier, obviously." She chuckled nervously. "I see her when I'm walking Frank."

"Are you sure it's her?"

"It's not just the coloring, but the limp; she was in some kind of accident, that hind leg is mangled." Deedee was on friendly enough terms with the owners. A tall, slender man with a scratchy beard who wore band T-shirts with names Deedee had never heard of, and a very short woman with purple cat-eye glasses and bold lipstick choices. Not that Deedee judged, but they were definitely the kind of do-good hipsters you'd picture when imagining the type of person who'd have the notion to import a stray from abroad. Weren't there any mutts left in Ireland?

"You know what to do?" Doyle was already straightening, already leaving her to her own devices again. He was proud of her. He trusted her.

Deedee did know what to do, and she nodded, invigorated, as she logged the lead in the system. She had always known, she just hadn't anticipated that her life outside of this office could collide with the crime they saw in here.

Did ya see that, Mac, you prick? she thought.

"Great stuff altogether." Doyle gave her a final nod of encouragement and left for his private office. As his door closed, a mocking "Finally!" was called across to her and met by a chorus of snickers around the room. It hadn't even been Mac that time.

As the nascent pride that had blossomed in her chest died, Deedee remembered that this was the dream. She was supposed to be happy now.

It didn't feel a thing like she'd thought it would.

3

CAITLIN

The puddles filled with streetlights. A pub crawl of Santa hats and waving glow sticks clattered past Caitlin as she entered Tooting Bec station. This close to Christmas, the city constantly teemed with revelers.

Mark's wallet held a wad of twenties, a baggie of white powder in the coin pocket. She clucked with satisfied faux sympathy. What an evening he'd been planning and what a joy to ruin it.

On the platform, the train was still four minutes away. Even as London froze, the Tube remained boiling. Heat—from people as well as trains—sank into the limestone of the tunnels and remained trapped there forever. Back against the wall, she pressed her bare palms to the tiles behind her, knowing that the heat impression of her temporarily victorious body, hot blood and beating heart, would still echo down here in decades to come.

At the rumble of the approaching train, she peeled herself from the wall. She'd need to kill a little time before she could meet Lola, but she was closer to relief. The brakes screeched as the carriages flashed by. The first wasn't even half full of passengers. The second was a little more populated, but her eyes snagged on something—someone—

in the blur. The impression of a sharp little jaw under a familiar tangle of brunette curls.

Roisin.

Caitlin hurried alongside the train, weaving her way through waiting passengers on the platform. She needed to catch up with Roisin. The doors beeped while she was still at the fourth carriage, where the crowds were thickest. Jumping on, she resigned herself to slithering forward through the fray. She ducked under arms, holding her nose against the warm stinks of body odor, perfume, cologne—a full assault on the senses. She weaved through knots of commuters, catching the odd beat of music or snatch of a podcast that leaked from their headphones. She slipped past laughing groups of tourists and averted her eyes from the easy pickings that tempted her: box-fresh iPhones peeping from pockets, handbags dangled carelessly, gaping open.

Finally, the second carriage. Emptier than she'd expected; her eyes found those curls immediately. Roisin, her head now limp and bobbing in sleep. Caitlin's breath caught in her throat.

No scent of bonfires now, no creeping shadows. This was real.

They entered the next station, and Caitlin, fearful of losing Roisin again, hurried to get to her before the doors opened. Yet, drawing closer, she could see something wasn't quite right. The features that should have been resolving into familiarity were warping instead. This Roisin was too pale and her hair was clearly dyed. Caitlin's stomach flipped and curdled as she drew closer and remembered.

Roisin would be grown-up by now. She wouldn't be some coltish teenager.

This was just some girl.

Teeth clenched, Caitlin dropped into the seat opposite the girl who wasn't Roisin. Shadows slid back into the corners of her vision. The girl's head bounced up for a second, then lolled back against the window behind her. A crumpled brown paper bag of fast-food wrappers was at her feet, a light jacket balled up next to her. She didn't look anything like Roisin now.

Roisin had been a coiled spring, wary and watching, existing in a cloud of breathless energy. What was wrong with Caitlin that she was seeing her ghost again? She caught her lower lip between her teeth and nipped and scraped at it, searching for that hot metal taste of blood. It had been six months at least, but Roisin was haunting her again.

A stop later and a man strode into the carriage, his face in his phone. Caitlin registered him in the corner of her vision without moving her head, the way a rabbit notices a fox; the way all women alone in confined spaces make note of strange men nearby. She kept still, chewing on her lip and pushing her nails into the meat of her palm. The man paused, swaying for a moment, as he chose his seat. His expensive leather shoes shone. He was clean-shaven, and had the kind of jawline that belonged on an ad campaign. The girl, her head still back, throat exposed to the ceiling, didn't notice any of this. The man slid into the chair next to her. The rest of the carriage was quiet, near empty. Caitlin felt like she was trapped under ice, stuck watching the girl who wasn't Roisin. The memory of chasing her through the train was unnerving. Smoke scratched in the back of her throat as the shadows gathered themselves once more.

At the next stop, the carriage emptied further. The man slumped. His knees opened wide and he spread his elbows out into the seats either side of him, nudging into the girl's side. His weight and the shuddering movement of the Tube tipped her head against his broad shoulder. He turned his attention to the girl, his eyes wandering over her slack face and limp body. Assessing her.

They were moving from the outskirts of London into the center; the train should have been filling up. Caitlin thought back a few stops; there had been people. Now it seemed that the world was shrinking—no, the world was the same size but the people were disappearing, as though the shadows were absorbing them, isolating her. Was any of this really happening?

The man shifted his body closer to the girl. He snaked his arm behind her head, along the top of the seat, his hand curled slightly above her shoulder. He was so close to touching her.

The girl shifted a little, as though she sensed him but lacked the strength to move. Her eyes stayed closed. Caitlin focused on her, studying her so she could evict Roisin from her mind and come back to the present. The girl was just a kid, but she was connected to something larger—to a set of loving parents at home, and a boisterous group of glitter-covered friends dancing under a disco ball somewhere in south London. She had taken something, or was just drunk, but this wasn't how she had thought her day would go. Or what she thought her life would become. Whatever was about to unfold, Caitlin would bear witness. She swallowed the blood from her mangled lip once, twice. There was always more blood, no matter how much she swallowed.

The man pressed a fingertip to the girl's cheekbone, which was higher and more delicate than Roisin's. There was no response from the girl, but the pressure of his finger drained the blood from the flesh he had touched, leaving a white circle behind. He watched as the girl slept on.

How many thousands of Tube journeys had Caitlin taken and how often had she passed men like this? The truth was, the world was full of them and the sooner the girl figured that out, the better. The truth was, you couldn't blindly stumble onto some train and expect to be saved from the horrors of the world. The world didn't owe her that and neither did Caitlin. Roisin hadn't been spared. Horrors were always waiting; horrors didn't care about Christmas or holidays or—

Birthdays. That was it.

The train was slowing once more and the man was slithering closer to the girl, and Caitlin remembered it was—would have been—Roisin's birthday. Except that Roisin had stopped having birthdays twenty years ago. Hot blood slid down her chin as a smile twitched across her face. No wonder she had mistaken this child for Roisin. It all made sense now.

They pulled into the station. Caitlin brushed her thumb across her wet chin. She ignored the man's wary eyes on her. The girl let out a soft groan. The train shuddered to a stop and a noisy hen party crowded into the carriage. Caitlin threaded herself between their outstretched limbs as they passed bottles to each other.

"Isn't she a bit young for you, love?" one of the hens called out in a braying northern accent, Liverpudlian or Mancunian. The kind of city Londoners looked down on. The kind where you looked out for your own.

"Do you know him, babe?" Another joined the clamor.

The doors slid closed and Caitlin turned as the scene began to unfold in the carriage she'd just vacated. The man with his arms up as though cornered by police, and the hens, unsteady in their stilettos, clucking over the girl. She turned away and made for the escalators, dropping one of Mark's twenties into the takeaway cup of a vagrant slumped in a corner.

Roisin still needled at her, still bristled beneath her skin. Her body wasn't big enough for the two of them; her lungs felt like they were seizing up, her heart constricted, her ribs strained to contain them.

Maybe that was just the exchange.

Maybe Caitlin would always share her life with the girl she had killed twenty years ago.

4

DEEDEE

Deedee emerged into the glittering night, colored fairy lights overhead reflected into the damp pavement like confetti under her feet. Town was plastered in laminated flyers for Sunday's winter solstice celebration. Usually Deedee did her best to ignore them. This time she squinted at one on a lamppost. An amateurish collage of Ferris wheel, hot dogs, and balloons, a weird clown figure protruding from the bottom right corner.

After forty years of it, you'd think they could draw up a decent flyer, she thought. At least she wasn't the only one bad at her job. After all, what did she bring to the force? Encyclopedic knowledge of the local dog population. She was pathetic. She turned from the shop window, but in the corner of her eye, the reflection that followed her was hunched and miserable.

A beered-up lad, draped in tinsel, stumbled out of a pub yowling "Silent Night." A gang of girls screeched and reeled outside Baroque. Deedee could tell they were locals almost from the smell of them, how they held themselves, their specific kind of going-out polish.

Twice a year, hippies and crusties, tourists and travelers flooded Bannakilduff. The existing community of New Age blow-ins, all potters or makers of chunky jewelry, set up stalls, ran drum circles, and took the true believers over to the coast to watch the sunset. For the locals, the event revolved around a late-afternoon parade, an opening ceremony, and the fairground that went on until the early hours.

Roisin was last spotted at the fairground, after the summer '99 parade. Deedee had been there with Sean and Maureen to watch Colm declare the festivities open. She hadn't seen Roisin, but she wasn't looking. She hadn't realized then that she had already seen her little sister for the last time.

She had gotten what she asked for. Roisin's disappearance was all her fault.

A tidal wave of accented revelers swept past her on the street, some kind of bar crawl, not locals, and Deedee itched to be alone.

They never found a trace of Roisin, not a scrap of evidence to point to what had happened. Like she just blinked out of existence. If that was the case, couldn't she just blink back into it?

What if it's time to give up?

One verified sighting was made. Roisin had followed Caitlin Doherty into the Hanging Woods. Two nine-year-old girls went in, only one came out.

Twenty years had passed this summer, and the Hanging Woods had been sold. Most of it would be cleared for a new-build housing estate. If there were any clues about Roisin left in there, they would be lost forever. Deedee was out of time.

Lost in maudlin thought, she turned north at the town square, off the high street, away from the partyers and toward the old part of town.

Garda training was in-depth and intense, and everyone came out of it changed, more confident, more able. Deedee had come out more aware of how much she could never know, more unsure.

There were the official rules, written broadly for everywhere, and then there were the community rules.

Official rule: missing children were high priority and not subject to any kind of delay in policing.

Community rule: Bannakilduff wasn't a big, bad city; naughty little girls who wandered off would turn up for dinnertime.

Thus, twenty-four crucial hours had elapsed before Garda McPherson and the rest had taken Roisin's disappearance seriously. They'd been caught up in another situation; Colm Branagh's hit-and-run accident, presumably a drunk driver from the solstice celebration. But even when they had investigated, they'd just accepted what Caitlin Doherty told them. Caitlin said she thought Roisin had been behind her as they both left. That something must have happened on the road between the Hanging Woods and home. A line of inquiry that returned nothing at all.

Then Caitlin left for some art school in England, never to return. With her gone, so was any chance of finding out more about Roisin's last day. Not that that bothered the guards at the time. Mac's dad had been in charge then, and there was no questioning any decision of his.

The streets were quiet up here, and Deedee slowed, headed for the cemetery.

She had a Google alert on Caitlin's name, but nothing ever came through. She was a ghost. She hoped Caitlin's mother Kathleen's attention-seeking genes would emerge eventually. Kathleen Doherty weaseled her way into all the local news. When there'd been a house fire some years ago, Kathleen had craned her head into all the press photos of the still-smoking remains.

Kathleen had returned ten years ago, when the girls would have been around nineteen. There was no triumphant homecoming; she seemed instead diminished by her absence. A roundness to her shoulders, not quite a widow's stoop, but certainly not the regal bearing she'd had.

"Caitlin's no need of me now," she had declared, dropping her bags on Colm and Maureen's doorstep. "On her MFA course in fine art at Goldsmiths, the best art university in England."

Deedee's phone pinged, and she knew without looking that it was the group chat. All her old friends were home for Christmas now, and within twenty minutes of meeting up, Deedee would be told the price of a pint everywhere from Sydney to London—and how much smaller and shittier Banna was than the rest. How far behind she was.

Inside, the church was dark, but the exterior was spotlit in cold white that lent the blackness of the cemetery pockets of visibility. Deedee didn't need the light to navigate by; her body knew the way to her parents.

BARRY O'HALLORAN
1962–1998
SINEAD O'HALLORAN
1966–1998

She spat on a tissue to clear off a hardened clot of bird excrement on the top of their headstone. Granny, who had taken Deedee and Roisin in, was at home in her urn in the living room. Roisin was missing. All that was left was this nickname, Deedee, that felt more and more ridiculous the older she got. It was a reminder that none of them would ever know her as an adult.

At thirty-four, she was already older than her mother would ever be, and what did she have to show for it? She had been out of her mind to think that she could retrain as a guard and solve her missing sister's cold case.

"She would have been twenty-nine today," Deedee reminded the headstone. Roisin had missed twenty birthdays so far, but Deedee would never stop counting them for her. If Roisin was here, they'd be celebrating at Maureen and Colm's. "Almost twenty-two years since . . ."

The accident, they knew themselves. Driving home late at night, too fast, too dark, there'd been a party in town, everyone had been merry. Those roads. It was a freak accident; her dad had driven those roads every day of his life in every condition and had never come to any harm. You couldn't blame a couple sips of a pint for any of it. You couldn't blame them.

Would she have stayed here if her family had survived? For a while, she'd nurtured a dream of moving to New Zealand, but Sean would never agree, and—secret, stupid hope—if Roisin came back, she would look for Deedee here.

What she needed was something to anchor her as a Branagh. Something like a baby.

Cows lowed somewhere in the distance, and then, closer at hand, Deedee heard a crunching underfoot. The sound of a plastic-wrapped supermarket bouquet being trampled.

She opened her eyes and saw a ghost.

A pale white face, mischief in the eyes; Deedee felt like she was falling, the shock sending her head spinning. Roisin, back and safe. Conjured by Deedee's wishing.

The feeling passed in a flash as the figure turned her head. In the moonlight, her hair was fine and blond and straight, and her face! Illuminated, she was nothing like Roisin at all. As Deedee watched, the girl was joined by a gaggle of other kids. They stomped without regard over burial plots, flowers, bodies. Screams of laughter echoed off the headstones, surrounding Deedee.

Deedee was rattled, her head still thick with all the day's resentments and disappointments. Before she'd considered it, she had darted forward. Her fingers scrabbled only momentarily before she grabbed the girl's arm.

The laughter stopped.

"What are you playing at?" Deedee demanded. Her hand wrapped almost entirely around the girl's tiny puffer-jacketed arm in a way that should have made her feel guilty.

"Get offa me!" The girl twisted in Deedee's grip. Deedee had been about to let her go, but now it would look like she was obeying the child. A couple of the kids lingered, watching, unsure of what to do.

The girl continued, voice dripping in condescension, "Omigod, we're only messing!"

Deedee shone the torch into her face. There was something familiar that she couldn't quite place until the girl sneered.

"I said get offa me."

She was the spit of Michelle Quinn: notorious gobshite and no friend of Deedee's.

"I should have known," Deedee said. "You're one of Michelle's, aren't you?"

"What's it to you, like? I'll call the guards on you in a second if you don't let go of me! S'assault!"

"Cop on," Deedee said. "Ye should all be home, not stomping around over graves. You should be ashamed."

Competing images danced in her mind: that she should be able to control these kids and demand their respect; but also, the O'Sullivan brothers lurking, the dark cemetery not unlike the blackness of the Hanging Woods that Roisin had disappeared into. Losses everywhere; full of bravado, these kids had no idea how vulnerable they were.

The girl squirmed and let out a thin, high whine. Deedee realized how hard she was gripping her, hard enough to leach the sensation from the tips of her fingers.

"Quinns have always been trouble, but if I catch any of youse hanging around again, I'll take you in for underage drinking." She shook the girl as she spoke.

"We weren't!" one of the kids piped up.

"You're hurting me!" Michelle's girl's voice was thick with tears.

Deedee let go and watched the child flee, her arm clasped against her body. The others followed.

"Get out of here!" She had expected defiance, rebellion. Finding none, her righteous anger deflated.

The intimacy of the place was ruined; the kids had made a mockery of her. Injured, she left.

She took a winding route through the residential streets that clustered around the high street. Christmas trees filled every window, wreaths hung on doors. When they were young, their parents had pretended that all the festivities in December were actually for Roisin. Being born so close to Christmas, they never wanted her to feel left out compared to our Lord and Savior Jesus Christ, which was fair really, as he did tend to get the headline.

Deedee's front door was undecorated, but baying and the scrabbling sound of dog claws on tiles heralded her arrival. Five years old when they'd adopted him and already considered unappealingly old and stinky, Frank was now ten and smelled worse than ever, but Deedee felt something loosen in her chest as she buried her face in his fur.

Sean appeared behind him, his familiar bulk reassuring. Deedee held out an arm to him, and he lowered himself down to join her and Frank.

"Oh Dee." He remembered, of course. "I'm sorry."

"It's not just that," Deedee began, but how to express it all? Humiliated, ashamed, sad. So much sadness.

Sean murmured something reassuring, and suddenly Deedee was sobbing. Frank snuffled at her tears, jockeying to get closer to her as Sean held her.

"Is there anything I can do?" he asked, a tinge of desperation to his voice. He was as uncomfortable with her tears as she was.

"I just need to get myself together." Deedee tried for a smile.

"At least," carefully, in the gruff voice that he knew would crack Deedee up, Sean said, "she wasn't stranded in the torrential rain after missing the last bus home."

Deedee snorted, transported back to Sean's most memorable birthday, his thirtieth, five years earlier, when they'd huddled together, soaked through, in a stinking coach station in Limerick for four hours until the first bus.

"Casualties of the craic." She looked up at him, his own eyes misted over behind his glasses. They'd been having too good of a time, she hadn't wanted to leave the pub until the very last minute, until it was too late.

Sean shrugged good-naturedly. She knew he was remembering the Moët champagne she'd produced from her overnight bag, part of his gift, that they had guzzled like it was a five-euro swill, letting it run down their chins and explode from their mouths in laughter. They hadn't cared how cold or hard the tiles were, or what the source of that station's stench was. A happy disaster.

When things were good between them, they were golden.

"Are you OK?" Sean asked. "I just got back from tutoring. I was going to pop over and help Ma with Da for a bit this evening—plus, she's fussing about the development again—but . . ."

"How is he? How was tutoring?" Deedee asked.

"Da's . . . Da." Sean replied. Colm Branagh had been severely infirm since the accident and Sean's ma was his primary caretaker, so Sean tried to help out as much as he could. "Tutoring's tough. I don't know what they're teaching them."

He'd taken on giving Leaving Cert maths tuition recently, his reputation as an accountant prompting local parents to start bothering him—after mass, at the SuperValu, in the pub, wherever they came across him. Finally, he had capitulated. It was a natural next step anyway, continuing the family tradition of service to the community.

"I could stay here," he offered, checking his watch. "For a bit, anyway."

"No, I should go out." If his parents needed him, then Sean Branagh would go. It was just a question of how much they argued about it before it happened, and today Deedee didn't have the spirit.

"Why don't you wear your new boots?" Sean beamed. He'd gotten them for her after a bad fight last month. "That'll cheer you up."

Secretly, Deedee called them the Guilt Boots. They'd cost her an awful night of tears and recriminations, followed by judgmental glares from the neighbors the next day. Everyone knew Deedee O'Halloran was a hothead who made a fuss about nothing.

"Good idea." She summoned a smile. "Show them off a bit. The girls are in town."

"The girls are back! The girls are back!" Sean chanted to the tune of the Thin Lizzy song, shimmying and waggling ridiculously until Deedee couldn't help but laugh with him. No one could make her laugh like Sean.

"Good luck with development stuff. Tell her she'll love having new neighbors—think of the gossip." His parents' place backed onto the Hanging Woods. Once the trees were razed, they'd lose their privacy.

Sean rolled his eyes and kissed her before leaving.

Once the door closed, she headed for the bathroom, phone in one hand, wine bottle in the other. The girls in the group chat were talking about what they'd be wearing this evening. She texted, *Jeans n nice top xx*

The girls meant well. It was just that they would always have a big moment about Roisin. A solemn face would catch her eye, then there'd be beer breath in her face, telling her *what a tragedy* it was. How it had affected them. How, after, everyone started locking their doors all the time. The younger kids never had the same all-day, free-roaming liberty as Deedee and her friends. As though those freedoms were equivalent to a lost baby sister.

Deedee kept a box of Roisin's things in the bottom of her wardrobe. She took it out now and picked up a roll of butcher's paper, secured with an elastic band. It was a map, rendered by Roisin in a mix of felt-tips and colored pencils and heartbreaking in the way that puppies with only three legs are, in the blatant naked trying of it. Roisin's ambition had far outstripped her ability.

The most detailed and densest part was the Hanging Woods, a diamond-shaped thicket in the top left, marked with various symbols that only Roisin understood. Larger than the others, a shell and a wizard's hat were dotted in the trees, a cat in the gatehouse, a skull in the clearing nearest the Branaghs'. Smaller symbols—mushroom, gem, horseshoe, hare—clustered in the rest of the woods. West of the woods was farmland—marked in the map with sausage-bodied cows and horses—that was now an expensive estate, the expansion of which was planned for the Hanging Woods. The feral Quinns, including the kid Deedee had met in the cemetery, lived there now. East of the woods, the Branaghs' estate, known as the Big House, was marked, with a couple of symbols in the garden, an X marking the darkroom shed. The bay was to the north, but Roisin had sketched out many of the town's landmarks south of the Big House, their granny's house marked with a heart at the top of South Street, which led from the rural wooded area down into town. Opposite that, a book for the library, a flame symbol for the firehouse, a halo over the cathedral.

Deedee always paused at the clarity of the symbols in town. There was a sense to the map, but why would Roisin have put a shell in the woods rather than on the bay? She knew that there had never been pets in the gatehouse either, so a cat didn't make sense. What had her sister been thinking?

She ran her fingers over the small half-moon scars on the side of her wrist, alongside her lightning-bolt tattoo, where Roisin had dug her nails in and taken chunks out of her during one of their last fights. Roisin could be brutal, but she was just a wisp of a thing when she'd climb into Deedee's bed at night crying over another nightmare.

Deedee had turned these memories over so often now that the edges were fraying and worn, details blurred. It had been the summer that all the local girls terrorized each other with chatter about a mysterious man living in the Hanging Woods. One girl had seen him first and told the others, and soon everyone had seen him. He had long, thin hands and fingers reaching through the trees to grab you, and a bright light shone out from his waist. Pinned in the spotlight, you'd freeze until he came and got you.

Her phone pinged once more, but her stomach flipped when she saw the sender.

Florian had sent a selfie, wrapped up in a beige jacket with the funnel-neck collar rolled down to approximate lapels. A tie was loosely knotted around his neck over a white T-shirt, and his hair was fluffy and unstyled. He held one finger aloft while he pulled a quizzical expression. The text alongside it read, *Just one more thing.*

Wow, you really are our station's answer to Columbo, she texted back. This was not disloyal of her, so she didn't even need to mention it to Sean.

More like Dumbo, he replied. Then, *Hope you're all right, D. Lemme know if you wanta talk. Always here to cheer you up xx*

She scrutinized the selfie, committing the details to memory. He was getting ready to go out but thinking of her. She took another swig from the wine bottle. She deleted the selfie.

Deedee would never leave Sean. That was what mattered.

5

CAITLIN

Caitlin emerged from the stifling Tube into streets full of the scent of roasting chestnuts and sugared doughnuts. A giddy, queasy energy tilted the world. The bar was a five-minute walk, but the pavements were full. She was grateful. Alone, it would be too easy to disappear into nothingness.

Her phone screen lit up. She ducked into a quiet doorway and waited for the voicemail.

"Caitlin," her mother gasped over the clamor of a pub, "why won't you pick up?"

Caitlin hung up. The same old anger kicked through her as she shoved her phone deep into her coat pocket. Her mother could be crying or laughing or hoarse from screaming in previous voicemails. Caitlin didn't have time for it, whatever it was. There was nothing she could do about it from across the Irish Sea anyway, and—

There. A woman passed by her, at the back of a group of braying yuppies, gold bracelets and bangles tinkling as she swept a manicured hand through glossy hair. A tailored coat swirled around her ankles. She radiated wealth and luck and the kind of idiocy that made a person think they'd earned that combination.

She would please the shadows.

A taxi passed slightly too quickly through the narrow streets, sending the crowds hopping up onto the curb, and Caitlin seized her moment. Rushing out of the doorway, one outstretched hand met the woman's lush coat while the other closed around a fistful of hair, and then they were both falling. The woman screamed. Caitlin screamed louder.

The woman landed on her knees next to Caitlin, who had caught herself on her forearms. She felt her palms tear open against the concrete, blood on the pavement. Relief. She was back inside her body, for now at least.

"What is wrong with you?" The woman scrambled to her feet. Her left knee was skinned, a trickle of blood clotting against skin-tone tights. That was good.

"What?" Caitlin summoned tears to her eyes. "You just knocked me over!"

"No! No, you knocked me over!" The woman looked down at her with disgust.

Caitlin lunged at her, catching her by the wrist. "Hardly! The least you could do is help me up."

"Get off me!" The woman shoved her, but Caitlin held her ground. She felt the woman's pulse pounding in her thin wrist. She also felt the shifting chains of bracelets, links loosening.

"Ettie! Come on!"

Ettie's group had carried on, barely noticing the loss of one of their own. Caitlin saw the hurt flicker across the woman's face. She released her. As she did, she dropped one of Ettie's gold bracelets into her pocket beside Mark's wallet. She grinned so widely that she reopened her bitten lip. That was a good sting, blood on her tongue.

"This psycho attacked me!" Ettie skittered after her, complaining about dry-cleaning bills and demanding an apology. Caitlin drew near to the woman's friends. She ran her thumb over the raw lump of flesh on her lip that swelled up where it had been skinned.

"Come off it, Ettie, she's bleeding." A tall, dark-haired man looked at Caitlin with concern. "Are you OK?" he asked in the kind of vaguely international accent of boarding schools abroad, families that divided their time by seasons: winters in Switzerland and summers in the South of France.

"Can't be doing with the drama today, Etts," a horsey-looking woman called back from the front of the group. "It's Christmas!"

Caitlin felt Ettie fume beside her. There was a resignation to the way her shoulders slumped, something lonesome in her exhale that told Caitlin this was how things always were and always would be.

Caitlin approached the handsome man.

"Sorry about this." He rummaged in his pocket and pulled out a handkerchief. "For your mouth." His smile was expensive, teeth too white, too big for his mouth.

Ettie huffed. "Let's go."

"I'll catch up." His eyes were on Caitlin. "I'm George."

His handshake was firm but gentle. She brushed her fingertips against the soft skin in the hollow of his palm as they released from the contact.

"Roisin." The name appeared in her mouth.

"This is low, even for you," hissed Ettie, storming past them.

"Are you OK, Roisin?" George asked Caitlin.

He was so alive. He radiated the warmth of expensive holidays, the glow of an easy, monied existence. She wanted to slip inside his skin. He blotted out the shadows and the thoughts of Roisin.

"Just wet, mostly." She brushed at her tights. "A little shaken, I guess. Thanks for your help."

Ahead of them, Ettie grasped the arm of the horsey-looking woman, who bobbed her head and patted her placatingly with a specificity that made Caitlin curious.

"A close friend of yours?" she asked.

George had a low, rumbling chuckle made for darkened rooms and private jokes. "I know her better than I'd like to."

Caitlin snorted. "Well, I better do something about this. I'm supposed to be going on a date . . ."

"Oh yeah? What's he like?"

They were alone now. Caitlin leaned into a closed shop front to allow the crowds to pass by. George joined her there.

"You know the type. Tall, dark, good-looking." They stood side by side facing the street.

"Sounds awful. What does he do?" George shifted his weight just enough to open his body out to hers.

"He's a fireman, can you imagine."

"Women and firemen. Just because they're, what? Brave, muscular, often rescuing kittens? What's so great about that?" George tutted. He turned fully toward her, leaning into her space.

"When you put it like that . . ." Caitlin mirrored his move, and they were face-to-face.

"How will you get through the evening with such a loser?" George drew closer to her, almost closing the space between their bodies.

"I'm sure I'll cope." Her breath caught in her throat.

"I was hoping I could perhaps make up for Ettie's rudeness." He sighed in mock despair. "Reaffirm your faith in human nature."

"Were you?" She breathed in his exhale.

"You couldn't simply . . . stand your fireman up?" The air was electric.

"Not unless it was in service of something really groundbreaking and utterly necessary. Like reaffirming my faith in human nature." Caitlin felt the heat of his body so close to hers.

"In that case, I think I can help." George offered his arm.

"Lead the way," she said. She thought of how she could be contained, safe against the pliability of his flesh, the delicacy of his skin. It could be enough to keep away the shadows and the ghosts, at least for tonight.

With George's arm firmly around her waist, Caitlin felt anchored. The crowds had thinned out and a waxing moon emerged from behind cloud cover. The damp air nipped at her nose and cheeks. These were real things.

"You often ditch your date if another comes along?"

"Only if a rougher bit of rough turns up," she replied.

"Oh, slumming it, are you?" George laughed.

Caitlin shrugged. It was nice to make him laugh.

The buildings became residential, streetlamps replacing fairy lights. They approached an unassuming mid-terrace with a small brass plaque inscribed "Invitation Only." Though she had never been there before, Caitlin recognized Southern Manse immediately. She straightened her shoulders and raised her chin.

"You don't mind if we meet up with the others, do you?" George shrugged apologetically.

Caitlin feigned hesitation. Ettie's stolen bracelet burned in her pocket. Ettie's man hung on her arm. She tasted victory, power.

"We don't have to, obviously," he went on. "It's just it's my friend Chris's birthday. And—"

"Maybe you could make it up to me later." Caitlin drew herself into George's chest, tilting her face up to his. She held the lapels of his coat lightly.

"Well, now I'm reconsidering going in the first place." He grinned, but he led them up to the door.

Caitlin's smile split her lip open again. She ducked her head to staunch the blood with his handkerchief. George pressed the ivory doorbell four times in quick succession. Caitlin dropped her hand from her mouth as the door swung open to reveal a long and dimly lit hallway. Maroon shag carpet swallowed their footsteps. She trailed her hands over the velvet damask-print wallpaper. Bass thudded from the shadows ahead.

"You know your phone has been ringing," George said. "Your whole left side is buzzing."

"I'm in high demand."

"There's more than just the fireman?"

"A lady never tells."

George nodded to the hostess, who didn't even check their reservations before opening the door behind her to reveal a narrow spiral staircase.

Descending, Caitlin saw that the bar area was arranged with a series of booths styled to look like tiny, old-fashioned living rooms complete with fringed lampshades on ceramic standing lamps and doilies for coasters. George's friends were easy to spot, a prime booth having been reserved for the birthday boy. There were more magnums of champagne on the table than people around it.

"You caught up!" A bald man blew kisses across the booth as they arrived, indicating the glasses and bottles on the table in invitation.

From the other end of the table, Ettie scowled at everyone.

"This is Roisin!" George began the introductions. "This is Scott, he's Chris's boyfriend; Chris, one of my oldest . . ."

"Easy on the old!" Chris placed a hand over his heart and pouted.

". . . dearest and perhaps most handsome friends," George corrected himself. "Hugo, Jazz, Chloe, and—"

"And you know Ettie already!" Hugo stood to offer Caitlin a handshake. He was ruddy and broad and wore a gold signet pinkie ring.

"Don't be a beast," Chloe sniped at him.

"Never! Only ever a beauty!" Hugo's response set off a spirited round of jokes. Chris filled two glasses and slid them to Caitlin and George. Caitlin took a single, polite sip. She wasn't a drinker, couldn't be after seeing how her mother was, and with the wine she'd had at the office, it wouldn't take much more to blunt her senses completely. She needed to stay sharp.

Across the table, Ettie beckoned George. He huffed but nodded, topping up Caitlin's glass.

"I'll be two minutes." He took his time about it, but he followed Ettie.

"Are you jealous?" Scott asked Caitlin, leaning into the space George had vacated.

"Congratulations on ruining Ettie's night," Chris said, raising his glass.

Caitlin clinked her own glass on his. "She ruined mine first. And I'm not the jealous type."

"Where were you headed?" Chris leaned in over Scott toward her. He had an inviting, gossipy air. "Somewhere cooler, more fun?"

"Is there anything more fun than being shanghaied?" Caitlin's speech fell into their patterns.

"Shanghaied!" Chris clapped in delight, then crooked his pointer finger into a hook. "I like it, makes me feel like a pirate."

"Where are you from, Roisin?" Scott cut in.

"Here." Caitlin stalled for time. "What about you?"

"He means, what school did you go to?" Chris translated what Caitlin already understood.

"Cheltenham," she told him, thinking of Ettie tossing her glossy mane like a thoroughbred. "And then St. Andrews."

"You must know Jazz, then?" Scott pointed across the table. "From Cheltenham, of course; she won't go further north than Cambridge. What year were you?"

"She can hardly be blamed for that, but yes, I *thought* she was familiar. Perhaps not in my year, but is there a sister?"

"Yes! Lucinda! She was the year above."

"Lucinda, that's it! Oh, I'll have to talk to her." Caitlin sat up straighter and craned her neck toward Jazz, who stared into her phone. Caitlin smiled brightly and waved. "It's so lovely to reconnect!"

"Let me get her for you." Scott angled his head, looking for eye contact with Jazz.

"Just a minute." Caitlin addressed them both. "As it's a special day, I thought perhaps . . ." She opened her purse and let them see the cocaine she'd lifted from Mark's wallet.

Chris's eyes brightened; the threat of exposure evaporated. "A gift! How thoughtful!"

"Enjoy."

"Are you coming?" They took the bag and slid past her out of the booth.

"Oh, none for me." Caitlin puffed her cheeks out and patted her midsection, a pantomime for *I'm stuffed*.

From the way they laughed, she doubted that these would be their first bumps of the evening.

Across the table, horsey-looking Chloe was gesticulating at Hugo while he quaffed champagne. Jazz twisted between them, pouting and staring heavy-lidded into the screen of her phone.

Caitlin scooted closer to eavesdrop.

"Why does she *still* come out with us anyway?" Hugo said. "If you ask me—"

"That's the point! No one's asking *you*!" Chloe snapped back.

"Roisin," Hugo addressed Caitlin, "please don't judge our friend George by the madwomen he unfortunately seems to associate with."

Caitlin laughed, hating Hugo all the more as he slung an arm around her shoulders and pulled her against him. His shirt was damp; she hoped it was from the rain. From this adjusted angle she could watch Ettie and George near the short bar. An argument. George shook his head, trailing behind Ettie as she stormed back toward the table. Caitlin could imagine their whole relationship.

Ettie entered a huddle with Chloe and Jazz. George took Caitlin's hand and waited for her to slide out of the booth. He bugged his eyes out at Hugo and then rolled them while Hugo guffawed. A wordless exchange of *Women are crazy!*

"Can't stay, mate. I'll text Chris," he told Hugo. "See you soon."

"Merry Christmas!" Hugo roared back, one hand wrapped around the neck of a magnum.

As they made their way back up the stairs, George apologized to Caitlin.

"Ettie was being unreasonable. She's barking mad. She even

accused you of trying to mug her." He shook his head. "I didn't want to stick around. Ettie has trouble with the truth."

"I can't imagine," she murmured. Inside her pocket, Ettie's bracelet jangled. "Chris will be glad to avoid the scene."

"Oh no, that's the worst part. Chris loves a scene. He would have loved nothing more than to clap gleefully as the accusations started flying." George laughed fondly. "That's why I knew we *had* to leave."

Out on the steps of the Manse, they paused. A crow sat on the railing alongside them, its head tracking Caitlin's movements as though judging her. She shook off the thought that it was an omen.

"Perhaps we can still salvage the night?" she said.

George stopped and looked at her searchingly. "Where have you been hiding all these years, Ro? You're so different."

She quelled the rising disgust she suddenly felt for George and for herself, and plastered a smile on her face. "Oh, most women are just crazy."

Behind her the crow took flight and disappeared into the dark sky.

6

DEEDEE

Scanning the O'Shea's crowd on tiptoes, Deedee squared her shoulders. The usual suspects filled the place: Kathleen Doherty, clutching a phone as another pint landed in front of her; Noel Hegarty from school, who'd be so drunk he'd wet himself standing at the bar before midnight; a cloud of familiar faces. And then there was Mags, waving from the back corner of the bar. Mags was startlingly beautiful, with jet-black hair and feline blue eyes. A careless kind of beauty that led to her always being served first in the bar, picked first to dance. Despite this—or perhaps because of it—she was the unpredictable one in the group, given to screaming matches in the chipper after a night out.

With Mags was Fi, who always had a packet of tissues and a spare hairband, and radiated trustworthiness and calm. Deedee's closest friend, despite the distance. It had been no surprise when Fi moved off to London to be a paramedic. Mags was based in Berlin but seemed to spend a lot of time now in London herself. Deedee hadn't really considered that the two of them might be meeting up, growing closer.

"Hope I'm not interrupting." She joined them.

"Interrupting? Thank you for gracing us with your presence," Fi joked.

"Here she is, living the dream!" Mags greeted her. "Congratulations, Garda!"

"Thanks, I had a bit of a breakthrough in a case today," Deedee said. "Really rewarding."

"Good for you!" Fi and Mags sounded sincere, and Deedee felt the knot in her stomach loosen. She was doing big things too.

They sank into the usual amiable chatter: what everyone else from school was up to, how things had changed or not changed, the kind of gossip even they cared about less and less with each passing year.

"Seen Michelle Quinn this morning. You'll know all about it already, Dee, but she's expecting another one." Fi was like this, always trying to be friends with everyone. Even if that meant betraying Deedee.

"The real surprise is that they've all the same father," Deedee snorted. "Or so she says. You know Mrs. Lynch almost didn't come to the wedding, couldn't stand to see Little Barry make such a mistake."

Michelle had been in the school year below Deedee and her friends but dated much older boys. She was willing to do the things other girls wouldn't; there had even been a boyfriend she'd sneak away with for whole weekends while she was still in school. Then somewhere along the way she had decided that actually she'd had no agency at all, had rebranded herself as a victim. Little Barry Lynch, who was actually quite tall and so named only to differentiate him from his father, Big Barry Lynch, was from a decent family. Women like Michelle always found a way to land on their feet.

Mags cackled appreciatively. Whatever else you could say about Mags, she was always up for a little bitching.

"I saw one of her litter in the cemetery earlier," Deedee continued, "pure trampling on graves. Dragged up, they are."

"Feral!" Mags gasped.

"Ah, kids are kids," Fi chided. "You know yourself how it is."

"How often were you out vandalizing headstones, Fiona? *I* certainly don't remember *us* ever doing that." Deedee spoke with finality. Michelle Quinn was not like them. Case closed.

"Vandalizing now, were they? Sure, you shoulda picked 'em up for it so, Garda Dee!" Fi laughed.

Garda Dee. The way she said it.

"Ah now, Dee's having breakthroughs with the notorious Bannakilduff bike thief!" Mags cackled.

"Finally getting to the bottom of the rotten core!" Fi continued. Then, after a glance at Deedee, "Ah, we're messing! Come on!"

Deedee shoved her chair back hard. "I'm off to the bar."

She could feel it building to breaking point and knew she should go home. Invective on the tip of her tongue, her hands shaking with the want to . . . what? To hurt. She was tired of being the one grieving and in pain. It was irrational, but she couldn't make herself care about rationality. Everything was raw; she was the walking wounded and it wasn't fair.

Grow up, she scolded herself, *you can't be throwing a temper tantrum.*

"Mine's a vodka soda!" Mags screeched. She was wrecked already, barely aware of the conversation. Deedee was too sober. That was the real problem.

She shoved through to the bar, barely feeling the odd splash of a drink against her arm when she pushed a little harder than necessary.

More than the drink, she needed to get her head together. She'd lost it once this evening already, shaking that kid. That had been justified, but she couldn't fly off the handle over a bit of teasing.

By the time she'd ordered, she'd also resolved to leave it. Just move on, not mention anything controversial. She even bought a vodka soda for Mags.

See? I am a good person. I do nice things.

"Deadly!" Mags grabbed the drink as soon as Deedee set it down. "I'll get the next round."

"Now, the prices in here!" Fi started.

Deedee checked the time on her phone. Yep, within twenty minutes.

"You'd be lucky to get a thimbleful in London for these prices!" Mags agreed.

"You're in London now?" Deedee asked. No wonder she and Fi were cozy. "When did that happen?"

What else were they keeping from her?

"Fancied a change." Mags shrugged. "Restless soul."

"Right." Deedee swigged her pint. She couldn't get drunk fast enough.

"I'm thinking of buying a flat," Fi announced.

Deedee looked at Mags, who showed no reaction.

"You've told Mags first?" she asked. "How very cozy."

Fi and Mags exchanged a glance, a private conversation happening behind their eyes, a decision made.

"You've got it all going for you now, Dee." Mags sat back in her chair and spoke with finality, as though truth was granted from her speech. "But *when* is the wedding and when is the baby in the baby carriage coming?"

Look at these two, Deedee thought. How smug they were to come back to this little town, which they had outgrown long ago, and condescend to her about her little life. The drink stoked this feeling, fuel on the flames.

"Soon." She spoke through gritted teeth. This was one thing she had over both of them. They were single. She was loved. "What would either of you know about that?"

Fi blinked rapidly, as though she'd just had an object thrown at her.

Mags laughed, her head back and shoulders shaking. It was infuriating. Deedee had meant to injure.

"What's so funny?" she demanded.

"Like anyone cares"—Mags wiped faux tears from her eyes— "about what happens in Banna-shit-duff."

It had landed then, the barb. Deedee grinned.

"Ah, Mags," Fi cautioned. Fi the referee, Fi the betrayer. "It's not as easy for everyone."

"Look. What happened with Roisin was really sad, right? But we can't tiptoe around you forever." Mags glared at Deedee.

What happened with Roisin. What happened to her parents. What happened to Granny. What happened at work. What happened in the cemetery. What was happening right now. Deedee was justified in feeling like shit, in throwing the odd dig in. She deserved to snipe a little if she wanted. Suddenly she couldn't stand to be here.

"Fine. I'm off to my partner and my home and my dog."

"Go on then!" Mags made a shooing motion.

"Dee, c'mon . . ." But Fi made no attempt to stop her.

Deedee jostled through the crowd with enough aggression to set people tutting after her. She wished one of them would openly challenge her. She wanted someone to give her an excuse, a real cut-and-dried interaction to justify her laying them out.

The anger radiated from her body like stink lines in a cartoon; the floor should have cracked and splintered under her feet. Her eyes blurred with furious tears. A feminine figure stood between her and the door; someone in a long fur coat who stank of some kind of powdery perfume and swayed as they yelled into a phone.

Deedee squared her shoulders. The woman was oblivious to her and Deedee was prepared to go right through her. Why should she be considerate of this selfish person?

The woman turned just as Deedee collided with her. Perhaps it was that the action of turning had already destabilized her, perhaps Deedee just pushed too hard, but whatever it was, the woman went down so quickly and so hard that Deedee fell too and landed beside her. Close enough to see the woman's head ricochet first against the doorframe and then against the pavement. Close enough to hear the crunch.

7

CAITLIN

BANNAKILDUFF
SUMMER 1999

Three evenings this week, Caitlin has been alone. Which means that she's gone through the bread, butter, jam, and Crunchy Pops cereal. Being alone is only fun for a little while, and never at night. A fourth evening is effectively too many. The warning signs are there: her mother's mood has been too good today, and now she hears the sound of Cyndi Lauper drifting from her room telling her that *girls just wanna have fun.*

Caitlin wrenches the fridge door open hard enough to send a satisfying shiver through the bottles of spirits huddled together in the rack. She drinks the last drops from a tiny bottle of milk. Now the fridge is empty. Although to be precise, there is a bundle of celery stalks and two tubs of cottage cheese. So, effectively empty. *Effectively* is one of the words Caitlin has been using recently. It's like *literally*, but better, because people say *literally* when things aren't even literal. Effectively—but not literally—Caitlin is pretty much a responsible grown-up, after all the lonesome evenings spent waiting for her mother to come home.

"This is why I'm so short!" she yells in the direction of her mother's bedroom. "There's no food here!"

No answer.

She stomps down the hall and flings open her mother's door.

"Mam!"

Her mother is seated at her dressing table, her glossy lips pursed and her kohl-lined eyes narrowed as she inspects her face in the mirror for imperfections.

"We have stacks of food here. You're just greedy."

"There isn't even any milk left!" Caitlin slumps in the doorway.

Her mother picks up the smaller handheld mirror, the one that magnifies everything, transforming the slightest bump on her face into a mountain. She brings it to her eyes, like a detective with a magnifying glass, but the only criminal here is her traitorous skin.

"Do you see this? Crow's feet! Whole crow's legs, as good as!"

"You look beautiful." Caitlin hopes the words work. "Really, really. A movie star."

That does it. Her mother rewards her with a direct smile and then places the mirror back and pushes away from the dressing table.

Her mother is beautiful, but recently Caitlin has noticed the cost of that beauty.

"Oh, you're too sweet, Caity baby." Her mother approaches her, and for a moment, Caitlin thinks she's about to be enveloped in a hug. No such luck. She scurries after her mother to the kitchen, watches her spoon cottage cheese into a small bowl. All their bowls are small. Portion control. "Here," her mother says as she hands her the bowl along with a celery stick. "You're dainty, that's a good thing. No one wants to be friends with the fat girl."

"I hate cottage cheese," Caitlin says, but without energy. Her mother must be right. She's out all the time because she has an *enviable* social life, which means that Caitlin wishes she had as many friends as her mother does, which is weird, and so she hates her mother a bit. Also, because Caitlin is very into Judy Blume right now and she read *Blubber*, in which the fat girl gets bullied and *effectively* no one cares.

But grown-ups can be tricky. It's not always easy to know when they're telling the truth or saying the right thing.

"One day, when you're thirty, you're going to call me and say, thank you, Mother, for fostering a sense of resilience, and discipline, and . . ." Kathleen pauses, one arm outstretched, her hand to her temple and her eyes focused on the ceiling as though seeing into the future, and for a moment, Caitlin wonders if she is. ". . . self-control in me, because now my life is great. *My* mother, well! She certainly never understood this kind of thing, and look how I ended up."

Caitlin is never sure how to take this speech, because her mother is so thin. Her mother is the kind of thin where people who don't know her might think she's sick, that's how thin she is. To have people think you're sick when actually you simply have amazing self-control is the highest compliment anyone can pay you. So effectively, her mother is a huge success. That means that *how I ended up* refers to being single and living with Caitlin.

"I think you ended up OK. I think we don't even need anyone else."

"Shows how much you know. And not everything is about you, Miss Self-Absorbed. Anyway, I'm seeing Michael tonight."

"Mick." Caitlin hates being right about her mother leaving.

"Michael." Her mother's tone is light, but the way her voice pitches higher toward the end of the word means danger.

"Everyone calls him Mick." Caitlin hates that her mother wants to pretend they're something other than they are, she and Mick. That nothing is ever good enough for her.

"How would you know? You know everyone now? You're the big social superstar in this house, are you?"

"Michael, then. Whatever."

"So you can sort yourself out something for dinner, right?"

"I knew you were going to say this! I can't eat anything if there's nothing here!"

"Aren't you the one who's like, literally, grown up?" Kathleen huffs, rolls her eyes, and juts her head sassily on her neck. The imitation stings.

"Celery is effectively negative calories, because your body burns more processing it than it has calories in it," Caitlin says, parroting her mother's diet advice. "So it's not even dinner. I'll go to Maureen's." She means it as a threat; she wants her mother to feel jealous.

Kathleen is looking at herself, rolling her neck to check all angles, barely even listening. "Your little friend was running around out there a minute ago. Go play."

"Even worse," Caitlin groans. "She's not my friend!"

"Beggars can't be choosers, darling." Kathleen has already moved on, into her wardrobe, to choose a wrap for her shoulders. She pauses to straighten the folds of her fur coat.

"That coat is ugly and Roisin's annoying," Caitlin announces. "I don't want to play with her."

Roisin's loud and bossy and no one else likes her either. Roisin doesn't realize there are types of alone, and even as she envies her mother's social life, Caitlin would rather be the type of alone you choose than not-alone with Roisin.

"Sometimes *you're* annoying, and this coat is gorgeous." Kathleen gives the fur a final tender pat before pulling out a silky shawl. "So you'll go to Maureen's, then."

"Maureen is such a great cook. She cooks every night." Caitlin tries for needling. Kathleen doesn't rise to it.

"Sounds good," she says, dropping a kiss in the air above Caitlin's head, so as not to mess up her glossy lipstick. "Mind you don't wear out your welcome."

Caitlin says nothing, because all the things she wants to say are crowded in the back of her mouth and they can't get past her clenched teeth. She looks down at the small bowl of cottage cheese and the celery stick, and she's not even hungry anymore.

"What? Are you trying to guilt me, with those big puppy-dog eyes?" Kathleen demands. "It won't work. I deserve to have a life, Caitlin. You can't hold that against me. I deserve—"

"No! I don't even care!" But Caitlin can't stop her voice from breaking, snapping in two, and then the tears start and her nose is running, and then *she's* running, out of the house. Her mother doesn't call out, so she keeps going, running down through the field behind the house toward the trees. She's in the Hanging Woods, which are very dark and scary, even now, but she doesn't care, because it would serve her mother right if she got dragged away by ghosts, because no one would notice if she never came back, and who would even care? No one loves Caitlin. Her thoughts rocket her straight into a clearing in the middle of the woods, where no one in the world has ever been before, and she leans over, hands on her knees, and vomits onto the ground. She straightens and screams, and a murder of crows caw-caw and take flight above her, and all she hears is beating wings, louder even than her beating heart.

"My goodness, I got the fright of my life!" Colm appears, a couple of logs under his arm. "Did you see the banshee? I certainly heard her!"

An old, scarred stump sits in the middle of the clearing, a small axe embedded in it. Colm deftly removes it.

A chuckle escapes Caitlin, and she wipes her nose with the back of her hand. "It was me."

Colm lives next door; he's Maureen's husband, Sean's da, Caitlin's favorite person. Just seeing him makes her feel calmer. His face is round and it's all smile, his eyes disappearing into joyful crescents. There's not much Colm can't fix.

"You?" He drops the axe and walks toward her. He's so tall, he's there in two strides. "No, it couldn't have been, that was much too loud a scream to come from such small lungs! That was a banshee if ever I heard one."

"Have you heard a banshee?" Caitlin palms her eyes dry.

"I've heard as many banshees as I've seen little folk." Colm twinkles. "And I'll let you in on a secret: this wood's full of those."

"Fairies?" Caitlin is doubtful. Obviously she knows how to spot a fairy ring, and she's never seen any in here.

"Oh, that's not all," Colm continues. The way he says things, it's not like the usual uneven grown-up way, where they say stuff and kids have to just listen and not question or anything. "You must've come across something already, no?"

Caitlin thinks carefully before responding. "I'm not scared, but I don't like the woods much."

"You're very brave altogether," Colm agrees. "It's not just the fairies and such, there's rabbits and woodpeckers and all sorts of interesting creatures running about in here."

"Really?" Caitlin's interest is piqued.

"Really. No messing now, that's the truth. I'd say you'd have a fine time exploring in here. Now, what's all this upset about?"

"I had a fight with my mam." The tears threaten to come back; she has to speak quickly. "Can I have dinner at your house?"

Colm looks toward the gatehouse, his mouth pursed. He's holding back from saying something.

"We'd love to have you," he says. "Just this morning I was telling Maureen that we'd need some help eating up the marble cake."

"Marble cake!" Caitlin grins, and then remembers that she's sad. One more thing she remembers. "Is Roisin around today?"

"Deedee's after collecting her for dinner." Colm shifts the wood in his arms, getting tired from hanging around talking to her.

Her mother is always warning her not to bother the Branaghs too much; that if she's not careful, they'll want to get new tenants into the gatehouse.

"Can I help?" She holds out her arms, flexing the tiny muscles as hard as she can for effect.

Colm shakes his head and pretends to put the handle of his axe between his teeth to free up his hand, squinting his eye like a pirate. Caitlin giggles. He returns the axe to a leather loop secured with a shiny silver buckle on his belt. Caitlin takes his big hand in both of her small ones. She's skipping as they leave the Hanging Woods together.

8

DEEDEE

It had been raining all day. Kathleen would have been drinking for all that time too, and she was already unsteady—everyone knew she was always lurching around. Deedee rolled onto all fours and leaned over her. The older woman's eyelids—mascara and eyeliner smudged haphazardly almost to her brow bone; she had no eyebrows—flickered.

"She's grand!" Deedee waved away the beginnings of a crowd that threatened to form. "I broke her fall!"

Liar, hissed the little voice in her head—guilt? *You did this.*

Then she was on her feet, tugging Kathleen up by her elbows, the older woman's head still lolling forward. Kathleen stank of a heavy, plummy perfume and she weighed nothing at all. Deedee thought of moths, powdery and fragile, until Kathleen brought her elbow out to steady herself and hit Deedee's nose hard enough to send her vision sparkling for a moment.

Fat drops of blood spilled from her bruised nose onto the collar of Kathleen's coat. Deedee struggled, but managed to tip her head back and loop an arm around the woman.

A strange, misplaced thought occurred to her: that soon she would be juggling a toddler like this, ducking tiny fists and scooping a miniature figure out of harm's way. The thought of such tenderness and fragility softened her.

"Kathleen, you silly thing," she clucked, only half pantomiming her innocence for the straggling crowd now, half believing it. "You've near broken my nose!" She pulled an old fast-food napkin from her bag and twisted it to plug her leaking nostril, then patted ineffectually at Kathleen's collar, hoping that the mottled brown of the coat would disguise that she had bled onto it.

No one was particularly paying attention to them; still, Deedee hoped to God no one had witnessed her purposely knock Kathleen down.

A couple of young local lads sniggered as they passed. Kathleen flapped a hand in their direction, whether as a greeting or to scold, Deedee couldn't tell, but the futility of it was pathetic to behold.

She helped the woman out, explaining to the smokers that Kathleen had had a little fall and taken Deedee out on the way. Her bloody nose was evidence.

Outside, she hailed a taxi. All day long she had just been taking it, putting up with all the shit. It had come to a head and Kathleen had been in her path. Now Deedee had to pay for it; she couldn't just leave Kathleen like this.

Inside the taxi, Kathleen came back to life. She ignored both her injuries and Deedee in favor of jabbing at the cracked screen of her phone. Deedee's own phone had died, so, unable to use the torch function, she tried to examine the side of Kathleen's head in the dim flashes of light from streetlamps and the headlights of other traffic. There was no visible evidence of injury, thankfully. She hoped that Kathleen's forearms and phone had broken her fall. Or—she allowed herself the moment of bitchy levity—the sheer force of Elnett hairspray.

"She's going to call! How's she going to call?" Kathleen shook the screen at Deedee. A clear plastic rose charm dangled from it. The phone slipped from her grasp and Deedee caught it.

"Who?" she asked, but Kathleen was back to muttering to herself. "Caitlin? Do you mean Caitlin?"

Caitlin's not going to call, she thought, and then questioned that assumption. Kathleen had intimated that Caitlin had notions of herself, that they'd had a blowup years ago, but maybe things had changed.

"Do you have Caitlin's number?" Deedee thought of her investigation, Caitlin the missing piece, Kathleen always pleading ignorance. She resisted the urge to shake some sense out of her.

They were slowing down outside Quinn's garage, still a good mile from their destination.

"Brendan, we're miles away!" Deedee called. "Keep going!"

"I *will* charge if she throws up, Deirdre O'Halloran!"

"Little Deedee O'Halloran!" Kathleen turned to Deedee as though seeing her for the first time. "I've been trying to reach her—she doesn't pick up—but it was an accident, it was all an accident. Sure, you know yourself how it is, you do one thing, then another, and suddenly—"

"Trying to reach Caitlin?" Deedee grasped this moment of lucidity.

"I'll charge you now, Kath, for every other time!" Brendan called back to them. "Thousand euro!"

"I've been looking in the woods!" Kathleen called back.

"You've got Caitlin's number, do you?" Deedee tried again, anxious that the window of clarity was quickly closing. She still held Kathleen's phone, but the older woman had lost interest in it.

"They can't build back there!" Kathleen cupped a hand around her mouth to whisper to Deedee.

"We'll get you home now, no bother." Deedee offered Kathleen her phone, but Kathleen's head was buried in her sequined clutch. It bulged with napkins and cardboard coasters and left an unsettling slickness on her hands that Deedee prayed was just spilled beer.

"It's all just one thing after another, and then poof! There you are!" Kathleen continued, beaming in from another conversation.

"Don't worry about Brendan." Deedee held the phone out and Kathleen continued to ignore it.

Fine, she thought, slipping it into her jeans. *I'll leave it in the house.*

"Don't have children," Kathleen blurted with unsettling prescience.

"They don't tell you what it's like. Not really. It's relentless. A life sentence."

Deedee summoned patience.

"I'm trying to be better," Kathleen continued. "I've got the big book and I . . . well, sometimes you make mistakes, but I've been looking for years."

Deedee knew that feeling. Kathleen might be hoping that Caitlin would call her, but from all she was saying, there was no relationship and no reason she would. Kathleen didn't have the answers.

They pulled up outside Kathleen's home. As soon as Deedee opened the car door for her, Kathleen emptied the contents of her stomach all over Deedee's new Guilt Boots.

"What did I tell you?" Brendan crowed.

"You're a prick, Brendan," Deedee snarled. She helped Kathleen out of the car and then slammed the door with force. "I'll remember this if I see you going a hair too fast."

Brendan lingered just long enough to be sure Deedee heard his snort of derision before disappearing back toward the town center. Deedee shook her feet to dislodge the mess from her boots, but they were already marked irreparably. She lit up a cigarette. This town, the insults were unending.

Kathleen lived in what was technically the gatehouse of the Branagh place, the Big House. Small and low-ceilinged with a hotchpotch air, it was originally a single-room dwelling with a partition; Colm's father had first begun extending it to add on a modern bathroom and kitchen in the 1950s, thinking of renters. Colm had further extended it, adding a second bedroom and enlarging the kitchen. Before Kathleen, it'd been rented to a young couple while they saved up for a deposit.

As town legend had it, Kathleen simply materialized one day, heavily pregnant, fresh-faced as a teenager, a tarnished silver ring on her left hand, and no word of a life before. Maureen took her in, offered the gatehouse temporarily—that was the Branaghs all over, generous to a fault. The ring had disappeared at some point, and no one ever got out of her who had fathered her daughter. With Colm recovering from his accident, the gatehouse had sat empty while Kathleen was away.

The shuffling sound of Kathleen dragging her balding fur coat after her as she staggered toward the house interrupted Deedee's thoughts, and she hurried to pick the coat off the ground. She tapped the ash off her cigarette before getting close to it. It was already full of cigarette burns and she could probably wring a brewery's worth of beer out of it, but it had been a fine garment once. Kathleen took her arm. Deedee navigated her up the drive and shook the old coat until it released the keys from its folds. The Big House was always so full of life and movement; Kathleen's was a world apart. It had the air of a faded seaside town or abandoned funfair, as though all vitality had drifted away and whatever remained was left to crumble unseen.

Finally, they made it inside.

"Jesus, Kathleen, it's freezing in here." Deedee watched her breath cloud in front of her face.

"You kids are always complaining." Kathleen wrapped her fur coat around herself and shuffled off into the first room on the left.

"Have you a window open?" Deedee followed her into the living room. Two yellowed floral armchairs, one buried in old newspapers and magazines, the other worn at the seat and headrest. A picture of Kathleen with an early nineties–style bouffant and her too-blond toddler daughter hung on the wall, yellowed with nicotine. Others were dotted around the room, charting mother's and daughter's lives. These, Deedee knew, were Colm Branagh portraits. Her own parents had envied that Kathleen was raising her child so close to their town's documentarian.

Kathleen patted the pockets of her coat, hunting for a cigarette. Beer mats from pubs all over the county covered a side table next to her armchair, all warped and stiffened from various spills. Perched on top of this mess was a single wineglass, its rim crowded with various shades of lipstick, an overflowing ashtray, and a half-full bottle of wine.

Deedee handed her a cigarette from her own pack and watched as Kathleen sneered at it.

"No menthols?"

Deedee shook her head. "Just normal." The wine bottle winked at her under the sickly overhead light.

"Not very refreshing," Kathleen grumbled, settling herself in the non-cluttered armchair. She held the cigarette at a careful distance and peered at it as though it were an eye exam.

"Take it or don't, but leave out the slagging." Deedee's buzz was well and truly wearing off, leaving her feeling even more frayed and impatient. She took a deep, soothing inhale of her own cigarette.

"I'll give it back then." Kathleen picked up the remote control and pointed it at the TV. The opening credits of *Pretty in Pink* were rolling. "Have you seen this one?" she asked. "'Tis a good one."

"I think so." Deedee checked her watch. Technically she had done her duty. She had delivered Kathleen safely home. The older woman didn't seem to be injured. Deedee could go home. But it was so cold. "Are you staying up then?" she asked. "You'd want to be tucked up warm in this weather."

"I might watch a bitta this." Kathleen pulled herself up from her chair and crossed to the other armchair. She pushed the newspapers off its seat and onto the floor. "Sit down."

"Just for a moment," Deedee said. Kathleen's loneliness had drained her. She was exhausted, and she felt entirely too sober. That wine bottle beside Kathleen bothered her. Her mouth was awfully dry, and Kathleen didn't need to be drinking any more tonight.

"I'll just get you a tea, Kathleen, will I?" She swept the wineglass and bottle away and headed to find the kitchen. As soon as she was alone in the hallway, she took a long swig from the bottle. It was paint-thinner unpleasant, but that didn't stop her returning to it and glugging down the end of it. There. That was better.

The kitchen was small but, considering the state of the rest of the house, oddly spotless. No splatter on the splash back, no crumbs on the counters. An ashtray lay on the counter beside the sink, and as she stubbed her cigarette out into it, Deedee pictured Kathleen standing here smoking, contemplating the view. From here, the front door and left-hand side of the Big House were visible, the gatehouse offset to the left of the plot. Then there was a length of the field behind, ending at the Hanging Woods.

No wonder she's unhappy about the new development plans, Deedee thought, dampening a tissue and cleaning the last traces of her bloody nose. She'd be losing her privacy, and her view of the trees.

Deedee clicked the kettle on and hunted for tea bags and mugs. The cupboards were full of junk-mail flyers and napkins from fast-food restaurants. Plastic straws and coffee stirrers filled the cutlery drawer. The fridge door was covered in newspaper clippings. She filled a glass with water to bring through with her.

"Kathleen, where're your tea bags?" she called out as she re-entered the living room.

Kathleen was curled up asleep on the armchair, still snuggled into her fur. Asleep, she looked even tinier, birdlike and fragile.

Deedee set the water on the small table. She'd done her good Samaritan bit and could leave now, but she couldn't quite make herself go. Kathleen was a nuisance, but wasn't she also a vulnerable person? What if Deedee left and found out in the morning that she had frozen to death in here? She'd never be able to live with herself.

Sean had left a decent stash of wood and kindling ready beside the fireplace, from his excursions to the Hanging Woods, but Deedee made a mental note to drop some more round another day. Kathleen's place felt like it hadn't been heated for a month. The thought of her alone, too proud to admit that she was freezing, was hard to bear. She would talk to Sean about this; the place needed modern heating.

While Kathleen slept, Deedee built a small fire, then set up the fire guard and made sure that there was nothing too close to it that could catch.

You're welcome, she thought, knowing that Kathleen would never actually thank her for her efforts. Still, she'd done everything she could.

Outside the back door, she lit another cigarette. A cold breeze whipped through the trees in the Hanging Woods, and she turned to huddle against the house. As she did, she saw the window of the back bedroom shiver in the breeze.

She felt a brief, pointless satisfaction at being right: there had been a window open after all; no wonder the place was arctic. She thumped it closed with her fist. Another thankless favor performed for Kathleen. She paused on the back step to finish her cigarette. She didn't want Sean to see her; she was still telling him she'd quit.

She made her way across the field, toward the always unlocked back door of the Big House. The Hanging Woods lay like a dark smudge at the end of the field. It had been searched after Roisin disappeared, but days later, after a rainstorm that would have swept away any scent for the dogs to follow.

She entered the kitchen. From the living room she heard the strains of the *Law & Order: SVU* credits, and knew Maureen at least was still up.

"Hello?" she called out softly. The muffled thud of Sean's feet hitting the floor in the living room followed, and he met her in the kitchen doorway.

"Hey." He indicated over his shoulder. Deedee closed the distance between them and craned her head. Maureen was just visible in the living room. She was asleep, her TV glasses askew on her face and her mouth ajar. Deedee softened with love just looking at her.

"What happened?" Sean gestured to the soiled boots.

"Kathleen. I'm sorry." Deedee winced, but she was lucky tonight. Sean's mind was elsewhere.

He took out cigarettes and offered her one.

Deedee shook her head. "You know I'm quitting."

He responded with a low snort and an I'm-not-touching-*that* shake of his head. Deedee stood close to him as he opened the back door to let the smoke out.

"Da's getting worse." He paused and stared up at the night sky, searching for the words. "I don't know how much time we have, really. Mam won't take it in, and I just don't know what to do."

"Christ." Deedee tried to keep her voice level as her heart broke. Colm meant as much to her as he did to Sean.

As though he read her thoughts, Sean shook his head again. "He's my da. Even though everyone used to run through here." He thumped his chest possessively. "He's *my* da."

"True enough." Deedee inhaled deeply and forced herself to exhale slowly, leaving the unspoken message—*not yours, not yours*—time to dissipate. "What's the doctor say?"

"What does he ever say?" Sean was bitter. "He's been on borrowed time for twenty years now. *Get it over with*, he might as well say."

"D'you think we should have a baby?" Deedee blurted. A thought half formed: more family, more connection, the look on their faces when she had not only the career and the man but the baby carriage too.

Sean's eyes widened. "Where has that come from?"

"I don't know. Sorry, I don't know what I was thinking," Deedee said. "Is that a no, though?"

"Jesus, Dee, there's a lot going on." Sean looked at her like she was a stranger.

It shouldn't have been an outrageous idea.

"I should go," she said. "Just dropped off Kathleen, she had a fall in town."

"Is she OK?" Sean asked. "Did she . . . Were you two talking about kids or something?"

"She's fine, she'll be fierce hungover in the morning. Could you drop me back, though?"

She hated to ask. Her instinct not to make trouble for him, not to make herself awkward here, not to endanger this only family she had left even as it too withered and died in front of her, was overpowering.

But the Big House was outside of town, only a fifteen-minute drive at this time of night but about an hour's walk, and much, much slower with her dead phone unable to be used as a torch to make sure she wasn't about to fall into a ditch or pothole.

He agreed, as she knew he would, but something hung in the air between them. She had thought they would be on the same page about all of this, hoped he'd welcome the idea. They spoke on the journey back, but she had no idea what about.

At the front door, she realized she hadn't told him she loved him, and he was already reversing, already focusing on the journey ahead.

She let out a low whine of frustration. The whole evening had left her feeling bereft of something she couldn't name. All that remained was a clawing, panicked need in her chest for Sean's reassurance. Inside the house, she plugged her dead phone into its charger, but the screen stayed resolutely blank, a punishment to her for allowing it to run totally flat.

Minutes ticked by on the clock in the kitchen, where she sat running Frank's velvet ears through her fingers, searching for solace. Jittery with insecurity, she turned out her pockets, meaning to put away and tidy up her things, and found Kathleen's phone. A long crack bisected the lower corner of the screen, but it was some old tank of an Android, and its battery showed at 90 percent.

Before she could think about it, she punched in the number of the Branaghs' house, the very same one she'd learned more than twenty years ago while still a teenager, and waited for the ring.

"Hello?" Sean had snatched up the phone almost immediately.

"Sorry." Deedee cringed. She hadn't thought about the loud ringtone echoing through the sleeping house. "I just miss you. I love you."

She waited for the bite of his response, knowing that she'd set herself up for the exasperated *We just saw one another!*

"I love you too," Sean affirmed, and Deedee felt the warm glow of assurance. "But I thought this was Kathleen, the number is showing up as hers."

Deedee explained, and they agreed that she'd come up to the gate-house tomorrow to return the phone. What was really important was Sean's attention, and his easy acceptance of her in the logistics of their lives. She wasn't alone. She was almost a Branagh.

Nothing else mattered.

9

CAITLIN

Ettie called while they were in the Uber. George's arm was around her, his weight heavy on the seat belt as he twisted and leaned his body toward hers. Caitlin knew it was Ettie by the way he winced and cut a guilty glance at her before tucking his phone back into his pocket. Or maybe it was someone else, another woman. The grim clandestine pleasure of fucking someone else's partner. The dark residential streets they cruised through swallowed up the ambient streetlight, keeping the interior of the car dark. She let her hand drift up from his knee, higher and higher on his thigh, until he coughed and nodded toward the front of the car. Though she couldn't make out the driver's face, she caught him watching them.

Smiling, she leaned in to let her lips graze his ear as she asked, "So?"

He grinned, and even in this light she was struck by how handsome he was. How satisfying it would be to nip and scratch at this body, to watch rosy beads of blood appear on such blessed skin. She needed that, that and the gravity of him to keep her edges contained. The too-big feeling of her skin made her teeth hurt; the effort of pretending that she was fine all day every day was draining. He reached for her, kissing her hard, his hand fisted in her hair.

Then they were outside George's north London townhouse,

tumbling out of the cab and through his front door. Caitlin's need was savage and impersonal. It always was. The idea of sex born from true desire or a sense of romance was the stuff of paperbacks sold to sad housewives. She had never bought into that. Sex was the chance to shove and bite and pull hair and conquer. It was her body consuming another. It pushed the shadows away and brought her fully into focus. It was she who gained and she who won.

George's eyes widened as she wrapped her hand around his throat and pushed against the underside of his jaw, but then a smile broke across his face and he gripped her flesh harder, thrust deeper. The men she'd met on dating apps and in bars were quick to place their hands around her throat and squeeze until she saw stars. She left their homes with bruises. She arrived with her nails sharpened to daggers, her teeth bared. Finally, pushing George down into the mattress as hard as she could while she worked on top of him, focusing on nothing but her own release, the tension broke inside of her.

Victorious, she fell into place alongside him on the bed. With the shadows firmly pushed away, the room came into focus around her. Hardwood flooring and minimalist white walls, sage-green bedding and pine furniture. A series of framed charcoal sketches and a Neil Young poster. No sign of anything particularly valuable.

"Wow." He reached to hold her hand. "That was . . . something."

"Oh, for me too." She yawned and tucked her hands under her head and away from his grasp. Idly she thought of texting Lola her apologies; instead of a pill to help her sleep, she had fed the shadows their much-desired blood and she felt a heavy sleepiness drift from her chest out to her limbs. Something had been purged.

"I think I'm scarred for life." He twisted his neck to examine the place on his shoulder that she'd sunk her teeth into, and frowned.

George was so dull.

"You'll be healed by vest-top season." She turned her back to him and he moved to spoon her. Relief flooded her body, the persistent bonds of wakefulness loosened further.

"I better be. Could be some awkward chat at the beach."

The beach. Caitlin hadn't been to a beach in years—decades. Her mother loved the sea, and so the push-pull of the tides was forever linked to the frustration and pain of being her mother's daughter.

"Clears your head." She didn't realize she'd spoken aloud.

"What does?" He propped his chin on her shoulder. When she turned to face him, their noses touched. It was comforting. She pulled back.

"Something my mother used to say. She loved the beach." Caitlin rolled into his arms and let herself unspool. George didn't matter; he had no idea who she really was. "Even in the lashing rain, she'd go every day if she could. Said it was the only thing that really clears your head when you're in a bad place."

"She was often in a bad place?" He was all serious-chat mode now, grasping for intimacy.

The faces of the many boyfriends Caitlin's mother had relied on flicked through her mind as she looked into George's eyes. Caitlin had never believed in love, but she could spot a sucker a mile off.

"Rarely," she said.

The truth: when she was dumped, which was frequently, and forced to be alone with just Caitlin. Reduced to being only "mother," not an object of lust. Kathleen Doherty could only see herself if she was being desired, was only real in the face of a man's validation.

"You're lucky. My mother has made being miserable her life's work," George joked. "But it's mostly because of my father, of course . . ."

Isn't that always the way?

Even when Kathleen had met someone who seemed different, seemed to love her, it hadn't lasted. The way she told it, Michael had been backlit, the sun streaming in behind him, just an angelic hand reaching out after she spilled a whole crate of peaches that she'd been stacking. She knew the grocer would have heard the crash and be out in minutes, well before she could clear it up alone. She'd begun crying before Michael intervened, waylaid the owner by asking him to check for something in the back, and then fell to his knees to help her pick up the rolling runaway fruit.

". . . It's not that I always agree with him . . ." George droned on.

Those peaches were ruined the second they hit the floor. It was impossible to tell from the outside, but bruises had developed under the skin at the points of impact. Their sweetness was already drained, and if they were bought, they'd only spark complaints. Kathleen, on her final warning, had destroyed the whole crate. If she came clean, if she hadn't met Michael, she'd have been fired.

". . . and she doesn't help herself . . ."

Caitlin had ruined it in the end, though they'd been planning to leave Bannakilduff anyway. The Academy of Visual Arts in Highgate, a monied north London suburb, had introduced an underprivileged kids' scholarship. Caitlin was a shoo-in, and Kathleen was delighted to move up in the world. Michael might have come with them, if only Caitlin hadn't gone to the Hanging Woods with Roisin that day.

". . . Ultimately, it's just that he has high standards," George concluded.

Caitlin wondered how often he did this: transformed any woman in his orbit into his unpaid therapist.

"That sounds like a lot," she said. "You've really been through it."

"You're so insightful." George cupped her chin and turned her face to his so he could stare into her eyes.

He could see her and hear her, yet it seemed like he was looking past her, hearing past her. She felt that she wasn't quite real, a ghost, and suddenly the crisp, fresh air of Bannakilduff came back to her, the scent of fuchsia in the hedgerows, the total darkness of the night. She huddled closer to George's warmth, nuzzling into the skin of his chest and inhaling the warm citrus scent of his cologne. This was real; she was safe here.

"What's up?" George asked.

"Nothing," Caitlin replied. But what was the harm in mentioning it? After all, George would only be waiting for her to stop talking so that he could start again.

She told him about the creature in the Hanging Woods.

"Did anyone ever see it?" he asked, his eyes alight with a sleepover delight. "Or could you just . . . not go into these woods?"

"Sometimes it would wait outside the houses at night. Whispering, but nothing you could understand. Maybe not even in English." Caitlin felt like a burden was lifting in the telling of the story. Now, in the freshly laundered Egyptian cotton sheets of a stranger, surrounded by buildings taller than any tree, it all felt faintly silly. "Mostly it was in the woods, though, or if you were walking home alone around dusk, that's when we saw it."

"We? You saw it?" George seized upon her language in a way that irritated her. He wasn't supposed to be listening properly. This wasn't for him.

"No," she said.

"You said—"

"Like, general we, the girls of the town. Of which I was one. No, I never saw anything," Caitlin lied once more. "But a few girls I knew, yeah. There was one girl . . ." She couldn't stop herself now, she was careening toward the horrible ending of it all, but maybe, maybe once she said it aloud, it would seem as ridiculous as all the rest of it. As unreal, even though she knew the truth. "One girl, she saw the creature and that was it. She never came back."

"Jesus, Roisin. That's a bit dark." George blanched and pulled away from her.

"What?" She frantically replayed what she'd said; when had she told him that Roisin was the one who'd disappeared? "How did you know her?"

"Know who?" He pulled away from her to look at her face, and a cold breeze rushed between them.

Too late she remembered that she had introduced herself as Roisin.

"Hmm?" She tried to sound sleepy and absent-minded.

"You just asked how I knew someone." His eyes were alert, but he stifled a yawn.

"Did I?" Caitlin snuggled back into him. "Who?"

"I don't know, you asked me."

"Can't have been anything important then." She searched for something to distract him. "Cool sketches over there, by the way."

"Oh, those. They're ancient. They're by an old family friend."

"Picasso?" she joked.

He winced. "Not quite."

She moved to get a better look without drawing too much attention to herself. The strokes were confident and bold, working with the negative space to create impressions of wider scenes. One was particularly familiar, but she couldn't quite place it. Her heart beat faster. There was something valuable here after all.

George misread her action and began stroking her hip. The second time was slower, more considered. She could just about see the sketches over his shoulder.

"We should get some sleep." He checked the clock on his bedside table. "We're basically on New Zealand time now."

Caitlin groaned. The window had passed; she had moved through sleepy relaxation back into wakefulness. She hoped Lola wasn't passed out uselessly somewhere, or too annoyed at her to return her calls at this hour.

Neither of them moved. Caitlin's phone buzzed loudly on the wooden floor.

Right on cue, she thought. Lola must be wondering about her. The idea warmed her.

"I hope it's the fireman," George said.

"Me too, actually." Caitlin padded out to take the call in the privacy of the kitchen. She was smiling when she picked up, let the smile seep into her voice, fondness and affection focused down the line.

The caller had a strong Cork accent, wide awake and businesslike, that made her feel doubly ashamed—for the intimacy of her tone, and for having given up her own accent.

When she replied, she sounded high-pitched, clipped, BBC pronunciation, embarrassing.

The sea came back to her as she listened. A wave crushing her, a riptide tugging her under, the feeling of being swallowed alive, airlessness. *Clears your head.*

She had always thought the news would feel like a release. She never considered that it would be like the severing of a line, like the ground disappearing beneath her feet. She hadn't realized until her mother was gone that she was carrying her somewhere inside her body, like her spine was reinforced with the knowledge that somewhere out there she wasn't truly alone.

The suffocation of George's home, bed, arms was suddenly overwhelming, and she grabbed her things as fast as she could while he sat upright, brow furrowed in confusion.

"I didn't get your number!" he called. In the dim lamplight, his tanned torso was a shadow on the crisp white sheets.

Good, she thought. One last regretful glance back in the direction of the sketches.

Outside, she thumbed through her phone, past the alert for the voicemail her mother had left, the last one she would ever leave, to Lola. In the taxi home, she fingered the broken chain of Ettie's bracelet. There was comfort in knowing some things could be repaired and made whole.

Lola met her outside her flat. Her mane of white-blond hair glowed under the streetlamp, but up close, Caitlin saw how it had gone peppery at the roots with regrowth. Gold piercings dimpled her cheeks, and she pushed her tongue against the gap in her front teeth as she concentrated, listening, intuiting Caitlin's needs, prescribing her wares, fee waived for now. Not sleep, she had decided, not yet; Caitlin needed to be alert, awake.

Caitlin needed someone to tell her what to do.

Lola's hands were tattooed on both sides: a sun on her right hand and moon on her left, constellations across her palms. Caitlin plucked the pills from the inky heavens Lola cradled, and swallowed.

It was time to go home.

PART 2

CAPTURE

There's a before and an after. The bit in the
middle is gone with the press of a button.

John Lyle,
The Little Photographer:
A Kid's Guide to Perfect Pictures

10

CAITLIN

Caitlin was eighteen when she left. They'd been living in east London at the time, in an already tiny house subdivided into flats, where most of the surfaces bore leftover cockroach poison resin hidden on their undersides.

Her reasons had been everything and nothing; every cutting remark but none of them in particular. They had an argument unlike the ones before, only because this time Caitlin slammed the door and didn't come back. It was early summer and she should have been getting ready to start at Goldsmiths, but instead she walked through the night until the dawn, and then years passed, and she never saw her mother again.

Now she never would.

Kathleen Doherty had been found dead in her home. No sign of intrusion or unnatural causes, but, the Cork-accented family liaison had explained, an unexpected death in the community required investigation from a pathologist before the patient—the body, the corpse—could be released.

Unexpected for who? Caitlin had wanted to ask. It was the call she'd been waiting ten years for.

As Lola had promised, there was no sleep, but then there was no feeling either. Hours passed in flashes. Everything was hard edges; her depth perception failed her and made her clumsy. She was constantly being reminded where her body ended and the world began, constantly being batted back into place. Her mother was dead.

Maureen had called in those blurred predawn hours of throwing strange objects—her favorite mug, an old sketchbook, a half-burnt candle—into her backpack. Caitlin could come back, stay at the Big House with the Branaghs, be collected from the airport, have Maureen's support with "everything." The call was disorienting in itself—Maureen was as estranged from Caitlin now as Kathleen had been—but the second she heard that familiar voice, Caitlin deferred to it entirely. She would stay with Maureen, do whatever Maureen suggested. Finally, a grown-up was back in the room.

It was only at Stansted that Caitlin realized that "everything" meant the wake, the funeral. A dim awareness that the remembrance of this should have been a dagger to the heart but registered in her cloud only as fact, and she finally saw what her mother had liked about the drink.

This close to Christmas, Cork Airport was packed with last-minute travelers, merry chaos everywhere, but no shadows. Had the pills vanished them, had her grief stolen them, or had they followed Kathleen to wherever she'd gone?

Maureen had texted while Caitlin was in the air to inform her that Deedee, newly a guard, would pick her up and bring her down to the Big House. Caitlin remembered Deedee with her school skirt rolled up at the waist, a cloud of Charlie Girl perfume, and a mean streak a mile wide. She'd always liked pushing the younger, weaker, smaller kids around.

This thought propelled her to pick up the shabby black suitcase from an unattended luggage carousel. Stealing it was soothing; it brought the world around her into focus. But mostly it was getting a guard to handle stolen goods that made her smile.

Deedee stood slumped against a wall beside arrivals. A beacon in her high-vis jacket, tall, her broad frame and ruddy complexion bringing to mind camogie sticks and shin pads. Even in repose, her blunt features expressed dissatisfaction. Seeing her sent an unpleasant jolt through Caitlin. Deedee twenty years ago, wild-eyed and lunging downward toward her, face twisted unrecognizably, tendons jumping on her neck. Screaming again and again, *Where is she?*

"You've not changed," Deedee said, in the here and now. Caitlin was almost surprised her voice wasn't still hoarse after all this time.

"You haven't either," Caitlin said.

Deedee narrowed her eyes, waited for Caitlin's face to betray her meaning: compliment or insult.

"They still call you Deedee?" Caitlin asked. How easy it would be to infuse that nickname with scorn.

"It's Garda O'Halloran now." Deedee gave an it's-a-living kind of shrug belied by the proud lift of her chin. "Come on." She spun on her heel and marched off, leaving Caitlin to trail behind her, the purloined bag bumping along last of all.

In the car park, they stopped at a small, mud-splattered car. Caitlin opened the passenger door, then hesitated. The seat was littered with an open takeaway burger wrapper smeared with sauce and onion slivers, stray chips in its seam.

"What's the problem?" Deedee swung herself into the driver's seat. She reached over and collapsed the mess inward on itself. "Sure, you can't find a bin, no?"

Caitlin reached through the fog to consider how best to play this. There was no benefit to immediately antagonizing her, so she smiled as she accepted the litter, then simply walked a few meters away and, hidden by another car, dumped it on the tarmac. Returning, she tossed the stolen bag into the boot before getting in.

"That didn't take long." Deedee nodded at her from behind the driving wheel. Her sleeves rode up, and Caitlin saw a patchy yellow-and-orange lightning bolt tattooed inside her right wrist, a patina of white scars speckling her fingers and knuckles where she'd nicked or burned herself in the kitchen.

"It didn't," she agreed. A Styrofoam cup rolled about the footwell. Caitlin crushed it beneath her heel. Would Deedee accuse her straight out? A crazy thought: landing in Cork only to immediately be arrested for littering. She bit back laughter.

"What's so funny?" Deedee asked. The radio played an oldies station, the final notes of "Total Eclipse of the Heart" crashing into the air.

Paranoid, Caitlin thought, but she said, "You're exactly like I remember."

"Is that so?" There was threat in Deedee's voice.

"Don't be offended!" Caitlin laughed. "Why would you be offended? Didn't you say the same thing to me?"

"Who's offended?" Deedee snapped. "Anyway, I hope you're not expecting a taxi service all the time."

"Too busy with the policing?" Caitlin asked.

They were heading for the country roads, routes that should take minutes as the crow flies winding around hills and fields for hours instead.

"I am, yeah. Just had a big breakthrough on a case, actually. Not something I can really talk about with civilians, but high profile." Deedee was on the defensive again.

"Wow." Caitlin kept her tone on the right side of impressed. "You know, I never really thought of Bannakilduff as having much crime."

"Surprising," Deedee remarked, "since you should have been involved with our biggest case."

Caitlin's tongue felt thick—with tiredness, with whatever Lola had given that was still in her system, with regret.

"Is that so?" She mimicked Deedee's earlier comment.

"I wasn't going to get into it so soon"—Deedee was clearly champing at the bit to get into it—"but they shouldn't have let you go, definitely not let you just fly off to England."

"I had to start school." This was true but sounded like a lie. Caitlin swallowed hard.

"Not before September." Deedee pointed at her.

"We had a rental lined up. We'd applied ages before." Caitlin felt her heart start to pound, forced herself to stop talking. Deedee knew, she must know; Caitlin couldn't outrun this forever.

"Whoops," Deedee muttered as she blew through a red light, angry horns behind her. "See, now, I was distracted, because you're coming off awfully unsettled, Caitlin, you know what I mean?"

Rows of houses painted in Easter pastels flickered past the window.

"I'm not after accusing you of anything, but you're acting like I am," Deedee continued.

Caitlin didn't trust herself to speak.

"It's bad policing, is what I'm saying." Deedee was enjoying this, and it radiated from her. "But why would you be worried about that?"

"You said I should have been a suspect!" Caitlin blurted. "But I was a kid too!"

"I didn't say that. When did I say that?"

"It was the first thing you said, that I should have been a suspect in our biggest case."

"Involved," Deedee said, glancing oddly at her. "I said you should have been *involved*. You were the last person to see her."

Caitlin froze. She hadn't slept in several days; she realized now she also hadn't eaten since breakfast yesterday. She tried to replay the conversation, to recall the exact cadence of Deedee's accusation, and found she couldn't. Her guilty conscience had heard the truth.

"Sorry, I'm just tired. It's been . . . a lot." But why say "involved"? That was tantamount to saying "suspect," wasn't it?

Was it?

"I'm sorry about Kathleen," Deedee said.

Caitlin nodded. They lapsed into silence.

"Weren't there sightings?" Caitlin asked. She couldn't help herself; Roisin was still at the forefront of her mind. One thing she knew she would have in common with Deedee: everything always came back to Roisin.

Deedee snorted, the suggestion unworthy of a response.

Caitlin knew there had been, because she had called one in herself, weeks after she'd left. She'd gone to a payphone with a pound coin and dialed the information line, told whoever answered that she'd seen Roisin. She'd been skipping, she said, she was in Kinafallia. She had thought she was buying herself more time, more distance from the disappearance. She hadn't thought of Deedee and her granny, the impact of false hope.

The landscape of cottages and fields, hand-painted signs for eggs and milk on the roadside, felt alien after so long. Everything was cuter and quainter than she remembered; she was returning a patronizing outsider.

The opening synth notes of Cyndi Lauper's "Girls Just Want to Have Fun" began, and a squeeze of grief stole the air from Caitlin's lungs. Deedee hummed along while Caitlin shut her eyes and breathed slowly through her nose.

"If you're allergic to dogs, you'll have to say."

Caitlin opened her eyes. "I don't think I am."

"That blanket isn't bothering you?" Deedee jerked her head behind them toward a blanket, more dog hair than fabric, spread across the back seat of the car. "Your eyes are watering. Looks like you're crying."

"Hay fever, I suppose."

"Funny time of year for it."

Off the tarmacked road now, they passed a tractor so long rusted to the ground that the dirt had turned orange beneath it. Caitlin could have sworn that tractor had been there when she left too. Ahead of them, the Hanging Woods.

Where is she? Caitlin would never stop hearing that scream. She averted her eyes.

"Do you think about her?" Deedee drove slower on the approach.

Caitlin didn't know whether to lie or tell the truth.

"What do you remember of that day?" Deedee pushed.

Caitlin took a deep breath. "It was hot. Roisin was talking about Shackleton, about exploring. About the summer solstice celebration. We saw Lee Casey on the road, like I said at the time."

Lee Casey, with his silver St. Christopher's medal around his neck and fistfuls of beautiful dream catchers made with materials from the Hanging Woods.

"Nothing else?" Deedee jumped in, impatient. "Lee Casey had an alibi."

Those dream catchers had chimed in a very particular kind of way, like the pebbles and feathers and sticks from the Hanging Woods carried a song all of their own.

Where is she? Caitlin wiggled her little finger into her ear, but she couldn't dislodge the scream. "No. Nothing new." Then, "People believe that alibi then?"

Believing Casey's alibi was believing Caitlin was a liar. It was uncomfortably close to raising the question of why Caitlin would want to find someone to blame.

"I couldn't speak for people," Deedee said. "I can only say for myself."

They swung around a corner; the Hanging Woods surrounded them. The long shadows of branches fell over the car, flickering across Deedee's face; there one moment, gone the next.

"For myself," Deedee concluded, "I think most people lie when they're scared."

The Hanging Woods rustled, thick with the stories of lonely farmers, visiting in the middle of the night with their nooses in hand. Sometimes they had been spotted from the road the next day. Sometimes they were only found weeks later.

The keening sound of wind through the old branches filled the car, ghosts rustling the undergrowth, pushing against the sides. Dwindling sunlight was blotted by the jagged boughs that stretched above them from the woods.

"Are you scared?" Deedee pulled over to the edge of the road to let another car pass, the engine grumbling to a halt.

Caitlin scoffed.

"Ah, of course not. You went in here all the time, didn't you? That day, for instance, you had been at the celebration, then you both came here. How do you figure that?"

Roisin shouldn't have followed.

"The project, mapping the town, we were working on that, I guess. We were just . . . hanging around. I don't know, we weren't even really friends."

"Looked like ye were friends to me, having a joint project. Always the brains, weren't you? What was that school in London called?" Deedee asked, deliberately casual.

The road was empty.

"It was an arts school." Caitlin willed Deedee to start driving again. When she didn't, Caitlin continued. "It wasn't great. Just turned nine, entering into the second-to-last year of primary over there. Everyone had friends, and I just had a weird accent and these nightmares every night. All right?"

It must have been, because Deedee tapped the steering wheel and started the car up. "They're planning a housing development here, you know. The Hanging Estate, maybe they'll call it."

"Can they do that?" Caitlin's stomach dropped. Could they pry her secrets from the Hanging Woods?

"Developer's been trying to buy for years; the price is right now. The owners, well. Niall Wilson's got gambling debts, Big Mac's getting a place in Spain with his bit." Deedee finally turned to look at her. "Would you go in there now, do you think?"

They were a single point of light against the blackness of the woods. Something rustled in the undergrowth.

"No." Sweat prickled on Caitlin's brow.

Deedee humphed in acknowledgment of her fear.

They pulled back out into the lane, with Caitlin sending a silent prayer of thanks at seeing the back of every tree they passed. Fear squeezed her chest at the thought of being swallowed up once more by the darkness of the Hanging Woods, like Roisin had been.

"Big Mac?" she asked.

"Garda McPherson, you'd have known him as," Deedee explained. "His son's a guard now."

McPherson had been a terrier of a man, oversized canines and sly, darting eyes. Wiry hair that crept from his cuffs over the backs of his hands down almost to his nail beds.

"That make the son Baby Mac?"

"Makes him a prick."

Caitlin resisted the urge to draw comparisons between Deedee and the younger McPherson. Silence between them as the wide-open fields reappeared, and Caitlin was dizzy with relief.

"Where'd you fly out from?" Deedee asked. Caitlin could feel it was a warm-up to more pointed questions.

"City," she lied, for no reason other than *fuck you, Deedee.*

"And what did you do in London?"

"Civil service." This tended to curtail further questions, even from actual civil servants. With the woods behind them, she felt more confident, more herself. Maybe the pills were wearing off.

"That's not what I meant."

Caitlin watched Deedee. She looked blank, her jaw set and eyes now forward on the road ahead. "Hobbies, then? I still do a bit of doodling."

Deedee couldn't have been asking what Caitlin thought she was asking; she couldn't know about her . . . less-than-legal activities. Surely not.

"I think we'll be talking a lot more, now you're back," Deedee said.

They had pulled up outside their destination. The gatehouse first, now ringed with yellow-and-black caution tape. *Unexpected death in the community*. Behind it, smoke issued from the chimney of the Big House. Cold white Christmas lights shone from the high roof, draping across the second-floor window lintels, offering only a glimpse of the life bustling within. It loomed larger now than it ever had, her mother's place suddenly so clearly a worker's home, only ever an afterthought to the manor.

"Lovely." Caitlin jumped out, her right hand with a key pressed against the side of the car. "Thanks for the ride." As she slammed the door, she twisted the key against the paint, stabbing in as hard as she could.

"Mind the door!" Deedee slapped the wheel in frustration, but Caitlin had turned toward the Big House.

A man waved madly at her from its door. As she approached, his features clicked into familiarity. Sean. He had a rugby build, large hands, and shirtsleeves rolled up over beefy forearms, a softness at the stomach. He pushed his glasses up with a practiced wrinkle of his nose. He wasn't handsome, but he had an appealing, open quality. Wide smile and lots of eye contact.

Though Deedee was climbing out of the car, Caitlin noticed that Sean didn't so much as glance at his girlfriend. He was helping Caitlin instead, pulling the suitcase from the boot. She was grateful for this, and for the distraction of his chatter; the lump in her throat had returned at the sight of the dark, empty gatehouse. She smothered a bone-jittering urge to run, and focused instead on walking toward the Big House, to safety.

11

DEEDEE

When Deedee had imagined getting the chance to talk to Caitlin Doherty again, she had envisioned herself as cool, calm, collected. She would lull Caitlin into a sense of security, build rapport, and eventually lead her into remembering some key detail. Something Roisin had said, some stranger who had lingered too closely. Obviously Caitlin hadn't had direct involvement with Roisin's disappearance. How could she have? A nine-year-old couldn't cover up a crime for twenty years.

Now Deedee watched Sean usher Caitlin toward the Big House, and realized that she'd probably lost her chance of playing that scene out in the future too.

She trudged toward the house, cursing herself, several paces behind Sean and Caitlin as they disappeared inside. Even out there, she heard Maureen exclaim in delight at the sight of Caitlin, and her heart sank even further. Maureen and Colm loved Caitlin; they'd almost raised her as their own while Kathleen spent years gallivanting around town. Would the space they had held in their lives for Deedee still be open if Caitlin walked back into it?

Deedee couldn't bring herself to enter the house. Quiet, grateful Caitlin was probably already taking her place. She deliberated for a moment, and then self-pity swept through her so totally that she felt exhausted. She turned back to the car, and with every step, another sad thought came to her.

Sean wouldn't even notice her absence.

None of them would.

They would be only too delighted to forget hotheaded, moody, mean Deedee.

Deedee had no one.

She was at the car when she heard Sean call for her.

"Yeah?" She turned. He was jogging, his long legs only a stride or two away from her. He *had* noticed her absence! Of course he had. She should explain herself. "I said I'd meet Fi . . ."

Sean leaned past her and opened the passenger door to pull Caitlin's backpack out of the seat well.

"Sorry about that." He gave her a quick, dry kiss on the cheek. "Have fun!"

And that was it. Deedee couldn't help but snort in anger at his retreating figure. Sean heard her, and there it was: the hitch in his step, the raising of his shoulders just a tiny bit, a literal bristle.

"You're welcome for the taxi service," Deedee called. She knew she shouldn't inflame him.

"Thank you." Sean stopped, halfway between her and the Big House, the backpack dangling from one hand. "I know we all *really* appreciate it."

He spoke as though she was unreasonable, rather than unappreciated. Difficult, not cast aside. It was infuriating.

"Good luck to you, but I'd say you wanta be careful with that one," she called.

"Not this again." Sean groaned. "They investigated! I know yesterday was rough, but you have to start accepting this."

"You don't get it." Deedee paused to gather her thoughts. *It's not about me being crazy, it's a real chance this time, she really might—*

"I don't get it? I'm the only one still listening to you." Sean couldn't—or wouldn't—keep the mocking note from his voice. "Did you already accuse her of foul play?"

"No! She misheard me!" Deedee could feel all the things she wanted to say, but none of them made sense. She should have just left, not said anything. Now they were in the thick of it, and leaving would be storming off or throwing a tantrum. She had to stay.

"Jesus, Dee, I was kidding! What have you done?" Sean closed the distance between them and drew himself up to his full height. He wasn't quite the athlete he'd once been, but all that bulk was still there.

"It's not like that." She had to tilt her head back to see his face. "We talked, I asked her if she remembered anything."

Sean exhaled slowly through his nose and Deedee knew that she was in trouble.

When things were bad with Sean, they were very bad.

"Look, it's fine, OK? I delivered her, I didn't say anything, we're fine." What Deedee had been trying to tell him didn't matter. He had to be defused. She placed her hand on his arm.

He looked down at her hand and then back to her face.

"It would be best if you left now." He spoke in his normal tone, but the stillness of his body felt dangerous, like a snake coiled to strike.

"I told you I was meeting Fi." Deedee crossed her arms over her body and tucked her hands up into her armpits. It was cold out, was all. She wasn't scared, even as she shrank into herself.

"Tell her I said hello." Sean stepped backward, away from her, toward the house.

Deedee felt her knees give a little with relief. She hated to argue with Sean, hated that she was so often the instigator.

"I will. I'm sorry, all right? I'm just a bit hungover, but tonight we can order in—"

"Of course you're hungover." Sean spat on the ground in front of her. Deedee jumped back. "I'll stay here tonight."

"Ah, c'mon." She kept the shake from her voice.

"No, I'll stay here. You've really upset me, you know. I don't know why you do this, but Mac told me you were so hammered last night, stumbling around, that you knocked Kathleen down."

Deedee's heart stopped. She hadn't even seen Mac. "He's got it wrong. She bumped into *me*, I got her home safely."

"So safely she was dead by morning, eh?" Sean shook his head. "I've always kept your secrets, the things you do when you get angry, but this, this might be a step too far."

"I was being a good Samaritan!"

"I told Mac the same thing. He agreed. He knows he's mistaken now. But when they release the body, what if it was the fall, Deedee? What'll we do then?"

"It won't be," Deedee whispered. It couldn't be.

"You wanta be careful, Dee. The way Kathleen was living, the way she drank, it's not surprising. But she started out like you."

Deedee gaped. She had that slowest-kid-in-the-class feeling again; how this situation had spiraled, how she'd ended up here. She felt herself on the brink of tears.

Sean clucked. "You've worked yourself up something awful, haven't you?"

She nodded miserably.

"C'mere to me." He dropped the backpack on the ground and opened his arms, his posture suddenly soft.

On shaking legs, Deedee went to him.

"Don't I always look after you?" he cooed into her hair. "You just apologize, go see Fi, and we'll chat tomorrow."

"Sorry, Sean," she said, pushing her face into his chest. "You're right."

At the door, he turned and waved once. Deedee wiped her eyes and got into the car. She had gotten herself into such a silly state. She needed to grow up a bit, think about something outside of herself, and Sean needed something to soften him up a bit more. A baby would fix all their problems.

12

CAITLIN

Caitlin heard Maureen before she saw her, the familiar tinkling of her many bangles, her head-thrown-back explosion of laughter, and felt herself relax instantly. When Maureen appeared before her with her silver hair in a long plait, and her weathered face—tanned, wind-blown, deeply lined, and beautiful—Caitlin surprised herself by pulling her into a tight hug.

"Welcome home, sweetheart." Maureen rubbed her back as though she were still a child. She smelled like lavender. Caitlin was surprised at how youthful she seemed. As a child, she'd thought Maureen was ancient, but seeing her now, she'd have put her in her fifties somewhere.

They made their way through the wood-paneled hall into the familiar country-style kitchen: decorative brass jelly molds in the shape of leaping fish over the stove, a row of snake plants in kilim-patterned pots lining the windowsill with yellow-green leaves, bright against the midwinter fields outside. An internal door to the left led through to the formal dining room, used solely for Christmas dinner, and ahead of her was the back door, which she had spent so much of her childhood running in and out of.

Something was slightly off, though, like everything had shifted a few inches to the right. Caitlin dismissed the feeling. The kettle still bubbled away. The carriage clock that Colm had been given in recognition for volunteering with the fire brigade ticked as loudly as ever. The Big House even smelled the same: like clean laundry, earth, a smoldering fireplace.

This was home.

"'Tis awful." Maureen settled her at the table in her usual place and put a tea in front of her. "I've already spoken to Paudie at the funeral home for you. You know the story?"

Caitlin had been told that a neighbor, Sheila Murphy, suffering from perimenopausal insomnia, had strapped on her head torch and gone for a late-night jog. Caitlin thought she'd been snooping but, whatever the case, she'd seen the house all lit up and, peeking in the window, realized something was amiss.

I just get these feelings sometimes. Caitlin could imagine Sheila retelling the story again and again, reveling in her role. *There's a lot more to the world than just what you'd see with your eyes.*

"Thanks," she said. "The guards said it could take a few days to . . . process."

"You poor thing, and poor Kathleen, God love her." Maureen clucked.

A sudden snapping sound from within the cabinet, and Maureen's hands flew to cover her mouth. She let out a groan.

"Now what that is," she explained, "is we've had a little mouse running around in the cupboards back there, and you know yourself, if you let one in, you're only leaving the door open to a thousand more."

Caitlin sympathized—she'd want to live in here too—but aloud she said, "Country living. I suppose in London it might be rats."

"Pests everywhere you go." Maureen busied herself bustling around the kitchen. "Anyhow, so that's to say, don't you be looking in those lower cupboards, just in case. Seany will deal with it."

Caitlin sipped her sugary, milky tea, made to her childhood preference. Knowing Maureen had remembered this warmed her through. To have been loved all along.

"Now then." Maureen gave a mischievous wink as she set a slab of marble cake down in front of Caitlin, as though she was still sneaking her treats behind her mother's back. "I got that for you, so you've to eat it up."

Caitlin grabbed it. Too-sweet chocolate and vanilla sponge that dried out on her tongue and coated her teeth. She couldn't stop; she pressed her thumb and fingers to the crumbs on the plate to collect every last one. Maureen said nothing, only brought the whole cake over for her.

Car tires crunched over the gravel outside and onto the road.

"Deedee's not staying?" Caitlin asked. Sean had been out there retrieving her backpack for several minutes.

"Never mind her." Maureen rolled her eyes. "Let me just tell you this: we'd your mother over there the last ten years and she was wonderful. She'd be here often enough, at that seat there."

Caitlin looked at the empty seat Maureen indicated and felt a deep sadness.

A shadow passed over it, and both women turned to the window to watch Sean trudge past, on his way to the back door. His cheeks were flushed and his breath puffed angrily ahead of him, but by the time he entered the room, he was all smiles. He held her backpack up triumphantly, and Maureen directed him to take it up to "Caitlin's room."

Every word loosened Caitlin's muscles, and she felt a sudden tug of fatigue. The house was hot, and she pressed the cool backs of her hands against her rosy cheeks. The uppers from Lola were clearly wearing off.

"Now, Colm will be only delighted to see you, but he's under the weather just now." Maureen kept a steady stream of chatter going. "But doesn't he get right to the front of the queue with Dr. Sheehan?"

"He should," Caitlin said. "He did a lot for the community."

"More than anyone else before or since, people say." Sean entered the room, collected his tea, and joined them at the table.

Colm's accident, the day of that awful solstice celebration. He'd told Maureen he was popping back to the car to grab the trophy for the costume contest, and had been hit by a speeding car racing past the parking area. His pelvis and hips were crushed. The vehicle, which must have been badly damaged, was never found, nor was its driver.

For Caitlin, the accident provided a distraction. Word hadn't yet gone out about Roisin; those perilous hours when she might have been found and Caitlin caught were lost. Caitlin had flown to London days later with rusty red blood embedded under her fingernails.

"Is he well enough for a visit?" she asked.

Maureen dithered, checking the time on the carriage clock. "He might be asleep still, after his tablets."

"Ah, he'll be devastated if he knows Caitlin's here and he's missed her." Sean winked.

A happy flush of pride overpowered Caitlin's lingering guilt.

Maureen steered her back through the hall and up the polished wooden stairs, chattering all the way. "We have a nurse come by twice a week to check on him, help with his physical therapy, all of that."

Upstairs, past a side table covered in a dusty silk flower arrangement, they reached the door at the far end of the hallway.

"He gets out a bit; he'd be taking a turn around the fields, though Sean maintains the boundary with the woods now and gets all the kindling and so on. He'd even go down to church on Sunday," Maureen continued. She swung the door open. "But it'll be his heart, they think. He's after getting awfully weak altogether, but I worry most about his heart."

The room was gloomy, the curtains half pulled. The scent of sickness hung in the air. Colm's figure in the bed was all wrong. He was gray and gasping even in repose. His gaunt face was slack below his cheekbones, the lower half collapsing like cliffs crumbling into the sea. Previously clean-shaven, now his chin bristled with a short, scrubby beard.

"Colm?" An involuntary question pulled from the throat of her child self.

"Colm, love, Caitlin's back." Maureen rifled through a medicine bag, her bangles thunking against plastic, pills rattling in bottles.

Colm's jaw dropped even lower, his tongue undulated. The fingers on his right hand twitched.

"Cait." His voice was barely an exhalation, but the corner of his mouth quivered toward a smile.

"Caitlin, yes!" Maureen looked up with the energy of a lottery winner. She turned to Caitlin. "Oh, he remembers you well!"

Colm croaked, and his chest arched up millimeters toward the ceiling, but he lacked strength enough to pull himself up.

"I'm back," Caitlin told him.

"You can take his hand, love." Maureen indicated Colm's hand, palm-up on the bed, and Caitlin slipped hers into it.

Locked inside this body was the man who'd taken care of her, loved her. She squeezed his hand. His fingers closed, his huge palm eclipsing hers. He squeezed back with a reassuring strength.

"He can talk usually?" Caitlin asked.

"Oh yes, it's only that he's a lung infection today." Maureen laughed. She drew a hand over her husband's forehead fondly. "He's a lot of opinions most of the time!"

"It's good to see you again," Caitlin told Colm. He tipped his chin down in acknowledgment and then cleared his throat. Caitlin leaned in.

"Long time," he said. His eyes fluttered open and closed, closing for longer each time, until Maureen patted Caitlin on the shoulder to pull her away.

"I'd say he'll be looking forward to a chat with you in a day or two now, won't you, Colm? After a rest, hey?"

Caitlin let Maureen push her from the room. When she glanced back over her shoulder, Maureen was swabbing his inside elbow. Colm's eyes were open and he locked his gaze with Caitlin's. Then Maureen pushed a syringe into his arm, and his eyelids shut definitively.

Back in the kitchen, Sean had refilled her tea and arranged a plate of biscuits in the middle of the table.

"You'll talk to us, won't you?" he asked anxiously. "Let us know how we can help?"

Caitlin nodded, though fatigue closed over her faster and faster.

Overhead, they both heard the door to Colm's room closing and Maureen's footsteps on the landing.

"Where's Deedee?" she asked, fighting a yawn.

Sean's jaw tightened. "Off to the pub, probably. You look knackered."

"It's been a very long day," Caitlin said.

Sean led her up to the spare room at the top of the stairs.

"I'm hanging around here for a few days." He paused and looked down at her fondly. "It's not so often we get to see you, is it?"

Caitlin squeezed his arm affectionately and he placed his hand over hers, held it there before releasing. He swung the door open to a riot of peach and lilac with grand mock-Victorian paneling. A large hardback book lay in the center of the bed.

"I remember this." Caitlin seized the book. "*The Little Photographer: A Kid's Guide to Perfect Pictures*! I can't believe it's still here."

She flicked through the pages, marked with her childish annotations, and felt a lump in her throat.

"I thought you'd get a kick out of that." Sean grinned and mimed clutching it to his chest, an impression of Caitlin as a child.

"Thank you." She pulled him into a hug. She owed the Branaghs so much.

He coughed politely and she released him, but he lingered.

"You remember your ma and mine running back and forth over that field with fistfuls of pictures ripped from magazines?" He indicated the loud decor.

"I can't believe it's still the same." Caitlin couldn't remember a thing about this house but the kitchen. Sean's story felt familiar, though. It could have been real.

"That kind of operation, you'd only ever want to do it the once." He rolled his eyes good-naturedly. "Give me a shout if you need anything."

Alone finally, Caitlin turned her attention to the stolen suitcase, breaking the zipper with a biro. Inside, she found clothes, chargers, whatever. Boring.

The frisson of achievement she'd had at taking it soured now that it was open. Reality was often a letdown. Like those sketches in George's flat. Stealing those would have been the same—a high of winning, and then the reality of "now what?"

She dug into her backpack for Mark's wallet and Ettie's bracelet. She didn't keep everything, and she wouldn't keep anything forever, but these things were anchors to who she was. What she could do.

Against her better judgment, she clasped the bracelet onto her wrist. She'd mended the link with a dot of superglue, but that wouldn't hold for long.

Restless, she rifled through the room. The chest of drawers held Deedee's old clothes, and Caitlin dimly recalled a time when Deedee had moved in here, after her grandmother had died. There was no sign that the room had been personalized for her, she noticed with satisfaction. No Blu Tack marks on the walls from posters, no hint of a teenager's style in the furniture or fabrics.

An image of the mouse in the kitchen cupboard came to her. *You let one in, you're only leaving the door open to a thousand more.*

The wardrobe was full of Colm's old photography things, including a film camera with four shots left. Caitlin turned it over in her hands and then carried it to the mirror and took a picture of herself.

Photography had been her first love creatively, but without Colm, it hadn't felt right. She put the camera in her backpack.

Outside, the day was getting dark. The winter nights were long and already snatching at the last rays of sunshine, though it was only midafternoon. That suited her for now, as she curled up on the bed. She would feel better if only she could rest.

13

CAITLIN

Caitlin has been busy with the Hanging Woods. She is literally becoming an expert on the woods. An expert is the best at
something, or the most knowledgeable. Not just anyone can be an
expert. Experts are smarter and more hardworking than everyone else.
Effectively, experts don't have very many friends because they spend
so much time researching and because they're more interested in ideas
than people.

Three weekends away from the summer holidays and Caitlin
needs to be ready for her big project. If she misses her chance now,
she'll have to wait all the way until the winter solstice, and she doesn't
fancy the idea of conducting her research in the dark on the shortest
day instead of the longest.

The expert has to journey to somewhere far-flung. Caitlin practices making a dangerous voyage, keeping low to the ground and moving slowly. Once the expert arrives at their destination—here, the
famous Hanging Woods of Bannakilduff, home to ghosts and beasts
aplenty—she tosses a branch onto the ground ahead. If it sinks, the
ground is quicksand. It hasn't been yet, but you never know. She also

carries a ball of wool, which is first tied securely around a sturdy tree at the outskirts of the woods, and then slowly unravels as she walks. Not only will she never get lost, she will be able to pull herself out of any dangerous situation, although sometimes she does find she gets a bit tangled in the branches. She forages for samples: leaves, berries. Once she picked up some strange stones that, when squashed between her thumb and forefinger, let out a horrible smell, so that's how she learned about rabbit poo, but this is the life of the expert. Experts can't get too precious about staying clean, but also it would not be a good idea for anyone the expert knows from school to ever, ever find out about that.

Then the expert takes to the library. Experience has shown that books about folklore are the best, while the atlas has a very limited usefulness to this particular project. Caitlin is working on her own encyclopedia of the woods. The most haunted place in Bannakilduff, probably in all Ireland. She is looking for ley lines, fairy rings, any other supernatural hazards that she should be aware of as she researches the solstices.

Soon the Hanging Woods are her place. The trees only look identical. She is navigating a path that gets deeper and deeper into the woods with each passing day.

On the third weekend, the ground is muddy from the rain. Caitlin has once more anchored herself to a tree and is making her way along her worn path when she hears it. A tiny sound, the slightest cracking of a twig. If she wasn't an expert, she might have assumed this was just an animal, but she *is* an expert, so she knows that another human is here, in the woods with her.

It's not that she's afraid, because she never really gets afraid. Sometimes, in the dead of night, after her mother falls asleep in her chair, she watches a late horror movie. She turns the volume down and sits right up against the screen and watches a hockey-masked murderer slash his way through a bunch of teenagers. Even though she can still hear the violin strings as she tries to fall asleep, she never even has nightmares afterward. So she's definitely not afraid now.

"Show yourself!" she shouts.

The Hanging Woods are still. Caitlin waits. Nothing.

But as she moves forward, she hears it again. Rustling now. She is being followed. She stops and whirls around. No one is there.

"Come out!" she challenges, as fiercely as she can. "Who's there?"

Still no one makes themselves known. Caitlin continues.

When the rustling picks up again, she turns and runs toward the sound. These woods are hers. She isn't going to be teased, pushed around, called names, or made fun of in here. No way. She sees a figure hunched over behind a tree and she launches herself on it, fists and feet and knees and elbows. This is her place and she will defend it.

"Ouch, Caitlin! Stop it!" The voice is familiar. Unwelcome.

"Roisin? What are you doing?"

"What are *you* doing? Why did you attack me? And why"— Roisin's eyes grow round and she covers a mean little snicker with one hand—"are you carrying around a ball of wool?"

"I wouldn't bother to explain it to someone like you, you couldn't even begin to understand." Caitlin tries for dignity.

"Looks stupid." Roisin's presence has punctured Caitlin's world, made her feel shrunken and small. As stealthily as she can, she tosses the wool ball behind her into the undergrowth.

"*You* look stupid. I bet that's rabbit poo on your legs too, not just mud." Caitlin isn't sure, but she pinches her nose and waves a hand in front of her face anyway. "Pee-yew!"

"My grandma is going to be mad," Roisin mutters, brushing herself down.

"No one is ever mad at you." Caitlin is scornful. Roisin doesn't know how good she has it. Orphans are so lucky.

"Have you seen any?" Roisin scans the clearing.

"Any what?" Caitlin asks.

"Rabbits. Have you seen any in here?"

"Tons. And mushrooms—once I found poisonous ones." She doesn't mention the fairy circles, the solstice stuff just yet. It's too precious, too secret a desire.

"You didn't?" Roisin's tone is mellowing into awe. She wants to believe.

"I did." Caitlin takes a chance. She pulls out her notebook/encyclopedia and flips to the page where she drew the poisonous mushroom.

Roisin looks at it and then hands it back. "Good drawings."

"I'm saving up for a camera." Caitlin would need money to save, and that's another thing they never have any of, but it feels grown up to say it.

"All the old explorers did drawings anyway. I'm drawing. I'm making a map." Roisin pulls out a notebook of her own.

"A map? Of the woods?"

"Not just the woods. Everywhere. The whole town. I've already done my house, see, and then here's the fields, and town, and the road up there . . ."

Caitlin flips through Roisin's book and it's clear that she has covered a lot of ground. Caitlin respects it, even as she thinks that the quality of Roisin's work doesn't match the quantity. Roisin is no expert.

"What do these mean?" She points to the area of the Hanging Woods. Roisin has marked it with a mishmash of symbols: a shell, a skull, a dotted path. "Stuff you've found?"

If Roisin has found a skull, Caitlin will be so jealous but also so excited.

"No, it's—"

"Roisin!" An almighty bellow rips through the trees, and both girls startle as a murder of crows takes off over their heads, their wings momentarily blocking the sun and plunging them into darkness.

"Roi-sin!" Again the call comes.

"You'd better head. This way's fastest." Caitlin is delighted to have a chance to show off how well she knows the Hanging Woods, and even more so when Roisin actually falls into line behind her.

In no time at all, they're on the edge of the woods bordering the Branaghs' house and the source of the racket is revealed.

Deedee O'Halloran, storming forward to take Roisin's arm. "The state of you!"

"The great explorer returns!" Colm Branagh claps a hand on Roisin's shoulder, and Caitlin feels the dislike she has for Roisin shift from something formless and vague into jealousy. When did Roisin become such great pals with Colm?

"Sorry," Roisin mumbles. "Thought you were off with Sean."

"You hush up," Deedee says, turning red, because everyone knows she's desperately in love with Sean Branagh. "Granny wants us home."

Caitlin moves backward into the trees. It's like she's invisible, like no one cares about her at all.

"Is it dinnertime, is it?" Colm stands, his hands on his hips, surveying all three girls. "In that case, I'd better get Caitlin in for hers."

Caitlin's legs feel jellied with relief. She does have a place here. She is home.

14

DEEDEE

The pathologist would examine Kathleen's body to rule out any potential foul play. Kathleen had been fine when Deedee left her. Anything could have happened—stroke, heart attack, liver failure, the list went on. It wasn't the blow to the head when she'd fallen. Hopefully.

After that, the wake and the funeral. Friday just before Christmas, the pathologist would be getting to it Monday earliest. That meant there was this weekend, minimum, but probably a week to put the screws on Caitlin. Unless on Monday the pathologist did say Kathleen had died from a blow to the head, in which case Deedee didn't know what she'd do.

She shook her head at the absurdity of the situation: this time next week she might have uncovered something crucial for the investigation—or she might be being questioned for manslaughter.

Uneasy, she parked and hurried to get Frank. He'd be fine for another few hours yet—it was only a morning alone, after all—but she was prone to dog-mammy guilt.

That phone call to the Branaghs just after she came home played on her mind. She'd used Kathleen's phone for that, which wasn't a crime, but what would it look like if someone was to investigate the situation?

Deedee hadn't even known anything had happened to Kathleen, she'd just innocently borrowed the phone, but what was she supposed to do about it now? She'd only been trying to help.

Outside O'Shea's, Frank took great interest in a dark mark by the door that could have been blood. But no, Deedee reminded herself. The only blood had been hers, where Kathleen had given her a nosebleed. She'd bloodied the collar of Kathleen's coat herself. Still, images of Kathleen sprawled out after her fall flashed through her mind. She scanned the area above the door, and there it was, the CCTV camera pointed right over the entrance. What was its range of capture? And on which side of the threshold had she actually hit Kathleen?

Fi was already there, a bottle of house white on the bar as she chatted to Gerry O'Shea. To Deedee's relief, she was already well on her way to tipsy. She waved to Deedee. Deedee glanced over her shoulder as she joined them. There was no camera inside the doorway.

"I'm just saying, Dee, we were watching *The Snowman*, and every single second they'd be asking me questions: 'What's wrong with this feller, can they all fly here?' 'Is he made of snow, is he?' 'Wouldn't your hand go right through him?' 'Sure, you'd be awful cold, giving him a hug!' Driving me demented!"

"I know it well," Deedee replied. "The other day I showed Maureen a funny picture of a cat, and she's all 'Whose cat is that now? Do you know that cat?' I said, I do, yeah, I see him down the pub all the time."

They laughed. Fi downed the end of her glass and emptied the bottle into a generously portioned glass for each of them. Deedee ordered another bottle. For the first time she noticed a camera behind the bar too.

"Shooting a reality TV show in here, Gerry?" she asked jovially. "Got cameras all over!"

"A deterrent," Gerry answered offhand.

Probably not even filming, Deedee thought with relief.

"Cheers to the Christmas holidays anyway," Fi broke in.

"Cheers to that," Deedee said, though the time hadn't occurred to her. "I've truly put a shift in ferrying Caitlin Doherty from the airport for Maureen."

"Aren't you good?" Fi said, but she was distracted, sneaking a look at her phone, suppressing a smile.

"Fi-ona! Who're you smiling over?" Deedee mimed leaning in to sneak a peek at the screen. The wine warmed her blood and loosened all her nerves.

Fi unleashed a huge smile. "He's called Ben. It's not officially a thing yet, but we've been seeing each other for about six weeks."

"I can't believe I didn't know! Pictures?"

"Let me find a good one." Fi scrolled for a couple of seconds, and then, "OK, so I promise he's actually much better-looking in real life."

"No, he's cute!" Deedee gasped appropriately at the picture of a thoroughly average man Fi showed her. "He has kind eyes, you know? And you're happy?"

"You know how it is. Early days and all that. Well—you missed the update last night." Fi looked archly at her over her glass.

"I had to go in the end." Deedee flushed; she might have been forgiven, but her actions hadn't been forgotten.

Fi nodded. "It was packed out like. I wasn't sure if you'd gone to the bar or fallen down dead. Half the place could have perished, and with the crowds in here, the first you'd notice would've been that your drink came within a reasonable time frame—apologies, Gerry! It's not your fault!"

Gerry, at the other end of the bar rinsing out glasses, looked up in confusion.

"You're a victim of your own success, Ger!" Deedee called out. He rolled his eyes and flicked his cloth toward them. He didn't mind them acting the maggot. Bannakilduff wasn't big enough for grudges. You could make any number of mistakes, offend half a pub, and still be fine the next day. To your face, anyway.

"Here, let's find a corner," Deedee said. O'Shea's was sparsely populated; too soon for the real drinking crowd to be in, but so close to

Christmas, it would never be empty. She steered them to a quiet booth at the back. Frank settled down under the table, his head resting on his paws.

"Caitlin's back to look after arrangements, I imagine?" Fi asked. "I was thinking of her earlier. Quiet kid, hardly remember her. All I can think of is, well, you know. Roisin and her, heading off into the woods that day." She looked at Deedee meaningfully before taking a long swig of wine.

There weren't a lot of people Deedee would have this kind of conversation with, and she felt Fi's caution, the space she created to let her stop.

"I asked her about it," she said. "She's no memory apparently."

Fi raised her eyebrows but kept her glass at mouth height, signaling Deedee to continue.

"Sean tells me I'm mad all the time, but there's something there. I can't quite grasp it, I just have a feeling." Deedee smiled ruefully. "But what's a feeling worth?"

"What of that school she went to? Now, maybe I'd be wrong, we weren't in her class either of us, but was she that much a genius?" Fi asked.

Deedee glowed to hear the tinge of suspicion in Fi's voice.

"I've not a notion, but she dodged the question."

"Hmm, well. I suppose we'll see. Get her out and put a few drinks in her, see if anything comes to light," Fi joked.

"I didn't expect such interrogation offa you." Deedee grinned. "You, who loves everyone."

"I make exceptions now and then," Fi said, but her posture changed now that Deedee had reminded her who she was. "But she was a traumatized kid. That'd make you lose your memory right enough. She never had a dad around either, did she? She'll be on her own now."

"Yeah," Deedee said cautiously. "But is it surprising? I mean, with how Kathleen was and all."

"No," Fi agreed. "She lived hard, for sure. Still. Sad."

Relief flooded Deedee. So they all agreed then. It was sad but it wasn't unexpected. It wasn't her fault.

"Here, another thing." She drew Fi closer. "Caitlin's just sort of . . . off. Like, she kept checking over her shoulder, even though there was nothing there."

The thought of Caitlin, painfully thin and pale, freaked Deedee out. Her huge, wide-set blue eyes had come straight from Kathleen and were all the starker against the dark rings that surrounded them. It was like the dead woman could still stare at Deedee. Caitlin brought to mind spiders, cobwebs, the deceptive strength of spun spider silk.

"Grief does weird things to people." Fi shrugged. "How long's she over for?"

"As long as it takes. Coupla weeks at least. Didn't say anything about Kathleen, got the feeling they hadn't even spoken in ages."

Another thing that got her back up about Caitlin. What would it have been like to have had a mother but rejected her? Deedee had lost her parents eighteen months before Roisin, and then her grandmother hadn't lasted much longer after that. So much loss before she'd even turned sixteen. She was always being left. She was never the one to leave.

"Whereabouts is she based in London? Did she fly from Gatwick?" Fi asked.

"City Airport." Deedee said. She'd been to London a couple of times to visit Fi, but not enough to have much idea of the place beyond the scale of it. She thought of Caitlin scurrying like a rat around the Underground, while back here, Kathleen froze half to death, growing lonelier and stranger by the day.

"City? To Cork?" Fi frowned. "Are you sure?"

"S'what she said." Deedee was only half listening. Indignation on Kathleen's behalf rose in her chest. If her own mam had still been around . . . A rush of images: her mother there at her Garda graduation, her mother tutting at her short skirts before she went out on the town in her late teens, her mother at her to do her homework. Her mother, there. You'd want to be a real piece of work to just abandon a mother.

"City doesn't fly out to Cork."

"It doesn't? Thought they all would." A flare of embarrassment disrupted her mounting anger at Caitlin, and then added to it. Now she was showing herself up as backward, untraveled, and uninformed.

"No, Stansted, Gatwick, or Heathrow, definitely. Not City."

"Lying bitch!" Deedee gasped.

"Bit strong, Dee," Fi cautioned.

Deedee's phone buzzed in her pocket. A text from Flo, who was certainly contacting her for work purposes, she assured an imaginary jury. That wasn't a big deal, surely.

Busy justifying it in her mind, she missed the rest of Fi's sentence.

"Oh-oh, is that Sean?" Fi crowed. "Look at you!"

Deedee snorted. "I should be so lucky. We're after arguing. No, this is just one of the guys I work with, Florian."

"Oh, I know him! The handsome feller with the French mother, is it? Deejays at Peachy's every now and then? Dabbles a bit in . . . party favors?"

"He doesn't do the deejaying anymore," Deedee corrected her. *But he's still dealing,* she thought. "Would you say he's handsome, then?"

"Yeah, I would, because I've got eyes in my head."

"Bit obvious, though, isn't he?"

"All right, so you fancy him, good to know."

Deedee realized they were drunk as she snorted with laughter.

"I'm going to tell Sean, give him a bit of a kick up the arse. A handsome Frenchman is going to have his woman if he's not careful."

"Oh my God, Fiona, shut up!" But it was too late now, they'd descended into a state of untouchable inebriation. Nothing was serious. Fi didn't have a clue.

Fi shrieked and grasped her arm, and the two of them were the funniest, warmest, happiest people on earth. The bottle of wine was empty.

A sudden tug from the lead looped around her wrist turned Deedee's chuckle into a yelp. Around them, O'Shea's had filled up and Frank had gone darting after a nearby dropped chip.

"I'd better get moving," Fi said. "God, you don't realize the time when it's always so dark like this, do you? But my lot'll want me home. Ma's doing a roast."

Deedee nodded. "I better head too. My pal hasn't been subtle that it's dinnertime."

"Oh!" Fi paused, one arm in her coat, one arm out, and sat back down. "I forgot to say, I know you don't like her, but Michelle told me she saw Sean at Martina's. Merry Christmas to you!"

Martina ran the independent jeweler's on the high street. People would travel into Bannakilduff to see her for her engagement rings, each unique and stunning.

"It could be a necklace," Deedee said, fully on Fi's wavelength.

"It could be a diamond-studded dog collar for Frank, but it's probably not!" Fi crowed.

"No. You think?" Once she married Sean, Deedee would become Deirdre Branagh, up at the Big House, looking down on creation. Or at least on Bannakilduff. The wanting of it made her feel queasy. Everyone respected the Branaghs. "You know, we've been talking about kids recently."

Which was true, technically.

"About time! Speaking of kids, I'm thinking of bringing Michelle out next time. She's nice, you just haven't spoken to her in about ten years. Which is impressive, considering the size of the town."

And that we're among the few who stayed, Deedee filled in mentally.

"Always been a head case, hasn't she? Remember when she was riding half the town?"

"Ah, Dee, cop on. We were all kids."

"Went around making up shite all the time."

Fi held up her hands in surrender. "I'm not getting into it. Are you heading now?" She hugged Deedee, but the air had soured.

Still, the thought of a proposal sent Deedee floating out of the doors, happy enough that she almost didn't look back at the camera over the entrance. Almost didn't see the blinking red light indicating that it was definitely on.

15

CAITLIN

While she curled up in the spare bedroom at the Branaghs', she felt the gatehouse's presence like a splinter under her skin, nagging at her nerves and kindling an old bitterness. The gatehouse years hadn't exactly been idyllic, but they'd been better than what followed.

After the fight with her mother in that shabby flat, and her storming out, Caitlin had sofa-surfed. Then, when the people she knew stopped answering her calls, she'd wandered into a house party in the student area one night. The students were so busy challenging each other to down whole bottles of Strongbow that she'd melted into the genial chaos. It turned out to be an end-of-term party, the inhabitants of the house leaving in the morning. The next day, Caitlin waited for the parents to collect the hungover students before she jimmied the back-door lock and crept inside. The soft furnishings were gone, but there were mattresses, and a fridge, and she could have squatted there longer but for a scare when the landlord finally came round to check the state of the place ahead of a new crop of students arriving.

Still, by then she had softened on Kathleen. She had a new understanding of how hard it was to be alone, properly alone. It would have been easier for Kathleen without Caitlin, and yet Kathleen hadn't been the one to leave. In her mother's absence, Caitlin remembered her fondly, edges softened. She began to feel foolish, immature. She wanted her mam.

But Kathleen was gone. A new mother and daughter lived there. The previous occupant had "moved home to Ireland." That could only mean Bannakilduff, the one place Caitlin could not follow.

She had stewed on that for at least two years. Even later, they'd never buried the hatchet—Caitlin's feelings were too deeply wounded to be repaired—but they had built up something fragile yet enduring over the years that followed, as she sensed her mother's decline and herself strengthening.

The last Kathleen had seen of her daughter, she'd been red-faced, hissing, "I hate you!"

The thought was too painful to sit with, so she thought of Deedee instead. How long had it taken Deedee to acknowledge why Caitlin was even in her shit-heap car? Deedee thought she had the market cornered on grief and loss.

A sudden slam made her jerk up from the bed. Something had hit the window; she caught a split second of something black disappearing under the ledge outside. She half expected to see Deedee when she opened the window, scowling up at her, projectile in hand. But no one was there. Cold air blasted into the room. A dead crow lay on the ground below, its head smashed from the impact. It felt like an omen. This crow, a messenger from the underworld come to tell her—

No. *Stop it*, she told herself. *It's just a bird.*

She coughed, her throat suddenly scratchy.

It's not real. There's nothing there. I am safe.

The old mantra almost, but not quite, worked.

The wrongness was back, the feeling bubbling in her blood. The shadows were close. She inhaled hard. The faintest hint of smoking embers, bonfire.

She drew her teeth over her still raw lip, looking for blood. It stung, but it wouldn't be enough for the shadows. She stared at the crow's corpse. One wing was outstretched as though directing her. To the gatehouse.

Unthinking, she clambered straight out of the window to sit on the sill. Outside, the pull was stronger, as though there was a string around her waist reeling her in.

She was nine, ten feet above the ground. A straight drop down would jolt her, maybe injure her joints if she landed badly. She rotated on the sill until she was facing into the room, her body dangling outside, leaning into the palms of her hands. Her socked toes wedged into the tiny spaces in the cement between the bricks and she kept her pelvis close to the window ledge. She was hanging, then one foot reached down, caught the top of the window ledge below. The other followed, her fingers only just about on the ledge above her, the bricks rough against her cheek, and her heart hammering in her chest.

It was thrilling. It had been years since she'd broken into or out of a home, but her body still knew how to keep calm, find its own path. She felt powerful, wondered suddenly why she ever used doors at all.

Then something was speeding toward her, another crow, its body like an arrow, and she flinched, her hands leaving the ledge above her head, her weight shifting from her toes to her heels. For one heart-stopping moment, the world paused and she was suspended in the air, until gravity caught up with her and she crashed bottom-first into the bushes below.

She lay still, all the air knocked out of her. She scanned her body and made tiny movements, looking for signs of serious injury. She'd landed hard, bruising her right hip and her back, but the bush had mostly broken her fall. Carefully she rolled onto her feet.

The freezing cold of the ground seeped through her socks, and small stones jabbed into the arches of her feet as she scurried. Her feet were sore and her hip ached, but her discomfort was eclipsed by frustration; a need to get to the gatehouse, to follow the crow.

The pain worked, though—the bonfire smell was fainter. The first inky tendrils of the shadows had receded, just a touch, from the corner of her eye.

The yellow-and-black caution tape was more vivid in the gloom. The gatehouse became shabbier the closer she got to it, the bricks looser, the cement between them crumbling. Caitlin hurried under the tape, just ahead of the shadows, lest the gatehouse blow away like dust before she reached it. She'd never needed keys to be able to get into a house, especially not this one. The latch on her window had broken years ago; a good thump to the frame would spring it open. She thumped. The window remained closed. She thumped again. Still closed. She thumped harder and harder, the side of her hand reddening from the effort, and still it was shut, but then she was just thumping and thumping and the ache in her hand and wrist was enough to keep the shadows skulking at a distance.

Try the back door.

She jumped away from the window. The words had come to her in a low hiss. The shadows had never spoken to her before. They were stronger here.

Wind whistled through the branches of the trees in the Hanging Woods. Images sprang to her mind: a single bare red bulb suspended from a low timber roof, walls enclosing her on all sides, the mud-black soles of small white socks with a frill around the ankle.

An orange cigarette stub lay on the back step. She watched herself reach out, turn the knob.

The gatehouse had been unlocked all along, and she was terrified, but her body entered the kitchen and closed the door behind her. It felt like she was on rails, moving to a choreography only her bones knew.

It was darker inside than it had been outside, and it would be darker still once she passed through the kitchen, so she lingered here a moment. The old light-blue cabinets were as she remembered, but the fridge door was covered in newspaper clippings. One about Lee Casey being released, which made Caitlin shudder to think about. Local news: the planned housing development, but also it appeared that her mother had been following a story about corruption in the local guards. Caitlin frowned, wondering what the connection was. Kathleen would only take an interest in something if it benefited her.

But then she opened the fridge and found nothing in it at all, not even a bottle of clear spirits—*they don't smell, these ones*—or cottage cheese and celery. Things had gotten worse; Kathleen had been willing herself out of existence. Caitlin felt the food she'd eaten with Maureen solidify into a ball in her stomach, weighing her down. Unbearable. She darted out of the kitchen and into the bathroom. Taking her mother's toothbrush from the sink, she knelt in front of the toilet bowl, and slid the body of the toothbrush over her tongue and down toward her throat. Her eyes watered, her nose ran, her body convulsed, and she heaved. It hurt. It was exhausting. Hot vomit tumbled over her hand and into the bowl. Even without the toothbrush now, her stomach heaved and she vomited again and again. Finally, she was empty, and lying on the cool tiled bathroom floor. Her mother's daughter again, hollowed.

She stepped back into the hallway. The gilt-framed mirror that hung inside the door—an image of her mother preening inside it just before she left the house—was dusty and reflected only the crucifix hanging opposite it.

In the living room, a sun-bleached picture of Jesus and the Sacred Heart alongside all the pictures Colm had taken of them over the years. A pair of black court heels by the door. Caitlin pushed her socked feet into them. Her mother's old fur coat, tossed over an armchair. She buried her face in it. The thing was rank—sticky with spilled drinks and shrouded in a mixture of old smoke and Dior Poison. A pang of loss kicked through her as she hugged it against her body. Her mother hadn't been perfect, but she had been hers. She slid her arms through the sleeves and embraced herself.

Her mother's dressing table dominated her bedroom. Kathleen had had an affection for the Golden Age of Hollywood. Caitlin picked up a perfume bottle with an attached rubber squeezer, still half full of the scent her mother bought in its modern packaging only to decant into this. It brought a lump to her throat, but she felt better as she spritzed herself with it. Everything was sad: the faded purple bedspread, the empty bottles under the bed, the well-thumbed copy of *Valley of the Dolls*. It felt like she'd walked into her mother's diary.

Back in the kitchen, the clock on the wall showed almost four in the afternoon. Caitlin moved to stand in the patch of fast-fading sunlight behind the sink and looked out over the field into the Hanging Woods beyond. An ashtray was positioned right in front of her.

As she stood there, in her mother's fur, watching her mother's view, she understood something about Kathleen.

From here, Kathleen had watched over Roisin's gravesite in the Hanging Woods.

Had she thought she was protecting Caitlin?

Caitlin huddled closer into the collar of the old fur coat and felt the texture of it change. A stiffening of the fabric. Pulling it back from her face, she rubbed one of the spots of discoloration between her fingers. A dark brown dust of dried blood stained her fingertips.

Blood on the collar of her mother's coat. From a head wound? Caitlin wondered how recent it was—would there be any way to tell? She supposed it would have flaked off sooner if it was from some older injury or misadventure. But no one had mentioned any external signs of wounding, or anything to indicate that an injury could have contributed to Kathleen's death.

If only Caitlin had picked up that call last night. At the thought of it, she realized that she hadn't seen her mother's phone anywhere. She frowned, patting the pockets of the fur coat. Not in there. She called it from her own phone and heard it ringing down the line, but the house was silent.

She looked at the ashtray again. A single orange butt nestled among the slim white menthol filters, like the one she'd seen outside on the doorstep. Someone else had been here.

16

DEEDEE

Stepping out of O'Shea's, Frank snuffling at her heels, Deedee reeled as the cold air hit her.

Shite.

It was 4 p.m., and she was much, much drunker than she had thought. But how? There had been half a bottle when she arrived, and then a second bottle, but that was only roughly four large glasses of wine, which was nothing. She'd had one quick one before she left the house. And this morning, she'd gone to do the recycling and found there was a bottle with just a tiny bit of wine left in it, so she'd downed that. But you couldn't count those. It would be like counting the odd nips she had on long drives.

She drifted along, contemplating the mental arithmetic of pubs, in the general direction of home, but without urgency until another sharp tug on her wrist. Frank had discovered a half-eaten sausage roll on the ground outside the chipper.

"Drop it!" Deedee ordered him.

Frank swallowed the whole thing.

"You'll ruin your appetite." She knew it was time to go home and feed him his macrobiotic, perfectly balanced senior dog food. It was only around the corner now, but the house would be dark and cold and unwelcoming. Besides, Frank had a point. She should soak up the drink with a bit of food.

"One kebab isn't going to kill you, is it, Frank?" she asked him.

He wagged his tail.

"Good man yourself."

The chipper was full of teenagers on their Christmas hols. Someone's phone went off, obnoxiously loud, and very nearby. Deedee tutted. It wasn't until everyone was looking at her that she realized it was coming from her, from her bag.

Kathleen's phone.

She had just missed a call from Caitlin.

She switched the ringer off.

Caitlin knew that the phone was gone.

Deedee collected her food and walked Frank to a bench overlooking the small park, the same one that she'd watched the edge of in CCTV footage a thousand times. Bundled-up toddlers careened around in the fast-fading afternoon light, while their coffee-clutching parents stamped their feet to keep warm.

Deedee dropped the plain kebab for Frank before turning to her spice box. She thought as she munched.

By and large, she was happy to skate on the surface of things. She would take people at their word because she didn't want to expend the mental energy of interrogating what she was told. It was much easier.

But the phone situation was more complicated. With its owner dead, some would say it was evidence.

She watched the steam rise from her food and evaporate as she thought about how bad this was for her.

Firstly, she thought, *while the phone was a link to Kathleen, so was Brendan the taxi driver*—and she was willing to bet that he would remember every detail of that interaction. Plus, there was no way that some busybody hadn't spotted them together.

She couldn't worry about that now. Instead, she looked through the phone. There were only a few apps—Google, some app for filtering pictures, plus Facebook and the National Lottery.

There were plenty of selfies, and pictures out of the back window of the gatehouse, aimed at the Hanging Woods. These pictures gave her pause for reasons she couldn't articulate or identify. She zoomed in on some, hoping for a pattern to emerge. Was it so unusual that Kathleen would be interested in documenting the environment in which she lived? Perhaps she woke up some days just full of joy at the beauty of the world. Deedee grimaced at the idea. It didn't fit.

The texts were mostly spam, the odd one from Maureen checking in, but Kathleen didn't seem too interested in messaging.

The same few numbers filled the call log. Kathleen had rarely received calls, but she'd placed many, and often, to Caitlin. Absurdly, Deedee felt betrayed. They'd had the whole drive together this morning for Caitlin to tell her that she was on good terms with her mother before Kathleen passed. Though it didn't seem that Caitlin picked up even half the calls that Kathleen placed to her, the last one had been just before Deedee bumped into Kathleen. Plus, there was the call to the Branagh house that Deedee had made, which came up now as "Landlord."

After that, there was nothing until the call from Caitlin just now.

It felt bad to remember the collision, so Deedee plowed on. There was one other number frequently contacted but who rarely answered, a Michael.

She navigated back to the photos. She had the same feeling she'd had watching Copper's legs in the CCTV footage of the O'Sullivan brothers. She couldn't surrender the phone until she knew exactly what had been going on. The answer was somewhere just out of reach, but she could find it. She could study the images, she could—

As though on cue, Copper ran up to them, looking to play with Frank, who was very unwilling. His appearance knocked all other thoughts from her mind, and she dropped the phone back into her pocket. The perfect opportunity for her to pick up the investigation had presented itself! Doyle would be so pleased with her for working even when she wasn't on the clock. *Policing's like that*, she thought, *a calling, a noble profession.* One never simply *clocks off* from that kind of duty.

"Hey!" She waved to the woman who was with Copper. The woman looked behind her before returning a small wave. Deedee shouted louder. "Hey!"

"Sorry," the woman said. She whistled for Copper as she approached. "She gets a bit boisterous."

"No, no, none of that." Deedee shook her head. "I was wondering if I could talk to you about . . . Excuse me." She turned her head and muffled a burp in her fist. "About if you've seen anything in this park."

"I mean . . ." The woman shrugged. "Not really?"

"Not today, no, I wouldn't ask you about today, because I'm here myself to see." Deedee tried to be gentle in her explanation. This woman just didn't get it.

"Right." The woman checked her watch. "I've got to get on, but I've seen you here before if that's what you—"

"Do you live around here?" Deedee asked. "Or how can I get in touch with you? Oh! We haven't even . . ." She pointed at herself, then at the woman, before sticking her hand out for the woman to shake. "I'm Deedee, well, Garda O'Halloran."

"Jules," the woman said. "Nice to meet you—formally—but I should really . . ."

"No, no, just a minute." Deedee tried to grasp the thread of the conversation, to steer it in the way she wanted. She couldn't think suddenly. Copper was barking again and poor old Frank pushed himself behind her legs and it all felt chaotic, and suddenly she just thought—

Feck it.

"Look, I need to talk to you, or your husband, partner, whoever, the man. Because of the drugs. The drugs coming into Bannakilduff."

"The . . . drugs?"

"Yes." Deedee nodded. Jules was getting it now! "It never used to be like this, but the O'Sullivans, Jason and Kevin, they're bringing them in, you know? And you've seen it."

"I don't know. I'm sorry, I'm late . . ."

Deedee didn't have her card. "Just call in to the station tomorrow, I'll be on shift."

Jules looked uncertain, so Deedee raked through her pockets. She pulled out a wad of bloody tissue paper from Kathleen knocking her nose. Jules jerked backward as though Deedee had been about to offer it to her. Which she obviously wouldn't, and it was honestly borderline very rude of Jules to think that.

Finally, she found a receipt and scribbled her number on it, almost punching through the paper. Jules pocketed it reluctantly. "I'll follow up, sure. I really have to . . ." She jerked her thumb to the right.

Deedee waved her away.

That went all right, she thought. She hadn't thought much of Jules and her dog, but maybe they'd end up quite friendly by the end of this. Deedee could have it all—new friends and career success. She'd prove everyone wrong.

17

CAITLIN

Ducking back under the caution tape, Caitlin wrapped her mother's old fur coat tightly around herself. Her bruised hip was stiff and sore. Full darkness had fallen over the shivering branches of the Hanging Woods, and she held her head at an angle, keeping it in her periphery as she walked away from it toward the road.

Strange cigarette butts in the house, blood on the collar of her mother's fur, her phone missing. Something wasn't right. There had been no mention of blood on Kathleen, no indication of anything but a natural passing.

In the expanse of grass between the gatehouse and the Big House, wearing her mother's fur coat and heels, Caitlin began to hyperventilate. She was so fucked up, like some kind of weird child-woman playing dress-up in her dead mother's clothes.

And she had jumped out of a window because she saw a dead crow. Jesus Christ. Her knees buckled and she sank into a low squat.

What is wrong with me?

The throbbing from her hip radiated down to her thigh, over to the base of her spine. Her whole rib cage ached with it; the drop had rattled all her bones.

The Caitlin she'd been last night wouldn't have jumped out of a window on the say-so of a dead crow. Or would she? If she smelled that phantom bonfire . . . *No.* She shook herself. It was this place; it was being back. It was because she was so exhausted.

She texted Lola to ask her what it was exactly that she'd taken before the plane ride, but this time of afternoon, Lola was likely still asleep. She kept vampiric hours.

Indecision seized her, a gnawing panic that she was under threat but that it was too late to do something about it. She had to know who had been in the gatehouse.

It's not real. There's nothing there. I am safe.

Her confidence drained through the soles of her feet into the earth. Where would she start to reconstruct the movements of a woman she hadn't seen in years? She was a stranger here—the town would close ranks against her.

The smart thing to do was leave. Whatever Kathleen had gotten into, it could only involve Caitlin if she stayed here. She could change her name, lose herself in the underworld of cash-in-hand jobs, survive the way she had before, with Lola. Pickpocketing, shoplifting, scavenging. Lola had spent enough nights curled up in the drafty warehouse alongside Caitlin that it didn't matter that Caitlin suspected she was funded secretly by some long-suffering but wealthy parents. The place she had now, a moldering basement in north London with shared facilities and too many inhabitants, Lola had fronted her the deposit, just as she'd given her the uppers to keep her going.

A car approached, its headlights twin North Stars in the gloom. Another messenger, like the crow?

If it stops before it gets here, I should stay here, go into town, figure this out, she thought. *If it passes, I should leave.*

Somewhere between superstition and a coin toss. The car seemed to slow down as she focused on it.

Please pass, she willed it. Behind her, the lights clicked on in the Branaghs' kitchen, and then the Christmas lights.

The car drew nearer.

Caitlin didn't need to wait for it; she could just go inside at any time, pick up her bags. She was in charge of her life. But the car would pass anyway; there was nothing else here to stop for.

And then it pulled up in front of her and its window rolled down.

"Is that you, Caitlin Doherty?" A man with a round face, red cheeks, a thin, gray comb-over leaned out of the window. "Sure, aren't you awfully cold out here? You needn't have waited outside. I can find my way to the front door!"

It had been a messenger after all.

She raised a hand in greeting and noticed that it was shaking.

The man pulled into the driveway.

The Branaghs' front door opened.

"Niall, there you are! And who's this? Caitlin, you gave me the fright of my life standing there!" Maureen held one hand against her breast. Caitlin saw her deliberate and decide not to comment on her appearance in front of Niall. "Come in, come in, you'll be perished in the cold!"

Caitlin followed Niall in.

"Go through to the kitchen!" Maureen urged Niall. She waited for him to shuffle his way through, and then turned to Caitlin. "The state of you! When did you nip out? Never mind now, Niall'll be over to see how you are, check in on the arrangements. Hurry back."

Caitlin understood that the news had spread. The neighbors would all be round to offer her their condolences.

In her room upstairs, she slipped her mother's heels off, feeling the hitch in her sore hip as she did. She patted the coat's matted fur before laying it out on the bed like some huge creature at rest.

From below, Maureen called up to ask if she'd have a tea or not, and Caitlin knew it was a hint to get a move on.

The kitchen was bright enough to make her blink, and warm enough to make her hands and feet tingle. Niall Wilson sat at the table flicking through a newspaper, looking as though he'd lived in this house himself his whole life.

"Caitlin." He cleared his throat. "I wanted to come by and see how you are. Kathleen was a great woman."

"Thank you," Caitlin said. She took a seat opposite him, shifting her weight away from the sore side of her body.

Niall continued, but Caitlin was distracted by the way his face moved. Like a rubbery mask. Spit collected in the corners of his mouth, white and frothy.

She remembered him, a friend of Colm's. Local councilor, general man-of-the-community type. Virtuous.

"Have you the plans all sorted?" He leaned over the table as though conducting a job interview, shrewd eyes missing nothing.

"I'm waiting to hear on the timeline." Caitlin put on her professional office voice and then cringed at the Englishness of it.

"Bright girl, you are." Niall nodded. "But weren't ye always? Kathleen'd talk the ears offa me any day about how well you did at art college. We'd ask when you'd come to visit and she'd just be listing off alla your achievements!"

Caitlin detected a hint of sneering in his voice, but his face betrayed nothing.

"It was hard to find the time to visit."

Every word she spoke made her feel more alien. She had erased her Irish accent as soon as she landed in the playground at her English school, realizing early that it would make her a target. She searched for it now, but her tongue refused her.

"We'll miss her," Niall said. "She'd the finest voice for a song. And she loved a chat!"

"A good neighbor," Maureen added. "Well liked by all. That's not nothing."

"We could do with more like Kathleen around here, and less of those solstice lot. Bad as tinkers, they are. Leave the whole place a state."

"Haven't they started coming earlier and earlier?" Maureen agreed.

There was a difference between the blow-ins, who made Bannakilduff their home, and the true outsiders—Caitlin wondered which category she fell under now. To be an outsider was a charged kind of identity, loaded with potential malignance. Sure, the locals would laugh with them and play up to the stereotypes superficially, but they never let their guard down.

"Oh no, you're one of us." Maureen had read the doubt on her face.

"'Twas here you were born, wasn't it? You can move away as long as you like, but the blood, that's Bannakilduff," Niall said, conveniently eliding that Kathleen was not Bannakilduff, was not anything.

The safety of being known. The cage of it.

The outsiders. Caitlin pictured Lee Casey, paint-daubed and wild, the newsprint rendering of him bristling with energy, vivid even in black and white. The papers had made him into a monster.

"Did I hear right that Lee Casey has come back?" Maureen said, as though clairvoyant. "Some people've no shame."

"He's allowed to be here?" Caitlin asked.

"He was cleared," Niall said. "But you'd never know the likes of him for cheek. He put in an application for wild camping!"

"Would you believe there's some who feel sorry for him?" Maureen tutted. "Those blow-ins weren't all here twenty years ago, but you'd think they'd a notion."

Caitlin smiled and nodded. The conversation continued around her, and she tried to chime in at the appropriate moments with the right kind of noises, but her mind was reeling. Lee Casey had known exactly where Kathleen lived, and the way people talked around here, gossip a vital part of the community experience, everyone knew that Caitlin had spoken to the officers right away and volunteered the information about him. Coming back now, twenty years later, that couldn't be a coincidence.

The Hanging Woods had called to him, Caitlin knew. They'd given up her secret, let Roisin's bones scream through the earth and shiver through the roots and branches.

Stop it, she thought. *Stop.*

Roisin was dead; the woods were only trees.

A different scene unfolded in her mind: Casey asking Kathleen why Caitlin had lied, telling her that those words had marked him ever since. A confrontation between them, and then—

And then Kathleen dead.

"Wild camping," Niall mused, shaking his head.

Caitlin looked toward the trees but saw only the reflection of the kitchen in the window. Casey could be skulking around out there even now, watching her. Waiting for his moment.

18

CAITLIN

BANNAKILDUFF

SUMMER 1999

Someone is living in the Hanging Woods. Caitlin can tell, she knows these woods better than anyone, better than God even, probably, and He has a bird's-eye view of everything. But Caitlin is on the ground, weaving her way through the trees. The string system she set up means she could navigate around the woods eyes closed, but her strings have been cut in places.

Someone is forging their own paths.

She has read the phrase "grim determination" before, but now she feels it. She squares her shoulders, sets her jaw, and marches straight into the trees.

The leaves quiver with it, this unseen presence. There are imprints, huge ones, in the ground. A trail. And with it, new treasures are appearing all the time.

A piece of turquoise. A yellow marble.

When she finds the peacock feather fastened to a low-hanging branch of the tree she ties her strings to, she understands it as an apology for them being cut.

The trail makes her feel strange, small. She finds herself hesitating. The trees are so dark after all, and the prints seem to lead everywhere. In front of her, beside her, behind her. Even now, the intruder could be watching her.

A twig cracks and Caitlin freezes. Heavy breathing, coming from somewhere ahead. Very heavy. Carefully she sneaks toward the sounds. She is rewarded for her bravery; a dream catcher is balanced against a tree, and in bending to grab it, she catches sight of a tent.

Dream catcher in hand, she races out of the woods, along the road, further out, out to the end of the track, where she crosses the carefully tended lawn of a bungalow to hammer on the door. She hears only her heart pounding in her ears, her own breath heavy and frantic.

After a lifetime, the door swings open.

"What?" Deedee stares at her.

Roisin's house smells like old people. Not dust, exactly, but also not not-dust. Musty, but floral, and like the stinging orange antiseptic you dab on a wound.

"Can Roisin come out?" Caitlin pants. "To play?"

Deedee rolls her eyes. She must be the tallest girl in the town. Caitlin feels the five-year age gap between them keenly. Deedee's wearing lip gloss and mascara even though she's just at home, which feels incredibly grown-up.

Roisin appears, elbowing past her sister.

"It's for me!" She glares at Deedee. "You're supposed to call me if the door is for me."

"OK, I will." Deedee steps back from the door and calls out at Roisin, "Roisin, your weird little pal is here! The only one almost as weird as you are! Is that better?"

"Shut up!" Roisin shoves her sister and, to her credit, shifts Deedee back a step. In response, Deedee grabs her arms to restrain her.

"Stop being a bully, Deedee!" Caitlin yells. She doesn't have time for this. "Just let us go. C'mon, Roisin."

"I'm not a bully!" Deedee releases Roisin anyway. Roisin takes the opportunity to swipe at her and scratch her arm before running out of the house. Deedee looks to Caitlin for confirmation, and says, "You saw that! You saw how she is!"

Roisin dances a couple of feet away, just out of grabbing distance, and yells, "Because you're a bully, Deedee!"

"Don't tell people I'm a bully!" Deedee darts out after her, but Roisin is too nimble, her eyes bright with the fun of taunting.

"I will!" she crows. "I'm telling Colm, and Maureen, and Sean . . ." She draws the names out as she says them, watching how they land, saving the best for last.

Caitlin wonders what Sean would think, whether Deedee even has a chance with him, for all her obsession. Sean has that Branagh glow that Caitlin has only recently become aware of. When he speaks, people listen.

Roisin shouldn't have said anything, because now as they run back down the road toward the Hanging Woods, there's no privacy. Deedee is running along with them, to get her side of the story across. With her stupid long legs, she's faster than Caitlin easily, and Caitlin is left in the sisters' dust long before they arrive.

She hears them as she jogs to a stop outside the Big House, girlish voices yelling and the deep laughter of the Branagh men. She waits, lets them get the drama over with before she joins the rabble.

"Ah, what's a little sister for if not to torment ye?" Colm says fondly, one arm around Roisin's shoulders.

Caitlin pretends she doesn't care. Colm is still her friend, and Maureen definitely likes her best too. They just have to pretend to be nice to Roisin.

Deedee is laughing along, like she wasn't just furious. Three livid red scratches run down her arm, but she doesn't point them out. "That's what I always say!"

"No it's not." Roisin has turned her face into Colm's ribs and her voice is muffled. "It isn't."

"Roi-*sin*," Caitlin hisses. They can't waste their time here. "Come *on!*"

"You've business to attend to, do you?" Colm asks.

"Yes," Caitlin replies.

"Your project, is it?"

She knows Colm thinks she's the smart one; she's his best girl.

"Kind of. But I need Roisin. It's just for us for now. Secret." She holds the dream catcher out of sight for reasons she doesn't really understand herself.

Roisin unsticks herself from Colm's side, as Caitlin knew she would at the word "secret." Caitlin grabs her hand and pulls her out of the house, past the darkroom, down to the Hanging Woods.

"Someone is in there, really in there. Like, living in there." She points out one of her severed strings.

"Bigger kids, maybe." Roisin shrugs.

"No," says Caitlin. She feels afraid of going back in, but less so now that Roisin is here. The only way to prove it will be to show Roisin. So, she leads her into the dark of the woods.

"I found this. It's a dream catcher." She hands it to Roisin as they walk, and then wishes she hadn't, because Roisin could decide not to give it back.

Roisin turns the dream catcher in her hands, inspecting the feathers.

"That's some of your wool in there," she notes.

She's right. Caitlin's wool forms the internal webbing held inside the circle made of pliant green twigs.

"It's a peace offering," Caitlin says. "From him." She imagines the iridescent, soapy shine of her dreams caught in the woven structure, held as though in arms.

"Yuck." Roisin pushes the dream catcher back to her.

Caitlin feels offended; the rejection lands like a judgment against her, and she stops, ready for an argument.

"I don't want my dreams caught," Roisin says with a shudder.

And Caitlin sees it through her eyes, the knots now of restraint rather than comfort, an outside force imposing control on the world inside Roisin's skull.

"It doesn't work like that," she offers weakly. But she doesn't quite know how it does work, only that it's something good, so she can't finish the thought.

Instead she fumbles in her pocket and finds the turquoise, holds it out for Roisin, who can't resist it.

That feels right, Caitlin thinks. *Something for both of us.*

The man in the Hanging Woods reeling them in with treasures.

19

DEEDEE

Deedee and Frank had found themselves quite refreshed by their stop-off at the chipper, and found the strength to stay out just a bit longer. Deedee had called Florian; he hadn't been out, but was up for hosting a few drinks at his, and the time flew. It had never been a big deal, what she and Florian did. Florian wasn't the kind of guy you left a boyfriend for, and he wasn't the type to look for trouble by being indiscreet. He was a good friend, but ultimately, Deedee knew that he simply didn't care that much about her.

There was no one else, had never been anyone else except Sean, and Deedee had trained herself to consider her time with Florian as something like smoking. A bad habit that hurt no one but her.

Now it was evening, and she was home once more, and no one even noticed she'd been gone. She texted Sean that she missed him. He didn't respond. She let his silence assuage her guilt about Florian.

She popped open a can of supermarket own-brand beer, enjoying the crack and hiss of it. At her feet, Frank snuffled his way through a bowl of macrobiotic dog food. He'd been significantly more enthusiastic about the kebab.

Deedee hoped Sean wasn't with Caitlin. There was something

about how he had looked over at her. Deedee wasn't the jealous type, but Caitlin wasn't trustworthy.

From the fridge: Gruyère, Brie, Cheddar, slightly suspect milk, and bacon. She switched on the radio, eighties hits playing in the background. Caitlin had lied about the airport.

From the cupboards: brown sugar, balsamic vinegar, maple syrup, onions, garlic, nutmeg. Maybe Fi was wrong about the airport.

She chopped the onions and put the kettle on. The beer steadied her nerves. She needed to think clearly. She googled. Fi was right: London City didn't fly out to Cork.

She put a pot of pasta on, the water liberally salted. She dropped the chopped onions into a frying pan. The bacon, brushed with maple syrup, went on the grill. Caitlin wasn't likely to have forgotten the airport she'd left from.

Frank sniffed hopefully by her feet. Deedee moved with a swiftness and sureness that belied her drunkenness. The lightning tattoo on her wrist flashed past her eyes as she assembled her meal. Working with her hands and concentrating on the simmering, bubbling pots always pushed her into a Zen state. She could focus.

The onions were softening, browning. Caitlin could have flown from anywhere.

The pasta threatened to boil over. Luggage tags. If only she'd looked at Caitlin's bags when she'd loaded them into her car.

The bacon waited under the grill. On the radio, Michael Jackson yelped and Deedee whooped back at him. From the fridge, another can. It didn't have to mean anything. Most things didn't mean anything.

A taster spiral of hot pasta burned her tongue. Roisin had disappeared and Caitlin was the last person to see her and none of it had to mean anything.

She turned the pasta off and left it sitting in the hot water. Roisin and Caitlin had been friends, Deedee remembered, they'd been together that whole summer.

The bacon sizzled under the heat of the grill. So that was another lie then, that they hadn't really been friends.

She added brown sugar and balsamic vinegar to the onions. There was something there, something just outside the edges of her perception. A warning flare.

Steam fogged up the windows. What else had Caitlin said? Not much, not now that Deedee really thought about it.

The onions were almost ready. She should search the internet, look for clues. Social media profiles.

From the fridge, another can. A Caitlin Doherty based in Yorkshire who worked in local news dominated the results. No hint of the Caitlin who was right now inside Colm's house with all the people Deedee loved.

A burnt smell in the air. Lots of people weren't very online.

Deedee coughed, her throat suddenly dry, but she was too absorbed in her thoughts to pay any notice. She'd gotten distracted from her fruitless search for any sign of Caitlin online. Somehow she'd found her way to Martina's website. Engagement rings. Round brilliant and pear-shaped diamonds haloed in other, smaller diamonds. Which had Sean chosen?

The alarm. Smoke, fuck, smoke. Where was Frank? The bacon had caught. Deedee smothered it with the lid of a pan. Her wrist came down on the hot metal of the grill. She smelled singed flesh. Opened the windows. The caramelized onions congealed in the frying pan. The pasta water was tepid. She waved a tea towel at the alarm. Next door banged on the wall.

"Shut up!" she shouted back.

The banging stopped.

The alarm fell silent.

An advert blared from the radio; she slammed her fist down on the off switch.

In the quiet, she twisted the angry red burn on her arm under the cold tap.

Frank waited hopefully by the charred remains of the bacon and was rewarded. Deedee ate plain pasta at her laptop. Her spirits were flagging. Her wrist throbbed.

She pulled Roisin's box out from her wardrobe, brought it to the living room, and dumped it out on the floor. She pushed around the newspaper clippings, missing poster, solstice party flyer, the photographs, the notes she'd made at the time, the old map Roisin had been working on, her drawings. She fanned everything out and stepped back.

In a movie, the clue would appear now. Deedee tilted her head and waited for it.

Newspaper clippings, flyers, the map.

The map.

She hovered over it. Symbols dotted Roisin's map. There were two categories, but neither was explained. The small ones included a tent, a gem, a hare, similar in size to the symbols that marked the fire station and the church. Then there were a handful of big ones: a cat, a shell, a pointy wizard's hat.

A skull.

Deedee shivered. The window was still open in the kitchen. She closed it, and then grabbed from the fridge another can of supermarket own-brand beer.

20

CAITLIN

Usually the boyfriends get bored and move on, but Michael is around more than ever now. He's always talking about how Caitlin needs to get into a "bedtime routine" so she can be well rested, as though that's any of his business. He gets up early too, and so, effectively, the first thing Caitlin hears in the morning is his stupid loud voice, humming.

A few weeks ago, Caitlin would have said that she wished her mother was around more. The fridge is full now; Michael even has Coca-Cola in there, and chocolate bars, and ham, and all sorts of things that were previously forbidden, and Caitlin doesn't even have to ask for it. She sits on the back steps of her home, sipping on cola and surveying the land that makes up her back garden while the smell of her mother cooking dinner drifts out toward her. Even the odd sound of Michael clearing his throat as he sits at the table reading is comforting. She feels on top of the world.

It can't last.

Michael won't stay.

The fridge will be empty again soon, her mother out every night, new shoes will appear by the door at night and be gone in the morning. Caitlin gets up from the steps and brushes the dust from her legs. She walks past her mother to the fridge and pulls out a Mars bar. The idea of it alone makes her feel a bit sick; she knows it won't taste as good after drinking her can of cola, but that's not the point.

"Caitlin, dinner is ready in five minutes, put that away," says her mother from her position over the stove.

Caitlin rustles the packaging of the chocolate bar as loudly as possible.

"Caitlin!" Her mother turns to her now, glares at her. At the table, Michael looks up from his book.

Caitlin holds her mother's eye as she takes a huge bite, a bite so big she can barely close her mouth. Chocolate and caramel oozing around her teeth, clotting on her tongue, it's too much. It works. Her mother is furious, although Caitlin isn't sure if that's because of the disobedience— especially in front of Michael; her mother likes to pretend to be perfect in front of him—or the chocolate. Her mother hasn't changed; she still doesn't want Caitlin to get fat or to get spots, which she will if she eats junk. Caitlin can barely swallow the mass in her mouth, but she manages, and just as she's about to take another huge bite—

"Didn't you hear your mother?" Michael says, his voice mild. "C'mere to me." He reaches out from the table and tugs her by the elbow toward him. He tips her head to one side and touches her ear as though stretching it open. "Must be full of wax in here," he exclaims. "Or no, is that . . . Could it be? My God, there's chocolate coming out of her ears!"

Caitlin can't help but giggle. She registers that he's removed the second half of the chocolate bar from her hand, but she doesn't mind. Then she's angry. She's not a baby. He's not her father. He's not even really *her* friend, he's just hanging around her mother.

"Ow!" she yells. "Ow, he's hurting me!"

"Don't be ridiculous," says her mother, as Michael immediately lets go of her ear.

"I'm sorry!" he says, astonished. "I barely touched her!"

"Hurts." Caitlin glares at him, one hand clamped over her ear. It does hurt, but not on her ear. It hurts that he will leave.

"I'm sorry, Caity," Michael says.

"Stop being such a little drama queen," her mother snaps.

Caitlin storms toward the front door.

"Five minutes, Caitlin!" her mother calls after her. "Don't stomp so hard!"

"I swear . . ." Michael must be apologizing to her mother now, but Caitlin knows her mother won't care anyway. She has swiped the end of the chocolate bar from Michael and she throws it out into the hedgerow across from the front door. Then she slams the door and stomps her way across to Colm's house. By the time she gets there and sees Maureen, her anger has dissipated.

"Hello, you!" Maureen sings out as Caitlin enters their house. "Are you here for your dinner?"

Caitlin smells beef burgers. Much better than whatever her mother is making.

"Yes please!"

Sean is setting the table, and Colm is helping Maureen to plate up. It's all very peaceful. Caitlin takes her place at the table, across from Sean. She has almost forgotten everything that happened only a few minutes ago.

That is, until Michael appears at the front door. There's the rumble of low male voices talking angrily at one another, then Michael is in the kitchen.

"Come on, Caitlin, you know there's dinner on the table at the house above." He's serious, and Caitlin realizes that she's never seen him angry before.

She squirms, but says nothing.

"Ah, she's no trouble here," Maureen soothes.

"She's got a plate full of food up above," repeats Michael slowly. "Her mother has gone to some trouble."

Maureen is wringing a tea towel between her hands. Sean is watching everything carefully. The beef burgers are cooling on their buns. Colm is nowhere to be seen.

"Well," sighs Maureen, "I suppose if your mother wants you back over . . ."

"She does," affirms Michael. Then, "She spends a bit too much time with you as it is, no?"

Something is happening among the adults. Caitlin isn't sure what, but there is a meaning zinging around that she can't grasp. She slides off the chair and crosses to the back door. Michael joins her and opens the door so that she leaves first. He says something in a low voice to Maureen before he leaves. Then he closes the door behind them.

He is quiet as they walk across Colm's property, but as they arrive back at Caitlin's house, he stops and stoops so that he is at eye level with her.

"Be very careful, Caitlin," he says.

"I am," she tells him, indignant. She thinks of how she always checks for quicksand in the woods, snakes in the undergrowth.

Michael shakes his head. It's like there's something he wants to say but can't translate to her language. He sighs and settles on telling her, "Not all the danger around here is in the Hanging Woods."

All Caitlin understands is that she's eating burnt kippers on toast instead of beef burgers in soft buns for dinner tonight.

PART 3

PROCESS

Details need time to come to the surface.
You can't rush it, but you can't leave it down
there forever.

John Lyle,
The Little Photographer:
A Kid's Guide to Perfect Pictures

21

CAITLIN

S alt in the plant pots. The unease of knowing that Lee Casey was nearby, that someone had been in her mother's house around the time she died, that these two facts might not be unconnected, all of it made Caitlin feel wrong. Salting Maureen's windowsill snake plants was proof that she could impact the world, even if she didn't feel in control of it. These plants would die, and only she would know why.

Niall was long since gone, Maureen up in bed already, Sean out. All that disrupted the quiet was Colm's occasional racking coughs. The kitchen held the heat, and she felt the warmth of it in her cheeks, soporific and soothing.

Finally.

As she turned off the lamp in the kitchen, she saw a light moving in the trees. It was magnetic, hypnotizing. She sat back down in the dark at the kitchen table and watched the Hanging Woods. Her eyelids were heavy, her body weighted with fatigue. She felt herself closing her eyes for longer and longer each time she blinked.

She could almost smell the soil, taste the clean air. In her mind, it was forever midsummer out there, and she was lying in the clearing beneath a sun-dappled canopy of branches, delighting at the sight, when a rabbit flashed whitely past.

The Hanging Woods had been a refuge, once.

Yet even in her mind, she couldn't help but feel the air become weighted with another presence, darkness drawing itself into form.

It's not real, she told herself.

But the wood of the breakfast table roughened to bark under her hands, and the clearing narrowed to a point around her.

Wake up, she thought.

She heard ragged panting and realized it was coming from her; her chest heaved but her jaw was locked, and she couldn't scream.

All she knew was that she was seconds from—

She woke up.

The oven clock showed 12:57. Her legs and feet were damp and the sour smell of urine surrounded her. She didn't dare look toward the woods.

Caitlin was an almost thirty-year-old woman who had just wet herself during a nightmare. The familiar drumbeat of self-loathing sounded. She had never felt more pathetic as she wiped down and disinfected the wooden kitchen chair and the tiled floor.

Upstairs in the spare bedroom, she changed her nightclothes. The bruise from her fall was black and swollen. She collected her soiled clothes and, after a moment, her mother's fur, and took them to the bathroom with her.

The overhead light in the bathroom buzzed. She kept her head low to avoid her reflection, the way her hair hung greasily over her pallid, waxy skin.

The water was hot enough to sting her hands, and she scrubbed at her nightclothes, then wrung them out and draped them over the lip of the bath to dry.

That done, she moved on to her mother's coat. With a damp hand towel, she cradled the coat and gently scrubbed the hem. The towel came back gray with old mud and dirt. She ran it over the arms, where it was sticky from splashed pints, and patted down the front. There wasn't much she could do about the cigarette burns that dotted the pelt, but it definitely smelled better after her attentions. She faced herself in the mirror. This much, at least, she had done for Kathleen.

Now 3 a.m., the night had taken on an endless quality, any sounds from outside drowned out by the ceaseless buzz of the bathroom lights, her mother's perfume hanging around her from the fur. It felt like she had nursed something wounded. The blood on the collar remained, a part of Kathleen that couldn't be taken from her.

Back in the bedroom, she laid the coat out alongside her in the bed.

Her thoughts were too loud and the bruising across her hip was too sore to allow sleep. Resting her sketchbook on *The Little Photographer*, she began drawing. Caitlin had always been able to lose herself in the focus of drawing. The clearing in the Hanging Woods appeared beneath her pencil, no trace of the rabbits or butterflies, only stark branches and threatening shadows. And a darker patch at the center where the soil had been freshly dug up.

But the blank page was a place she could control. On the next page, she thought of Roisin as she would be now. A series of images flashed before her eyes. Roisin a teenager, with perpetually rolled eyes and singed, straightened hair. Roisin a little older now, in walking boots and waterproofs, standing proudly at the top of a mountain. Things got fuzzier when Caitlin tried to think about Roisin in her twenties. There was so much potential.

She translated that onto the page. Eyebrows raised in challenge, mouth closed, and jaw set, the Roisin she created was confident and capable. She stared at the image. She had never really considered the full enormity of the potential she had destroyed. She sketched more and more Roisins, filling pages with them for hours until her hand cramped.

She hadn't realized how hard it would be to be back, or how the parade of visitors would start up so soon—first Niall, then Bernadette Tiernan, who had been Caitlin's teacher in second class, then Hugh and Sheila Murphy. Smiling for each of them took something from her and left her hollow.

At almost 6 a.m., a low groaning noise sounded through the house, building in urgency until the light clicked on in the hallway. Sean's heavy steps shuffled quickly through the house to Colm's room. He was such a good son. Guilt simmered in her belly and she buried it before it could take hold. He was a good son to a good father. She was a bad daughter to a bad mother.

Then the door to Colm's room closed and Sean's footsteps moved to the kitchen. Caitlin gave him a few minutes before joining him. He sat at the table, yesterday's paper opened to a partially completed crossword.

"Morning," he half whispered. He raised a pot of coffee to her.

"Thanks." She grabbed a mug and let him fill it for her.

"Mm-hmm. Jet-lagged, are you?" he asked, pushing the paper between them so she saw the clues.

"Something like that." Caitlin wondered how the truth would go down: *I have nightmares that I'm back in the woods. The monster never stopped hunting me.*

Instead, she said, "Seven down, Yosemite enthusiast. Ansel Adams."

"The photographer? It fits. Still into all that?"

The coffee was good, rich and reviving, and Caitlin felt safe with Sean. The night was over.

"Once a *Little Photographer* . . . Actually, wait there a second." Caitlin hurried off to her room and returned with the camera. She took Sean's picture as he looked up at her re-entering the room, the crossword still before him.

He smiled. "That answers my question then."

"D'you think you'll get another tenant now that . . ." Caitlin wondered which fit better: had her mother *passed away*? Was she *gone*? Or could Caitlin bear the thumping finality of the word *dead*?

"Don't worry about that. Take your time with . . . with whatever you need. It's nice to have you around." Sean didn't look at her, but the tips of his ears glowed pink.

"What else are you stuck on?" Caitlin tapped the paper to avoid acknowledging the generosity of his offer.

"Fifteen across, final trip of Shackleton." Sean chewed thoughtfully on the biro.

"Antarctic." Caitlin could almost hear Roisin chattering about the explorer still.

"Nowhere near long enough." Sean turned the paper toward her.

"That was definitely it."

"If you say so. I'm more of a Sudoku type, but Ma beat me to it."

"Does it feel different? Down here, now. You know, with her . . ." Caitlin jerked her head toward the cottage.

"She was quieter recently. Remember her music?" Sean smiled.

"The whole neighborhood knew when she just wanted to have fu-un." Caitlin snorted. The bones of the cottage would rattle with Kathleen's music. It felt good to share a chuckle about her mother's idiosyncrasies, until the sadness hit her once more. Kathleen would never sing again.

"I'd been wondering recently if we shouldn't get in touch with you, to be totally honest. She'd been acting a bit off. Couple days ago, she came by and her hands were black with mud. She'd been in one of those floaty Laura Ashley numbers and the hem of it was all mud too. Smudges of it on her face, in her hair."

The idea of her beautiful, coiffed mother half mad and scrabbling through the dirt on her hands and knees made Caitlin feel like she was suffocating. She dropped her head into her hands, but when she raised it once more, Kathleen was sitting opposite her. The vision spoke without opening her mouth. *No one can ever find out about this, do you understand? Do you know what they'll do to you?*

Caitlin gasped, and the vision flickered. This was her mother as she had always been, groomed and in control. She glanced at Sean, who had noticed nothing.

"What did she want to talk about?" She ignored her mother. The question of whether this was a hallucination, a ghost, or a brain tumor would have to wait.

Shush! No one will believe you. The vision glared at her. *Haven't you caused enough trouble?*

"I don't know if I ever found that out exactly. That wasn't the unusual bit. I'd see her in the woods when I was collecting kindling." Sean rubbed the back of his neck, embarrassed. "I'm sorry, maybe we should have told you. It's just . . . you never seemed to want to come back. I—we—respected that. And don't we look out for our own around here anyway?"

Stop crying! Don't be stupid now! The vision snapped into context. Her mother as she had been the day Caitlin ran into her kitchen and announced that she'd killed Roisin in the Hanging Woods.

"I'm not crying," Caitlin hissed at the vision, who tutted but also lost a degree of materiality. Evidently she felt that the point had been made. "I mean, no need to get upset," Caitlin said to Sean, who had looked up in puzzlement. "I know you all did your best."

He reached across and put his hand over hers. The vision of Kathleen Doherty winked out of view with the warmth of his touch. Caitlin glanced up at him and caught the way he looked at her when he thought she wouldn't notice. Even under these conditions, appealing to men was a language she spoke fluently. She turned her head as though bashful while arching her back enough to emphasize her bust, then pretended not to notice Sean's eyes flicker over her body.

"You're so thoughtful. And kind. Thank you." She squeezed his hand and rolled her head around to hold his gaze. "I hope Deedee knows how lucky she is."

"Not at all." Sean cleared his throat and slid his hand away from hers. He couldn't make eye contact.

Caitlin glanced back across the table to make sure her mother wouldn't reappear. Her gaze fell upon a bank of pictures on a shelf. Sean's baby pictures, school photos, a graduation picture. Sean and Deedee beaming together at the bottom of the Eiffel Tower. Shaggy-haired teenage Sean giving a thumbs-up from the driver's-side window of his first car.

"Oh wow," she said. "Look at you!"

"You're lucky you never had an awkward phase."

Then Caitlin found herself, first in a picture with her arm slung over Sean's newly teenaged shoulder when she was around seven years old, tucked toward the back of the sideboard. There were more: Caitlin and her mother in this very kitchen, Caitlin's first school picture.

"I can't believe these have been up all this time," she said.

"You know how much he loves pictures."

The next one stopped her in her tracks: Caitlin and Roisin, next to each other on the stone wall outside the house, a blur of blond hair just whisking out of the picture. That final summer, captured here. It was a little tilted, the subjects not quite as centered as they should have been. Michelle Quinn had long blond hair like that, but Caitlin couldn't remember her being part of the gang. Back then, Caitlin had been a little afraid of Michelle, who was three years older but far more worldly.

In the corner of her eye, a light flickered out beyond the fields, in the Hanging Woods again.

"What's that?" She pointed out the window.

"Hmm?" Sean squinted. "Nothing?"

"You don't see anything? Like, a light?"

"A light? No. They're starting development early, though; probably a foreman or someone."

"Must be." Caitlin knew it wasn't. The light was unearthly, and besides, what about the light she'd seen in there last night?

"I should start getting ready." Sean indicated the clock on the wall, which now showed a quarter to seven. "Hoping to start early, finish early."

"Deedee will be glad to have you back."

He grimaced. "Something like that."

She waited until a couple of minutes after she heard the bathroom door close before unlocking the back door. The Hanging Woods were dark and still now, but something had hunted there twenty years ago. Maybe it still had an appetite.

22

DEEDEE

God, what a night. Deedee felt like shit. The clock on her bedside showed 4:58 a.m., and she was about to throw up. She barely made it to the toilet in time. She rinsed her mouth at the bathroom sink and slunk back to her empty bed. Reaching out for the paracetamol on her bedside, she swallowed two tablets dry. Her bedside glass was empty, but she didn't have the strength to refill it.

Last night came back to her in flashes. Sean had popped in to check on Frank—or had he been checking on Deedee? He couldn't have known that she was with Florian, and even if he did, she had a cover story ready. They were colleagues, after all. Did he suspect anything? Frantically Deedee rewound through her memories, scanning for signs that she'd said anything, that he had noticed something, and came up empty-handed. Still, she deleted Florian's number from her phone.

She and Frank had been snoozing on the sofa when Sean arrived, the kitchen a mess, the living room a mess, mud on the walls in the hallway apparently—*blame the dog walker!*—plates in the sink—*when was the last time you washed up?*—blood on the worktop—*nothing, stop overreacting!*

Furious banging on the wall; both of them turned to face it: *would you ever feck off!* Laughter then, a common enemy. Tears; she was sorry, he was magnanimous, her wrist hurt. She pulled her arm in front of her face; he'd put on a bit of canvas bandage and it had stuck fast to the oozing wound. She hissed now as she peeled it off and dropped it on the floor. *Give it a bit of air,* she thought.

Then Maureen had called, worried about Colm, or Caitlin, and Sean had gone again. Once Sean married her, Deedee would suggest they just move up to the Big House. She'd go teetotal too, so she could care for Colm, to support Sean and Maureen. Things would be easier.

Deirdre Branagh could be a new person. With thoughts of booking a manicure, so she was ready if Sean did propose, she fell back asleep until Frank woke her, two hours later, grumbling for his breakfast. He didn't care that her head was still spinning and her stomach contents felt like they were sloshing. He still needed her to get up, give him his biscuits, and let him out for a quick, snuffling amble of the garden. The walker would be popping by at lunchtime to take him out. Deedee yelped in pain as she hurried to get dressed and pulled the starched material of her work shirt over her wound. She ran past the chaos in the kitchen—for all his complaining, Sean hadn't been moved to help her clear it up—chomping a wad of mint chewing gum between her teeth. Roisin's map still lay out on the carpet where she had been looking at it. She scooped it up and tucked it into her bag, worried that Frank would damage it in her absence, surprised that he hadn't already.

The station was a single-story redbrick building, with a nineties sense of modernity that set it apart from the cozier, more traditional frontages of the high-street businesses around it. Deedee loved it. If a building could have held its hands behind its back and asked, "Well now, lads, what's the craic here?" before moving on a tangle of hoodlums, this building would have done it. The noticeboard in the foyer had been edged with tinsel and the officer on duty behind the reception desk wore a pair of felt reindeer antlers.

Deedee popped more gum into her mouth as she entered the office. Everyone had unnaturally keen noses for the booze around here.

The start of a morning shift was invigorating, the air charged with potential. She headed straight for the coffee machine. Deedee prided herself on never being hungover, but she was more tired today than usual.

A colleague she didn't recognize was already there, pushing the button for espresso. She was a shorter woman with a bouncy, balls-of-the-feet kind of energy who didn't seem like she'd need any more caffeine. A large plastic Santa face winked down on them both.

"Looks great, doesn't it?" the colleague remarked to Deedee. "All the Christmas stuff. We didn't go all out like this in Kinafallia."

"It does," Deedee agreed.

"Jo Martin, just moved," the woman introduced herself.

"Deirdre O'Halloran. Local, but I'm a recent grad."

"Well, congratulations to you. How have you found it so far?" Jo removed her cup and stepped aside.

"It's not quite how I thought it would be, but I love the buzz of it, you know?" Deedee punched her order into the machine.

"It's a lot more community-focused all right," Jo agreed.

"Ah, our Dee, just where you belong." Mac strode past on his way out. "I'll take mine to go. Ah, I'm only joking!"

A drive-by insult; there was no point replying. When a man kicked off, it was no big deal, but let Deedee even just disagree and they were all circling around her, saying "Whoa!" as though she was an unhinged horse. Anything she said was ammunition.

"I used to work in a restaurant," Deedee explained.

"Terribly amusing stuff to an eejit, isn't it?" Jo smiled and bumped her shoulder against Deedee's. "They'll get used to you in the end. I'm guessing that one's in the family business?"

Deedee nodded. It wasn't unusual, a lineage like that. It could be dangerous, though. Mac was sure of himself, of his place, and Deedee had been discovering that perhaps that confidence could be a weakness, something like her own lack of curiosity. You had to be a questioner in this job—of yourself as much as others.

"Oh, he's fine really." She forced herself to smile, tried to not show any cracks. She was a professional. Jo smiled back and nodded a goodbye.

Deedee hadn't made a new friend in years. It was hard to, she supposed, when you already knew everyone in the town—and they knew you too. But she could see herself hanging out with Jo, going for drinks, up to Cork city for a bit of a rave sometimes maybe. She'd have to remember to ask her what kind of music she liked. She was so lost in thought that she hadn't realized her drink was ready and a queue was forming behind her. She pulled her mug away from the machine too quickly; the coffee spilled over onto her hand, hot enough to make her hiss as she shook it dry. Another burn for the collection.

She'd barely had time to clean herself up a bit and log into one of the station computers to check her email before a briefing was called by Doyle himself. She grabbed her notepad and hurried over to listen.

"Morning all. We've had a report in of a missing child. I'm passing around the picture now, please take it with you. Lily-Mae Lynch, ten years old, went to bed at nine thirty in the evening. Mother says she felt a breeze when heading up to bed herself at around one a.m., but she didn't check the kids' rooms. Call came in about ten minutes ago: window open and child gone. House backs onto the development site over by the Hanging Woods, so we'll start our search there."

Whatever else was said in the briefing, Deedee didn't hear it. Lily-Mae was blond, just like her mother, Michelle Quinn, and the older Quinn kid Deedee had admonished in the cemetery yesterday. She had a shy smile and a scattering of freckles across her nose and cheeks. She didn't look much like Roisin, but she was the same age, disappeared from the same area twenty years later. Roisin's disappearance had been considered an aberration, a one-off. Now the conditions had aligned once more, history repeating itself.

Deedee remembered that irrational strike of fear she'd felt in the cemetery that the girl would end up in the Hanging Woods somehow. She had been right to worry.

Caitlin Doherty returns, and another little girl disappears.

Her mind raced, seeking connections between the two. The shuffling and scuffing sounds of others around her standing up, the briefing over, punctured her thoughts. Still, she didn't notice Doyle until he was inches from her face.

"Not you, O'Halloran." His expression was grim. "I'll need to speak with you in a minute. Martin, we need you here on the phones. Let the local lads do the sweep at this stage."

His phone went off and he held up one finger to Deedee in a "wait here" motion before walking off to take the call.

As if they had all the time in the world, Deedee thought. She knew exactly where she would go when she got out there: to Caitlin Doherty. The coincidence was too much.

"D'you reckon anyone'll call in?" Jo asked.

"Yeah. As much to try and fish for info from you as to tell you they think they've seen something," Deedee said. But she was already preparing the argument she'd put before Doyle to make sure he let her get out there.

"I heard some of the lads talking a load of old shite," Jo said. "Something crazy like that the woods are haunted? Are they having me on?"

"That's the word around here." Deedee was brought back to the conversation by Jo's tone. She didn't like it. The stories about the Hanging Woods were nonsense, but they were the nonsense of the people who were actually from this town.

"Are you for real?" Jo asked. "What's it really about?"

"It's just part of growing up here," Deedee said. "You think that's weird, haven't you heard about the solstice parties? Load of the hippie artist types have a bonfire twice a year, plenty of chanting and dancing about."

"Now *that* I know all about." Jo grinned. "It's part of the reason we moved down here. My husband and his family *are* those artist hippie types. We're all dusting off the Tibetan singing bowls for Sunday night."

"Of all the places you could go, Bannakilduff for the solstices is something else!"

"Hey, it makes them happy! Where would you suggest?"

Images of lush green landscapes, mountains, lakes, sunshine, and warmth kindled immediately in Deedee's mind. *New Zealand,* she thought. *We could've got the visas to go for a couple years. Worked on a farm in between, spent all our free time outside, far away from everything here. We could have stayed forever, even.*

"Maybe as far as Kinafallia." The dream was too precious to be shared, even now.

"Exotic!" joked Jo. "But no solstices there."

"We used to go to the summer ones when I was a kid. Those were a much bigger deal." The summer solstice was a week or two before school finished, and the kids would treat the party as an informal end-of-term bash. It was safe enough, but they were always left to their own devices, where they could snaffle a nip of booze here and there and then watch the fireworks as dusk finally, finally set in.

"Ach, I never got to go in those days," Jo said.

"It wasn't the same after my . . . well, after a girl went missing." Deedee hadn't thought of this in years, but her mouth was running away from her now. Without disclosing the connection between herself and Roisin, she told the rest of the tale.

"Of course, the biggest news story of our childhoods, eh?" Jo said. "My parents knew Lee Casey."

Deedee was stunned; no one had ever claimed a relationship with Casey so casually. "What was he like?"

"Kinda weird, but he seemed harmless. He'd be reckless; he once tried to jump out of the window of a bar to land on the roof of a building next door. That sort of circle, though, eccentrics aren't unusual."

"Lee Casey," Deedee repeated under her breath, flashes of the images she'd seen of him. First the before: red paint streaked across his bare chest, tattered shorts, shaggy head thrown back as though howling at the moon. Then the somber version, in a tired suit, close-shaven, dead eyes. "He must've been some creep to stand out then?"

"He'd had a breakdown or something that year. No one saw him as much; he was hanging around the woods—well, you know that bit."

Deedee did know that bit.

"Is he different now?" she asked.

"Even more of an outsider," Jo said. "The accusations have . . . stained him. He's in town now for the first time since."

"Is there something you're not saying?" Deedee asked. Casey had an alibi. He'd been part of a drumming circle, with several other participants to vouch for him. She thought of the map, still tucked in her bag, the tent symbol. Could it have been Roisin marking Casey's campsite?

"Those kinds of things, they're all a bit loose, aren't they? Like half the drumming circle will have been off their heads, so if he did nip out, would they really have noticed?"

"They wouldn't even have had to lie, they would have just thought he was there," Deedee said.

Jo nodded. "Exactly. But if they're right, and it wasn't him, why did the other kid say she saw him in the woods?"

"Official line? It's a child caught up in a traumatic event, not remembering clearly. The case was closed five years after Roisin's disappearance. But"—Deedee spoke faster, eager to vent her theories—"it's possible that she was lying about Casey, trying to create a distraction. I know her, I picked her up from the airport the other day."

"She's here too? What's your feeling there?" Jo asked.

"Compulsive liar, minimum. Terrible witness." Deedee thought about the inconsequential airport lie. "It's possible that the lads figured the same, that she wasn't reliable. But without Casey, they'd no case, so maybe they just hoped it would work out."

Deedee didn't think nine-year-old Caitlin could have murdered

Roisin and covered up the crime so thoroughly that decades later there was still no evidence. She was only sure that Caitlin knew something. She was protecting someone, or covering something up, but Deedee had no idea who, or why Caitlin would do that.

"You know yourself it shouldn't happen, but sometimes you think you've the right guy, everything adds up, and then he gets off . . ." Jo's voice trailed away, but Deedee followed her thoughts.

"It's more of an art than a science sometimes," she said, knowing that policing shouldn't be about gut feelings or the right face at the right time but also that sometimes any answer was better than none. If Casey had been sentenced, would Deedee have felt differently her whole life? Would the loss have felt less acute?

Casey could have had some kind of incident with Roisin, stashed the evidence somewhere, returned later that night after establishing his alibi, she thought, but her theories became less and less clear the more she considered them.

"I don't know the feller—like I said, he's weird," Jo said, a note of caution in her voice. "But being weird's not a crime."

"There's something not quite there." Deedee clicked her fingers. It was all on the tip of her tongue, and yet so far out of her grasp. "But I feel like it's all connected. The timing of Lily-Mae, Caitlin being back, Casey being back . . ."

"If your idea is that the disappearances are linked, who do you talk to first?" Jo asked.

"We're talking about Lily-Mae here?" Deedee said.

"Of course, you couldn't be doing anything else," Jo replied carefully.

"Caitlin will only lie to me," Deedee said. "With Casey there's a lot of loose ends, but if he had that breakdown, maybe I can pressure him. Last time this happened, the lads fumbled the interrogation, let him get away. I won't."

All the training, all the shit the lads give me, it was all to find Roisin.

No one else was even pursuing an idea that the disappearances were linked yet.

"Look, the walls have eyes and ears around here, of course, but what about if we stop off for a quick drink after the shift ends? Would be good to pick your brains," Deedee said.

Jo laughed. "A lunchtime pint, is it?"

"Just one. It's almost Christmas after all."

"Don't get me started," Jo sighed. "I've all my in-laws to sort out as well. Are you married? I don't recommend it for the blood pressure."

"Not yet," Deedee said. She glanced around her. The phones were still quiet. It was just them. She told Jo about everything with Sean: his secretive behavior, Fi's theory.

"So, you might be in line for even more congratulations!" Jo exclaimed.

"I know, it's mad, isn't it? But we've been together so long. I . . ." Deedee hesitated; was this about to go too far? She chose her words carefully. "I wouldn't have necessarily stayed in Bannakilduff but for Sean. His dad was badly injured years ago, and he's needed a lot of help since."

"Ah, go on, you've something in mind." Jo could read her easily. "I'll get it out of you over that pint."

"O'Halloran." Doyle interrupted them, and beckoned Deedee after him.

His office was a small cubicle at the top of the squad room. A pane of glass stretched across the top two thirds of the wall. He pulled the blinds shut.

"O'Halloran, we've just had a woman call in. She said that you told her Jason and Kevin O'Sullivan were dealing drugs. She laid out the case we've been building. The whole investigation is compromised."

Out-of-body horror seized Deedee. It was all coming back to her. Copper. Jules.

"I don't think I need to tell you how bad this is, Deirdre." Doyle couldn't meet her eyes.

"Sir, I didn't . . . I was trying to do something good." Deedee heard her voice crack as she spoke.

"How could you be so stupid, Deirdre? You know the position you've put me in?"

"I'm sorry. I didn't . . . I'll never do it again." Deedee held up her arms in surrender.

"You're right, you won't. And look at the state of you! You're bleeding."

"What?" Deedee touched her face, as though she'd been in a fight.

"Your arm."

Blood had crusted over the cuff and sleeve of her shirt. She shoved it under her coat, embarrassed that everyone had seen it. "S'fine."

"What happened to you here?" Doyle held out his hand, wanting to see the wound. Reluctantly she unbuttoned the cuff, pulling the sleeve up slowly to reveal the wound without disturbing it. "Deirdre. Did you do this to yourself?"

"No! I was cooking and, and some oil spilled . . ." She wasn't sure which was worse: if Doyle thought she was self-harming, or if he knew she'd gotten drunk and nearly burned down her house.

"O'Halloran, you've put me in an impossible position."

"No, look, I can make it right. I can help." Deedee pulled her wrist back and jumped up from the chair.

"You can't help anyone right now." Doyle looked up at her sadly.

Dread froze Deedee in place where she stood.

"Garda O'Halloran, you are suspended. Your conduct yesterday has endangered an ongoing investigation and members of the public. You are to go home immediately and await further contact."

Deedee was speechless.

Everything she had worked for, all the shit she'd swallowed, everything was evaporating. Doyle was still talking, but she couldn't hear him. The room blurred as hot tears rolled down her cheeks.

It was over.

"Dee? Dee, sit down." Doyle guided her back to the chair, patted his pockets in search of tissues. Finding none, he simply sat back down across from her.

"I'm sorry," Deedee said. *I didn't mean to, I only wanted to help, I wanted to make you proud*: all the things she couldn't bear to let pass her lips.

"Dee, you have got to clean yourself up. And I don't just mean this. You think we don't know when you're coming in still half-cut?"

Deedee gaped. Her emotions came in waves: defensiveness, embarrassment, denial. Anger.

"I thought I could help you get a grip on things, but clearly not."

"You can't do this now. Not when another girl has gone missing."

"This isn't about Roisin." Doyle spoke with finality.

Deedee wiped her cuff across her face. She sniffed hard.

"Look, Caitlin lied about Casey—" she began desperately.

"Stop," Doyle told her. "Go home."

"If I go home, someone else has to—"

"Christ! Roisin is dead! You don't tell me how to run an investigation, O'Halloran!" Doyle's patience had run out. "The arrogance of it! You, who wouldn't even be here but for me!"

The words landed with both of them at the same time, and Deedee watched as it was Doyle's turn to look horrified.

She nodded and left his office. This was only confirmation of everything she'd ever feared, but just as she felt how it stung, she also felt a brief, peaceful reprieve. She'd been right all along.

She had never belonged here. She would have to do this on her own.

23

CAITLIN

The TV is still on when Caitlin wakes up, but the screen has gone to static because of the storm. The grating sound mingles with the soft patter of rain outside into a noise that makes her teeth itch. Curled awkwardly in the big armchair, her muscles have stiffened. Her mouth is dry. The door is open and the hallway is dark.

"It's just the hallway," she whispers to no one. "I'm not scared."

Saying the words makes her feel braver in the blue glow of the TV, the only light on earth right now. Inspiration strikes her: she could pretend that her mother is already home. Yes, if her mother is home then she is definitely safe. She will do that, she decides.

"Mam." She stretches one leg out, feels her foot land safely on the worn carpet. "I'm going to bed."

A scraping sound answers her, and she withdraws her foot back up into the safety of the armchair. It's metallic, coming from the front of the house, from the front door. Someone is outside. Someone is trying to get inside.

Caitlin's first thought is of the Hanging Woods behind the house. That pattering sound mightn't be rain at all; it could be blood dripping from the blade of an axe, it could be drool falling from the jowls of a monster.

The scraping comes again, louder this time, more determined.

Caitlin is alone.

And the back door is unlocked.

The memory of how she failed to lock it after she came home this afternoon freezes her blood in her veins.

The scraping is louder again, the door handle rattling now. Frustration and anger have replaced stealth.

Time is running out. Caitlin uncurls herself from the armchair and crouches on the floor. The front door has a long glass pane down the center. She will need to move quickly in order to not be seen by the thing outside.

What happens to little girls who go missing? They are eaten up by monsters.

She fixes her eyes on the living room door and shuffles on her knees toward the hallway. At the threshold, she freezes. The hallway is darker than it should be, the window in the door blocked by a shadow cast against the glass. Tall and person-shaped, the bit where the head would be is pressed against the glass, looking for her.

Is it him? The one leaving her dream catchers and crystals and marbles?

What price has she agreed to pay by accepting his offerings?

Still hunched on the floor, pure terror grips her. But for as long as the figure stays at the front door, she knows that it's not at the back door. She might still be able to get away from it, out to the road. When she hears it move around the house, she will bolt to the front door and escape. The plan soothes her enough to get her breathing under control.

They both stay where they are for what feels like hours. Everything in Caitlin's body is focused on survival.

Finally, the figure backs away from the glass. Caitlin raises her weight onto the balls of her feet, her fingertips resting on the carpet like a sprinter. The shadow recedes further, and yes, Caitlin was right, she hears it stomping around the house, heading for the back door.

She springs into action. She is at the front door so quickly that she bumps into it and the noise makes her gasp, but she is there. All she needs to do is unlock it.

She reaches for the keys, hanging on a nail on the wall, but fumbles and knocks them off, leaving nothing but air where they should be dangling.

The footsteps outside are quicker now, as though they heard her and know what she knows—that she is vulnerable now, trapped.

She looks down, praying to see the silver glint of the keys in spite of the darkness. She drops to the ground, searching with her hands until she finds them, but once more her shaking fingers send them tumbling.

The footsteps are almost at the back door.

The keys are in her hand, but she can't quite get the right one.

As though it can smell her terror, the thing outside chuckles. A low, slow, unmistakable chuckle.

Caitlin feels her guts spasm in horror. There are two keys in her hand and neither seems to fit the door, both skittering and rebounding off the metal.

The click of the back-door handle turning.

She fits the key into the lock.

Her sweat-slicked hands can't turn it.

She is going to lose.

This is not the kind of story where the girl gets away from the monster.

The back door squeals as it creaks open.

Caitlin wrenches the front door open. She can still do it, she can make it, she can run.

In the moonlight, a figure is coming toward her, making hungry snuffling noises. From behind her, she hears a heavy foot cross the threshold and land inside the house. All along she thought there was one creature trying to get to her, but now she sees that there are two, that she never had a chance at all.

She screams as loudly as she can.

"Caitlin Doherty, what on earth do you have to scream about?" The figure in front of her grabs her, and it's her mother, her mother has come home. "You'll have the whole county awake, my God!"

Speechless with fright, Caitlin falls into the safety of her mother's arms.

"It's raining, come on." Kathleen is snappy and short-tempered. Her date must not have gone well.

Caitlin pulls on her arm. The thing is still in there.

"Get off!" Her mother brushes her away as though she is nothing. "Stop this nonsense!"

"There's someone in there!" Caitlin cries out.

Kathleen clicks on the hall light and Caitlin waits for the monster to be revealed.

"What are you thinking, Caitlin?" her mother scolds. "Is that the TV on all night in there?"

Caitlin peeks. The hallway is empty. The lights are blazing. Her mother has turned off the TV, the static noise is gone.

"Everything all right, girls?" Colm, emerging from behind the house. He must have come from his front door as soon as she screamed.

"Sorry to wake you!" her mother greets him from the back door. "Caitlin had a bad dream."

From her position in the open front door, Caitlin can see that Colm looks very awake already. He's wearing his waxed jacket, and the silver buckle of his belt glints in the moonlight. He hasn't been asleep yet; he looks like he's only just coming home.

"Poor creature," he tuts, turning back to his own place.

Caitlin closes the front door firmly behind her. In front of her, her mother is slamming the back door.

"If we get rot in the floorboards because you've left that back door open all evening, Caitlin Doherty, I will not be responsible for my actions."

"I didn't!"

"Do you know that this is the very last thing I need? And *you're* crying? *I* should be crying! Oisinn Quinn was down there talking up a storm of shite, the lying cretin, and Michael just sits there and doesn't say anything!"

"What was he saying? About cars?" All Caitlin knows about Oisinn Quinn is that he's a mechanic, so if he's going to get in trouble, it follows logically that it would be about cars. Overcharging, maybe, or saying he'd fixed them when he hadn't.

Caitlin doesn't know a whole lot about cars, to be honest.

"Never *you* mind, Little Miss Nosy, but just know that a man should always stand up for a lady. Get to bed. Now."

Sniffling, Caitlin turns on her bedroom light and checks under the bed, in the wardrobe, just in case. She finds nothing. She runs a hand down the seam where the curtains meet, before remembering Colm. She peeks, expecting to see that the Big House is still lit up, Colm and Maureen pottering around. But the curtains are drawn, the place is in darkness, shut up for the night.

This time the monster opened the door. She doesn't want to know what it will do next time.

24

DEEDEE

Suspended, pending investigation, but they both knew Deedee's career was over. Although how the investigation into her conduct would go was anyone's guess. If any of that shower of eejits had been good at investigating in general, she'd never have had to get involved in the first place and—

"Are you OK?" Jo asked. Deedee was quickly and efficiently packing her things. She could feel Doyle watching her, as though she would cause a scene. Jo coughed politely.

"I'm fine," Deedee replied, too quickly. "I'm just heading out now, though. I'll catch you at O'Shea's after your shift?"

"See you then." Jo seemed concerned, but she was taking everything in. Would she use this as currency later? Tell everyone how Deedee had made an exit, shape a new rumor about her?

"Listen, the solstice lot—Lee Casey and them—are they staying in the Starboard, do you know?" Deedee didn't want to rely on Jo still being friendly with her later, and she didn't want to wait either. She wanted to begin her investigation into Caitlin now.

"A few are, much as the owners hate that," Jo said.

The Starboard Hotel was old, and always looked on the verge of being swept away by the sea. It was the de facto wedding venue, debs venue, afternoon tea location. Deedee struggled to imagine it filled with solstice party pagans and hippies, all tie-dye canvas trousers and unwashed hair.

"Would Casey be there?" she asked. "Out of interest. Just wondering who'd put the feller up; you said he's few friends."

"I wouldn't go looking for him," Jo said carefully, "but the rental cottages on the cliffs are more likely. Less folk around."

"Good to know," Deedee said. "I'll be sure to avoid those cottages then, eh?"

Jo waved her off. Behind her, Doyle stood framed in his big office window, watching her go. He would be eating his words when she found Lee Casey.

She'd get the truth out of Casey, figure out what—or who—Caitlin was hiding, and then she'd quit.

She was about to be a Branagh. She wouldn't need this stupid job, or any other. They'd all be feeling sheepish pretty quickly. The thought reinforced her spine, allowed her to walk out with her head held high.

Barely even 8 a.m., there was only one coffee shop open. She popped in and ordered an Americano to go. While she waited, she pulled out Kathleen's phone. It had dropped to 63 percent, even with no one calling or texting and Deedee only opening it every now and then to scroll through the pictures and examine the texts. She still felt sure there was something there.

Then Kathleen herself passed by the window.

Deedee caught it only from the corner of her eye. The tiny, hunched figure shuffling by in a fur coat. She shoved the phone into her pocket, where it suddenly felt heavier than ever.

"No milk with that?" The barista yawned as he tapped her order into the register. Deedee managed to shake her head no.

"Did you see that?" she asked.

The barista blinked at her.

"See what?"

"A woman just passed by, you didn't see her?"

"Wasn't looking." He turned to the coffee machine.

Deedee went to the door. The wound on her wrist protested as she shoved it open, and she gasped. The skin around the burn was pink and inflamed, while the wound itself was yellowish and oozing but no longer bleeding.

When she looked up, the street was empty.

She had been mistaken.

Kathleen was dead.

She shook her head as she returned inside. It was the phone freaking her out, her own guilty conscience. She grabbed a napkin from the side, and reminded herself that she had nothing to feel guilty about. Dabbing at the wound, she achieved little but to draw fresh pinpricks of blood to the surface. Deedee was used to burns and scrapes and cuts, but something about this one hurt more.

She took her coffee, dropping a tip into the jar on the counter.

Doyle might have been right; she must still be half-cut. Seeing things.

The coffee and the cold air cleared her head. She climbed up toward the cliffside cottages. Casey had been here; she might've passed him in the street. Would she have recognized him? He could've lost all his hair by now—or grown it out to three-foot-long white-guy dreadlocks.

The arrogance of him, to believe that he could just walk back into Bannakilduff and get away with whatever he liked. He probably thought of them all as fools, yokels, just a bunch of idiots. With every step she took toward the cottages, Deedee invented another insult that Lee Casey had thrown at the people of Bannakilduff, and got angrier and angrier.

Three cottages in a row, each with a lockbox for keys and small signage. *Cliff House. Summit Point. Land's End.*

A mammoth Land Rover was parked next to the first cottage. Deedee peered into it. Child's booster seat in the back, baby wipes set up on the dashboard. Not Lee Casey's car.

At the next cottage, two bikes leaned against the front of the house, a sleek black racing machine and a dark-purple woman's bike. Jo had described Lee as a loner still, unlikely to have a girlfriend.

The last cottage, then. She strode up to the door marked *Land's End*. She had worked herself up into such a state of anger at him that as she pounded on the door, she was ready to greet him with a punch straight to the nose.

Lee Casey opened the door shower-wet, in khaki shorts and a vest. He was leathery from sun exposure and his leonine mane was shot through with white at the temples. Celtic knot tattoo on his right shoulder, a tribal-style sun inside his left forearm. His face was fuller than in any of the media photographs, and his cheeks rosier, but he was missing a tooth on the top right side of his mouth. Deedee felt glad that perhaps someone else had already dealt him a blow to the face.

"Hello?" Soft voice, brow steepled in worry. Spicy incense drifted out of his open door.

"Lee Casey?" Deedee confirmed. "Garda O'Halloran. I was hoping to speak with you."

"They've already been, the guards?" Casey was a nervous up-talker, every statement a question. "They came about an hour ago about the little girl. They should have my statement on the record?"

Deedee had been so sure that no one else would have made the connection that to hear she was actually slower than her team winded her.

"Is that so?" she demanded. "Why do you think they came to you?"

Casey dipped his head, looked at the ground. "Because of . . . the past?"

Shame radiated from him.

Shame, but not guilt.

"I didn't see anything then and I haven't seen anything now, either." He met her eye.

Deedee wished she trusted her instincts enough to take him at his word.

"How do you explain it?" she asked. "It's quite a coincidence that you're in town every time a child goes missing."

"People find patterns where they look for them," Casey said, "but I don't have anything to hide?"

He stepped aside, welcoming her in. Deedee hesitated, peering about to assess for danger. The cottage was warm, a fire kindling in the grate, a mug of tea steaming on a table beside an open notebook. A yoga mat lay on the floor. Colorful crystals clustered on the windowsill.

"Charging," he said as she glanced at them. "Full moon coming?"

Honestly, she had expected weirder. That was exactly the kind of shite all the solstice lot came out with. She watched him take a seat in an armchair beside the fireplace and crossed over to sit opposite him.

"What exactly did you tell the guards?" she asked.

"I was here last night; the locals don't seem too interested in my readings these days, but I still have online clients? I was booked all evening."

"Into the early hours?"

Casey nodded. "Americans, Canadians—even a guy in French Polynesia! I've traveled a bit? My last reading was with a New Yorker at one a.m. our time—that's evening there? It was a good one too, really good. I hope I don't lose a client over this, when they talk to her."

"I woulda thought your reviews would be the least of your worries," Deedee scoffed. "Did you see this coming?"

Lee Casey cocked his head to one side and considered her. Deedee felt her hackles begin to rise, and perched on the edge of her seat, ready to spring forward if he came toward her.

"I don't think you're really here about this?" Casey picked up a flyer with Lily-Mae's photo printed on it. "There's something else, isn't there?"

"What do you think?" she asked. Did he recognize Roisin in her?

"You have a sadness about you," Casey said. He put the flyer down and picked up a stack of tarot cards. "Pain, loss, not recent. Old wounds. Meditation would help you."

"A lot of people think that. For the anger mostly."

"That's a cover." He shuffled the cards. "Anger, fear, sadness, anxiety; different shades of the same color."

"My sister is—was—Roisin O'Halloran." Deedee waited for the reaction.

Casey paled. He put the cards down. His shoulders hunched up to his ears and he shook his head.

"I'm sorry for your loss? But I don't know anything about that."

"You seem sure she's dead."

"I'm not sure of anything?"

"What were you doing at the fairground in the first place?" Deedee asked.

"I'd made these dream catchers. That summer I was newly recovering? I needed something to do with my hands, so I was always knotting up dream catchers, to keep me from thinking about ..." Casey passed one hand over the inside of his elbow. The skin there was lumpen and discolored.

"I didn't know," Deedee said.

"I hid it." Casey's mouth twitched, screwed up to one side, and then relaxed again. It looked involuntary, though whether it spoke of nerves or lying, she couldn't tell.

"And you saw Roisin?" she asked. She watched him carefully for signs of discomfort, but he looked right at her.

"I gave a statement; you should have the records? I told them someone else was there—the kids were always talking about the monster? It wasn't me. But I wasn't the only one in there."

"How did you know what the kids were talking about?" Deedee demanded.

"I heard them?"

A memory of Roisin crashing around the house, so loud on her feet for such a small person, the nonsense songs she'd sing, constant noise. The quiet afterward so complete it was painful.

"What about Caitlin? Why would she say she'd seen you if you weren't there?"

"I wish I knew! There must have been someone else who looked like me?" Casey seized on the conversational thread like he'd thought about it a lot.

"You don't think she was lying, no?" Deedee asked.

"Why would she lie?" From Casey's reaction, it was obvious that this idea was new to him. From that Deedee deduced that there had been no tensions then, he'd never suspected Caitlin's involvement.

"What were they like together?" She realized as she asked that she was curious. Who Roisin had been as a friend was a mystery to her. A facet of her sister that she would never know.

Casey made a helpless gesture. They were just a couple of kids, he seemed to be indicating. How should he know?

"They never approached me, but they watched me making the dream catchers. And I deliberately dropped things—a couple turquoise crystals for luck, some bundled twigs? Stuff to discover, treasures?"

Deedee unrolled Roisin's map for him.

"Do these symbols make sense to you? The tent, is that your campsite?"

"Looks about right, yeah." Lee studied the map, then indicated a small round symbol in the trees. "That's where I left a dream catcher for them, right behind the small house, on the edge, so they'd find it."

"What about the shell? Did you leave them a shell?" Deedee asked.

"There's meaning to everything—" he began.

"Sure, the universe or whatever," she interrupted.

"No, here. Some of the symbols are small, those I recognize. Like the dream catcher, or there's a little gem where I think I dropped a turquoise for them. The shell is big, though, that's different."

Deedee looked at the map again and understood what he meant. "The church, the fire station, they're small too. Objects or buildings are small symbols. The big symbols are something else. People?"

"The big wizard's hat is where I'd forage; the kids watched me there."

"You would have seemed magical to them, the crystals and all that. Like a wizard," Deedee said.

"Does that theory hold for the others? What about the cat in the gatehouse, could that be whoever lived there?" Casey asked.

"Caitlin lived there," Deedee said. "Caitlin, Cait, cat? It's a theory."

It felt right, like the breakthrough she had been waiting for. Adrenaline pulsed through her veins; she felt like punching the air. *I can do this, I can work this through.*

"So the shell is a person," she said, "and so is the skull."

"The skull doesn't seem like good news," Casey said. "It's probably him? I told the officer—the guard—who spoke to me back then, that there was someone else there."

"Do you remember their name?"

"It'll come to me? But he wasn't interested really." He spread his hands in a gesture of hopelessness. "He told me to leave, not come back?"

"Why come back now?" Deedee asked.

Casey fidgeted, clearly uncomfortable. "I've had a hard time recently with my . . . recovery? I thought, if I came back here, I don't know. I never picked up a needle after that summer."

Something about that sounded off to Deedee.

"Seems like this was a pretty stressful place," she said.

"But everyone knows I had nothing to do with it. The guards, they knew? The one who spoke to me, he had a very sad aura too."

"Seems there's a lot of that about."

"Name from literature, wish I could remember, it's on the tip of my tongue. Like an author, Sherlock Holmes?"

"There's no Holmes on the force." Deedee was getting nowhere. "Thank you for your time."

"No, not the character . . ."

"Well, let me know if you remember," she said, standing up.

Casey held up one hand for her to wait and ran over to his crystal collection. "I have something for you?"

Deedee waited in the open doorway, her back exposed to the coast.

25

CAITLIN

You ruined that man's life. The voice spoke from behind her, at the table that Sean had left. Plummy perfume, menthol smoke. She was alone in the kitchen, wasn't she?

"I didn't do anything." Caitlin stayed at the window; she didn't turn to face the ghost.

Officially, 'twas you who saw him out there. No bonfire smoke smell, no shadows; this was new. Christ, she hoped she wasn't going to have to argue with her invisible mother for the rest of her life.

"I did see him out there."

He had built a little structure. It had shocked Caitlin; the idea of someone scurrying around in her woods, gathering its materials for themselves. Then it felt like a betrayal, that the woods could sustain and shelter another.

Tell the truth.

She hated him for this. Despised him. Infiltrating her woods, her place, stomping around like it was his own.

You wanted to kill him.

Could you blame her?

He knows what you did.

Smoke filled the room, filled Caitlin's lungs; she coughed, choked on it. She could picture it: Lee Casey, older now but still probably only in his forties. Her mother, also older and flattered by his attentions. Drunk anyway, no longer too particular if Casey was going to be buying the booze.

Lee Casey in their cottage. Caitlin imagined him growing antsy in the taxi. If he hadn't known who Kathleen was already and sought her out for that reason, if he had just stumbled upon her in the bar, he would realize as the car approached. He would know.

Lee Casey, smoking orange filter cigarettes in the kitchen, looking out and remembering how the Hanging Woods had ruined his life. How Caitlin had ruined his life.

You'll have to do it now.

"Yes," Caitlin agreed. She would have to get to him first, before he came for her.

She hustled out of the house into the predawn twilight. The signs had been directing her all along; she only had to trust in them now. She was slower than usual, the jolt to her hip bothering her with every step. She could feel the bruise wrapping around the back of her body, pulsing.

The walk into town was just under an hour on a good day, with the way the roads twisted, and this was not a good day, but the cold air was a balm to her fevered thoughts.

An early-morning jogger dressed in a neon high-vis running vest nodded as he passed her, which she took as a good sign. More confirmation that she was moving in the right direction. As she emerged onto the outskirts of town, past Quinn's garage, the traffic lights turned green. Glowing beacons in the dim twilight, affirming her once more.

As she walked, she thought of all the other Caitlins she'd been in this town. Four years old and skipping ahead of her mother, off to get new shoes for school. Eight years old and walking in on her own, a pound coin clutched in her fist, head full of thoughts of sweets and comics. And now, not quite thirty, looking for monsters.

Monsters.

Her step faltered. Was Lee Casey a monster? There had been a monster in the woods, Lee Casey had been in the woods; she had told everyone they were one and the same. Yes, he was the monster, she remembered now. He had taken Roisin, and now he had come for her mother. This was what she needed to remember.

Stick to the story.

She smelled her mother's perfume again, heavy and heady.

Say nothing.

Confusing, contradictory advice.

Caitlin didn't remember hating Lee Casey; she remembered feeling jealous of him. The idea of living in the Hanging Woods, knotting strings and manipulating sticks into dream catchers, had been the most beautiful thing she could think of. She had envied him, yes, but hated, despised? The rush of emotions that had filled her back in the Big House and propelled her this far dissipated.

But he killed your mother.

Did he? She tilted her head, listening for more clarity, but none came. The perfume smell lifted. She was alone again.

The town was shuttered still; it was barely eight. There was an open coffee shop, and she passed the guards' station, but signs of life elsewhere were few.

She paused, breathed deep.

"Where is he?" she whispered.

She felt exposed, suddenly, standing alone in the middle of the pavement. Like she could be struck down at any moment. She ducked into a tight alleyway and pressed herself against the bricks, anchoring herself to something real, something solid.

A sign would come, she just had to be patient.

Then there it was.

Deedee walked past, her face grim, her eyes and nose red from the cold, a coffee cup held at her chest. She leaned forward into the wind, fighting the elements.

Caitlin waited a few seconds and then followed her.

It was reckless, she knew. At any point, Deedee could turn and see her, and she would have nothing to say.

But Deedee didn't turn.

Deedee kept walking, so Caitlin kept walking, and then they were at the coast. A steel-gray sea roiled, waves crashing against rocks. From here, she could see all the way to the Starboard Hotel.

Deedee turned away from it, up toward the cliff path. *That was good*, Caitlin thought. The angry sea felt like a bad omen for the Starboard Hotel path. On the right trail, the route would present itself, unfurling clearly just for her, leading straight to Lee Casey.

On the cliff path, Deedee forged ahead, all quick, efficient strides, the ground flying beneath her. It was impossible to deny that she was Caitlin's omen. Deedee would lead her to Casey.

Caitlin struggled to keep a steady pace; her hip protested as she made her way over the uneven ground, so she hung back. Deedee strode toward a huddle of dirty white cottages. Smoke issued from the chimney of one. As Caitlin watched, the plume of smoke darkened into a black shadow. She sniffed. Bonfire smell.

Deedee deliberated before the cottages, peering at the exteriors, looking for clues. Reading signs of her own. Finally, she knocked at the door of the third cottage, the one issuing smoke. The door opened, and she disappeared inside.

Caitlin left her hiding place and followed Deedee's path. The steep incline and cold air stole her breath, but she forgot even the throbbing of her side as she climbed higher. She passed the first two cottages.

And there, only a few steps ahead of her, she saw a rock, solid and hefty. She picked it up and tested the weight. It felt right in her hand. She ran her thumb over a pleasingly jagged side of it. It would do, it would do the job nicely.

A tall figure stood in the shadow of the doorway of the third cottage. Caitlin knew that it had to be him. The signs had taken her this far; there had been too many coincidences for this not to be fated.

It's me or him, she thought, *if he's here for revenge . . .*

She raised the rock over her head.

Just like the last time.

26

DEEDEE

The handful of crystals Lee Casey was about to offer her clattered to the ground. His eyes widened in shock, and before she could react, he yanked her inside the cottage. Something solid whistled past her ear, grazing her shoulder. She heard a grunt behind her as someone fell.

"Kathleen?" Deedee gasped at the pile of ragged fur and matted bleach-blond hair on the path outside. A heavy rock lay beside it.

"Stay back!" Lee Casey shouted, brandishing a Buddha statuette in one shaking hand. His phone slipped from his other hand, but he continued shouting anyway, "I'm calling the authorities!"

"Hang on." Deedee approached the fallen figure. Kathleen was dead, so this had to be . . . "What kind of eejit are you, Caitlin? You coulda brained me!"

She kicked the rock away, just in case Caitlin still had any ideas.

"Lee Casey. He's been there every time, Deedee!" Caitlin propped herself in the doorway. Gaunt and gray, she looked like she had come back from the dead herself. "In the Hanging Woods, at my mam's . . ."

"I don't know what she's talking about!" Casey glanced nervously at his crystal collection, but none was as large as Caitlin's rock.

"When was he at your mam's?" Deedee tried to follow; unpicking Caitlin's troubled streams of consciousness could provide a crucial clue.

"When she died!" Caitlin howled. The sun disappeared behind threatening gray clouds, leaving her spotlit, her limbs at odd angles, hands grasping the doorframe.

"I don't even know her mam?" Casey fumbled with a vape, dragging on it and sending an acrid cloud of apple-scented smoke into the room that undercut the drama of the moment.

"The smaller house next to the estate by the Hanging Woods," Deedee translated for him. "When did you get into town?"

"Yesterday morning." Casey said it quickly, easily. His instinct hadn't been to hedge, or try to figure out how not to incriminate himself. It had been to tell the truth.

"You can't believe him," Caitlin warned. "He's dangerous!"

The know-it-all tone of her voice made Deedee snappy. "The only one who's been a danger to me so far is you."

"My boarding pass." Casey held out his phone to show them.

Caitlin paled, her eyes bugged out, and she looked around the room as though just realizing where she was.

"Caitlin Doherty." Casey recognized her finally. "Why did you say I was there?"

"I saw you," she whispered, "with the dream catchers, the knots, living in the woods."

"But I wasn't there that afternoon," he insisted.

Caitlin covered her face and shook her head. When she finally took her hands away, she had composed herself. Her tone was crisp and imperious. "I suppose you would say that."

Before their eyes, Caitlin morphed. Her jaw rose, her mouth puckered into an impatient sneer. The lady of the manor, above guilt, passing judgment instead on her lessers.

She was lying again.

"Sorry to trouble you, Mr. Casey." Deedee grabbed Caitlin's arm and wrenched her away from the cottage. "Caitlin, let's go talk about your attempted assault on a Garda, shall we?"

Caitlin scoffed but let Deedee remove her from the cottage. They set off back down the cliff path, toward the town center.

"He must have faked it somehow," she insisted. "Someone was at my mam's house that last night. I can prove it. I have cigarette butts—that's saliva evidence right there—and there's blood here." She tapped the collar of the fur coat with her free hand.

Deedee stumbled on the loose gravel of the path and staggered to regain her balance. Caitlin took the opportunity to snatch her arm back.

Somehow, in all of Caitlin's paranoid madness, she had done her own investigation. And it had only taken her twenty-four hours to realize that there could be more to Kathleen's death than she knew.

She had better instincts than half the lads at the station.

Deedee needed to be careful.

"You sound mental, properly mental. This is conspiracy theory shite." It had sounded better in her head than it did aloud.

"How would you explain it, then? The butts, the blood?" Caitlin sounded curious.

Funny story, your ma actually whacked me in the nose and I bled all over her coat but still somehow felt guilty enough to take her home and look after her, and see where that's got me?

"Kathleen herself smoked, so that's no proof at all, and who's to say what's on that coat or how long it's been there?" Deedee hoped her desperation didn't show. Having Caitlin's attention felt unpleasant. "You're grieving. Looking to blame someone for your loss."

"Or I'm right and there's more to this. Something happened to my mother."

"You were committing assault." Deedee wanted to get Caitlin off this train of thought as fast as she could. Nothing good could come to her with Caitlin's scrutiny on her.

"I was going to scare him," Caitlin answered quickly. Too quickly. "That's all."

She had morphed back into the woman Deedee had picked up at the airport. Self-assured and calm. Something was settling in her blood, like she was a snow globe that had been shaken.

"You were going to hurt him." No matter how Caitlin wanted to spin it, Deedee knew the truth.

"Me? I'm tiny, Dee! I couldn't if I wanted to." Caitlin looked up at her, and she did appear tiny, bundled in the fur.

Deedee's head spun. Caitlin wasn't finished careening around in her own investigation, she just didn't yet know that it was Deedee she was looking for.

"What about the girl in the woods last night?" She tried to distract Caitlin and regain control of the conversation.

Caitlin cocked her head to one side.

"Did you think you were helping her?" Deedee asked. This version of Caitlin was perhaps more predictable, but clearly still dangerous.

"I don't know what you're talking about," Caitlin said at last. "I was inside with the Branaghs all last night. You can ask them." That commanding manner lingered at the edges of everything she said, but she was lagging behind, her steps painful and labored.

"Oh, I will." Deedee waited for Caitlin to fall into step with her again. The hitch in her stride was from an injury to her right side. "What happened to your leg?"

"You're bleeding," Caitlin replied. "It's disgusting."

In all the tumult, Deedee's wounded wrist had erupted, and blood was soaking into the cuff of her shirt. She swore. She also lost the momentum of their conversation, and her authority, as her professional image crumbled.

"I guess Casey's on edge here," Caitlin continued, smooth as you like, eliding mention of the girl. "And I have an old injury; it plays up in the cold weather."

Deedee floundered, at a loss for how to react to such blatant lying, and still reeling from Caitlin's attempts to seriously injure her. Deedee had never considered Caitlin to be violent. Cunning and manipulative, sure, but she'd never seemed the type to get her hands dirty. Knowing this about Caitlin threw new light on the events surrounding Roisin's disappearance, not to mention Lily-Mae's. Clearly she was dangerous; who knew what she might have done—last night or twenty years ago.

Caitlin was completely relaxed, fixing Deedee with a wide, sincere stare. "Thanks for being there, to make sure things didn't get out of control. He's unpredictable."

They stood at the bottom of the coast path, looking down at the churning sea. Fat drops of rain pattered from the dark clouds above them. Hunkering down into her jacket, Deedee turned away. She was sick of Caitlin—no, repulsed by her.

I'm afraid of her. She buried the thought as soon as it came to her. Still, she put her head down and jogged back into town, hoping to lose Caitlin. Caitlin followed, panting raggedly with the effort. They arrived back to the high street to find the shops had opened, golden squares of light daubing the wet pavements, the day still dark enough to need the illumination.

Hands shaking, Deedee lit a cigarette. At some point Caitlin would have to stop following her, surely.

"You smoke?" Caitlin asked.

Deedee paused, the cigarette between her lips. Caitlin watched her carefully.

What did she just say? Deedee felt like the biggest dope on earth.

"You need to leave Bannakilduff." She ignored the question, tried to act cool, like she hadn't just put herself on Caitlin's hit list by lighting up in front of her. Though, what did that prove? Deedee wasn't the only one who could have left orange cigarette butts at the gatehouse, surely.

"Just . . . not a lot of people our age smoke these days," Caitlin said.

"Round here we do." Deedee exhaled deliberately toward Caitlin, wanting the smoke to push the other woman away, make her back off for a moment, physically at least. "You mightn't be familiar with how we do things."

She saw the tiniest twitch in Caitlin's jaw and fought the urge to smile. That was one thing Deedee did have over Caitlin. The victory didn't last long.

"I know more than you think." Caitlin laughed, a tinkling dinner-party-chatter laugh. "And what happened to Roisin was all your fault. We were only there because of you."

Horrified, Deedee watched Caitlin leave, telling herself she wasn't rattled. Telling herself that Caitlin was wrong.

But for once, Caitlin wasn't lying. It *was* all Deedee's fault.

27

CAITLIN

Saying it was Deedee's fault that they'd gone into the Hanging Woods that day had been a stab in the dark to try and get Deedee off her back. Caitlin had struck lucky, though; there was something there. Deedee was definitely hiding something.

She walked as smoothly and confidently as her bruised hip and side would let her, gritting her teeth through the throbbing pain that rattled into her spine with each step. Behind her, Deedee watched her go, and Caitlin was determined not to let any weakness show. Especially now that she had discovered one of Deedee's weaknesses.

She reached for the reassurance of her bracelet and touched bare skin. The bracelet was gone. It could be anywhere, buried in the mud of the coastal path, already claimed by the sea.

As far as omens went, this was a bad one.

She rounded a corner out of Deedee's sight and let herself fall exhausted against a shop front. She felt battered. It had all made sense at the time; she had only followed where she was led, but somehow it had gone wrong. She was lucky that a real cop hadn't found her. She was lucky that she hadn't managed to hit anyone with the rock.

It was obvious that Deedee did blame herself for what had happened to Roisin. It had been a guess, but Deedee was easy to read.

All that bitterness and anger, of course she hated herself above all else.

She focused on the Big House. If she could just drag her aching body there, she would be safe. But the morning's activities had taken a toll on her and she found herself moving slower and slower the closer she got to the house. Far more than an hour had passed before, red-faced and panting, she arrived back.

"God above, the state of you!" Maureen gasped as Caitlin entered the kitchen. "What's the matter?"

"I fell on my walk." Caitlin didn't care if Maureen believed her; her concentration was taken up by trying not to feel all the ways in which her body hurt. "I'm OK."

"Sit down, sit down. Now I always knew you'd be one of those go-getters!" Maureen made fists and mock-punched the air above her head. "Are you one of those who'd be out jogging in the parks at four, five in the morning? No? Well, let me say this: I'm glad of that. I'm glad of that because you always see on the news, isn't it the early joggers and the dog walkers who find all the dead bodies? Mind you, speaking of, the guards are out in the woods. Didya hear anything on your walk?"

"I went to Paudie, to see about arrangements. Just to be prepared for when we hear back from the pathologist." Caitlin helped herself to a banana from the fruit bowl, then sank into a seat at the table and let the warmth of the Big House seep into her bones. It was a struggle to keep her head from dipping, her eyes from closing.

Maureen maintained a constant chatter as she cracked eggs and placed bacon into a frying pan. Caitlin's stomach growled.

"This banana's enough for me," she said. She took the tiniest bite possible.

Maureen laid a fried-egg-and-bacon sandwich before her. "Ah, you have room for a sanger, of course you do."

"I feel a bit unwell, to be honest." Caitlin's mouth watered at the smell of salt. She had slipped up yesterday, lost control and demolished all that cake. She couldn't risk the same thing happening again.

Lights filled the Hanging Woods now, all headed toward the clearing, the one Caitlin had revisited last night.

No. She had been in the kitchen; she hadn't been in the woods since . . . well, since.

And she hadn't seen her mother at the table.

And Roisin wasn't on the Tube.

But she had tried to assault a man this morning. She had found her way to Lee Casey, and if Deedee hadn't been there, she would have done it again. She would have taken that rock and smashed it into his skull.

The Caitlin who had done that, the tireless one who followed signs and crows, she seemed far from the Caitlin who sat at the table now, bruised and hungry. An eerie lurching sensation in her stomach as she considered again what would have happened if Deedee hadn't been there.

Was it possible that the nightmare was real, that she had gone into the Hanging Woods last night? She would have been looking for Roisin; had she seen a sign that Roisin was in there?

Deedee had asked her about a girl in the Hanging Woods. If Caitlin had come across a girl in the woods last night, what would she have done?

It was a nightmare, she thought. *There was no dirt under my nails, no mud on my feet.* Not like the image of Kathleen that Sean had described for her, how her mother was roaming disheveled around the woods. Searching for Roisin, still trying to keep Caitlin's secrets.

Desperate for distraction from her thoughts, she took a huge bite of the sandwich. The flavors burst over her tongue. It tasted fantastic, but she didn't care about that. She stuffed the rest of it into her mouth, her cheeks bulging, gristle and salt nearly choking her.

"I'd say you'll feel better for that," Maureen said. "You're only a scrap of a thing."

Caitlin's skin prickled at being observed, and she felt the need to purge. Instead, she swallowed, her esophagus bulging painfully.

Maureen needed to be distracted before she gave her any more food. The camera was still on the table, where she'd left it after snapping a picture of Sean this morning. Caitlin picked it up.

"Say cheese!" She raised the viewfinder to her eye and caught Maureen in the midday sun, standing over the stove.

"Oh no! I look a state!" Horror-struck, Maureen's hands flew to smooth down her hair. "Oh Caitlin, you can't! You're as bad as Colm!"

A knock on the front door silenced them both and saved Caitlin from the temptation of another sandwich.

"Another one popping in to see you, no doubt!" Maureen swung the door open, taking a breath, ready to gently admonish their visitor.

A young guard was at the door.

He introduced himself as Garda Carroll, then stared directly at Caitlin and Maureen in turn, as though they were already suspects. Caitlin waited. Had Deedee made good on her threats and actually reported her? Or had she herself done something last night in the Hanging Woods?

". . . not feeling well." Maureen's words drifted through the fog.

"Sorry," Caitlin said. And then, "My mother is dead."

The guard let a sympathetic expression twitch across his face: a slight downturn to his mouth, flicker of downcast eyes. "I'm sorry to hear that."

Heavy polished boots on the welcome mat. Boots in her mother's house, shining like beetles, just inside the front door. Images from years ago mixed with the reality of the moment, and Caitlin's head spun. She focused on the boots in front of her. This was real, this was now.

"Florian here—sorry, Garda Carroll—he works with our Deedee. He's very good." Maureen squeezed Caitlin's shoulders, anchoring her to the moment.

"Congratulations," Caitlin said. If she was a suspect, they wouldn't still be standing here chatting.

Florian cleared his throat. "Did either of you see or hear anything from inside the Hanging Woods last night or this morning?"

He handed her a photograph of a little blond girl, and Caitlin pictured her, alone in the Hanging Woods, golden hair shining in the moonlight. Maureen spoke, but it sounded like she was far away.

Time skipping, repeating, unspooling, unraveling. Her mother at the table. Something hunting in the Hanging Woods.

Caitlin in the Hanging Woods.

Do you know what they'll do to you? Her mother's voice.

What about the girl in the woods last night? Deedee's voice.

Last night, sitting at the kitchen table, lights moving through the woods.

"In the trees." Caitlin heard herself before she realized she'd spoken.

"What did you say?" Florian asked.

"They've started clearing the trees," translated Maureen on Caitlin's behalf. "For the development."

"Nothing else?" Florian's voice was smooth and gentle, but the part of her brain that operated like a feral animal registered the suspicion crossing his face. "Anything helps."

"Caitlin just arrived from London, she's not had time to see anything," Maureen said.

"Lee Casey is here, isn't he?" Caitlin jumped in. "That seems like a strange coincidence."

It was a clumsy attempt at distraction, a return to the days after Roisin's disappearance, when she was desperate to not be noticed. She was too rattled. She wasn't in control. That sandwich, that lack of discipline.

Florian looked at her carefully. "We're exploring all avenues at the moment."

Caitlin glanced at the picture again. The blond hair in the photo from the summer Roisin left. She blinked, and the face was familiar.

"Michelle Quinn?" she whispered. Michelle Quinn, already with a bad reputation before she was even a teenager, hanging around them that summer.

"Yes, Michelle's her mother." Florian paused. "Do you know the family?"

Caitlin shook her head.

"The girl's the image of the mother, isn't she?" Maureen cut in, saving Caitlin from explaining herself. "Married Barry Lynch in the end. That's the Quinn women for you, that blond hair. Don't the boys have the same white-blond hair but with foxy beards?"

"Mind showing me around the exterior of the property, Mrs. Branagh?" Florian jerked a thumb to the right. It seemed like he'd already decided Maureen wouldn't have too much of value to say.

"Of course! Would you have a tea as well, while you're here?" Maureen seemed delighted at another chance to host.

"Maybe after we've had a walk," Florian said. Caitlin noticed that his eyes had widened slightly in exasperation.

Caitlin followed them to the right, past the window for the living room and around the side of the house. There was nothing to see, nothing amiss at all.

Caitlin had implicated Lee Casey years ago because she had to, because she had accidentally killed Roisin, and here he was again, a convenient patsy. If the police kept up their searches in the woods, there was a chance they could find something linking Caitlin to Roisin's death. She couldn't take that chance. She pushed the memory of the harmless-seeming man she'd met this morning out of her mind.

If it's him or me, then he has to be guilty.

"It's a shame." Maureen tutted over the picture. "They must be out of their minds with the worry."

"Where was Lee Casey last night?" Caitlin asked. "I'm sorry, it just seems a bit much. You probably don't remember, but he was involved with a previous disappearance."

"Is that right?" Florian gave her an appraising stare. "And what do you know about that?"

"Niall Wilson was up here last night; he mentioned Casey was back," Maureen explained. She made it sound very reasonable, very natural. "And that gets you thinking, doesn't it?"

Caitlin loved Maureen so much. Maureen wasn't even aware of it, and she was still protecting Caitlin.

"Have you seen someone matching his description?" Florian addressed them both.

"I might have," Caitlin said.

"It'd be hard to tell now, in the dark." Maureen spoke at the same time.

Florian watched them both.

"Well, if you become sure, let us know." Florian handed them each a card with his contact details on it.

Caitlin turned it over in her hands, mentally interrogating the possibility of calling in a sighting of Casey, entering the woods from the opposite side, perhaps. She'd have to disguise her voice, but . . .

They had arrived at the back of the house; the darkroom stood before them. A box of a shed only a few feet long and wide; there was a large, rusted lock on it. Florian stopped to peer at it with his hands behind his back.

"The house is close to the Hanging Woods. I'm only wondering if she might have taken shelter in here. The nights are fierce cold."

"In there?" Caitlin was doubtful. The lock looked secure.

"I'll fetch the key," Maureen popped back into the house.

"He wanted to stay in the woods," Caitlin said, as they waited. "Lee Casey, that is, in case you didn't know."

"What's your relationship to Casey?" The friendliness had disappeared from the Garda's face as he inspected hers.

"None." Caitlin summoned indignation. "I'm a concerned citizen."

Florian nodded and walked around the darkroom shed. There were no signs of disturbance, or any other entrances or exits.

Maureen returned and fitted the key into the padlock. It took her a few attempts to turn, rusted as the lock was, but the door opened and Florian shone his torch inside. Its beam hit a narrow space, tinier than Caitlin remembered, with a shelf running around the perimeter, and boxes beneath that she knew contained various photography tools and chemicals.

They were all silent, Caitlin and Maureen waiting for the Garda to say something.

"Thank you for your help, ladies," he said finally, as they completed their circuit of the house. "We may be in touch if we've any further questions."

"Not a bother," Maureen said as she closed the door back up. "I hope she's found soon."

Florian waved and jogged back to his car.

Caitlin and Maureen looked at each other. Maureen had no idea that she'd saved Caitlin again.

28

DEEDEE

Deedee was weighed down with the horrible responsibility of being alone with the knowledge of how dangerous Caitlin was.

She had gained one advantage today: she believed in Lee Casey's innocence. Addicts could be manipulative and weren't exactly known to be the most upstanding citizens, but she'd seen no evidence of him lying. Whereas Caitlin had been desperate.

Deedee was close to home; she could get the car, drive up to the Big House and talk to Maureen about all this. There was plenty of time, but as she considered the logistics, she felt fear calcify her bones. Maureen would believe Caitlin; she'd been taken in totally by that con artist. If Deedee wasn't careful, she'd blunder into really damaging her own relationship with Maureen. The thought stung.

It felt like she'd lived twenty years since waking up this morning, and her wrist was throbbing with pain. If she could steady her nerves, she'd be better. She knew O'Shea's had opened an hour ago. She could nip in for a quick one, just to straighten herself out, before going up to the Big House. She'd still probably be there before Caitlin even.

It was a sound plan.

"Howya, Ger," she called out in greeting as she stood at the bar. She pointed at the top shelf. "I'm after a swift hair of the dog."

Noel Hegarty was already there, a pint in front of him two-thirds drunk. He grunted at her in greeting. He was a sad sight, hunched and gray, killing himself slowly. Deedee tried not to judge him.

She sipped her whisky and felt the warmth burning through her, felt it tingling in her brain, and something clicked.

Caitlin hadn't been at Lee Casey's because she thought he'd killed Roisin; she'd been there because she thought he'd killed her mother. She knew that someone had been at the gatehouse, she had the cigarette butts, she even had Deedee's DNA in the blood on that fur coat. But how had Casey gotten into her crosshairs? How had Caitlin even known that Casey was in town, let alone where to find him?

Deedee ordered a second whisky to help her mull it over.

Caitlin hadn't necessarily known where Casey was; she'd just followed Deedee. Deedee had even seen her, the figure in the fur passing by the coffee shop. So, Deedee was on Caitlin's radar, and Caitlin was an unpredictable psycho who knew her mother had been out the night she died. It was only a matter of time before she figured out where and with whom. If Caitlin was just to go about asking questions, there was every chance she'd get nowhere with it, that folks'd mess her around or not want to involve themselves. But the CCTV was a witness that couldn't lie to her.

"Ger." Deedee called him over. "Got a question for you."

Gerry snorted dismissively, as though she was just another drunk. Then, remembering her job, he said, "Are you asking in an official capacity?"

"I am," Deedee said. The third whisky was going down nicely. "What do those cameras capture?"

"The door and the entrance. These behind me do the tills and the area around the bar. Why?" Gerry leaned in, forearms on the table, hands knitted together.

"I'm working a case," Deedee replied, voice low and confidential.

"Right now?" he asked, dripping irony. He moved about the bar, polishing the taps, wiping the surfaces.

Deedee raised her eyebrow at him. "It's about the O'Sullivans. You ever get them in here?"

"I'd turn them away, but I've no bouncers or what-have-you, so." Gerry polished up pint glasses and placed them back on the shelf behind him.

Deedee nodded slowly. "That'd make sense all right. I'm hearing they were here on Thursday night."

"Sure, *you* were here Thursday night," he laughed. "Weren't ye?"

"Now that definitely wasn't in an official capacity." Deedee laughed along with him. "So, I'd need a bit of footage. How often do you delete?"

"It's automatic after three days." Gerry waved as another patron entered.

"Do you reckon you could pull Thursday night for me?" she asked.

"I'm not sure I should." He looked doubtful and indicated her glass. "You're after downing several of them; you're sure this is an official thing?"

Deedee became aware of the pub filling up around them, the lunchtime crowd filtering in. She shrugged as though none of it meant anything to her.

"I'll come back for it later, so. When I'm on duty."

"You're going on duty like this?" Gerry stopped and focused on her.

"Ah, later like another day, you know what I mean."

A wave of orders from the new arrivals at the bar distracted Gerry. When he had a break, he returned to Deedee. "So, you come back then, in your full get-up, with your pals. And in the meantime, I'll keep that tape safe."

Too late, Deedee realized that perhaps by interceding she'd actually made her situation worse. The tape would have been wiped by tomorrow; she'd have been able to throw Caitlin off the scent till then.

She opened her mouth to protest, but Gerry was watching her too closely.

"Great," she said instead. "That's perfect, thank you."

She ordered one more and carried it over to a small table by the window to wait for Jo. She watched the melting ice in her glass and wondered why nothing ever worked out for her. *Caitlin would have been able to pull that off.*

She hoped Caitlin wouldn't be traipsing in here next and actually getting those tapes.

"Ach, Dee, I heard you're on leave." Jo slid into the seat opposite her, holding a gin and tonic. "Do you want to talk about it?"

Deedee didn't want to talk about it. She wasn't sure where she'd start.

"Doyle's a prick," she said finally. "Real, real prick."

"Cheers to that." Jo raised her glass.

"C'mere to me while I tell you," Deedee said. Jo was the only one on her side. She began to explain her connection to Roisin, but Jo interrupted.

"I know, I figured it out after you left, when I looked the case up. I shouldn't have said where Lee was."

"I don't think he was involved," Deedee said. "I went up there, I met him for myself."

"I know you did." Jo put a bracelet on the table in front of them. "My mother-in-law said he'd dropped this down to the house; she brought it in to me while she was in town for last-min gifts. Said it was from a friend of mine who'd come calling?"

The chain-link bracelet with insignia on the pendant, and emeralds. Caitlin's bracelet. Deedee must have knocked it off Caitlin's wrist when she yanked her out of there.

"You'd a weak link here, see?" Jo pointed out the place in the chain. "So, what'd Lee tell you?"

"He thinks the guards knew more'n they let on." Deedee pocketed the bracelet. It felt good to have something of Caitlin's, to know more than Caitlin knew for once.

"What do you think?" Jo asked.

"I've been racking my brains about that summer for years, looking for clues. I keep coming back to the things Roisin said. She told me that they had a friend in the woods, and she told me there was a monster in there too. I just assumed she was playing games as a kid, but if Lee was the friend . . ."

Deedee explained Caitlin's appearance.

"Why wouldn't youse team up, solve this together?" Jo suggested. "I could help, be your man on the inside."

"She's untrustworthy." Deedee hesitated, wondering how much she could share.

I'm actually a bit afraid of her.

No, those words could never pass her lips.

"Look, cards on the table." Jo spread her hands against the tabletop. "I called in a couple of favors in Kinafallia. Had a bit of downtime with everyone else out this morning and the phones dead silent, and also, I got to thinking about Roisin."

"What about her?" Deedee asked.

"It's messed up, isn't it? This isn't a big place, someone must know something. I never had a sister, but I can't imagine what my life woulda been like without my brothers." Jo was too close to that awful pity. Deedee had to cut her off.

"What did you find?" If Jo had been on this for one morning and found out more than Deedee had in her whole time as a guard, Deedee would feel humiliated.

"It was pretty much like you said, but there was one thing you didn't mention that I wanted to make sure you knew."

Deedee nodded, not trusting herself to speak, knowing that *tell me tell me tell me* would come out if she did.

"One other girl who gave evidence and I'm not sure why. Michelle Quinn. The notes from her interview are lost, so we don't know what she said."

"She wouldn't have been much help, she's a shaky grasp on the truth." Deedee could dismiss anything Michelle said easily. *Next.*

"Hold on there, do interview notes often go missing? It seemed like everything else was in place," Jo said.

Deedee paused.

"These days, no, I don't think so. But back then?" She considered it. "It was one of very few big cases we had, the lads mightn't have been so careful."

Jo looked doubtful and Deedee felt it too. Maybe someone would have been careless with a routine matter like public intoxication, but the biggest case Bannakilduff had seen? No, there was something to Jo's suspicion.

"I'll be honest, Dee, I don't like it. I don't know what it is, but I think there's something bubbling under here. This whole town. These guards, man. Too many family connections. I don't trust it. Old boys watch out for their own. Mac would sell you or me down the river for the merest hint of an advantage to him. I'm not convinced Doyle is much better. And Florian . . . I shouldn't say, but I used to know of him back in the day and I'm not sure he's changed much."

Deedee nodded; her expression closed to show she would brook no gossip about her friend. Jo was right, she shouldn't say. Deedee got the feeling Jo knew that Florian's days of drug dealing had never ended. He'd be supplying weed and MDMA to half the crusties and hippies at the festival this weekend, and a blind eye would be turned to the whole thing. Neither of them should say it aloud, though.

"You're close with Florian?" Jo asked, and Deedee understood what she was really asking.

"We've known each other for a long time," she said.

"Of course. And you're near enough a Branagh now, right?" Jo said, testing. "Because maybe, if you can, it would be good to just be a Branagh. Forget everything else."

"What choice do I have?" Deedee raised her glass. Jo pushed hers aside.

29

CAITLIN

If they found Roisin now, after all these years, would they know? Caitlin sank down on the seat of the old telephone table. She looked down at her palms. Her heart line, the crease beneath her first three fingers, fading as it reached toward her pointer finger. She couldn't remember Roisin's palms, where the heart stopped and the life ended. She could never forget the weight of what these hands had done. How the yielding of skull beneath rock felt.

"What's the matter?" Maureen stood in front of her holding a sagging cardboard box of Christmas decorations. "Hurt your hands, did you?"

"No, no, I just—I don't know. I was in a daydream." Caitlin accepted the box from Maureen and set it down on the floor.

"Are you sure you don't want to go for a lie-down?" Maureen asked. "Isn't it an awful shock to have them lot coming round?"

"I thought you'd be used to it with Deedee," Caitlin joked.

"Ah, you know what I mean. The proper lot." Maureen waved a hand in dismissal of Deedee. "Well then, I've a few little jobs for you."

The first job was decorations. Maureen seemed to have stashed boxes all over the house, with a logic known only to herself. Some were in the attic, some under the stairs, one in the coat cupboard. The activity helped clear Caitlin's mind. She had a purpose.

"Ach, the feckin' mouse!" Maureen exclaimed, holding up an old ornament Sean must have made as a small child: an angel made from an old toilet roll tube that was missing chunks. "It gets into the very walls of the place, I swear to God."

The damage seemed minimal to Caitlin.

"I hear it, you know." Maureen glared at the chewed angel. "Scratching away."

Caitlin hadn't heard a thing.

"Get a cat?" she suggested.

"Maybe in the new year," Maureen agreed, throwing the angel into the bin. "I suppose this yoke has had its day anyway."

They worked for an hour: twining tinsel around the banister, dusting off the figures in the nativity set. Caitlin felt almost normal by the end of it.

At 2 p.m., they stopped for a tea break.

Maureen had drawn the blinds in the kitchen. Caitlin wondered if she remembered this all happening before. The guards hadn't taken Roisin's disappearance seriously at first. Roisin had gone missing inside the woods in broad daylight, on the longest day of the year during the summer solstice party. No one had even noticed she was gone at first.

Caitlin couldn't think of the Hanging Woods without thinking of bare limbs, sun-scorched noses, and the freedom of broad daylight.

Maureen spread strawberry jam on buttered toast. "It's a Saturday treat." She winked at Caitlin. "They say he oughtn't to have sugars or fats, but what else is there? There's very few pleasures left for him, and I said to the doctor, you can't deny him a bit of bread and butter and jam. I let him know, all right!"

"What exactly is . . . ?" Caitlin searched for the right way to phrase her question.

"What's wrong with him, you mean? The car shattered his legs, his pelvis." Maureen's hair fell forward, obscuring her expression. The hand that held the knife trembled as it spread a final thick layer of jam. "He had a punctured lung, and they say he's healed, but he's never been the same since. The shock of it damaged his heart."

The conversation was fragile—Caitlin sensed it could shatter at any moment—but it felt incomplete. She didn't want to hurt Maureen, but she also had the sense that Maureen wasn't being completely truthful.

"It was awful." Maureen hadn't moved. She still held the knife. "I thought he was dead. I didn't know what I would do."

"I can't imagine," Caitlin murmured. The atmosphere felt taut.

"I was so young when we married, not even sixteen," Maureen said. She stuck her thumb in her mouth to suck off a smear of jam. "Even for those days, I was young, but we'd already been together years. He's been my life. To have that happen, it's like it happens to you too. It's like something hits *you*." She looked fierce, but she was directing her words out toward the officers in the trees. "No other living soul in my position would do anything different. Because you marry someone and you're in it for life and you . . . well. You just keep living."

"You've been great," Caitlin offered, hoping it was the right thing to say. "I'm sure you've been strong."

"Strong, nothing! You just keep living. Now." Maureen whipped a tray out from a drawer. She loaded it with an egg cup of tablets as well as the food. "You take this through. He'll be only delighted to see you."

Caitlin carried the tray carefully, afraid that a stumble would upset the egg cup and send the tablets flying. She knocked twice before she entered. She was uneasy, aware for the first time of the huge age difference between Colm and Maureen. Maureen was closer in age to Kathleen, and Colm had to be at least ten years older. The friendship between the two women suddenly made sense. A shared loneliness, perhaps, one with an absent partner and one with a partner she couldn't always relate to.

In the bedroom, Colm was green with the reflected glow of various pieces of monitoring equipment, including something with wires that attached to his chest. It whirred and hummed. His mouth opened and closed, and his eyes moved about the room.

Caitlin approached the bed. The nightstand on Maureen's side was cluttered with hand creams, an eye mask, dreamy pastel romance novels. She didn't sleep there every night—the machines were too obtrusive—but she still spent a lot of time by his side. Colm's nightstand was bare. Caitlin placed the tray on it.

"Hi," she whispered.

Colm smiled, and Caitlin let her worries go. Maureen was devoted to him; they were very much in love. Times were different then.

"Can you sit up?" she asked him.

Colm exhaled slowly. Something rattled in his lungs.

"Is there a, um, does the bed raise itself up?" Caitlin glanced behind the head of the bed, then knelt down to feel for a switch. She had to contort herself around the equipment. Her fingertips skittered over the hard plastic of what could have been a remote. Grasping it, though, she realized it was a videotape. She pulled out more. Above her, she registered the sound of rustling, a grunt of effort from the bed. There was a box too, softened with age and full of negatives.

"Caitlin." From the other side of his equipment, Colm had pulled himself to a seated position. He sounded old, but his voice was strong.

"Colm!" She made her way to standing as carefully as she could. The negatives and videotapes were still at her feet. She left them. "How are you?"

The effort of shaping the words and pushing them out into the air was clearly huge, but he managed to tell her he was happy to see her.

"I'm happy to see you too." She offered him the plate; now that there was time to talk to him, she didn't know what she'd say. "Your toast."

Colm had fed her when she was a baby, holding up toast triangles to her lips, wiping her chin between bites. She had a mad urge to do the same for him now, but he reached out and took a piece before she could. His hands were unsteady, but his grip was sure. Caitlin was anxious to do something for him. She poured him a glass of water to help him take his pills, and then handed over his now lukewarm cup of tea.

When he was finished, she supported his shoulders as he lay back down. His neck and upper back were still thick with muscle, but his eyes fluttered closed almost as soon as his head hit the pillow. Caitlin stepped back. His fragility didn't seem to be in his physical body, which even now held the impression of strength and power. It was in his spirit.

Maureen had prepared Colm's pills in the kitchen, and a quick look around the room showed no sign of medicines in here. That was counterintuitive; surely the best place to keep them was near the patient? Unless Maureen didn't want anyone to see exactly what Colm was taking. Usually the disparity between what she'd been told—that the weakness was physical—and what she'd observed would trigger a prickle of suspicion, but this was Maureen.

Caitlin returned the tray to the kitchen. The sound of canned audience reactions carried through from the living room, where Maureen crocheted in front of the TV. Colm's medicine bag was next to her yarn bag.

She slipped outside the back door and watched the lights blinking out in the Hanging Woods. The guards were packing up; the search was over.

She knew the girl was dead. She knew it the way she'd known she'd find Casey, because everything that was happening was related to what she'd done to Roisin. Dread and guilt sat heavily in her stomach. The Hanging Woods had hungered for more and she had done nothing to stop it.

It was still midafternoon, but night was already drawing in, though the relentless dark clouds and rain made it feel like it had never quite gotten light at all today. Fitting that Lily-Mae should disappear into such consuming darkness, much more so than Roisin dying under the bright sunshine.

Caitlin stepped back inside. As she did, the light hit the key to the darkroom just so, and it was a bright reflective spot on the counter. It was a shame to have the darkroom locked up considering those boxes under Colm's bed, plus the camera that she'd been messing with, finishing off the film. She still remembered how to process and develop; she could complete Colm's work for him. Something to leave Maureen with after she left.

The shadow of a man passing by the window to her left. Sean's return pushed her to action, and she snatched the key up.

"Hey!" Sean brushed the rain off his coat. "It's filthy out there."

"The guards were round asking about the missing girl," Caitlin told him. "One of Deedee's colleagues—Florian?"

"Ugh, that guy." Sean shook his head in disgust. "Slimy type, isn't he? Thinks he's God's gift. I don't know how he got the job in the first place."

"He took a look around the place."

"Inside?"

"No, just the perimeter. And the darkroom."

"Hope he got a splinter. Bit of tetanus." Sean grinned.

"Is he like Mac, then?"

"He wishes. No, Mac's sound. Florian's more likely to end up on the wrong side of the bars." Sean sat with a sigh. "I need to pull that old shed down anyway. Maybe this weekend."

"It's not hurting anyone, is it?" Caitlin asked.

"No, but no one's going to use it again." Sean looked gloomily out the window and Caitlin followed his gaze.

The world was so small here. Just this house that held all her happy memories but had never been hers, and the gatehouse, loaned by Colm. Everything else was empty fields and the Hanging Woods. Every inch of her happiness was borrowed or stolen.

The knowledge shrank her. There was the Caitlin who had fought and scraped and always made it on her own by the skin of her teeth, and there was this other, tiny Caitlin who was just lost and sad. The former was fading away.

"They found the little girl," Sean offered.

"I knew they would," said Caitlin. "In the clearing."

"Nah. She'd gotten the first bus into Cork city."

"What?"

"Turns out Devin Sykes is in town for a gig tonight. You know, he was on one of those old singing show yokes—the one whose granny had her heat cut off because she'd spent the last of their pennies buying him a ticket to the auditions."

"She was in Cork?" Caitlin's dream had been so clear. And she had seen a light, the light of the creature in the woods, hunting once more.

"With a horde of other screaming teens." Sean raised an imaginary placard and whisper-screamed. "*Dev-in! Dev-in!* He came out of his hotel and waved like the Pope. She's only thrilled."

"She was never out here."

"The granny might have been dead, actually. One or the other. You know him, of course you do." If Sean noticed how disturbed she was, he didn't let on.

"I really don't." Caitlin needed to think. She'd been so sure of what had happened. The London Caitlin was receding further and further away, though, leaving the Caitlin who hunted fairy forts and feared the dark to fight their battles.

"*You can leave me, deceive me, but you, you know you need me. You can travel the world, but you'll always be my girl,*" Sean sang. "Vaguely threatening, really."

"Never here," Caitlin whispered to herself. Then, to Sean, "We used to think the woods were haunted. Full of hanged men."

"Morbid, horrible little things we were." Sean grinned. "I don't know if the kids still tell those silly stories."

There had never been quicksand out here. The spectral corpses of tragic farmers couldn't have been real either. But the thing, the creature that stalked through the trees, the monster, she had seen that. She had felt its breath on her skin; hot, stinking, invasive. Her stomach flipped and tears sprang into her eyes.

"Hey, you OK?" Sean asked.

Caitlin nodded and let herself be guided into his embrace. Sean was real, and he was safe. She remembered George, the comfort of flesh and blood. She pushed her face into his chest. His heart beat hard beneath his jumper. She felt his neck crane down toward her, the lightest touch of his nose to the crown of her head.

30

DEEDEE

Some people were actually better drivers once they'd a drink taken. Deedee settled herself behind the wheel of the car. She was more cautious with a bit of alcohol in her system, really. She closed one eye and then the other: no double vision. As usual.

The rain had picked up while she was talking to Jo and the rhythmic swishing of the windscreen wipers was calming. The missing girl had been located and there had been nothing said about Roisin's case. Deedee had let herself think that maybe this would have meaning for her and Roisin, but she'd been wrong again. She was so often wrong that she couldn't yet feel bitter about it, though she knew she would soon feel cheated—why should Lily-Mae return and not Roisin? For now, she was numb with disappointment. The grief of not knowing was all the sharper after the hope of resolution.

Then there was the question of Caitlin. Deedee had been so sure that she'd been involved somehow, just as she was sure that Caitlin knew more about Roisin. Could she have been wrong on both counts?

Still, she owed Roisin. It wasn't hope that drove her now, but duty. The visibility with the rain and the early sunset would make it hard for her to investigate the Hanging Woods herself now, but not impossible.

Roisin's rolled-up map sat upright in the passenger seat next to her and she glanced at it every now and then for reassurance. The spot Roisin had marked with a skull had to hold some kind of meaning. Deedee envisioned a shaking, sifting motion trembling through the earth, loosening some key piece of evidence from the roots and rocks, presenting it before her.

If only, she thought.

If only she had listened to Roisin. Those nightmares she had dismissed as stupidity. Thinking of it made her want to pull over into a ditch and howl, but instead she dropped her speed further and crawled along the country lanes toward the Big House.

Soon enough she'd be driving back to the Big House every day. Then she'd be driving these roads with two kiddies in the back. They'd have blue eyes like Sean and dimpled cheeks like her. She could give them everything that she'd only too briefly had: two loving parents to chase them for homework and cheer for them at sports.

She turned a corner in time to see another car speeding toward her and yanked the steering wheel. Her car clunked across a ditch and a hedgerow obscured her vision as she furiously honked the horn at the other driver. Her hands shook on the wheel and she glanced behind her, for a moment half convinced she'd see two tiny sets of swinging legs and wide, scared eyes. The other car was gone.

No, not everyone was a great driver like her, that was the trouble.

The adrenaline had cleared her head and she felt totally sober. Once she accepted Sean's proposal, this would be it for her. She'd never so much as visit New Zealand. She'd know exactly what every Christmas for the rest of her life would look like, that he'd get her the same Chanel perfume for every birthday until one of them died, and that every Sunday they'd have a full roast with beef—never chicken or ham. These kinds of thoughts could be a straitjacket or safety.

Deedee parked outside the gatehouse, its caution tape struggling to hold up under the deluge of rain. It would be easier if she could just slip around the Big House and into the Hanging Woods without anyone seeing her.

As she put her hood up and left the car, her torch gripped in one hand, the thrill of adventure overtook her. They couldn't stop her investigating. Doyle wasn't in charge of her.

Sean's car was parked outside the Big House, unusually early. Its presence gave Deedee only momentary pause. She sneaked, unnecessarily quietly considering the noise of the driving rain, around the exterior of the house until she stood at the back left corner, the house on her right. A bright square of light from the kitchen illuminated the small concrete walkway and the patch of lawn beyond it. She peeked through the window.

Two figures stood inside the kitchen in an embrace. A tall, broad man with his arm around the slim waist of a small golden-haired woman. Cozy, like. Deedee would have recognized the man, his bearing, all of it, from a thousand miles away, but the shock pulled her out of her hiding place. The next thing she knew, she was near pressed against the window. The couple in the kitchen turned, the man drawing the woman against his body protectively, and Deedee saw them together.

She saw the moment Sean clocked her and dropped Caitlin.

He waved, all artificial brightness.

Deedee ducked below the window. Roisin was forgotten while she reeled through what she'd seen.

The back door opened and Sean called out for her to come inside.

Rage replaced shock and Deedee curbed her urge to stomp into the house. Caitlin was responsible for this. The raving, murderous Caitlin had disappeared again for now and the aggravating, sneaking Caitlin was back.

Her hands clenched and flexed and she gritted her teeth so hard her jaw felt like it would pop out of place.

"What was that?" she demanded.

Sean glanced backward into the kitchen, but Caitlin was gone.

"What is it now, what's the drama?" His face dropped with no one else around to put on a show for.

"Looking very cozy, the two of you."

Here we go again, she thought. She couldn't stop herself, even though she knew this wasn't going to end well. At the same time, she truly felt that if they could just be clear with one another, if he could just reassure her instead of lashing out—

"You're mental."

"No, she's nuts, Sean. She attacked—"

"Oh, you'd be a fine one to talk about attacking!" His eyes flashed in warning, and she read *pathologist report, Kathleen, assault* in them. "Depending on what happens, your whole career could be over."

"I couldn't give two shits about that," Deedee spat. If only he knew that her career was already over. All she had ever tried to do was the right thing. *And I have never once been rewarded for it.*

"Remember who keeps your secrets," Sean warned.

The reference winded Deedee. The last morning she'd had with Roisin flashed before her eyes: her little sister's face screwed up as she shouted, Deedee pushing her. How small Roisin had been, how easily teenage Deedee could shove her around.

"You told her," Deedee said. "You told her about our fight that morning."

"Why would I do that?" Sean scoffed.

"How did she know about it? She said Roisin went into the woods because of me!"

"The obvious answer is that Roisin told her." Sean spoke slowly, as though to a simpleton. "I finished a little early today and thought maybe I could be in my own house, speaking to an old family friend, but obviously not."

"You're making me sound unreasonable!" Deedee protested.

"Because you are!" Sean huffed. "I'm never enough for you, am I?"

It was awful. She could see logically that he'd been patient with her. She knew that this needn't play out nastily. Yet his irritation inflamed her, made her want to fight, and it all knotted itself together with her sorrow over Roisin.

"You feel more *enough* for her, do you?"

"There you go again! Where is this coming from?"

From years of watching you, Deedee thought. *From spending my life observing how you move, from knowing your body as well as I know my own.* It was the sort of thing they should have joked about, the idea of one of them having a crush as harmless as one of them wanting to live on the moon. Deedee could see herself ruining everything.

"You like her." She felt pathetic.

"Her mother just died. Our family friend just died. Cop yourself on." Sean left her on the threshold, and she trailed him into the hall. It was a Christmas wonderland, decorated to the nines.

"Hello, Deedee love!" Maureen greeted her from the living room, a romance novel open in her hand. The Michael Bublé Christmas album played and tinsel sparkled around the doorways.

A flash sent spots into her vision. Caitlin waved as she set a camera down. "Needed to finish the roll."

"Hi, Maureen." Deedee hugged the older woman tightly. *Love me,* she thought. *Don't leave me.* "When did you get all the decorating done?"

"Ah, Caitlin helped me earlier, the dote." Maureen beamed. Deedee inhaled her familiar lavender smell. "Do you like it?"

"Hope it's not an issue." Caitlin fussed over a bow.

Deedee couldn't help but stare at her hands, the delicacy with which she tweaked the ribbon into place just so. This morning those hands had been grasping a rock, ready to kill.

"An issue? How could it be? Dee's awful at the decorating, clumsy oaf that she is!" Maureen laughed merrily.

If Colm was here, he would have softened the joke, said something so that Deedee knew she was part of it. In his absence, the comment stung and formed one more injury against her than Deedee could stand. Caitlin had taken her place and Deedee was unwelcome. She couldn't bear it.

"I have to go."

"Let me get the mop," Caitlin said behind her, with a tut.

Deedee stomped a little harder hearing it and let the back door bang behind her.

She had come here for Roisin, not for Caitlin, and she would find out what Roisin had been trying to tell her with the map.

31

CAITLIN

The problem with Deedee—aside from that she was a massive bitch—was that she was so focused on what she had lost that she was blind to what she still had.

Caitlin ran the mop across the kitchen and hall floors, erasing the faint boot prints that Deedee had left. Roisin was Caitlin's loss too. Roisin was the thing that she carried with her everywhere she went. Deedee had a career, a partner, a whole family in Colm's house.

Even as she thought it, she knew it wasn't quite true. Maureen had made it clear that Deedee wouldn't have been her choice for her precious son. But then wasn't that Deedee's fault too? She didn't make it easy to like her.

"Ah, you shouldn't have." Sean lounged in the doorway. The front of his hair stuck up where he'd raked a hand through it in frustration with Deedee.

"Didn't take long." Caitlin put the mop away and stood before him. "Did she give you a hard time?"

"Only every single day."

She reached out and smoothed down his mussed hair, and he startled at her touch.

"Sorry," she said. She withdrew, her hand held in the air at chest height.

"It's OK, I just wasn't expecting it," he replied. He gently squeezed her still outstretched hand.

It was, Caitlin thought, a bold move for a man in a long-term committed relationship.

"How do you handle things?" she asked. "Does she ever ask you how you're doing?"

Sean clearly liked to see himself as long-suffering and put upon, so all Caitlin needed to do was reflect that back in a way that made him feel not only seen but also heroic for his actions.

He answered at length, but she didn't listen, only watched how he let his hurt and his concern play out in his gaze, eyebrows steepled as he struggled to comprehend Deedee's supreme selfishness.

"How does that make you feel?" she asked.

"It doesn't feel like a choice anymore," Sean said, "or not a choice that I would make today, but there's so much history there."

"Who would you be," Caitlin asked, "if you were free?"

The key word was "free," the reinforcement of Deedee as a shackle and Sean as a prisoner. If he balked at it, the misstep would be hard to recover from; it would make him feel small. The seconds before he responded were make or break, for Caitlin had decided what to do, where she could hit Deedee in the most catastrophic way.

Sean sighed heavily, accepting this vision of himself as martyr. She'd done it.

"The thing is, there's something Deedee hasn't told anyone about the day Roisin disappeared." He lowered his voice, as though anyone could walk in on them.

Caitlin felt her heart stop. If Deedee had seen something, or if Roisin had told her something, what would that mean for her? She tried to keep her face as neutral as possible, in case this was a trap Sean had laid for her.

"Does anyone know but the two of you?" she whispered back to him.

Sean shook his head no. He looked torn as he considered whether to tell her.

Caitlin's mind raced. She wondered if she could hurt him if she had to. She thought about the rock she had brought down on Roisin's head, how the girl had bled; she thought about the panic that had followed, how she'd run home, but this time there was no home to run to.

"Can we talk about this . . . somewhere else?" he asked. "I just don't want Ma walking in, you know?"

Caitlin knew. The best thing would be to get him somewhere secluded.

"The gatehouse," she said. Before he could disagree, she added, "I know we shouldn't, but isn't it ours? Yours and mine? Surely they can't tell us what to do?"

She the lowly tenant, he the landlord and above anyone else's rules.

"There's been no sign of anyone investigating anyway," he said.

He pulled on his jacket, Caitlin grabbed the fur coat, and they set off, running the short distance through the torrential rain. Deedee's mucky white car was parked outside the gatehouse, and Caitlin briefly worried that she might be inside already, waiting for them, having anticipated Caitlin's plan.

As she led Sean through the unlocked back door, she waited for any sign of Deedee, but the house was still, the air undisturbed.

In the gatehouse's tight kitchen, Sean seemed to expand and fill the space, a hulking presence looming over her. She had never realized quite how small it was in here.

"I'm sorry I just spewed all that at you," he said. His sheepishness shrunk him in on himself slightly, enough to remind Caitlin that she had the upper hand. "I know it's a lot, and it's not something anyone can understand."

Everyone's personal tragedy is greater than their audience's powers of comprehension.

"You know what might help you with your troubles?" Caitlin asked, holding out her hand. "Let me read your palm."

Touch; she needed to rebuild the physical connection with him, keep his barriers down. Normalize touching each other.

"Are you serious?" Sean laughed, but he flushed too.

"Give me your right hand. That's the one for the future."

Sean held out his hand. Caitlin lightly circled his wrist with one hand and gently straightened out his fingers with the other. His hand was damp from the rain, and as she leaned over it, her hair dripped straight into the center of his palm.

"Good, strong lines. Indicates health and longevity. This is your head line. No surprise, it's entwined with your life line. Strong family ties, duty. The kind of person who puts others first." The trick to performing a good cold read was to believe just enough in the magic of it. Yes, she knew the particulars of Sean's situation, but also, look, the lines here were conjoined. That wasn't something she'd made up. "That can lead to great sadness. You're always doing the right thing by society's standards, so sometimes you miss out. Like not taking risks. Solid, reliable, dependable."

"Where does it mention that I buy a swimming pool?" Sean joked.

"The line of incredible wealth? That one's very short actually."

The palm reading had worked, for her at least. She felt herself pulling her old armor back on. Caitlin the con artist, the thief, the one who got the last laugh was back.

"Wait—was that it? That's the whole reading?" Sean feigned outrage. "I'd want my money back if I'd paid for that."

"Ah, there's nothing to surprise you there anyway."

"Go on, give it a better go." He put his hand back out and Caitlin obligingly bent over it. "Where's the love line? What's that one say?"

"Here." She stroked a fingertip across his palm. "Do you see the break in it?"

Sean nodded.

"A change. An ending. It doesn't have to be a breakup. Maybe you renegotiate the terms of your love life into something that better suits. Or take a break. It could be the end of loneliness."

"And how far away is that, would you say?"

"It's up to you."

The rain drummed on the roof like it was about to break through, and the tiles they stood on shone with the ever-expanding puddle of rainwater that ran from their coats and boots. The pale, fast-fading daylight stretched one lazy finger into the hallway, as though lighting the way to Caitlin's old bedroom. It was like being at the bottom of the sea, everything murky and indistinct, the open door into the living room revealing only vague shadows in the gloom where furniture should be. Caitlin entered her bedroom and Sean followed.

Everything was different because Caitlin was; yet everything was the same because as soon as she set foot back inside the room, she felt herself returning to who she had been.

Sean was close behind her, and then they were face-to-face, the door to the room shut behind them. The first kiss was tentative, awkward. Caitlin pushed through the discomfort, imitating passion and need, nipping at his lower lip and emitting soft moans, leading him past the point of no return. Then the surprising urgency of Sean's movements, his hands snaking under her clothes, desperate for the heat of her skin. He pressed against the bruising on her body, without noticing. The pain focused her mind. This was victory; she would find a way to let Deedee know. She smiled, and Sean misunderstood. He paused to cup her face sweetly and she fought the urge to recoil. There was something about his face from this angle, the way it tapered to a point at a chin she'd never realized was so sharp, that made her think of a rat. It was in the way he pawed too, large, clumsy hands.

Outside of this encounter, she could see the appeal in Sean—his muscular form, his powerful height—but the chemistry was off. They didn't fit together at all, but he didn't seem to realize that. Pushing herself to participate was like forcing her toothbrush down her throat, a punishment that pulled her out of her skin. It was also a punishment for Deedee; this theft could never be taken back.

She summoned the memory of George from a few days ago, another life. She imagined herself back there, with that other man, as they slipped under the covers of her old single bed. That had been victory; this was surrender. In the gloom, Sean was just a shadow. She didn't even have to shut her eyes.

Afterward, the old springs of the mattress jabbed at her sides; the white flare of pain from her hip passed into numbness as her body acclimated to it. The air was cold but she was cozy. The wall pressed against her on one side, the surface of it softened by age and damp. Sean on her other side, his heart thudding against her face, his breath warming the top of her head. He was soft too, but not crumbling, not insubstantial. The walls of the cottage could all fall outward and he would still be there. With that thought, she felt the gentle tug of sleep pulling her in. Her eyes were heavy, her heartbeat slow, the tension drained from her muscles. She was slipping down into unconsciousness.

"I knew we'd be together one day, even back then. I was so jealous of him, that he could have you and I couldn't."

Sean's words didn't make sense, and they came from somewhere very far away. There was no *him*, no need for jealousy. Caitlin wasn't interested anyway, had never been interested, but now it was because she was finally sleeping. He was whispering, perhaps to her, perhaps to himself, or perhaps even to whoever "he" was. Caitlin felt herself drift off as he said, "All I had to do was wait."

32

CAITLIN

The morning after the monster arrived at the door, Caitlin is ready at dawn. She's turned the situation over and over in her mind, and though it never gets less strange, the strangeness begins to feel familiar. Something was creeping around her home last night, but as a kid, it doesn't matter that she knows that. She needs to get the adults to believe it. She needs proof.

In the kitchen, she assembles her supplies. They're not perfect, but she will have to make do. In a plastic bowl, she mixes shredded paper, salt, and water together; the idea is to make a kind of papier mâché.

What she produces isn't exactly what she was hoping for, but she's out of better ideas. She scans the damp ground outside the back door.

There's definitely mud by the door, but it's hard to distinguish any marks in particular. She sets the bowl down on the step and then jumps over the mud onto the grass, dropping to her knees to inspect the ground.

She finds shoe prints. She expected to find hoofprints, or some kind of large, other-worldly paw impressions, monster tracks. Still, she pours out the mixture.

It isn't quite a plaster cast, but it will do. Now to wait for the sun to dry it out.

"Caity?" Her mother is moving around inside the house. Caitlin took longer than she thought. She jumps over her cast and into the kitchen just as her mother enters it. "Have you been playing in the dirt?"

"Yes," Caitlin agrees. She holds her mixture-covered hands behind her back. "I'll go clean myself up now."

"Do that," her mother snaps. "You're old enough to know better, you're not a baby. Colm and Maureen will be expecting us in"—she checks the slim gold watch on her wrist—"fifteen minutes. We'll go in whatever state you're in."

Caitlin scurries off to the bathroom, scalded from the comparison to a baby. Could a baby have created their own plaster cast for catching monsters?

Hands damp, she throws on her smart trousers and a white blouse with a frilly collar. Most people don't really dress up for mass, but they're not most people.

"Now, Caitlin!" her mother calls from the door. Her mood hasn't improved. Caitlin scurries after her to Colm's car.

"In the middle," her mother tells her, and Caitlin climbs into the back seat, next to Sean. Her mother joins her, and they're off.

"You're looking lovely today." Her mother addresses Maureen. "And you too, boys. Isn't Sean getting so handsome these days?" She glances at Caitlin.

Caitlin shrugs, embarrassed, until her mother elbows her.

"Yes," she says. There's a strange, stilted quality in the car, everyone on edge.

The tips of Sean's ears turn pink as he mumbles, "Thanks."

"I don't think anything will happen," says Maureen, almost to herself.

"No, no, I shouldn't think so," Caitlin's mother agrees.

"Certainly not at mass," Maureen continues.

The adult world, a place of slights that Caitlin doesn't under-stand. Sometimes women in the congregation have looked badly at her mother, or approached her with wide smiles that disguise their words: *Stay away from my Barry.* Or Cillian, or Liam, or Patrick.

But today the whole car is tense, Colm's jaw stiff and his gaze rigid. Even Sean is uncomfortable. It's not about her mother today, she deduces.

"What?" she asks, not knowing how to even form the question.

"Don't mind Caity," her mother says. "She was up late last night, she's still half asleep. Had to drag her out this morning."

"That's not true," says Caitlin.

"It is," replies her mother. Caitlin knows what she means. *It is if I say it is. You say what I tell you to.* Truth can be stretchy, like chewing gum.

The rest of the journey passes in a tense quiet, no one seeming to quite know how to behave or what to say until they pull up to the church. They're late, Caitlin realizes, the rest of the congregation al-ready inside and the opening chords of the first hymn sounding out into the car park. They slip through the doors and shuffle into the back row. Something is very wrong.

They are the first ones out after the service. Usually they're mobbed with people wanting to talk to Colm, but today everyone is distant, turning their faces from them.

Caitlin drifts away to listen in on Fiona Donovan's family as they cross the courtyard.

"I don't believe a word of it," Mr. Donovan proclaims.

"But you haven't seen anything, Fi?" Mrs. Donovan asks her daughter. "Or Deedee?"

Fiona shrugs, clearly uncomfortable. "I don't know anything."

"If it was anyone, it'd be one of the O'Hallorans. I'm not saying I believe it, but those two are at the Big House the whole time. And Kathleen's girl. But Michelle? The Quinns're trying it on." Mr. Donovan says the last part loudly, though there's no audience but Caitlin, skulk-ing behind.

"You're sure, Fiona?" Mrs. Donovan stops and takes Fi by the shoulders. "You won't be in trouble."

Mr. Donovan walks on a few steps before realizing he's left his wife and daughter behind.

"Yes." Fiona is pale, her eyes round and worried. "And Deedee hasn't said anything."

"Girls talk," proclaims Mr. Donovan. "Sure, if it was true, we'd all know about it. The Quinns are after Colm's money only."

Caitlin has heard more than she can put straight. The Quinns. Colm. A dark rumor. She remembers her mother's remark about Oisinn Quinn causing trouble. Something to do with their business, the garage? She sees Michelle Quinn sometimes, yes, but she's closer to Deedee's age and Caitlin doesn't know her well. Sometimes she hangs around Sean's crowd, part of the revolving horde of kids at the Big House.

She slinks back to her mother's side, trying to think of how to scrape together these scraps of information into a question she can ask.

Her mother stands very close to Maureen, whose arm is linked with Colm's, while Sean hands out the parish newsletter. The first person to approach them is Jerome Hickey, the owner of Hickey's shop in town.

"Ah, it's good to see you." He embraces Colm, pats Maureen on the arm, and nods at Sean, Caitlin, and her mother.

"And you." Colm doesn't smile back.

"Never let the so-and-so's grind you down, isn't that what they say?" Jerome winks. "Don't be too hard on Mick Doyle now, I'd say he's only after doing his job."

Then the floodgates are open, and one after the other, the men of the town drift over to Colm, all slaps on the back and nods.

"Right you are," says Niall Wilson, the local councilor. "I never liked the lot of them. Is it true they're after a bribe, is it? Shameful."

With every greeting and kind word, Colm grows taller and taller.

When Michael emerges from the church, Caitlin expects him to join the line. He just shakes his head in their direction. Beside her, her mother tenses.

"Can't a person even go to mass now without the likes of him hanging around?" Maureen mutters. Louder, she adds, "You'll note who's not here, Michael Doyle!"

"All right, Maureen," says Michael.

Colm lays a hand on Maureen's arm to settle her.

"For God's sake, say nothing," he mutters.

But Michael comes over.

"There's no need for the dramatics now," he says. "When a crime gets reported, the guards have to—"

"Get away from us." That's Caitlin's mother. Michael looks injured.

"It's my job, Kath." He pulls her mother away to one side and Caitlin drifts along behind her.

"Your job?" Kathleen spits. "You'll have us homeless."

"Is that so? You know all about the investigation, then?"

"I'm investigating," Caitlin says.

"Quiet," says her mother.

"What are you investigating?" asks Michael, kneeling to come down to her level. "Something strange?"

"A creature—" Caitlin begins.

"Don't you fill her head with any more nonsense than is already in it, Michael Doyle!" Caitlin's mother hisses. "Leave us alone." She grabs Caitlin by the arm and pulls her back into the circle of men laughing along with Colm. Michael drifts away, alone.

"He's a horrible man," her mother tells her. "You're not to believe a word he says. Or the Quinns, for that matter. Liars and thieves."

There it is again, that stretchy kind of truth.

33

DEEDEE

Deedee's rage carried her into the Hanging Woods. The driving rain poured over her face, obscuring her vision until she could only run head down, headlong, into the trees. There, the branches canopied into enough of an umbrella that she could finally raise her head. All about her were the thick trunks of ancient firs. The earth beneath her feet was spongy, thick with moss and mulch.

She was lost. In her haste, in the rain, she had barreled into the woods without paying attention to exactly where she was. The crucial clues in Roisin's map were the clearing's proximity to the house and its position relative to the boundaries. The map was still in the car, although the weather would have ruined it anyway. She should have had it laminated.

The chest-tightening and shortness of breath she felt couldn't have been claustrophobia, because she was outside, but as she whipped around and was faced with the same view on every side, it definitely felt a lot like claustrophobia. She sat on a protruding root, her jeans absorbing cold dampness.

Get a grip, she told herself.

With shaking hands, she lit a cigarette. She focused on the plume of her exhaled smoke, on just taking drag after drag of the cigarette until only the orange filter remained.

Deedee had never believed in the monster, had never even been the kind of kid who could believe in any of the standard childhood characters—the tooth fairy, Easter Bunny, Santa Claus. It was that lack of curiosity, that inability to consider *what if*, that meant she now refused to consider the *what if* of getting lost in a patch of woods that she had known her entire life.

When she stood up again, she was soaked. She turned to knock some of the mud from her clothing and heard the jingle of the bracelet that Caitlin had lost at Lee Casey's place still in her pocket. She ran her thumb over the raised insignia on the pendant, felt the rough settings of the emeralds, and her mind focused further. There was something inscribed on the underside of the pendant, but it was too dark to see out here. She turned, found light penetrating the trees behind her. Her location clicked into place.

Behind her, the trees had been thinned out for the start of construction. Which meant that the thickest area, the area that bordered the Branaghs' place, was in front of her.

Think about it, she urged herself. *You're looking for a clearing*. She pictured the map. The clearing was closer to the Branagh house. She had run headlong from the back of the Branaghs' in a fairly direct line and she now stood with the Big House in front. The clearing was to her right, closer to the boundary on the gatehouse's side.

Rightward then. The Hanging Woods weren't so big after all.

She pushed toward the spot she'd pictured, mud sucking at the soles of her shoes, the first rumble of distant thunder overhead.

Vague memories of trees attracting lightning troubled her. The whole experience was deeply uncomfortable; a storm would be a great excuse for abandoning her mission. But she couldn't give up on Roisin so easily.

There was no sense of time inside the trees, only more trunks.

Deedee kept her patience, measuring a vague approximation of distance based on her strides. She noted the shapes of the trunks and branches that she passed by, maintaining a sense of control over her circumstances.

Abruptly the trees opened around her, and there she was, in a wide, circular clearing. Nothing there but an old tree stump. The rain had eased off, and she ventured inward, toward the stump.

Around her, the Hanging Woods seemed larger and more imposing now that she wasn't in the thick of them.

It was at this moment that she realized her stupidity. If the skull symbolized a person who had been in this clearing twenty years ago, what had she expected to find there now? The same individual still lurking?

"Fuck!" she screamed into the sky.

The Hanging Woods remained unmoved around her, not even a bird taking flight at the sound of her scream. She kicked the stump in a fit of petulance. Its surface was crisscrossed with scars, a particularly deep one in the middle. The cuts looked unnatural, man-made, as though from a blade. She recognized the pattern: wood-chopping.

Sean collected kindling for the Big House and the gatehouse from these woods. He must be using the stump to split thicker logs, she realized.

She'd investigated the map but still come up empty. She stared around at the trees once more, willing them to move and reveal whoever the skull symbol represented.

Of course, they didn't care what she wanted.

There was only a bunch of trees circling a stump the Branagh men used for splitting logs. Nothing more. No evidence, no monster.

Sometimes policing could be like this, she consoled herself. After all, following a lead was the important thing, whether it made sense immediately or not. She was muddy and damp through to the skin, but she was a Garda—for now, still, technically. This was her duty, and she owed it to Roisin to check everything.

"Maybe Sean's seen something," she muttered to herself, thinking even as she did so that he wouldn't have. Deedee was chasing the tail of something long gone.

She headed out of the trees, back toward the Branaghs' house. The way was easier coming out of the clearing, as though more highly trafficked. She had failed at this, but she had one easy win in her pocket. She could return Caitlin's lost property, maybe have another go at her about her behavior at Lee Casey's. Even though Caitlin didn't have anything to do with Lily-Mae, Deedee still didn't trust her. She was still one of Deedee's personal persons-of-interest.

The Branaghs' kitchen was empty, and she heard the low murmuring of Maureen on the phone in the hall. Only Maureen's shoes were at the door. Caitlin and Sean had gone somewhere then, together. Deedee pinched the bridge of her nose, summoning patience, reminding herself that what she and Sean had was bigger than whatever his fascination was with Caitlin. Reminding herself too of Florian, her own secret.

She removed her boots and walked into the hall. Maureen sat at the old telephone table; she raised a hand in a frosty greeting at the sight of Deedee.

"One sec," she said into the phone. She pushed the receiver against her shoulder and addressed Deedee. "You needn't worry about the floor, Dee."

"I need to return something to Caitlin. Is she around?" Deedee held up the bracelet.

"I'm not sure." Maureen's forehead wrinkled and she made to say something into the phone, to tell whoever it was that she'd call back, maybe, so Deedee started up the stairs.

"I'll leave it in her room," she said, seeing the opportunity. "Sorry to disturb you."

Maureen returned to her call, a reproachful look in her eyes.

Caitlin's temporary bedroom was neat, the bed made and a small pile of folded clothes balanced on top of her closed suitcase. Deedee put the bracelet on the bedside table, next to a sketchbook.

She would have left then but for remembering that lie about City Airport. This was her chance to get real, solid evidence. Something not even Sean could deny. She checked the tag on the suitcase.

It was marked *CDG to ORK*.

She googled the unfamiliar airport code. Paris Charles de Gaulle.

Caitlin hadn't come from London.

Deedee felt a prickling sensation on the back of her neck and down her spine. She looked at the tag once more; the name on it was Anais Peurvois, a Parisian address.

No, Caitlin *had* come from London, she'd arrived right on time; Deedee had seen her with a swathe of other passengers just disembarked.

She had stolen the luggage.

Deedee had been right all along. Caitlin was a liar and a thief. The confirmation of this ignited a need; Deedee hungered for more evidence.

Moving quickly around the room, she lifted the mattress from the bed frame, checked down the back of the bedside table, and pawed through the backpack.

A battered black wallet emerged from the backpack, the cards within all belonging to a Mark Lewis. Deedee lingered for a moment over the headshot on a building pass to a company called Vector Point Marketing Solutions. A plain-looking man with an aggressively trendy haircut and a smug look. She reminded herself that Caitlin was the enemy here, and pocketed the wallet.

She picked up the bracelet and examined it. It was too nice, too expensive. There was no other fancy jewelry in Caitlin's belongings—no other jewelry at all—and no designer bags or shoes. The engraving on the pendant was H.W-L., initials that didn't match Caitlin's or the name on the suitcase. Like the suitcase and the wallet, it was stolen. Deedee pocketed it.

Victorious, Deedee would have left then but for the sketchbook, which she flipped through only from a vague idea of thoroughness.

The early pages were portraits of people riding the London

Underground, tired men and women with their suit jackets rumpled from the day and their faces blank; and scenes from cafés, where a small jug of milk or a sachet of sugar was foregrounded with queues of people sketched in the background. Each picture had a black ink blot or shadow edging over it so that once the viewer had taken in the detail of the scene, the eye naturally slid to this lingering darkness.

She skipped forward in search of the latest drawings and was confronted with a picture of Roisin. Unmistakably Roisin, but older, her corkscrew curls tamed into a messy bun, her eyes full of humor but her mouth straight, like she'd just told a joke and was waiting for the audience to get it.

Deedee sank onto the bed. She couldn't look away from the image. She even saw a little of herself in it, the squared-off jaw that both sisters had inherited from their father.

Page after page was filled with sketches of this imagined Roisin. Roisin as an adult. Roisin alive. She tore them out and folded them into her pocket alongside the address tag from the suitcase, Mark Lewis's wallet, and the bracelet. She needed a quick nip of something fiery and strong, just a little taste to help her collect her thoughts.

34

CAITLIN

It was a victory, Caitlin told herself as she roused from the semi-sleep state she'd fallen into. Sean was getting dressed, his limbs sprawling through the air, taking up the whole room. She felt like cowering. Instead, she sat up and reached for her own clothes.

"Those bruises look bad," he commented, only mild curiosity in his voice.

"I slipped down some stairs the other night. I was out. At Southern Manse, you know?"

"I don't," Sean replied, "but they want to get some banisters installed, eh?"

Just dressing, the tug and release of muscles working under her battered flesh, sent darts of pain from her hip and back through her whole body. Caitlin hid her winces in the jumper she pulled over her head.

"What was it you were going to tell me, by the way?" She aimed for a casual, conversational tone. "About Deedee?"

"Oh, that," Sean said. "Roisin was running away from Deedee that day. Some silly spat between sisters, but she's blown it up into a whole drama."

"There has to be more to it. She blames herself?" Caitlin asked.

"Some days. Others she wakes up convinced Roisin was kidnapped." Sean spoke lightly, as though none of it mattered to him. "There were sightings, you know? I guess she puts a lot of stock in those."

Caitlin remembered her own phoned-in fake sighting. It triggered a difficult swirl of emotions; she didn't like Deedee and she had no right to feel sorry for her—wasn't she in this exact moment trying to sabotage Deedee's life?—but still. What a weight for her to have been carrying around since a child.

"It's pretty funny, really," Sean continued. "To her, it's this huge, terrible dark secret, when it's just nothing."

He had finished dressing now and stood before her, suddenly awkward.

What have you ever done to help her understand that it wasn't her fault? Caitlin thought. She knew the answer: nothing.

"You go ahead," she told Sean. "I might stick around here for a minute or two."

"I'm not sure that's safe," Sean said. He glanced over his shoulder toward the living room. "I've been wondering whether there's mold or something in here, something that contributed to Kathleen's, uh, well…"

"Death," Caitlin said.

He couldn't meet her eye as he handed her jeans to her. His cheeks were pink again, and it wasn't because he was flirting with her.

"Did she say something?" She slipped on her underwear under the covers. "That evening, did she say anything to you?"

Sean would be Kathleen's go-to with any house issues, with Colm infirm.

"No, why, did she say anything to *you?*" Sean asked, too quickly, too alert.

"She left a voicemail."

"And?"

Caitlin hadn't been able to listen to it. Whatever she said that night, Caitlin had already heard the slurring in her voice, the prelude to resentment and anger; it was the last thing she would ever hear her mother say to her. Realistically, she knew the message wasn't a heartfelt declaration of love or remorse, but until she actually listened to it, she could keep that fantasy alive.

"She didn't mention anything. She was at a bar." Caitlin clicked her fingers at Sean as though prompting her own memory. "You know, the one, in town . . ."

"O'Shea's?" Sean supplied. "Yeah, that's a popular place all right."

"That's the one." Caitlin filed the name away.

They left the gatehouse by the back door, ducking under the caution tape again. Sean made to head off for the Big House, at a pace just slightly faster than Caitlin could comfortably keep up with.

"Actually, could you drop me in town?" she asked his retreating back.

He considered it, his back still to her. She knew he wanted to refuse. The air between them was awkward; he didn't know how to hold himself. Caitlin prayed that his social graces and manners would overwhelm his clear desire to be away from her.

He darted back into the house to grab his keys. Her wallet and phone were in the pockets of the fur coat, from which most of the rain had dripped off rather than dried. She waited in front of the gatehouse. The rain was tapering off, Deedee's car was gone, and she had a lead. She could talk to someone at O'Shea's, find out if her mother had left alone. Make sure that Lee Casey hadn't been seen with her.

Sean refused to let her wear the coat in his car due to the dampness of the pelt, and he took the corners at speed, cutting down the drive time to ten minutes and pulling over at the edge of town to avoid the last-minute evening shopping traffic.

Caitlin got out and limped her way toward the high street. O'Shea's was a big, traditional-style pub with large glass windows on either side of the door. She smoothed her hair back and held her head high as she entered.

There was a mix of patrons inside, from older folks propping up the bar to impossibly young-seeming crowds of lads in too-tight polo shirts and girls covered in too-dark fake tans. Caitlin thought again of her upcoming thirtieth birthday, felt herself already becoming invisible. She fought her way to the bar. A couple of student-looking teenagers were deftly pulling pints and taking orders alongside an older man, presumably the proprietor. It was him that she needed to speak to.

Before she could, she saw the older man spot something behind her, at the entrance, and his eyes narrowed in anger.

"Out!" he roared. "Out!"

A ripple of heads turned toward the door, to see what the fuss was about.

Two large, bodybuilder-type men, as similar as brothers, one with a black rose tattoo all over his neck, had entered the pub. The patrons gave them a wide berth, but formed a circle that wasn't easily pushed through.

"C'mon, Gerry," the tattooed one said, a whine in his voice.

"You're a sad cunt, Gerry," the other sneered. "As if we'd wanta be in here anyhow."

The crowd was motionless until they left.

Caitlin took Gerry aside, introduced herself as an officer from the London Met, said that she was working with Mac on a case, could she have the CCTV from Thursday.

"So, it was true, was it? I thought Dee was just being a gobshite." Gerry motioned her to follow him up a rickety wooden staircase to a small office at the back of the building, where a dated monitor showing a split screen of four camera views sat. Dusty filing cabinets filled the rest of the available space.

"Garda O'Halloran?" Caitlin asked.

"Little Deedee. She was in here earlier asking about it. Would you tell me, is it about the O'Sullivans? 'Cause I've never noticed them in here before, but you saw yourself, they tried it tonight."

Caitlin connected the dots between the unsavory types who'd been ordered out and some kind of ongoing criminality Deedee had been looking into. There was no way Kathleen had gotten involved in drugs, was there? She was a bit long in the tooth to be starting to branch out from alcohol.

"I couldn't say," she told him, "and honestly, O'Halloran shouldn't have said anything either. I'll take that up with her superior." Whether that was true or not, Caitlin relished some imaginary power over Deedee.

"She's a good enough girl. Forget I said anything. She just gets your back up a bit," Gerry said. He sat at the computer and clicked through, accessing the footage from Thursday.

Caitlin gripped the edge of the desk as she watched him manipulate the time codes.

"Could you fast-forward to around six p.m.?" she asked, thinking of the call from her mother that she had missed, already so early in the evening.

Gerry did so, and Caitlin saw Kathleen at the bar, jabbing her phone. She watched as Deedee entered, crossing past the bar and disappearing into the crowd.

"Anything?" Gerry asked.

"Keep going," Caitlin directed. Hours sped past as Kathleen drank and chatted to whoever had had the bad luck to end up next to her, before she pushed herself away from the bar. Caitlin watched her so closely and with such focus that she gasped as the camera above the exit showed Deedee crashing into her, sending the older woman sprawling to the ground.

35

CAITLIN

No present awaits Caitlin on the morning of her ninth birthday. It's not unexpected—her mother has been in a state of mourning since her big fallout with Michael. Caitlin commends herself on her maturity as she swallows any sense of disappointment. The worst thing she could do would be to let her mother know she was unhappy.

Anyway, they've been talking a lot about their big move, about Caitlin's new school. She's not sure which one her mother means, but she won't miss Bannakilduff school; she's never quite fit in anyway.

With her bedroom window open, Maureen's radio drifts toward her from next door. The back door must be open over there, the house happily humming away. She can smell sausages, can practically hear the bacon sizzling. She can't resist.

"Oh, here she is!" calls out Maureen as Caitlin slips into the kitchen through the back door. "Lads! It's the birthday girl!"

In Maureen's kitchen a cuckoo clock swings on the wall, tea towels embroidered with chickens are neatly folded to one side. Something is always bubbling on the stove or baking in the oven. Maureen envelops her in a hug, oven-gloved hands and all.

"Now let me take a look at you." She barely needs to stoop any-more; Caitlin has been shooting up. "Will you ever tell me, just be-tween us girls, what keeps you looking so good in your old age? Nine already!"

Caitlin laughs, embarrassed and delighted.

"If she tells you, Ma, you must tell me," Sean says. At fifteen, he is a giant and getting bigger by the day. He scuffs a huge teenage hand in her hair affectionately.

Caitlin basks in the moment like a happy cat.

"Happy birthday, Caitlin!" Colm, a beautifully wrapped present in his hand. "Will we give you this now or wait until after you've eaten?"

Maureen is already setting her a place at the table.

Sean says, "Ah, go on, open it, will you. I'm dying to know and all!"

Maureen and Colm loop their arms around each other's waists as they watch her tear into the paper.

"*The Little Photographer!*" Caitlin has admired this book of Sean's for years.

"Would you look at that!" Maureen says, suddenly—magically—holding another present. "What'll you want to go with that?"

Sean whoops. Caitlin cannot make a sound.

Maureen glances at her husband, an unspoken acknowledgment that he was right flickering between them. Colm grins and grins and grins.

"You're big enough to look after this properly," he says, as Caitlin pries the box open with trembling hands.

Everyone knows that she has been fogging the glass of Hickey's electronics shop's window, staring at this camera. Compact, it fits perfectly into her hands, made for her alone.

The oven timer dings.

"Hash browns!" Maureen is all business, bustling away to the oven. Together they sit for the meal.

After breakfast, Maureen hustles everyone out of the kitchen so she can begin cleaning. Sean has promised Caitlin that she can come into town later this morning with him and his friends. Until then, she heads to the garden and practices with the camera. She raises the viewfinder to her eye and squints, pointing the camera at the house, the shed, the trees, flowers, her finger flexed on the button but never quite hitting it. The first picture must be just right, and the pleasure from lining up the shots is its own reward.

"Here, let me show you what comes next." Colm has appeared beside her, though she could have sworn she was alone in the garden.

He nods his head toward the shed. The room is dark, with tinfoil covering the windows. A bare, red light bulb swings with the movement of the door.

He stands back and lets her enter first. She hears the door lock behind her as the red light clicks on. The darkroom is small; she could almost touch all four walls from where she stands, if Colm wasn't in the way. She reaches her arms out and marvels at her own skin, perfect and freckle-free under this light. In front of her are the trays waiting to be filled with chemicals. Behind her, Colm is shuffling around. There are still photographs hanging up on the line. Pictures of Sean, smiling and waving. Pictures of Caitlin. She steps closer. The picture hanging in front of her is definitely of her, but she doesn't remember it being taken. She's in profile, sometime over the last couple of weeks, on the steps outside her house.

"Ah, you like that one, eh?" Colm says, and he reaches around her to pluck the photo down.

"I didn't know you were there," she tells her friend.

"Well, I'm always here, aren't I?" He grins, and his teeth are so white. "Don't you think it's a good one? The lighting was great. You can keep it if you like."

"No, that's OK. I just didn't realize."

He indicates the chemical troughs with one hand while the other slips the photograph into his back pocket. She turns to the troughs and feels him approaching behind her. He smells of soap, but underneath it there is a stronger smell, a tang of something older and more powerful. The space between their bodies is a whisper.

"Let me show you how to develop photographs," he says. Caitlin's mouth is dry because it's so hot in here, with no air.

From outside, she hears the clatter of teenagers, the loud jokes and raucous laughter. Sean's friends are here. The spell is broken.

"You'd better go." Colm steps back from her, already turning toward the door, his smile wide once more. "Can't miss the lads, eh?"

Caitlin only nods, her muscles shaky, but already she is questioning herself. What happened? Nothing.

Outside, the sun is too bright. Sean stands with Deedee O'Halloran, her sister Roisin and her friend Fi Donovan. A couple of local lads jostle with each other. Only Roisin notices her emerge from the shed. Caitlin gives her a small wave. Roisin doesn't wave back.

Caitlin makes her way to the gatehouse, feeling strange. Despite the bright sunshine, the rooms are dark, her mother still in her room, but a white envelope sits on the doormat inside the front door.

A birthday card for Caitlin, with a picture of a party-hatted bear clutching the strings of a load of balloons. It's from Michael, and beneath the printed *Happy Birthday!* message, he has written, *Be safe.*

36

DEEDEE

Fi and Mags were in O'Shea's. They'd organized it in the group chat. Deedee had begged off, claimed to have work stuff on, but really, she felt weird about going back there again. She might as well move in there at this rate.

What about Fitzy's? she had texted.

Gross, from Mags.

Are we twelve? from Fi.

"More pubs than people and we're always going to the same feckin' one," Deedee muttered as she walked. The links of the bracelet jangled in her pocket as she weaved through the festive shoppers. A raucous youth choir sang carols outside Quinn's garage. She sidestepped a gang of kids clamoring at the window of Hickey's electronics shop. Ahead of her now, Martina's jewelry shop.

Deedee could use a break from the drink anyway, even if she wasn't too busy working. She felt virtuous as she entered Martina's shop. A young lad with a buzzed head and his hands shoved in his pockets hovered the whole top half of his body over the diamond rings. A teenage girl tapped excitedly against a case of necklaces while her smiling mother rolled her eyes but nodded. Deedee shouldered her way up to the counter, where Martina was overseeing her Saturday girl as she placed a ribbon-wrapped box into a small canvas gift bag.

"Dee, how are you?" Martina still had the faintest trace of her Austrian accent even after all these years.

"Howya. I was wondering, actually, could you help me out maybe with tracing where a piece of jewelry came from?"

Martina shrugged. "It's not really my specialty. Duffy would know."

"I thought I'd try you first." Deedee was on significantly less friendly terms with Brian Duffy at the pawnshop since she'd pulled him over for speeding recently. Five miles over the limit was still over the limit. "Can we go in the back?"

"I wouldn't want to leave her, Dee. Come back at closing?"

"I'm in a hurry, is all," Deedee said.

"I can manage for a bit," the Saturday girl chimed in. "You said I was doing really well."

Martina wavered.

"She'll be fine, won't you . . . ?" Deedee trailed off to allow the girl to introduce herself.

"Claire. Yes, yes, I can do it."

"Claire, of course. Good woman, you are." Deedee turned to Martina. "It'll take five minutes."

"I'm taking the keys to the cases. Come and get me if anyone wants anything, OK?" Martina told Claire.

"I will." Claire was grave. She stood taller, her head held higher, and surveyed the customers in the room.

"Come on then." Martina unbolted the swinging counter door and held it for Deedee to go through.

"Thanks, Martina," Deedee said. "She's doing a grand job already."

The back room was shoebox-sized. Martina seated herself at a table that held a desktop computer, a stack of binders and folders for paperwork, and a small Tiffany-inspired lamp. "Let's see it."

Deedee passed her the bracelet. Under the warm glow of the lamp, it was even more stunning. The centerpiece was a large, round pendant engraved with a shield shape that split into three, with the middle one like a dagger. Noting these details, Deedee felt productive, like she was doing something important.

"Beautiful." Martina reached behind the monitor to switch on a long, thin task lamp and flooded the desk with bright white light. She pulled a loupe out of a drawer and inspected the bracelet. "I don't know what exactly you're hoping I can tell you."

"Are there any . . . I don't know, maker's marks?" Deedee asked, gliding one hand through the air as though highlighting a name. Her coat sleeve slipped down.

"God, what happened to your arm?" Martina gasped.

"Nothing." Deedee dropped her hand. Now that she had been reminded of it, the wound hurt again.

"It looks infected, it's all red," Martina continued.

"Nothing a little drink doesn't help with!" Deedee laughed, trying for carefree. It didn't land. "It'd be great to know who this came from, or where it was made."

"I don't know the designer, but it's antique-styled contemporary." Martina pointed out a small "M" stamped on the clasp. "There's your branding. What's the coat of arms?"

"No idea. Engraved initials, yeah?" Deedee blustered, embarrassed not to have realized it was a coat of arms sooner.

Martina flipped the pendant. "Yup, owner is H.W-L."

There was a thud on the door and Martina leapt up. "Ah, Claire needs me out there. Look after that arm." She was at the door, ushering Deedee through. "I'm not messing, it looks horrible."

Back in the shop, the mother and daughter who had been inspecting the necklaces were ready to buy and Claire was raring to go.

Deedee left the shop with the bracelet still cupped in her hand inside her pocket. H.W-L. As she walked, she googled *jewelers beginning with M* and watched a thousand results come back. An impossible task. She'd learned nothing. Too late, she remembered Fi telling her

Sean had been spotted in Martina's too. She could at least have asked about that.

Her failures piled up on her once more. She was such a loser.

She scrolled half-heartedly through the search engine results once more, before giving up. Fuck it.

At O'Shea's, she settled in with her gin and tonic and leaned forward to catch the end of Fi's conversation. "So, he's told his parents about me, we're all going to dinner in the new year!"

Things were going well with that guy Ben she'd mentioned the other day. Deedee wanted to roll her eyes.

Just wait, she thought. *Just you wait until you've been together a thousand years.*

"Dee!" Mags gasped, her hand pressed to her heart. "I've just remembered! What's the craic with you and Sean?"

"Yeah, Dee!" Fi joined in, flush with generosity now that she was among the chosen, the loved.

Dee took the straw from her drink and swigged directly from the glass to hide her face as her friends laughed.

"No, no, nothing like that. I don't know. Maybe we were wrong."

"No," Mags asserted. "Definitely not wrong."

"Did youse hear Michelle Quinn's kid got lost today and they'd half the country out looking for her?" Deedee threw it out there, the only thing she could think of to get them off the subject.

"Which one? What happened?" Fi asked.

Trust Fi to know all about that skanger Michelle's kids, Deedee thought. Between this wholesome "everyone's my pal" thing she was on recently and her gushing over some guy, she was getting awfully dull.

"Lily-Mae," Mags told her. "I saw old Mrs. Lynch in town this afternoon; she musta gone out purely to talk about her granddaughter. She was scarred, like."

"Poor Michelle," Fi clucked.

"I dunno about that," Mags mused. "I mean, you remember how she was. Maybe the kids are going the same way."

"Exactly," Deedee piled in eagerly. "They were never any good."

"Come off it." Fi was stern, the good humor of the evening fading quickly. "She was a child."

"She didn't act it," put in Mags.

"She definitely wasn't interested in dolls!" Deedee said.

"Honestly, Deirdre, I'm surprised that you of all people would be bringing it up." Fi was warning her.

"Why me? Because she said a load of old shite years ago when she was having a breakdown over being a pregnant teenager? Or sorry, maybe she was only trying to blackmail a well-off family." Deedee didn't like the implication.

"Aye, we've all decided it was a load of shite, but you'd be an idiot to not be worrying now about that sort of thing coming back around, what with all the 'Me Too' stuff." Fi seemed sober now, with the mood crashing down on them.

"Well, now that's a point." Mags tapped a finger on her chin in faux consideration. "I've often thought we were closer to Hollywood than anywhere else in Europe, I'll be honest."

"Colm isn't going to get 'Me Too'd! He can barely even walk!" Deedee said.

"And why is that?" Fi asked in a dark tone. "You ever wonder what happened there? My parents were friends with the Quinns, and I'll say no more, but no one was ever caught, were they?"

"No one was caught for anything that summer," Mags snorted. "Purely decorative Garda force. No offense, Dee."

"You've made your point. Let's not fall out." Deedee raised her hands in surrender. "I'm sorry, Fi. I'm a gobshite."

"Aww, she loves you, Fi!" Mags clapped. "Make her get the next round!"

"I'll do it after you tell us about the plans to meet Ben's parents," Deedee said to Fi.

"OK, right so . . ." Fi began.

Deedee let the chat wash over her, following Mags's lead on

reactions. Her mind was whizzing in a thousand different directions. She had never paid attention to the rumors about Colm. It was well accepted that it had all been some kind of malicious nonsense. The Branagh family's wealth made them a target.

She excused herself and headed for the toilets, where she locked herself in the cubicle furthest from the door and pulled out her phone. The music from the main room was faint in here; it was easier to think. Her investigation suddenly felt urgent again. She googled Mark Lewis and Vector Point first, hoping for an easy win with a professional networking profile, and was rewarded immediately.

Mark Lewis looked just as arrogant and smug in his various profiles as he had on his ID. Deedee messaged him with her number, telling him she'd found his wallet.

A rush of loud music and cackling as a group of girls entered the toilets. Two went into the other cubicles but there were others waiting outside the doors.

Deedee moved on to H.W-L. Researching family crests of England, she quickly became overwhelmed. There were too many to trawl through; she would never be able to do it. She thought harder.

Outside her cubicle, the girls were yelling at each other to hurry up.

Fi was always tracing where photos came from. She used reverse-image look-up to check on the guys she was supposed to go on dates with. Deedee snapped a picture of the crest and googled how to reverse-image search. It couldn't be that tough if everyone was doing it.

A hammering started on the door of her cubicle. She blocked it out, even as irritation swept through her.

The reverse-image search brought her to a number of web pages about crests, but also, even better, to a jeweler's Instagram page.

The "M" brand was Mallory's, jeweler to the elite, and two years ago, Lois Mallory was honored to share her commission for the Winchester-Lavery family. The net was closing around Caitlin now.

God, just a little G&T and Deedee was flying. *Some people really handle their drink better than others*, she thought.

The rattling of her cubicle door intensified, and manicured hands gripped the top, as whoever was waiting prepared to jump up and peek over.

Deedee opened the door, sending the girl who had been hanging off it stumbling away giggling as another of the girls rushed in.

She paused before returning to the table. She didn't think she could handle hearing more about Fi's great new guy and whatever Mags was going on about. Besides, the two of them were great friends without her now. They didn't need her. Neither did Sean.

She texted Florian and he responded quickly. He was home. It would be good to chat to him, get his opinion. Professionally, of course. She was lying to herself.

Florian lived in a small bungalow on the other side of town, so Deedee hopped in a cab. A mix of fizzing excitement and smoldering dread suffused her.

"Dee!" His hair was ruffled, as though he'd just woken up, and his feet were bare.

"Thanks for this."

He closed the door behind her and she spun to face him, their bodies close together.

"You're not even going to chat me up?" He grinned. "Straight to business, is it?"

"You were hoping for sparkling conversation?" Deedee looped her arms around his neck. "Could we have the cuppa after, maybe?" Her phone was going off in her pocket, the girls probably wondering where she was, but then she was sliding her hand up Florian's neck and along his jawline to cradle his skull as he brought his face to hers. The topography of this journey, tendons and pulse and soft downy hair at the nape. The tenderness of it could have broken her in two, so instead she wrapped her arms around his shoulders and closed her eyes and surrendered to the sensations.

Never again, she told herself. She knew it was a lie.

37

CAITLIN

Roisin isn't afraid of ghosts, but Caitlin thinks she would be if she'd seen any. Until you've seen a ghost, it's easy not to be afraid. Roisin counters that she wouldn't be, because there's no such thing. Each of them always leaves this recurring conversation more secure in her own superior knowledge: Caitlin's belief that the world of seen things is shrouded in a layer of deathly imprints and unknowable things; Roisin's that science can explain everything.

Michael, who has been back on the scene with Caitlin's mother for a few days now, would side with Roisin.

"What about the bodies then?" Caitlin asks, triumphant. She holds her arms out wide, demonstrating the trees around them and how they might positively burst with spectral corpses. They are in the woods, carrying their school backpacks with supplies—pens, pencils, oddly shaped rocks and colorful mushrooms collected as specimens in old sandwich bags. Outside of the woods, it's another blistering summer's day, the hottest in years. Inside, it's cooler and darker.

"What bodies?" Roisin scuffs the toes of her shoes through the mulchy soil underfoot, kicking up clumps of dirt, the way she does when she's bored of Caitlin.

"The dangling ones, right here in the woods."

"That's not a true thing, Caitlin!" she hoots. "I can't believe you actually think those stories are true."

"How would you know? You don't see the woods all night long like I do. They're outside my window." Caitlin's trump card. She is still the world's foremost expert in these woods. They are too deep into the trees to see her window, but she points toward it anyway. If they could see it, they would see Michael and her mother, gentle with each other these days, on a little picnic blanket facing the Hanging Woods. The arrangement chafes a little, because Caitlin feels herself observed, but it seems to have brought peace, so she doesn't mind.

"I've been here at night." Roisin speaks quietly. "But you don't have to be to know it's nonsense."

"You'd be too scared to be here at night," Caitlin says, as though she doesn't have regular nightmares about something emerging from the woods and fogging her windowpane with its breath.

"Not because of ghosts." Roisin is saying these things as though they're being pulled out of her. It throws Caitlin, the sudden shift in her friend.

"You admit it!" She leaps from one foot to another, pointing and whooping. It's too much, but she wants to provoke a reaction from Roisin, to bring them back to normal.

"Stop it!" Roisin hisses, glancing about them. "He'll hear you!"

Caitlin's smile fades. "The guy camping?" They have watched him now, and decided that he poses no threat. He still leaves his odd little things for them to find sometimes, but he has never come near them, and Caitlin has begun to think of him as a skittish deer, something to be regarded from a distance.

Roisin shakes her head, and Caitlin feels a new kind of fear.

"No, of course not. The other one. You know him."

Caitlin does. "But he's nice."

"He does things."

Everything feels muffled, like a heavy snow has fallen over them. They've dropped into another sort of space, suspended together in a world that looks just like theirs but couldn't be more different.

Perhaps because of the stillness and the quiet, the sound of boots shuffling through the soil is loud. Both girls gasp. Roisin claps a hand over her mouth. Caitlin clutches Roisin's arm. She feels a horror so intense that it knocks her out of body; she feels like she is floating above them, looking down at whatever happens next. The feeling is not unfamiliar. She fixes her gaze on the ground in front of her, as though if she doesn't see anything else, then nothing can see her either.

The boots are approaching, but the sounds echo strangely off the trees. It's hard to tell where they're coming from, only that they're between the girls and their usual path out of the woods.

Roisin breaks from under the spell first. She turns and runs deeper, deeper into the woods.

Should they split up? Should Caitlin move toward the boots—try to sneak out? If she screamed, would Michael and her mother hear her first, or would it only draw the monster on to her? She is beyond rational thought, so she pelts after Roisin. Soon all she can hear is her own breath and her pounding feet as she darts around trees. A clearing, a clearing is ahead. Something in her mind associates this space with safety. The passing thought of a protective circle of white salt, an impenetrable place. Roisin is gone. Caitlin lands in the clearing and drops to her knees. The world is spinning and she's seeing herself from above again, a bird's-eye view of how exposed she is, how wrong she was. With nothing left but fear and shame for being so stupid, she collapses onto her belly and rolls herself against a log. The bark rasps her skin through her T-shirt. She covers herself in leaves, streaks muck across her face. She is alone.

The footsteps arrive. Heavy and purposeful. Caitlin gets a sense of the enormity of this being from how the steps land, how they send shock waves rippling toward her. She peeks and sees the shadow of a big man, slowly walking the perimeter of the clearing. She doesn't dare to look at his face. As he walks, he seems to stretch and grow, getting bigger despite moving further from her. There is a tension to his posture, a feeling of something coiled ready to strike. When he briefly turns toward the weak shaft of light entering the clearing, an answering light glitters from his waist. Caitlin screws her eyes shut once more. Nothing good could come from witnessing this.

The air grows colder around her, and she shivers under the leaf cover. Evaporated sweat or adrenaline or both, she's not sure, but the footsteps are gone and the woods are normal once more. Which is to say, she hears birds again, a gentle breeze rustling the leaves. When she gets up, her whole body aches from the strain of it all. She limps toward the outskirts of the woods, cradling her arms around herself.

Roisin is there, at their entrance point where Caitlin's fields back onto the woods. She says nothing. She is watching Michael and Caitlin's mother as they laugh on the picnic blanket, empty plates from the house in front of them, lost in a world of their own and oblivious to the Hanging Woods.

"It's just us," she says.

Caitlin understands what she means. Despite what they say, the adults are no help at all when it comes to the monster.

PART FOUR

HANG

Now everyone can see what you've made.

John Lyle,
The Little Photographer:
A Kid's Guide to Perfect Pictures

38

CAITLIN

Caitlin steeled herself before she entered the kitchen, sure that Sean would be awkward; blushing, stammering.

What if he thinks he's my boyfriend now? Yes, there was delight in imagining how Deedee would react when she found out, but also, there was horror in considering how to handle this.

She smoothed her hair, took a deep breath, and stepped over the threshold. Was it her imagination, or did the snake plants on the windowsill already look sickly, drooping and curling at the edges as they reacted to the salt she'd poured into their soil? The sight steadied her.

"Good morning, sunshine! There's your fry now." Maureen pulled out a chair from the table and set a plate of bacon, sausages, eggs, and hash browns in front of it. "Did you want black pudding too?"

"Just toast." Caitlin sat as instructed and gestured to her plate. "I mean, generally. Sorry, this is a bit much for me."

"Are you sure?" Maureen fixed her with a searching stare. "You could use a bit more feeding, couldn't you? Small thing like you, you don't need to worry about getting fat!" She patted her own flat stomach. "Not like me, huge great lump that I am!"

"No way!" Caitlin exclaimed.

Simultaneously, Sean said, "You're only gorgeous, Ma."

"Aren't you two good?" Maureen struck a pose and then whisked an additional plate piled with toast in front of Caitlin. "Now, I won't move that fry, but you needn't eat it, and if you do, we won't judge you, will we?"

"Nope." Sean smiled briefly and then turned back to his phone.

"Morning," Caitlin said to him. When he didn't respond, she added, "Is that Deedee you're texting?"

"No," Sean said. "But we'll see her at mass. Ma, we'll need to be going soon, you know how busy the roads get."

"Ah, it's only ten minutes away." Maureen waved him off.

Caitlin watched Sean from the corner of her eye. He was completely composed. No, he was uninterested.

It's guilt, she thought. *He'll crack soon, maybe in front of Deedee. He won't be able to keep this up.*

"Are you eating anything, Maureen?" she asked.

"Me? I had near enough a whole loaf of bread!"

"Ten-minute warning. I'll be warming up the car." Sean stood up from the table and took his plate to the sink.

"Warming warning!" Maureen chuckled. "Don't mind him, Caitlin, he gets very uptight. Take that toast with you. I'm just going to check in on Colm before. He's not able for it this morning."

Maureen gone, Caitlin sprang out of her seat to the back door, where she tossed her toast out for the crows, a peace offering. The fry remained on the table, untouched.

She took the back seat of the car and felt childlike, vaguely ridiculous. Sean kept his head buried in his phone, the radio playing just loud enough to discourage conversation. Perhaps that was for the best. The minutes before Maureen arrived were excruciating in their slowness.

"The snake plants look a bit off." She angled for a reaction as Maureen settled herself into the front passenger seat.

"What plants?" Maureen asked.

"In the kitchen."

"I hadn't noticed," she said.

Caitlin scraped at her still-healing lip, searching for the taste of blood. She felt powerless, and that made her furious.

They pulled up to the church twenty minutes early, and the crowds parted as Sean and Maureen walked through. Colm's position in society, his charity work, was still potent. Maureen grinned broadly and introduced Caitlin to several of the people who were stopping them, and Caitlin become aware again of how intensely on the outside she was when she saw the surprise after she greeted people. She sounded English: clipped, nasal, soft "o" sounds. It was the verbal difference between perching on the edge of a chair and sprawling on a couch.

She'd lost the looseness and the lilt of her Irish accent. It wasn't possible for her to be of this town when she had spent twice as many decades trying to forget it as she had living in it. She was from here, but even that was tenuous. Her roots weren't like most people's, deeply wound under the ditches, lanes, fields. There was no trace of her life, only her secrets.

The urge to run burned through her.

Sean chatted and schmoozed like a politician, ignoring her. His plan was clear: he would pretend nothing had happened.

Unbelievable. What a worm.

Caitlin's thoughts were an angry buzz. He had been all over her, so solicitous, and now? Did he think he had played her for a fool? Did he think he had had the last laugh on her?

She watched him hold court, a group of guffawing men around him. He was so confident, his chest puffed out and his laugh booming around the churchyard. Then she saw the girl. She was young, twenty, perhaps, in a dress that was definitely too clingy for church, with the unlined, peachy skin of someone who could still binge-drink for six hours, throw up for another two, and make it to church looking fabulous. And she was watching Sean like he was the only man on earth.

There's no way, she thought.

Sean spotted the girl over the heads of the men around him and smiled warmly at her, tilting his chin up in greeting. She responded by touching the silver chain around her neck and mouthing, "Thank you." Caitlin felt like the world tilted upside down. Sean was not only seeing this kid but buying her jewelry.

"You've got two choices." Deedee appeared in front of her. Caitlin, momentarily overcome with a sense of kinship, felt like screaming at her to turn around and ask her boyfriend why he was buying necklaces for a twenty-year-old. "You and I can talk about all your . . . indiscretions, or I can just take them straight to the guards. Either way, I hope you've said your goodbyes."

"No idea what you're talking about," Caitlin said. "Sean is over there."

Deedee only glanced, guiltily, toward him. At close quarters, she looked run-down and exhausted. Her eyes were bloodshot, and when she scratched vigorously at dry patches of skin on her cheeks, her sleeve rode up, exposing a vicious-looking wound on her wrist.

Caitlin felt a detached curiosity. What had Deedee *this* worked up? Did she already know about Sean?

"I'll see you out here after mass," Deedee said.

"Probably you'll see me in there too. I imagine we'll be sharing a fucking pew."

"I think you should come somewhere with me." Deedee probably thought she was telegraphing steely determination, but she came off needy, repulsively so.

"Absolutely not, but thank you for the invitation." Caitlin wanted to get as much distance from Deedee's intense and grasping need as possible.

"Trust me," Deedee said, but she didn't follow Caitlin into the church.

39

DEEDEE

Mark Lewis called at 6 a.m. Deedee was already awake, languishing in a clammy hangover that made her wish for death. She didn't remember what had specifically caused today's dread, only that there was one inoculation against it. Sometimes she left a beer near her bed, but that didn't seem to be the case this morning, and she had been trying to summon the strength to ferret one out for over an hour now.

"You have my wallet?" Mark demanded.

"I do," Deedee croaked.

"What's this number? Is this a scam?"

"It's Irish, I'm in Ireland." Deedee rested the phone on the pillow, creating a distance between his booming voice and her aching skull. "Do you know a Caitlin Doherty?"

"Cait-lin," Mark drawled. Deedee could hear the leer. "You could say that."

Caitlin must have awful taste in men, Deedee thought. "How do you know her?"

"We worked together," Mark said. "I turned her down, actually. I'm on my grind. Gym, work. Got a PT session in a minute."

Deedee cut him off before he could tell her the boring details. "Yeah, me too. Listen, when'd you last see your wallet?"

She heard it dawning on him that Caitlin was there when he lost his wallet, that she had taken it. "It's probably revenge," he said. "For knocking her back."

Deedee didn't entirely regret having gotten in touch with him, but she was glad to get him off the phone. First the suitcase, then the bracelet, now the wallet, Caitlin had robbed at least three people. The knowledge fueled her enough that she staggered down to the kitchen and located a couple of beers.

The beers helped her to forget how awful she felt, but this morning they emboldened her too. She had woken back at home; she never stayed at Flo's. Frank's snuffly snoring was the only sound in the house, and for the first time she didn't feel badly about herself, about what she'd done.

She didn't fear being discovered today. She felt an internal shift, like she was tying up loose ends.

She rehearsed her big speech as she walked up to the church.

Doyle, I have reason to believe that Caitlin Doherty has been defrauding several individuals, and I further believe that she has information pertaining to Roisin's investigation. This is a matter of some urgency.

Instead, she found Caitlin, and her planned speech turned into a whining confrontation.

Inside the church, the congregation murmured and shuffled. In a couple of seconds, the priest would begin his procession up the aisle to the altar. Outside, Deedee waited for Doyle. The organist struck the opening chords to "How Great Thou Art" and Deedee stubbed out her cigarette. His tall frame huddled in the chill December morning, Doyle almost barreled straight into her. Deedee caught his arm and he shook her off.

"We're late!" he hissed.

"I need to talk to you. I have some information, about Roisin," Deedee hissed back, then, remembering herself, she added, "Also, Caitlin's a thief."

Doyle startled. "You need to let go of this."

Something in how he emphasized the word "need," the desperate look in his eyes, and Deedee understood that he was hiding something.

"You've been lying to me," she said, in wonder. How could Doyle, stalwart, loyal Doyle, have led her astray?

The congregation sang and the smell of the incense drifted out to them. Neither of them moved.

"Yesterday, you said Roisin was dead," she continued. "You've never said that before."

"You don't want to open this box, Deirdre," Doyle warned her.

"What about Michelle Quinn? Her interview notes are missing."

"Drop it," he ordered.

"Doyle . . ." Deedee began, but her words died in her throat as she pieced it together.

A name to do with Sherlock Holmes, Casey had said. Arthur Conan Doyle; he meant he'd spoken to Doyle. He meant that Doyle was in on it all along.

The last notes of the hymn faded away. The congregation shuffled, taking their seats in the pews. With a last warning look, Doyle slipped past her into the church.

Deedee felt paralyzed, her mind whirring too fast for her to process.

Michelle's missing interview.

Michelle.

Shell.

The shell on the map. It was so obvious, she should have put it together as soon as she realized that Caitlin was the cat.

The last line of investigation was the woman Deedee had spent her life hating. Could she really go over there and expect Michelle's help?

She owed it to Roisin to try.

40

CAITLIN

It had been years since Caitlin had attended mass, but the rhythm hadn't changed. As the priest sermonized, she considered the dark-room. Last night she had sneaked in and set everything up ready to process the images from the camera roll she'd finished. The only issue was the developer, which was several years beyond its shelf life.

If she could slip out now, she could run to Hickey's shop and buy developer. On this last weekend before Christmas, Hickey's was one of several shops opening for a couple of hours of frantic, last-minute shopping. She could be back in time to catch a lift with Sean and Maureen, and then she'd duck into the darkroom while they were busy after mass. She was almost ready to gift them Colm's final images.

"Not feeling great," she murmured to Sean. "Need some air."

He glared at her and put a finger over his lips. Insufferable. If this was how he truly was, Deedee might end up thanking her for having wrecked their relationship. Caitlin ducked her head and shuffled past the couple of people sitting between her and the left-hand aisle. Though no one turned to look at her, she knew that did not mean she was unnoticed.

Outside the church, she broke into a run, pelting down the stone steps onto the high street, heedless of the ache in her hip and back. She was learning to live with the pain of it now, to push past her discomfort. The town was sparsely populated, most people at church, those remaining crammed into the handful of open shops. Banners hung over the street advertising the winter solstice festival celebration.

In Hickey's, she caught the eye of a gawky lad who looked incredibly flustered. She was precise and exact in what she needed, making it easy for him to find the developer and hand it to her. She thanked him and made as though to go toward the cash register, before realizing that both he and the cashier were busy with customers, so she sneaked the box into her coat. She had the money, there was no reason to do it, but equally, there was no reason not to.

She ran back to the church as the last hymn was being played and waited it out as Sean and Maureen held court outside. Finally, having spoken to almost every parishioner, they headed for the car.

Back at the Big House, Sean stayed in the driver's seat while Maureen and Caitlin got out, explaining that he was heading off for a tutoring job. Though she couldn't be sure of it, Caitlin would have bet anything that his student was that young girl who'd been staring at him outside the church. Inside, Maureen checked on Colm while Caitlin made excuses and pretended to go back to bed.

The whole house was quiet as she slipped out the back door and into the darkroom.

It had been years since she'd tried this, but she soon rediscovered the rhythm to making prints. Her hands moved of their own accord; she remembered it in her body if not in her mind.

First the enlarger. The negative projected onto the paper. She focused on the edges: straight lines, crisp focus.

"Don't get distracted by the image; perfection lies in the details." She recited from *The Little Photographer* under her breath, adjusting the enlarger's lens.

Then the chemical bath—developer and stop. A wash to remove the chemicals followed by a hang dry.

She processed the first image on the strip, watching the picture swim to the surface. A test shot, taken from inside the Hanging Woods, facing out toward the cottage. She saw her own bedroom window appear and smiled at its familiarity. She had forgotten the small flower patch her mother had staked below her window, but there it was, a tangle of tough rock roses.

She had been able to smell these roses in her room, they were so close. How could she have forgotten that? She pulled the photo out and hung it up on the string that ran the length of the darkroom and back again.

The next image had been taken shortly after that first one, right up against the cottage. One of the rock roses was foregrounded, each soft petal defined and captured. Colm's eye. Caitlin felt a fond prickling of pride. He had been good. Maureen would be glad to have these.

She was still thinking these bittersweet thoughts as the third image swam into focus. There was a moment of suspended animation. The acrid chemical smell filled her nostrils, the red light making everything look smooth and unreal. She blinked several times. She was seeing things. Terrible things.

A child through the window. Bare skin, barely formed figure, captured in the act of dressing. She was looking at herself.

She pulled the picture out and hung it on the string.

She was mistaken. This was in her mind. She had to develop the rest of the film, prove to herself that nothing was wrong.

Her face was clear in the fourth image.

She processed negative after negative, faster and faster, barely waiting for the shadows of the image to clear before hanging them up. Flashes of herself, of Michelle, of Roisin, until she hit her own pictures, the ones she had taken in the past few days.

The relief of seeing her face, as it was now, in the mirror selfie she'd taken first.

The final images: Maureen's face over the stove with her lips curled into a smile but her eyes small and spiteful; Sean, the huge bulk of him, so much larger than she remembered, so like his father, leering at her; Deedee, the lightning bolt tattoo on her wrist visible as she raked a hand through her graying hair, her face slack and sad.

She finished pinning the images up and looked at the truth.

41

DEEDEE

Michelle lived in one of the new suburbs, where the driveways were full of Range Rovers and all the kids had violin lessons. The house was double-fronted and two stories high, sterile white with black window frames. Deedee had been expecting crumbling corners, dusty carpets, biscuits half dissolved in mugs of tea. The old Quinn place had felt like a clown car, overrun with children and color and texture.

Michelle wore cream leggings and an oversized cream sweatshirt, very clean-living fitness influencer. She did not greet Deedee.

"Kids not about?" Deedee said.

"At church with their granny," Michelle answered. "Why, trying to arrest them?"

Shouting at the little girl in the graveyard felt like a lifetime ago, but Deedee found she was still angry about it. "You think that's an appropriate place for kids to mess, is it?"

"You said you'd lie about her drinking," Michelle snapped back. "It's not exactly behavior fitting of a guard, is it?"

It wasn't, Deedee agreed. So much of her behavior hadn't been.

"Well, join the queue," she said. "Look, I didn't come here to argue with you. I heard something about . . . about that summer."

"What summer?"

"The summer Roisin went missing. I spoke to Lee Casey, and he said the guards already knew it wasn't him. I didn't believe him, but then I found out that you were interviewed too."

"Then you know," Michelle said. "I told the truth then, I've been telling the truth for years."

"The interview notes are missing. Whatever you said, it's not in the records."

Michelle's cool, detached facade was replaced with genuine shock and dismay.

"What did you see?" Deedee pressed on.

"You only want to know because of Lee Casey." Michelle shook her head in disbelief. "You'll believe him, eh?"

"Did you want to get your side out or not? I'm offering you a chance."

Michelle closed the door in Deedee's face.

Stunned, it took Deedee a moment before she hammered on the door again and again, until it was flung open.

"I couldn't give a shite about getting my side out there," Michelle hissed. "My side isn't worth anything in this town!"

"Roisin mentioned you on a map she was making. She drew a shell in the Hanging Woods. That's you, isn't it?"

"Roisin was a cute kid when she wanted to be," Michelle said.

"What can I give you, Michelle? What can I do?"

"You've got nothing I want!"

"Your daughter was running around in that cemetery, not much older than Roisin was, and I freaked out. I thought I saw a ghost because Roisin's been gone now longer than I had her and I'm never going to know what happened, whether she's alive."

"Oh Deedee." Michelle looked at her with so much pity. "You know she's not."

Hearing it again was worse somehow. Deedee felt her strength draining, and she swayed, just a little.

"What do you know?" she muttered without rancor. What she needed wasn't here. She needed a drink—Listerine would do at this point—to grant her distance from this, to whisk her away to somewhere grief and loss couldn't touch her, where nothing could touch her.

She was one house-length away when Michelle caught up with her.

"For God's sake, come in." She took Deedee by the elbow and marched her through a very gray hallway into an equally gray living room.

She noticed Deedee looking and said, "Gray and white are very serene colors."

"But the kids?" The place was immaculate, no sign of the disorder of family life.

"They're in school—early—every day, they get good marks on their tests, they're tall enough, they're healthy. All right, they're not angels, Lily-Mae put the fear of God into us yesterday, but they're not bad kids."

"You're proud of them."

"Makes you wonder what if. I was a duffer at school, but there was a lot going on."

Deedee had never really spared a thought for Michelle, or not a generous thought, at least. Staying here where everyone talked about her behind her back, judged her, considered her trash.

"I won't change my story," Michelle said. "That's why you're here. Protect your investment, isn't it? I've heard you were off in Martina's back room having some big secret jewelry meeting."

"What's that got to do with this?"

"There are no secrets in Bannakilduff, Deirdre. I heard he's getting sicker recently. You want this to die with him?"

"With who?"

"Colm Branagh."

"C'mon." This again. Deedee didn't want to hear Michelle's lies about having an affair with Colm. "You ended up with Little Barry Lynch and this place. Isn't that enough financial security for you?"

"I never cared about the Branagh fortune, and that's why I told the guards exactly who was in those woods." Michelle began to pace. "You lot wrote us off as knackers. Load of screeching kids, dad in the betting shop, but we were loved. I was loved, and my mam and dad believed me from the start. No one else believed me, but no one else had to. You see what I'm saying?"

"What are you getting from this?" Deedee asked.

"My life ruined is what I got. Painted as a liar, but I've been telling the truth—screaming it from the rooftops for twenty years." Michelle dropped onto the sofa, deflated. "You can take it or leave it."

"I know how he was. I was there too, I was young too, there was opportunity." If Deedee could be logical, lay it out like this, Michelle would have to back down.

"Exactly. He had all that access and you're wondering what happened to Roisin? No parents at all, grandmother who couldn't keep track of you." Michelle shook her head sadly. "I spend my whole life worrying about my girls. There was none of that for me, not with the shifts my parents worked."

"Colm never came near me. Never," Deedee said.

"He likes them younger. About the same age your Roisin was when your parents died; what was that? Seven, eight? That's when it started with me."

Deedee wanted to be sick.

Michelle continued. "He spent a lot of time with her after that, didn't he? Had you bring her down."

"That can't be true." Deedee racked her brain, looking for signs. Yes, Colm was always very close to people, but he was like that with everyone. Yes, he had . . . looked at her, once or twice, in a way that felt uncomfortable or like it had gone on for too long, but that wasn't a crime. Her experience of Colm had been so positive, so nurturing.

"There was no one Roisin could turn to, was there? That's what they look for. I've read about it. Vulnerable kids who aren't protected. So, he looked at youse and then he looked at me and he thought, well, close enough. Maybe he even thought it was the reputation that would do for me. And he was right, wasn't he?"

Deedee closed her eyes and summoned an image of Roisin's map, the markings on the Hanging Woods.

"Where did this all happen? Like, the location, specifically," she asked.

Michelle answered without hesitation. "There's a clearing in the Hanging Woods, in line with the gatehouse, he would meet me there."

Roisin's map—the skull in the clearing. She'd been trying to tell Deedee all along.

"Ask Caitlin," Michelle added. "I don't know why she went along with the Lee Casey thing, but she knows the truth. She must."

Deedee wanted to apologize, she knew she should, but if she started, where would she end? She felt sick with her own complicity, how she'd spread rumors about Michelle, how she'd protected Colm.

"Where is Roisin?" she asked.

"I don't know how it happened." Michelle cleared her throat. "I think he got rid of her. Forever."

A wave of grief choked Deedee, threatened to pull her under, and then she remembered, she had a life raft.

"But the hit-and-run! Colm's accident! How could he have been in the woods at the same time?" she demanded.

"Colm was in the car park; maybe he'd already been to the woods. My da, he was pissed off at how everyone was fawning over the Branaghs, so he goes to leave, but who strolls right in front of his bumper? Colm, sneaking around. Everyone was distracted." Michelle looked Deedee straight in the eye. "He knew we'd never get justice. That's why he ran over Colm. I only wish he'd killed him."

42

CAITLIN

*I*t's not real, there's nothing there, I am safe.

She could repeat the words forever and it wouldn't make a difference.

It had never been true.

The monster had been real, and Caitlin had never been safe.

43

DEEDEE

Outside, the sky was a perfect soft blue, scudding clouds only accentuating the beauty of the day. Yesterday's storm was long gone, and Michelle's neighbors were tumbling out of their homes, bundled up in coats and scarves against the chill wind. The solstice celebration was starting.

The Hanging Woods bordered the estate, and on the other side was Deedee's whole world. She sat inside her car with her hands in her lap, willing Michelle's words out of her head.

Oisinn Quinn with his garage could have fixed up the car so they'd never find any evidence of the hit-and-run. The events had run like this: Colm sneaking away from the solstice celebration, knowing that the whole town would be there, for a prearranged meeting with Roisin. Except Roisin couldn't shake Caitlin that day, so both girls went into the Hanging Woods, and then . . . What? Colm murdered Roisin in front of Caitlin, only to be caught by Oisinn on his way back to the celebration?

It felt like Michelle had worked the story over the years, smoothing out the jagged edges, the bits that didn't make sense. Deedee needed more.

Michelle's living room curtains twitched, reminding Deedee where she was, and she knew she could delay no longer. Bannakilduff had never felt smaller; all too soon, she was pulling up on the gravel outside the Big House.

What did it mean if Michelle was telling the truth, if Colm was the thing preying on children in the woods? It meant that Deedee had devoted her life to caring for the person who'd murdered her sister, finding comfort in the embrace of the monster.

If she believed it.

If she chose not to, she could continue her life as usual. Marry Sean, be a Branagh, say nothing. The map wasn't real evidence; you could bend the images on it to mean anything. Roisin was just a kid.

Roisin was just a kid.

If Caitlin corroborated Michelle's story, that would be it, too much proof to ignore.

Deedee entered the Big House by the front door, not wanting to pass too close to the Hanging Woods, not now.

"Hel-lo!" Maureen sang out from the kitchen, over the rushing sound of the tap running as she rinsed off the breakfast plates.

Deedee's every step was weighted with the knowledge that this was the last time she'd be warmly welcomed in this house.

"Didn't sit with us today?" Maureen asked from the sink, her hands submerged in suds. "Feeling rough from Saturday night, eh?"

She didn't look evil, like someone who could hide a predator and a murderer for twenty years.

"I was a bit late," Deedee replied.

"So were we, nearly. I tell you what, didn't someone—naming no names, but you know yourself—leave a whole huge plate of food out there? Didn't eat her breakfast; left four sausages, a pile of bacon and eggs, and three big hash browns, you get the picture anyway, just left them there on the table!"

Deedee could picture what had happened, Maureen telling Caitlin to leave it if she wanted to, Caitlin believing her.

"I need to talk to her, actually," Deedee said. "Is she around?"

"Not feeling well, apparently, though if you ask me"—Maureen lowered her voice to a conspiratorial whisper and tapped the side of her head—"I'd say the problem's up here."

Usually when Maureen tapped the side of her head, she was signaling that Deedee had said or done something stupid again. Seeing the action used against Caitlin, Deedee realized how much of the Branaghs' judgment she had internalized. How the attrition of low expectations had worn away at her.

"I'll knock." She turned to leave.

"Aren't you in a huff today?" Maureen prodded, "You'll make a great pair, sure. Before I forget, Sean's after going to do tutoring with Lucy Kearney; she's back from college."

"Thanks. How is Colm today, by the way? Better?" Deedee asked.

"Up and down." Maureen wiped her hands on a tea towel and led Deedee into the living room.

Deedee waited for the details. None came. "It's just that Sean told me he'd to stay here last night to help out."

"Isn't he good?" Maureen picked up the doll she'd been crocheting. She didn't answer the question.

Deedee didn't bother checking the spare room; she'd clocked that Caitlin's shoes weren't by the door. Hopefully Caitlin wasn't trying to brain anyone else, but she could be anywhere.

What had coming back here been like for her? If she had witnessed a murder, what had that done to her? Let alone the rest of it, the things that Deedee couldn't bring herself to consider.

She stepped out the back door, looking into the Hanging Woods, and mulled over her options. Caitlin wouldn't have gone far, not with her injured leg.

The faintest red glow came from the tinfoil-covered windows of the darkroom.

Deedee drew closer and saw the darkroom lock on the ground. From within, she heard a constant, even-toned muttering.

"Caitlin?" she called.

No response.

She opened the door.

Photographs hung from string lines that webbed out all over the shed. Red light cast an unpleasant, eerie glow over everything. The muttering was clearer here; Deedee made out the words ". . . nothing there, I am safe, it's not real, there's nothing there, I am safe . . ." but she couldn't see Caitlin.

A ledge that acted as a workspace ran all around the walls of the shed. It was barely big enough to contain two adults comfortably.

"Caitlin?" Deedee called. She stepped fully into the shed.

A breeze, and the door banged shut.

"Deedee." Movement, down on the ground. Caitlin's small white hands appeared first from the darkness beneath the ledge, and then her blond head, and then they were chest to chest.

"I found a camera, in the wardrobe." Caitlin held out a photo of Deedee, from yesterday, listening to Maureen and Sean joking about how she wasn't good enough. She continued. "But these others are from that summer, the last one."

Deedee stepped back and saw the web of photographs for what they were.

There were faces, yes, but so many of the photos were bodies disembodied. Small limbs, still dimpled at the elbows and knees. Bruised shins and muddied knees. Little girls. There were so many little girls. Or the same little girls, over and over. Her eyes watered; shock or horror or just sadness, overwhelming sadness. There, in the midst of it all, Roisin caught her eye and held it. Her funny, sulky, brave, mean little sister had been caught by this camera lens. That day, whatever day it had been, her wild hair had been smoothed into a ponytail, but wisps of it still flew about her face. There was a breathlessness to the photo, as if she'd just whipped her head around and caught the photographer, but something else too. Sadness, resignation.

Michelle had been telling the truth.

"How?" Deedee wasn't sure if she was asking how Caitlin knew or how the pictures had been taken or how this could have happened. She wasn't sure of anything. The walls felt closer than ever, Caitlin's wide eyes staring up at her.

"The Hanging Woods, you can see them in this one. You *can* see them." This last bit seemed to be directed at an invisible third party.

Indeed, now that she looked beyond the immediate horror of the subjects, Deedee saw the tree-lined border of the clearing.

"Colm?" she asked, even as she knew that it always had been. Colm on the edges of everything, so stealthy that you didn't know he was there till the camera flash.

Colm chopping wood on the old stump in the clearing.

"My mind plays tricks on me. I couldn't remember the roses below my window, and I smell bonfires—see shadows—all the time." Caitlin gestured expansively and sent the strings of images shaking. "But this is real."

As though hearing herself for the first time, Caitlin seized upon the row of negatives, a ballpoint pen in her fist. In a frenzy of activity, she scored deep grooves and scratches into the plastic film surface. Only a few crazed seconds later, the tiny windows of the negative strips were obliterated. Still, Caitlin grabbed scissors and sliced through what was left.

Deedee yanked the door open and stumbled back into the weak sunlight. Inside the Big House, the Branaghs were all safe and cared for while Caitlin struggled to cope with the reality of her past and Deedee threw up into the grass.

Cattle lowed. A car cruised past, a tentative driver slower on the bends than most of the locals would be. Nothing had changed. Everything was different.

From the bottom of the garden, the Hanging Woods watched.

She heard the shed door open and swing shut once more. Caitlin stood next to her, her gaze somewhere out above the trees.

"I want to go away, but I can't think of anywhere."

"I know the feeling," Deedee said. She was beholden to this new, terrible knowledge.

"I was looking forward to finding pictures of me here, part of the family. An honorary Branagh. I thought it would prove that I belonged. I thought anything I found would be just . . . normal. Nice."

"You don't want to be a Branagh," Deedee said.

"He taught me. In there. I just needed developer," Caitlin said.

"All this time, it was Colm?" Deedee asked.

"They'll never believe us." Caitlin addressed that invisible third again. She'd lapsed into a sleepwalker quality. Disassociating. She grabbed Deedee's arm, thin fingers digging in. "Can it unhappen?"

"What happened to Roisin, Caitlin? Where did she go?" Deedee asked, knowing that she would not hear what she wanted to.

"I didn't know you thought she was alive. I'm sorry, Deedee. If I had known . . ."

There was so much coming at her, Deedee felt like she had aged a thousand years.

"I live with Sean. I live with his son," she said. *I nursed the man who murdered my sister.*

"Sean is no good either, you can't trust him. He's . . . Yesterday we slept together," Caitlin said. "I wanted to hurt you, but it doesn't matter anymore, does it?"

"No, it doesn't." Deedee and Sean were over; the reality of that was a hard stone in Deedee's stomach. She knew she should be furious at Caitlin too, but that anger felt very far away and hard to access.

"He killed her?" she asked. "All this time . . . Colm killed her?"

Caitlin seemed to be searching for the words, her eyes wide and desperate, face twisted with dismay and grief.

"I was supposed to meet him, she wasn't supposed to follow, but she did, she wanted to help me, I think, she wanted to tell people . . ."

Deedee couldn't bear to listen to it; she wanted to skip to the end.

"So, she threatened Colm to his face and he killed her," she finished for Caitlin. Saying the words aloud made it feel real, and the reality of it, of what an idiot she'd been, how cruel the Branaghs had been, swept her up.

Caitlin twisted her hands and stammered, but Deedee was already leaving her behind. She'd heard all she needed to.

44

CAITLIN

N o one would have believed me," Caitlin whispered to Deedee's back. Even Deedee, even now, hadn't heard her side of things. After so many years of keeping the truth locked away, it wasn't easy for her to talk about what had happened.

Everything was too much. Deedee stalked back to the Big House, presumably to confront the Branaghs, and then she'd find out the truth—they'd tell her about Caitlin.

Unthinking, unseeing, Caitlin walked toward the Hanging Woods.

Beyond the lurching horror of seeing her own victimization recorded in black and white, there was pain in acknowledging the innocence of her young self. She had subconsciously considered her essential personhood to be separate from her body—an idea that she was always resilient, always strong, without understanding that her particular resilience sprang from having been that child who suffered.

She was twenty-nine, and she was nine, and she was everything she'd ever experienced, and she was tired.

The ground beneath her feet was sloping downward, the surface uneven with roots, and when she looked up, the Hanging Woods were there.

There had been times where Caitlin felt like she had nothing. So many of these times that she had trained herself to think of them as freedom; having nothing meant only being able to gain. She was confident in her ability to survive. Her friendship with Lola was built on that shared sense of capability. Now she had been stripped of her armor.

She wasn't strong and savvy and invulnerable.

She was a victim.

That was how people—women—who had experienced this sort of thing defined themselves. Victim, survivor, what was the difference? The thing you were subjected to, the crime visited upon you, that marked you for life. That became your identity: pitiable or brave, victim or survivor, a binary that left no space for simply being. Her whole life reduced.

There was nothing left of Caitlin.

Her cheeks were flushed despite the freezing temperature. She thought of her mother, beautiful and raving and covered in mud, emerging from the trees. Caitlin knew what Kathleen had been looking for.

Roisin was in there.

The whistling sound of a firework ascending and the boom-crackle of an explosion overhead. A rumbling cheer carried across the flat farm plains. The winter solstice celebration had begun.

It was the darkest day of the year. Caitlin would pass through the trees and enter the world of her nightmares. She knew exactly where to find Roisin, but even if she hadn't, she could hear her now. The rustling up ahead, like childish feet scampering through the undergrowth. A high-pitched giggle floated over to her and she turned toward it.

Caitlin laughed, and the woods swallowed the sound.

I'm coming, Roisin.

She remembered leaving these woods twenty years ago, the sensation of a sob caught in her chest, the feeling of unreality. She felt it all again. Time collapsed and flattened, everything happening at once.

Could she be walking through the woods again at the same time as her child self was running through them? It was like the London Tube, how the walls held the heat of everyone who had passed through the stations; she and Roisin had always been held here too.

The years fell away, or maybe they didn't, but grown-up Caitlin was drawn again down the same path she had taken that day. Roisin would meet her at the clearing and this time they could talk properly.

Roisin had wanted to talk to her.

Roisin had known.

Caitlin had been jealous, understanding only that Roisin seemed to be favored. Suddenly Colm's best girl. It was this thought that she'd comforted herself with: at least Caitlin must be the favorite now, at least this secret was only between Colm and Caitlin.

Roisin had known, though.

She had thought they could team up, find a way together to expose the rot. She had come to understand the weight of secrets. Already she understood that the fractures of Colm's crimes were not the type that could be knitted together easily. Roisin was ready to tell everyone.

It happened, didn't it?

Caitlin whipped her head around, but the voice was in the past. She hadn't understood then that it wasn't her fault; she hadn't understood until maybe this moment.

He did it to you too, didn't he?

Roisin had wanted them to be saved.

Caitlin had wanted them to be spared, for it never to have happened at all.

She hunched into herself. The voice was in the past.

"I can't even sleep anymore," she whispered aloud. Not without protection. Her thoughts snagged on Sean, on what he'd said when she was finally falling asleep.

I was so jealous of him.

Sean knew what his father was.

Full dark now, and Caitlin was surrounded by identical tree trunks. She hadn't been thinking when she went after Roisin back then; she wasn't thinking as she chased her ghost now, either. She was mixed up, she didn't know what was happening. Or she did know now, but she hadn't just a couple of minutes ago. As soon as she could find her way out of the trees, she would go back, gather the photographs, and take them to the guards. She would end this. She turned around to go back the way she'd come and saw the red string tied around the trunk of the tree in front of her.

It must have been there all along, but it also couldn't have been there. She touched it; it was dry and rough and unmistakably hers, from her exploration. It should have decayed after years of exposure out in the Hanging Woods, yet here it was. She traced it around the trunk until she found the loose tail. Then she picked it and followed it. She knew it wasn't real, but now she also knew where she was going.

45

DEEDEE

Maureen was standing in front of the open fridge when Deedee entered the kitchen from the back door.

"Will you have a sandwich, Dee?" she asked.

"No thank you," Deedee said, as though everything was normal. As though she hadn't seen proof that Colm had been abusing children, including her own sister; as though she didn't know now that Roisin was never coming back.

The front door opened and Sean called out "Hello!" from the hallway. He was flushed, and as he entered the kitchen, he waved both of his hands through his brown hair, mussing it.

"Wild windy out there!" he said.

He was lying. How often had he been unfaithful? As often as Deedee had been? What had been the point of any of it?

"Good weather for drying!" Maureen chirped.

Deedee had always just listened to what these people said without questioning them. If Sean and Maureen said it was pouring, she'd put up an umbrella without needing to feel a drop of rain herself.

"Good tutoring session?" she asked Sean. Lucy Kearney; at least she was over eighteen.

"Frustrating." He pulled her into a hug. He smelled clean, soapy. "Kid needs a lot of help. Almost pulled my hair out!"

Deedee pasted on a smile. Sean dropped into his chair at the table and picked up his crossword.

"But now, my true calling. Dee, do you know Shackleton's final trip?" He pointed the pen toward her as though it were a microphone.

"No one knows. Look it up, for God's sake." Maureen spoke without turning toward him.

"Antarctic," Deedee replied. This, she would miss. These moments where they could orbit each other without having to see one another. Comfortable familiarity, taken for granted.

"No," Sean groaned. "That's what Caitlin said too. It's South something. Unless the others are wrong . . . Hang on."

"I was wanting to talk to you." Deedee picked up a tea towel and plucked a damp mug from the draining board.

"Careful now, don't want that smashed," Maureen cautioned. Deedee had once, fifteen years ago, dropped a cup.

A lifetime with these people, who she had always thought to be good people. Fine people. The best of us.

Whatever happened next, she knew she had to keep her cool. Though she was still unsteady and queasy after the horrific images from the darkroom, Roisin needed her. She remembered their fight on the day Roisin had disappeared; how she had thrown her sister out and set everything in motion. She couldn't let her down again.

"Let's reopen the darkroom instead of getting rid of it," she said. "It might help Colm to work in there." She watched Maureen and Sean carefully for their reactions. She hoped they didn't notice the quaver in her voice or the tremble in her legs.

"Now, to tell you the truth, I don't know that he'll ever be going back out there," Maureen said.

"Ah, you never know, there might be life in the old feller yet." Sean grinned, teasing his mother. "Or maybe I'll get into it, pick up the hobby. Save me the job of tearing the place down."

"Sean." Maureen spoke sharply. "Stop playing the maggot."

"Why not, Maureen?" Deedee asked. "Why not open it again?" Her mouth was dry, her tongue thick and heavy in it; she wanted to run.

"It's all digital anyway these days," Maureen said.

"What was his favorite thing to photograph?" Deedee asked.

Mother and son exchanged a look, the briefest, tiniest flash of worry passing between them.

"Where's all this coming from?" Sean asked.

And with that, Deedee knew that they had been aware of it all, all along.

46

CAITLIN

The Hanging Woods had fallen silent at some point, perhaps hours ago. Caitlin felt she'd been walking forever; she was thirsty and tired, pulling ever more heavily against the string to guide her along. It couldn't actually have been hours, though the darkness down here made it impossible to tell.

"Out here," she corrected herself aloud. "Not down here." There was no down; she wasn't even far from the houses, yet she felt cut off from society.

And so tired.

Every sleepless night she'd ever had weighed on her.

By the time the string ran out and she emerged into the clearing, an impossible summer sun hung high in the sky over her head.

She held her breath.

Nothing moved.

It was warm, she realized. She wasn't cold at all.

First sign of hypothermia, she thought. But she was lying to herself.

She had slipped out of the winter of 2019 and into the summer of 1999. She had moved through time, or time had moved through her, and she was back here on the day of Roisin's disappearance. The string that shouldn't have existed had taken her here.

The old stump waited at the center of the clearing.

The crashing sound of Roisin making her way to the clearing from the other side. They would meet in the middle.

Caitlin reached for her phone and wasn't surprised to find a large rock in her pocket instead. It wasn't yet smudged with Roisin's blood.

A breeze rustled the leaves, like a relieved exhalation.

"We were kids," she addressed the clearing. "I don't know if this is real, but I was just a kid, and so were you. I didn't think . . ." She paused. What hadn't she thought? "I didn't think kids could hurt each other like that—or be hurt like that. I didn't know it would be real, would be forever. But it has been forever."

On this spot, twenty years ago, Roisin had come to find Caitlin. She had looked excited, as though she had some wonderful news to share.

"We need to talk to Maureen," she had said.

"She'll be mad," Caitlin had replied.

"We can just be friends together." Doubt flickered across Roisin's face. Caitlin had not reacted as she expected.

"He doesn't even like you!" Caitlin spat.

Roisin took a step back. "I'm going to tell her anyway."

In the present, Caitlin remembered the feelings: betrayal, spite, anger, grief. The hugeness of it all, so much feeling and nothing she could do.

She had felt like nothing, like she didn't matter to anyone. She wasn't enough for her mother, and she hadn't been enough for Colm. No one was just hers.

Roisin had wanted Caitlin to come with her and tell on Colm because she thought they were alike, but she was wrong. Roisin would have Deedee when everything came crashing down. She was mean sometimes, but she was still Roisin's sister. And she would have her granny. Caitlin had nothing. Her mother would know it had been her fault; she would understand the shame that Caitlin felt, the guilt and the fear. Her mother had Michael now too; she could start a new family.

Caitlin didn't want to be alone.

Standing in the clearing, under that unreal summer sun, Caitlin considered not only how Roisin might have grown up, but how she herself might have grown up if this hadn't happened. Colm's abuse had interrupted her life, impeded her development; the secrecy and shame of it had warped her soul.

But twenty years ago, Caitlin had waited for Roisin to turn her back. What Roisin planned would impact both of them, and Caitlin didn't have a say in it. Just like how her mother had planned their move to London and Caitlin hadn't had a say in that either.

She was tired of feeling powerless.

A push first. She hadn't pushed that hard, but the old stump was behind Roisin, tripping her so that she sprawled on the ground, winded.

"I'm sorry!" Caitlin had rushed to her. The push hadn't felt good, like she had imagined it would.

"You won't stop me," Roisin had said, "and you're not my friend anymore!"

It was that final declaration that had driven Caitlin to pick up the rock and bring it down right in the center of Roisin's forehead.

Blood everywhere, so much blood, running into Roisin's eyes, which were still open.

It was the worst thing Caitlin had ever done, and it couldn't be undone.

Twenty years ago, Caitlin had run from the clearing to tell her mother that she'd done something awful, except Kathleen hadn't been there. She'd found Maureen instead, so she'd sent her to Roisin while she hunted for her mother.

Maureen had told Kathleen it wasn't Caitlin's fault, not really, and together the women had covered it up.

In the center of the clearing, beside the scarred old tree stump, Caitlin dug. That huge, unreal sun was gone, and her skin froze even as she sweated over her labor. The hole grew larger and deeper until it began to swallow her up, and she welcomed it, welcomed the idea that she would end up down here with Roisin.

Except . . .

Roisin wasn't there.

Caitlin sat back on her heels, exhausted.

There was nothing but roots and stones and insects. No bones. Nothing that suggested anyone had ever been there.

No bones. No Roisin.

Her hands were hot with pain, swollen, one nail ripped off entirely and the others cracked and broken.

Roisin was gone.

47

DEEDEE

Stupid, oblivious Deedee, that was who she was to these people, who they expected to see in front of them.

"Caitlin mentioned that she still had that old photography book youse gave her. *A Kid's Guide to Photography* or something?"

"Yeah?" Sean said. Deedee had his attention.

"Thought it was the kind of thing that even I might be able to pick up, with a handbook designed for little kids." Deedee laughed. "The words won't be too hard in it!"

Sean and Maureen laughed. Deedee heard the spiteful edge.

Maureen put her arm around Deedee's waist and pulled her into a side hug. "Ah, now, don't be silly!"

"I dunno if there's a simpler book out there," Sean said, pulling the thread of Deedee's joke. He was playing along, but he really thought it; they were both laughing at her and her stupidity all the time. As they made her help ferry Colm to his appointments, as she fed the monster who had murdered her sister the medicine that kept him alive.

Roisin was gone, but Deedee was trapped.

"You do come out with some ideas, Dee." Maureen patted her fondly on the arm.

"I'll take down the shed today," Sean said.

"Perfect." Maureen smiled at him, and there was only warning in it.

"I'd better go," Deedee said. Both Sean and Maureen looked at her too intently.

"You've to have these sandwiches now I've made them," Maureen declared, bringing plates to the table.

"There's no rush, is there?" Sean asked.

"Frank gets lonely," Deedee said.

"I'll come with you," Sean said. "Check in on the poor old creature."

The pictures were still hanging up in the darkroom, incontrovertible evidence of Colm's crimes. She needed to get them before Sean or Maureen did.

"I didn't find Caitlin," she said. "Reckon she might have gone visiting? Or gotten lost. She doesn't know town so well these days."

Go find her, Deedee silently willed them. *Go far away, into town, leave me here.*

"Ach, she can be a bit much." Sean's lip curled in disgust. "Hanging around."

"I thought you got on really well." Deedee felt calmer than she'd felt in years. There was no point tipping her hand. *Florian,* she reminded herself. *I'm not the fool here. I'm no angel myself.*

"Well, you know . . ." Sean trailed off, shrugging. "I don't want to embarrass her, but she does hang off me a bit, doesn't she? I don't want her getting the wrong idea."

Deedee blinked at the tacit confirmation that Caitlin had told her the truth and Sean was laying the groundwork to tell Deedee that the other woman was a liar.

"What maths were you doing with Lucy Kearney?" she asked suddenly.

Sean paused, caught off guard. "Oh, nothing you'd understand."

Deedee forced herself to laugh along with him and Maureen.

"No, really. Because Florian, at the station, he's got a nephew. Same age as Lucy. Says he needs some help; will I pass your number on?"

"I'm not exactly swimming in free time . . ."

"No need to tell me that. I haven't seen much of you at all, but you've found the time to tutor Lucy."

"I'm only saying."

Deedee felt herself cracking. She didn't have the capacity to hold everything she was feeling. All the frustration and powerlessness, the waste of her years, the loss of this only family she'd ever really had.

She had to do something drastic.

"I'll just look in on Colm, say goodbye for now," she said. A normal enough occurrence.

She heard them muttering the moment she left. If they knew it existed, they would destroy the evidence as soon as possible. She couldn't let them.

Colm was asleep when she entered, but he stirred as she closed the door behind her. She crossed toward him quickly, her eyes scanning the monitors by his bed. Heart rate, oxygen levels; he was already so fragile.

"Colm." She spoke softly, and his eyelids fluttered as though he was coming round from a deep sleep. "What have you done?"

His eyes were the same watery blue they'd always been. His medicine bag sat on his bedside table. She'd never bothered with it before; Maureen usually kept it close at hand, "in case of emergencies," she'd say. Now Deedee wondered if there was something she could give him to make him seem unwell without endangering him. Still, she worried for his health, a hard habit to break. Not everything in there looked to be prescription, and there were a lot of sedatives. She frowned as she rifled through boxes and loose blister packs of tablets, small canisters of pills with American brand names.

"Where'd she even get this stuff?" she wondered aloud. She pictured Maureen on her iPad, ordering drugs online from abroad.

"Deedee." Colm stirred at the sound of her voice. "Good girl."

"Colm, do you remember the summer Roisin disappeared?" Deedee wanted him to make this go away, make everything OK. The sedatives she could deal with later.

He closed his eyes and turned his head away.

"No, no, stay here with me now." Deedee gently shook his shoulder and he rolled his head back to look at her. "I just need you to tell me that you don't know anything about what happened. To her."

"No one knew," Colm said, his voice weak and whispery.

"Listen, there are photographs, you understand? Your photographs." Deedee bit her nail as she watched for his reaction. "Do you know anything about any photographs, any . . ." There was no word she could think of; she didn't want to use the accurate terms, like "molestation" or "sexual assault," so she landed at ". . . carrying on?"

"Destroy them." Colm looked alert now. "No photos."

"Why, if there's nothing to hide?"

"Long ago." He looked relieved. "Over now."

"What was long ago? What's over now?" Deedee wondered how long it would be before Sean came in.

"I shouldn't have." Colm's eyes were sharp even as he turned the corners of his mouth down in contrition. "Maureen keeps me here. I'm . . . paying."

"That's a confession," Deedee whispered. "Maureen looks after you, Colm. What do you mean, she keeps you here?"

"Old man now, harmless." Colm's sorrowful act faded. "She keeps me weak. Tired. Doesn't trust me."

The bag full of sedatives. Maureen was Colm's jailer.

"Did Doyle know?" Deedee asked.

Colm smiled at her.

"Dee!" Sean called out.

"Did you kill Roisin? Did you kill her as well?"

Colm shook his head.

"Is that a no to killing her? No to killing her but yes to the photos, to the . . . the rest of it?"

He held her eye and nodded. An air of challenge to him.

"No."

She wanted to believe him, to spare herself this one extra betrayal.

It would be easier. The pain of having cared for him all this time was unbearable enough, but what if she could rationalize it? Could she see him as a flawed man, think of all the good he'd done in the community, regard him the same way Maureen and Sean did? Would it be forgiveness or turning a blind eye?

"I'm just an old man."

There was that smile again playing over his lips. There was a mischievous glint in his eye. His finger was poised over the call button at his bedside, the one that would summon an ambulance.

She wanted to believe him, but she couldn't.

She slapped his hand away from the button and he gasped in surprise.

"I'm going to kill you." She moved in close to his face. To let him live, to smooth things over was impossible. "I'm going to watch you die."

White-hot rage blocked her vision, every muscle in her body tensed, ready to pounce. He had decided that his life was worth more than Roisin's in his entitlement to her body and in his obstruction of justice, how he had never confessed. He had only stopped victimizing young girls because he physically couldn't.

"Now you're helpless; you're the one who can't fight back, aren't you? I'm going to smash every bone in your body." Deedee punctuated her words with pokes to his chest.

The machines attached to Colm whirred louder, faster, lines spiking up and down.

"Then I'm going to tell every motherfucker in this town that Michelle Quinn was right. Caitlin is going to testify, and everyone will know that Colm Branagh was a disgusting, child-abusing, child-murdering rapist and he was undone by his own sick, fucked-up pictures."

Colm gasped, his body starting to seize and twitch.

"The best bit is that you taught her how to develop all the evidence we need."

A tiny white speck appeared on his lip, and then another, and then he was frothing at the mouth, his eyes bloodshot and rolled back in his head.

The machines beeped loudly, and Deedee heard the chairs scraping back in the kitchen. She stuffed the medicine bag under her jumper before Maureen ran in.

"He's having a heart attack!" Maureen screamed.

"Da!" Sean fell at his side and cast about for the bag. "Where's his medicine?"

Deedee left the room as they searched, the sounds of Colm's machines blaring.

48

CAITLIN

It didn't matter if she couldn't find Roisin—it only meant that Kathleen had already been there. As an adult, Caitlin found a new sense of horror at how Kathleen must have suffered for helping to cover up what she had done. Digging a child's grave and then having to find its exact location twenty years later, facing the guilt she had lived with. No wonder she drank.

Caitlin thought of that gasping phone call again. Maybe that was what Kathleen had wanted to tell her so desperately: that she had found Roisin again, and moved her to keep Caitlin safe now that the woods were being dug up for the development. Though it was unlikely to be a conversation Kathleen had wanted to have in a pub.

Caitlin was so tired. And hungry. A lifetime of running from the past, starving her body in punishment for what Colm had done.

The hole she had dug looked just about the right size and depth. Experimentally she curled up in it, and the smell of earth filled her senses as her body absorbed the cold and the damp of it. It would do. They could just cut her down from the tree and cover her over when they found her.

With some effort, she roused her weary bones from the ground and unbuckled her belt. It slid out of its loops with a soothing shush of a sound. She had plenty of branches to choose from.

Wasn't this the Hanging Woods after all?

49

DEEDEE

Adrenaline surged through Deedee as she ran back out through the kitchen. She had already set in motion events that could never be undone, and every vision of the future she'd had until now was over.

Colm had killed Roisin, and now Deedee had killed Colm.

She needed proof, witnesses. Caitlin had disappeared, but around here there was nowhere to go but into the Hanging Woods.

Deedee dived into the darkroom before she had a chance to back out of it. The pictures fluttered in the wind she created, the sound of wings beating against glass. She grabbed picture after picture. Her hands filled with the skin, flesh, faces he had corrupted, lives destroyed.

How was it possible that the man who had been nothing but good to her could be so cruel to others?

She remembered her first time with Sean. The trapped heat of a summer's day, the sweetness of them both shedding their inhibitions in the joy of discovering one another, both teenagers together, and dizzy with the new sensations they'd encountered. There were thousands more tragedies in what those girls had gone through, Deedee was sure, but this was the first thing she thought of. There had been purity to her own experience, the realization that the shame and guilt she had been primed to expect on the heels of the occasion had never arrived, would never arrive.

Except Sean had known even then what Colm was.

She left the darkroom and ran down to the Hanging Woods.

Across the fields, at the solstice celebration, the band started up with an old classic. She had to strain to make it out, but the notes that the wind brought her were familiar: "Great Balls of Fire." Jo would be there. Deedee couldn't go to Doyle, but could she go to Jo? Was there a statute of limitations? It was the sort of thing she should have known, but while she could recite all sorts of citations for littering or speeding, this kind of thing was quite literally well above her pay grade. She pulled out her phone and texted Jo.

I found out something important about my sister's disappearance.

She stumbled over a tree root and Colm's medication fell out of her jumper. She kicked it into a hole that could have been an animal's burrow.

"Caitlin!" she called.

Everyone thought Deedee was a bad cop. She had no nose for it, she was terminally incurious. She didn't really care about law and order; she just wanted to fit in somewhere, be accepted and respected. She *knew* she was a bad cop.

But Doyle was a great cop.

Doyle was renowned. He was such a good cop, he was the top cop. Head of the station, head of the area.

The photographs bundled in her arms, she made her way deeper into the woods.

"What would Doyle do?" she muttered to herself. The thought had a calming effect. "What *did* Doyle do?"

Doyle covered it all up. Deedee could lose a suspect, absolutely. Probably not long after finding him in the first place. Doyle, on the other hand, he didn't get to where he was by misfiling papers, or losing his suspects. Doyle found a decoy to muddy the waters.

"Caitlin!" Deedee tried again.

Michelle said her dad had run Colm over as revenge for what he'd done, so was Doyle also party to covering up an attempted murder? The practicalities of it, it was a lot.

"Caitlin!" She pushed through branches and came upon a clearing, with a long, shallow trench of a hole dug into the center of it.

The skull, the map, this clearing.

The final piece of Roisin's puzzle clicked into place.

She heard the rustling of a heavy object traveling downward through a tree, branches snapping as it went, then a human gasp as the object came to an abrupt stop.

Across the clearing, about ten feet away from her, she saw a small figure hanging from a tree, gently swaying though there was no wind.

50

CAITLIN

Dying should have felt like slipping under the waves. It should have felt like floating, like being borne aloft on feather cushions. This was why her mother had loved the sea, Caitlin realized. The proximity to being washed away; cleansed and disappeared.

Dying felt like fear and lost control. Caitlin's mind might have felt ready to go, but her body fought. As soon as the leather belt bit into her throat, her hands flew to her neck and her legs thrashed to find some way down from here.

It wasn't as simple as realizing that all her problems were solvable, that she needed only to have a little more faith that this too would pass. It was just the ancient, animal will to survive at any costs, the same thing that had animated her for so long.

Her vision blurred.

She smelled the bonfire smell once more.

She heard sirens wailing far away.

The shadow appeared in the center of her vision. *For the last time.* It was coming directly for her and there was nowhere left to hide. She watched it get bigger and bigger while sparks flew and the belt crushed the life from her, and then the pressure eased.

Someone was holding her legs. Someone was speaking, but it was as though she was underwater, the desperate pounding of her heart and last rasps of breath blocking everything out.

Fingers scrabbling at her neck.

Too late, too late, she thought, slipping down, down, down into unconsciousness.

51

CAITLIN

BANNAKILDUFF

SUMMER 1999

The car smells of hot plastic, even with the windows all the way down, and the seat is scratchy against her bare legs, but Caitlin doesn't mind. Her mother is sitting in the front seat, happy and laughing and singing along to the radio. Her mother's hair has blown around, a bit of it stuck to her lipstick, the sort of thing that would usually make her really, really mad, but today she just keeps laughing. Michael sneaks glances at her. Every time he does, it's like just looking at her makes him happy.

"What do you want to do at the beach, Caity?" he asks. In the mirror, his eyes are smiling.

The question stumps her. Her mother loves the beach; she likes to sit on the sand and watch the waves lapping against the shore. Caitlin likes paddling, digging holes, and eating ice creams as quick as she can before they melt and run all over her fingers. None of those activities are very ladylike, though.

"See the sea." She settles on something close to what her mother will say and therefore correct.

"Only looking at the sea, is it?" Michael probes. "Not even dipping a toe in?"

"Well . . . maybe a toe." Caitlin doesn't want to seem unreasonable. "But only one!"

"Only one?" Michael sounds very serious, like he's going to be tested on this information later. Caitlin respects it.

"That's the rule."

"Which toe would that be, now? Would it be the littlest one?"

"Yes. Only the tiniest, littlest toe. Anything else is not"—she shakes a finger—"ladylike!"

Michael laughs. "Might I put two toes in then if I'm not a lady?"

"Oh yes, *you* could put both your feet in and walk out, out, out until the water is as deep as your head!" Caitlin feels like there are springs in her bottom; she is boing-boing bouncing up and down on the seat. Michael is so silly, and he plays along so well with her games and jokes. "Deeper than your head!"

"I had better not catch you up to your head in the water, Caitlin Margaret Doherty," her mother warns. "You're not to get this car all wet, you understand?"

The springs fall away. Caitlin slumps back in her seat.

"I wasn't talking about *me*," she grumbles. But her mother heard beyond the words she said to the secret wish she was making.

"Ah, what did you put her in her swimmers for if not to go in the sea?" Michael asks her mother in a quiet voice. "She'll dry, like."

Tense silence, the radio suddenly too loud, the wind in the car suddenly too chilly.

Caitlin stares out of the window. She cannot, under any circumstances, be seen to gang up on her mother with Michael. The whole day is at risk if her mother feels she is being ganged up on.

"Oh, all right then." Her mother gives in. "You can go in, but be careful."

Caitlin nods as hard as she can, so hard that her whole brain might be sliding up and down inside her skull. "Thank you, thank you. You're the nicest, kindest, bestest mother in the world!"

Her mother rolls her eyes and tuts, but she is only playing at being embarrassed. She loves it when she gets compliments.

The rest of the journey is smooth, and quick. "Girls Just Want to Have Fun" comes on, and Michael turns the radio up loud enough to scare the birds from the trees and they all three yell along at the top of their lungs until they are hoarse and panting. They park easily, in a space right near the beach, and Michael produces a shiny red-and-yellow bucket and spade from the boot.

"You'll spoil her," her mother mutters. Louder, she says, "That's a bit too young for her."

Privately, Caitlin agrees. She is, effectively, too old for buckets and spades. But a gift is a gift, and having them makes it all feel more special. No, not special. More ordinary. She skips down the beach, and she loves the feeling of the bucket swinging in time with her steps. Michael and her mother are holding hands and walking more slowly behind her, but she knows they are watching her.

It is so good to be watched over, to be thought of. To be loved.

Though it's a nice enough day, there are few people on the sand, so Caitlin practices her cartwheels. She can chain them together, one after another after another, until she collapses, dizzy, on the sand. She digs down until she hits water, until her hole is big enough to swallow her up to the waist, and then she makes a ring of sandcastles all around her, to protect her. She runs into the sea, and it's so cold that she runs right back out again, making her teeth chatter madly and rubbing her arms as though she is at the North Pole, and she is so funny that her mother and Michael clutch each other as they laugh.

They eat cheese sandwiches and crisps on a picnic blanket for lunch, and Caitlin is positive that she eats more sand than anything else, but she doesn't mind one bit. Michael buys them ice creams and her mother even lets her get strawberry syrup on top!

They drive back eventually, and the car is quieter. Caitlin rests her head on the window and closes her eyes.

"Thank you," her mother whispers.

"Is she asleep?" asks Michael.

"Tired out. Thank you, it means a lot."

"It's nothing. Thanks for having me."

"I'm glad that you're here."

"Let's not talk about it."

"I don't want to talk about it. I'm only saying that it's nice. You being here. It being over."

"Kath, it's not over." Michael's voice is tired but gentle.

"She's been accepted," her mother says.

There's quiet for a moment. Caitlin is heavy with sleep, but she feels the incompleteness of the conversation, strains to stay awake.

Finally, Michael speaks.

"He won't stop."

Caitlin can fight it no more; she falls asleep in the back seat.

52

DEEDEE

The photographs fell from her hands and carpeted the clearing as she grabbed Caitlin.

She weighed more than Deedee had expected, and she had looped a thick leather belt around her neck, too thick to simply snap. Deedee held her waist, trying to create slack in the line that held her to the branch. It wouldn't be enough to save her. She pulled at the belt buckle, stuck fast into the leather and squeezing the life out of Caitlin.

Deedee cried out in frustration. She needed at least one arm to hold Caitlin up, but she couldn't undo the buckle with only her spare hand. The wind fluttered the edges of the photographs, threatening to blow the evidence away.

An ambulance wailed its way toward them, heading for Colm. Sean would have the darkroom and any other negatives destroyed unless she got back right now. Deedee could make the case without Caitlin; she had enough evidence of Colm's crimes against the girls that she could get the story out.

She didn't need Caitlin alive.

I have to choose, she thought suddenly.

Roisin or Caitlin; past or future.

Caitlin, who had slept with Sean, stolen from anyone she came across, done all she could to sow the seeds of discord and chaos everywhere she went. Caitlin, who had been victimized herself and then taken away from the only home she'd ever known, punished for being a victim. Even Kathleen had left her alone in England.

She couldn't do that. Deedee was not the kind of person to walk away, not if it was in her power to help.

She pushed herself up onto her toes, reached above Caitlin's head and pulled the belt taut. The bough bent just slightly, while slack remained in the belt. Stretching her arm like this stretched the skin, reopening the wound on her wrist and sending hot blood flowing down her sleeve. She screamed, then wrapped the belt around her fingers, making sure that a loose loop remained near Caitlin's neck. Caitlin's eyes were closed, her breath rasping quieter now. Deedee couldn't tell if that was a good sign. She leaned her weight into those trapped fingers, feeling the bending of the bough just slightly, and then more and more.

The sounds of the winter solstice celebration; crackling bonfires, laughing children, all of it a thousand years away from her as she yanked and tugged on the bough. Her fingers cracking and knuckles twisting. Her upper arm screamed at her and her shoulders burned with the weight on them.

One final tug, and then they were falling to the ground, Caitlin and Deedee, the bough still attached to Deedee by her fingers.

She rolled her shoulders, trying to get her body back into place. She slid her fingers—now white and withered at the tips—out of the leather and used her other hand and thumb to undo the belt buckle around Caitlin's neck.

Caitlin was still, her face pale and her lips blue. Deedee pried her eyes open and saw they were bloodshot, lifeless.

The rain began. Fat drops of it falling onto both of them and the photographs. Deedee looked at the photos again. Something was wrong with them. Several of them were now blank, only the vaguest impressions of an image still in evidence on them. Those impressions were quickly blurring under the rain.

She had done it again. She'd ruined another investigation and she hadn't even saved the victim. She'd just ensured that Colm would go free and Roisin's murderer—for she was sure now that Colm had murdered Roisin—would never face justice.

The photographs had faded away to nothing, and Caitlin was dying in her arms.

53

CAITLIN

Icy raindrops landed on her skin as the pressure around her neck was released, but Caitlin felt far away. She had the sense that she was missing something crucial, but she couldn't think what it could be. She was so tired, but something was nagging at her. A stinging slap brought her back into her body.

"Caitlin!" Deedee's face filled her view. "What were you thinking?" Deedee slapped her again, and it felt less medicinal in nature.

Caitlin struggled to sit up. Leaves rustled beneath her. Deedee was running all over the clearing, picking up scattered photographs.

"They're blank." She tried to speak, but succeeded only in moving her mouth. She coughed, and tried once more, with more success.

"I don't know what happened," Deedee said.

"Was it real?" Caitlin croaked. A lightheaded feeling swept over her and she lay back down.

Deedee slapped her again. "Yes."

Caitlin touched her cheek. It radiated heat.

"I can't believe you did that," Deedee said. "Hanging yourself at a time like this."

Caitlin had developed the photographs as he had taught her to but in the frenzy of developing, she'd been skipping steps, hadn't she, rushing to get past the horrors.

"Fixer," she gasped.

"What?"

Without fixer, the photos fog up. Speaking was too hard, so she settled for "Forgot . . . a step."

"Why did you do that to the negatives, scribble on them?" Deedee wailed.

"No copies." Caitlin tried to shake her head and felt her neck protest.

As long as they existed, I would never have been safe. I would have been trapped in there forever, hurt and alone.

"There's nothing left to prove it?" Deedee buried her face in her hands.

Caitlin's mind felt quiet for the first time in years. Deedee had searched for her, found her, rescued her.

Roisin's voice in her mind: *We can just be friends together.*

"Sorry."

"It's not your fault. I panicked." Deedee was brusque, but Caitlin recognized shame in that tone. Embarrassment for how she had treated Caitlin, now that she knew.

Caitlin listened hard but no other voices appeared to drown out Deedee's answers. She looked around. It was just them in the clearing.

There was one thing she could do for Deedee. Roisin wasn't in the clearing, but Sean had said that Kathleen had been searching in there before her death. Kathleen must have moved Roisin, worried about the developers finding her and linking her to Caitlin.

If Kathleen had moved her, where would she have put her?

"I think I know where Roisin is," she croaked.

54

DEEDEE

Her phone began to buzz as soon as she left the woods, but Deedee ignored it. Next to her, Caitlin's breath was still labored. *She must have done something to her windpipe,* Deedee thought, then: *God, that's an annoying sound.* She cast a guilty look at Caitlin, embarrassed that even after the afternoon they'd had, she hadn't evolved past finding things that Caitlin couldn't control irritating.

"I saw the CCTV in O'Shea's." Caitlin's voice was a rasping whisper. "You?" She indicated the gatehouse ahead of them.

"Yes," Deedee said. They had gone beyond lying to one another. "I took her home after. I hadn't meant to hit her. She got her own back, though, she knocked me in the face and gave me a nosebleed."

"She was OK?" Three words in a row were an effort.

Deedee spoke carefully. "There was no lump, no bruise on her head. But there was this."

She held out the phone.

"It's Kathleen's. I thought there might be something on it, something that would link you to Roisin's death. I thought maybe you . . ." She couldn't finish the sentence. It seemed too ridiculous and too unfair. How could she have blamed Caitlin for Roisin's death?

Caitlin took the phone and began scrolling.

"I've checked, there are no confessions or anything," Deedee said.

Caitlin turned the screen toward her, showing her the photos of the Hanging Woods that Deedee had pored over. This time she looked closer. Most of the earth in the clearing had been turned over. The other pictures showed similar: everywhere the men had been removing trees, someone had been digging into the earth.

"Searched," Caitlin said. "Must've found her."

She opened the gatehouse door. It was dark enough inside to need to turn on the light, and the bulb buzzed over their heads. Heavy, sweet, plum-scented perfume still hung in the air.

Deedee coughed, and Caitlin rounded on her. Her face was full of wonder; she looked like a child again. It made Deedee's heart ache.

"The perfume? It's intense."

"She's here." Caitlin turned, taking in the empty room.

Deedee was skeptical and opened her mouth to say as much. But then what was the harm? Let Caitlin feel close to her mother.

Caitlin entered the living room to the left, so Deedee opened the closed door on the right. It was Kathleen's bedroom. In the dressing table drawers, she found papers, notebooks. Bundles and bundles of pages wedged so tightly within that the drawers barely opened. She slid a page free.

I remember the first time we met, with the peaches all over the floor. I felt so overwhelmed. It was like every peach was something I had done wrong: no education, a daughter with no father, an ex who threatened to kill me if I kept her, a mother who never spoke to me after I left, on and on. No future. And then, one by one, you helped me pick them up.

She turned the page over with a frown; it was densely packed with writing, but there was no name on it. She had no idea who it was addressed to. She put it down and slid the next one out.

I saw you today. I haven't aged as well as you. Women never do. I wanted to say something, but you slipped away before I could.

She flipped through the rest of the pile. Phrases leapt out at her: *I hoped you could forgive me,* and *I wasn't the only one who did wrong.* Kathleen had been heartbroken over someone.

She kept digging through fragments of thoughts and half-conversations until she pulled out a large book titled *Alcoholics Anonymous: The Big Book*. The title echoed with her last conversation with Kathleen. *I've got the big book*, she had said. She had finally realized she had a problem. Tucked inside the cover was a list:

WAYS TO MAKE AMENDS:
1. Fix relationship with Caitlin
2. Find the child
3. Deirdre

The problem with going through other people's things was that they often made sense only to the person who owned them. But this, *Find the child*: Caitlin was right, Kathleen had been looking for Roisin.

"Caitlin?" Deedee called out. "Does any of this make sense to you?" She handed Caitlin the notes as she entered.

"Yes," Caitlin said, flicking through them. "Michael."

"Michael who?"

"Doyle."

"Kathleen went out with Doyle? Like Superintendent Michael Doyle who investigated?"

"They argued about it." Caitlin gathered the papers into a neat pile. She gestured drinking from a glass.

Deedee led them back toward the kitchen.

"It doesn't make sense. Anything in the living room?"

"Bottles." Caitlin winced. "Newspaper articles. You, Michael, the guards."

"She was keeping track of us." Deedee felt shame that she had never thought of looking in on Kathleen. "Would she have asked him to cover this up?"

"Bleeding." Caitlin indicated Deedee's arm.

Deedee had the feeling that Caitlin was evading her, but her palm had filled with the blood that now ribboned around her forearm as she lifted it.

"This burn, I must have knocked it." She hurried to the sink. Drops of blood trailed after her.

"Looks bad." Caitlin handed her a tea towel.

Lightheaded, Deedee held her wrist under the tap, and felt panic set in. That intense perfume smell was making her head pound. She wrapped the towel around her wet arm and held it over her head. Caitlin sipped water. She looked as bad as Deedee felt. In the quiet of the kitchen, this felt companionable.

A sudden commotion in the living room. Caitlin and Deedee glanced at each other as the sounds of rustling and banging echoed down the hall toward them.

"Did someone come in?" It wasn't possible.

Caitlin moved toward the noise as though pulled on a string.

"Caitlin." Deedee wanted to warn her, but how could she, without knowing the threat? Instead, she followed, drawing level with her.

They would face this together.

As they approached the living room, a black shadow darted out of it at head height, and they screamed and ducked. A very stressed crow careened into the kitchen, while several others squawked in confusion as they flew around the room.

"Chimney," Caitlin said. Her voice was still weak and croaky, but improving.

"Open the windows and doors, get the birds out!" Deedee instructed her.

A bundle lay in the fireplace, dislodged by the crows. Deedee knelt beside it. The bundle was blackened with soot, and with a sudden awful sense of realization, she remembered building the fire that night.

The gatehouse had been freezing cold because Kathleen wasn't able to use the fireplace, and she hadn't asked Sean to fix it because she didn't want him finding whatever she had hidden in here.

Though she had intended to help Kathleen by setting the fire and closing the faulty window on her way out, Deedee had instead trapped her in a cottage that would have slowly filled with carbon monoxide. If the coroner found that Kathleen had suffocated, Deedee would know that she was responsible.

Why hadn't Kathleen warned her?

Because Kathleen had been asleep, *Pretty in Pink* still playing on her TV. Deedee hadn't consulted her, had just gone ahead and lit the fire, closed the window, sentenced Kathleen to death.

Behind her, Caitlin shuffled around, shooing crows out of the window and the front door. Deedee turned her attention to the bundle.

What had Kathleen needed to hide so badly?

The bundle was something wrapped up in a blanket. Stiff items inside shifted as she lifted it. *Some kind of doll,* Deedee thought. There was a pattern on the blanket, a repeated motif of small pink and purple hearts on a background that had been light once. It was familiar, but she couldn't quite place it. Dried mud flaked all over her hands.

The blanket was folded so that the corners were tucked over each other. She peeled it back layer by layer, until the contents were revealed.

A doll, she thought again, looking at the smooth, round shape she had uncovered. *How weird.*

The last crow was ushered out. Deedee heard the window close and Caitlin approach, watching over her shoulder.

She raised the ball close to her eyes and felt a long, thin piece of it remain behind on her lap. It was like a delicate shell. Up close she could see the details: shallow craters and ridges curving across an organic surface.

She looked down at the piece that had detached.

Teeth. Four little incisors on a short jawbone. This was the detail that forced her brain to resolve the delicate round shell into the pitted curve of a skull. Unmistakably human, and horribly small, too small for an adult, so small that it could only be a child.

After the discovery in the darkroom, she couldn't imagine finding anything worse or more horrifying. Her hands shook and vomit rose in her throat as she cradled the bones. After all these years, she had found her sister.

55

CAITLIN

Caitlin realized what Deedee had discovered half a second before Deedee did. Not enough time to save her the horror of understanding what she was holding. They both froze, and long seconds passed.

"I'm sorry," Caitlin whispered.

Deedee lifted her head. Her face was a mask of pain. She cradled the bones, tracing the lines on the skull with her fingertips.

"I let you think it was Colm," Caitlin said. "But she followed me, we argued. I pushed her."

"You?" Though Deedee had known Caitlin was involved, had even suspected this, she found that now she couldn't believe it. Yet there was one part of it that made more sense now. "Doyle covered it up to help his girlfriend?"

"Doyle? No."

Caitlin had left Roisin unconscious in the clearing and run back to the house. She'd looked for Kathleen, but of course she wasn't there. When Caitlin had most needed her, she'd been at the celebration with everyone else. Caitlin had gone there next, and found Maureen at the entrance, looking for Colm. Maureen had gone to help Roisin, while Caitlin found Kathleen.

"All this for you to waste your life as a pickpocket, sleeping around with other people's men?" Deedee rounded on her. "For you, who just tried to throw her own life away?"

"It was an accident," Caitlin said.

Deedee said nothing, only stared at the chimney and the bundle in her arms. Some complicated thought process was going on there, and Caitlin was afraid to find out what the end result would be.

She had her mother's phone, limping along at 9 percent battery after several days of being unused, and she checked the call log. Michael. Kathleen was old school; she had filled out his address in her contact book. Deedee's car keys were on the counter in the kitchen. Caitlin put the address into the maps app and set off.

Deedee would never forgive her, and she shouldn't. It was right. Caitlin was unforgivable.

The journey took fifteen minutes, and then there he was, after all this time. Michael. He wasn't as old as she had thought he would be; graying at the temples and lined around the eyes and mouth, but still ruddy-cheeked, still solid. Her mother had been stooped, with starbursts of broken blood vessels all over her bloated cheeks. Life had been that much harder on her.

There was a version of the world where Caitlin would walk inside this house and find her mother, still beautiful. Where Michael would greet her with a hug and already know all about her life.

Instead, in this world, he stepped back in surprise at the sight of her.

In this world, Caitlin introduced herself.

"I know," Michael said, still standing in the doorway. "Well. You'd better come in."

In a small sitting room, Caitlin sat in a leather armchair underneath a framed print of a ship on a stormy sea. The place felt empty. She wondered if Michael ever saw the other world she had envisioned outside his door.

"Here." He reappeared with two mugs of tea, a packet of custard creams clamped between his elbow and his ribs. He sat on the end of the two-seater opposite her. "Sorry, I've no marble cake in."

Caitlin's smile faded quickly. This visit would end with her officially confessing to killing Roisin, the past finally accounted for. She stalled for time, every minute newly precious.

"Sore throat," she explained as she sipped.

"Take your time," Michael said.

"Might be a long story." Sadness unfurled in Caitlin's chest. When she left this house, it would be in handcuffs.

"I'm sorry about your mother," Michael said. "It must be an awful shock to you. We hadn't spoken in a long time."

"Me neither." Caitlin shifted in the armchair; the seat was worn, the padding squashed in the center. The sofa across from her was pristine. Michael sat alone in here. "When she called, she was always just drunk and ranting about things that didn't make sense. I stopped answering."

Michael waited until Caitlin made it clear that she too could sit in silence. "It wouldn't have changed anything if you'd answered."

"No." She knew that he was right, and yet she felt that he was wrong.

They sipped their tea together in silence.

"Michael," Caitlin asked, "what if we'd stayed?"

"Who can say? I loved your mother, I loved hanging out with you. I don't think I would have stopped being with you both, but you know. Life happens."

Outside, a cheering group of kids ran past.

"We found something." Caitlin spoke into her mug.

"Oh?" Michael put his own tea down.

Caitlin shook her head.

"You don't have to say," he continued, "but it seems you might want to."

It was time. Michael said nothing while Caitlin spoke, only nodded at the odd moment. She began with the darkroom, what had happened in there to her, to the others. How she'd survived by disassociating, blocking it out. Then what she had found, what she had brought to the light, and how the photographs were ruined now.

Finally, she told him about Roisin. The real story, the whole thing. How Roisin had wanted them to tell the guards and how Caitlin had worried they'd be punished, her mother evicted. How she was guilty.

"Wait," Michael broke in. "What did you tell Maureen?"

"Only that I'd hurt Roisin," Caitlin explained. "I don't think she knows anything else. About Colm, that is."

"Maureen was Colm's first victim," Michael said. "His father made him marry her when she turned up pregnant at fourteen; it was what you did in those days. She lost that baby, but they were married by then. It was a few years till Sean came along. We always thought . . . Well, there was the odd comment, but no accusations. I thought Maureen had put a stop to it."

"You knew what he was." Caitlin tasted betrayal. Michael had been one of the only good adults she'd known, and even he had been part of this.

"I wish you'd come to me," he said.

"I hit Roisin in the head, and she died," she continued. "Maureen tried to help her, but it was too late. Mam told me about burying her in the clearing."

"You hit her in the head?" Michael frowned. "Your mother called me, I came down. I thought I was helping. I thought you'd have been mistaken. But it was a head injury?"

Caitlin nodded.

"Caitlin, Roisin was strangled."

"No, I hit her. She fell down, she was bleeding."

"She had a cut on her head all right, but her lips were blue, her eyes were . . . Well, it was very clear that she had been strangled. You only hit her?"

"There was so much blood, I freaked out. I knew she was gone." Caitlin couldn't process what Doyle was telling her.

"Christ, Caitlin, I never . . ." Doyle looked at her, stricken, fear all over his face. "Kathleen told me you'd done it accidentally, some game you were up to. She begged me to help. I thought I was giving you a future."

"I didn't deserve one." She wrung her hands miserably.

"The blow to the head didn't kill her." Doyle was slow, emphatic. "Someone strangled her."

Caitlin understood then. Roisin's death might have been her fault, but she didn't kill her friend.

56

DEEDEE

Deedee sat with Roisin for what felt like a lifetime. The gatehouse was silent around her, the noise of the solstice celebration somehow deadened by the walls. All the dreams that Deedee had had for her sister were irrefutably gone. It was over.

Deedee rewrapped the bundle and placed it on a side table. Her movements felt dreamlike, slow. She left the gatehouse and entered the Big House by the front door.

Maureen met her at the door still wearing her coat.

"He's stable," she said. She had an overnight bag open at her feet, Colm's things for a short hospital stay. "But his medication is missing. I don't suppose you'd know anything about that?"

"Maureen." Deedee wondered how she would be able to tell her about Colm.

"Why would you do such a thing? Why would you do this to us?"

"Maureen, I found Roisin." She spoke quickly, not letting Maureen get a word in. "I know Caitlin killed her, I know you and Kathleen covered it up. I know about Colm."

She watched Maureen's face morph to something darker, pinched. She looked older, her features suddenly severe and unforgiving.

"Nothing happened. Roisin was a liar, like the rest of them. My boys didn't do anything. Neither of them. The problem was always the women, the girls. That canny little Michelle. There're bad seeds in this town. His actions were not my responsibility, and neither were the actions of those girls."

"You knew."

"This is my husband we're talking about, the father of my son; this is my life."

"Your life? You still have your life."

"And Roisin would have hers if she could have stayed away! If she had shut up! She didn't have to hang around here, she didn't have to go along with it, but she did! And then she expected me to turn on my own husband, endanger my family! I had to do it!" Maureen drew herself up in an effort to look dignified, but she was shaking, whether with fury or shock, Deedee couldn't tell.

"She told you. Caitlin was wrong, she only knocked her unconscious."

"I said she must be confused. I offered her a way out but she kept on talking. And she was going to drag Caitlin into it, she had to be stopped. I just wanted to stop her from talking."

"You could have saved Roisin," Deedee said, knowing it was true by how it landed, how Maureen flinched. "But instead, you killed her?"

Deedee hadn't realized that her heart could break any more, that there was more grief and sorrow in her, until she was picturing her little sister looking to Maureen for help. How confused she must have been, how frightened, when instead of support and kindness, Maureen had responded with violence. Roisin's last moments on this earth were marked by betrayal.

"She could have saved herself. You could have saved her, but you were too busy hanging off of Sean. All of you girls, out for yourselves."

"She was nine." Deedee's ears were buzzing like a bomb had gone off; she felt disembodied. It was too much to take in.

"And so was I once! But I took responsibility for myself, I took matters into my own hands, and I kept him."

It was sick. Deedee barely recognized Maureen now to look at her; she had been twisted and warped by her own traumas into something hideous, devoid of empathy, unable to understand the magnitude of the horrors that Colm had perpetrated on those around him, the lives he'd destroyed.

"I've been protecting you, protecting all of them since then," Maureen continued. "You really think a broken pelvis would keep a man bedbound for two decades? No, I kept him there."

"You've been sedating him," Deedee said, but she didn't believe the rest of Maureen's words. Maureen wasn't protecting the girls; she was protecting herself, her family, her reputation. "You knew what he was, and you let me just waste my life on him."

"Waste your life? That's rich! You have never been good enough for any of us! You have lived off of our goodwill!" Maureen ranted. Deedee had never heard her shout before, and it was strangely powerful, so different to her speaking voice. "If Roisin would have shut up—"

From outside, there was a loud splintering sound, once, twice, three times. The sound of a mallet hitting wood, the sound of evidence being destroyed.

Sean had finally made good on his promise to remove the darkroom.

Deedee had wasted too much time with Maureen; she had wrecked everything again. The condition of Roisin's bones was too deteriorated for forensics, and DNA was more likely to implicate any number of others—Kathleen, Caitlin, even Deedee herself—than to help her case. Colm would get away with it—they would all get away with it—if she didn't stop Sean.

57

CAITLIN

Caitlin falls asleep thinking of the sea. Cool sheets on sun-flushed skin, the phantom rocking sensation of the waves lulling her; her beach day has exhausted her and she knows that she will sleep like the dead. Grains of sand still nestle against her skin inside the suddenly too-small pajamas that ride up above her tummy. It was a proper beach day, she reflects with a smile. She remembers pelting barefoot into the sea, her feet moving so fast she thought she'd trip.

Wrapped up in the darkness like a blanket, she feels the totality of the night weighing on her, hours and hours of it left before breakfast. She should close the window, but the old net voile flutters in the frame, dancing on the sea breeze. In the sunlight, the voile is yellowed with age, but now in the twilight, it shines like silver and moves like magic.

The window glides inward against the net with a shush. A warm breeze sighs inside, and settles around her bed.

In the blackness, she feels him watching her. The smell of another person, musky and earthy, something familiar made strange in this location. Caitlin knows she must be dreaming.

When she peeks, the room is darker than ever. A shadow blots out the moonlight. Worse, the shadow grows larger, fills the window. The wooden windowsill groans as gloved hands curl over it and the shadow slips inside her bedroom.

To scream, Caitlin would need to draw breath, but the shadow sliding into the room squeezes the air from her lungs. *It's not real,* she tells herself. *There's nothing there. I am safe.*

The air shifts to accommodate him as he pushes into her home.

Caitlin wants this to be a monster. More than anything, she wants this to not be happening, but it is, and if it must, then she wishes it would be a monster. A fanged creature covered in hair, with red eyes and leathery wings sprouting from its back. She risks a glance at the window and sees a familiar belt buckle catch the light at the figure's waist. Colm sees her looking and smiles, places one finger over his lips.

They both hear the cough, the heavy feet hitting the floorboards in the room next to hers. Michael, getting up. Colm's smile vanishes, and he is sliding back out of the window when his elbow hits the window frame. The footsteps pause, and then Michael whispers, "Caitlin?"

Colm stumbles as he hits the ground, and quick as a flash, Caitlin slams the window closed. Michael hears, goes running to the back door.

"Hey!" He calls out across the fields behind the house, loud and angry. "Hey!"

The sound of scrambling and scuffling, the thwack of fist into flesh, and Caitlin stuffs her own fist into her mouth, teeth on knuckles. Her mother is going to be so mad at her.

"—out for a walk!" Colm gasps.

"Outside the little girl's bedroom?" Michael is breathless too.

"It's my land! I can go where I want! This is assault!"

A horrible laugh from Michael. "If there's been any kind of crime committed here tonight, it's not been by me."

"What's this?" Caitlin's mother, at the back door.

"A misunderstanding!" Colm says, his tone now almost cheerful. *We're all in on a joke,* his voice is saying. *Come on, lighten up.*

"Kath, I just caught him outside—"

"Caught! I wasn't caught! Can't a man walk around his own property when he can't get to sleep of an evening?"

"Michael." Caitlin's mother has sided with Colm. Caitlin hears that in her voice, her *this is ridiculous* tone. "It's late, let's sort this out in the morning. It's his field to walk in. He's hardly a criminal."

"Kath." That's all he says, but the way he says it, Caitlin knows that this is the end of Michael and her mother. It's weighed down with disapproval, disappointment, dislike.

"Sorry about this, Colm. Come on, Michael." Caitlin's mother is shuffling back inside. Caitlin hears her return to her room and close the door. Michael stays outside, watching as Colm leaves. She hears him retreat, then close the back door, pause outside her room.

"Caitlin?" Michael opens the door just a crack, his face worried and serious. "Are you all right?"

"I'm sorry," says Caitlin. "I should have closed the window, I forgot."

"Has this happened before?" he asks. "You're not in any trouble."

"No," she says. "Never."

Michael nods, and pats the doorframe. He is thinking, but she can't understand what about. He mutters, more to himself than to her, "Someone needs to do something."

"I had a really great day today," Caitlin says. "At the beach."

Michael smiles, but only with his mouth.

In the room next to hers, she hears the rumble of them talking well into the night.

When she wakes up the next morning, Michael is gone, and her mother is on the phone to a letting agent in London.

58

DEEDEE

Leaving Maureen in her front hall, Deedee ran to the back door and burst out through it, stopping in Sean's eyeline.

Sean kept swinging. One wall was breaking down. The rest would follow. Maureen lingered behind her, clearly torn between returning to her husband in the hospital and defending her son from Deedee.

"We have the photographs," Deedee bluffed. The only chance she had to salvage evidence was if anything was left in there, or if any of the negatives could be recovered.

"You don't have anything," Sean spat.

"Sure we do. Colm knows it too."

He threw the mallet aside and advanced on her. Deedee held firm. Sean had always wanted to appear to be a bumbler, but she'd seen his real face several times. He saved his worst self for her. Still, she had never seen him like this. He raised a hand as though to hit her, and then balled it into a fist and shook it in frustration next to her face. She wondered whether it was because Maureen was still there, watching them, that he didn't strike her.

"What did you do?" he roared.

"I asked him to tell me the truth." Deedee felt a weightless kind of calm. This, whatever was happening between her and Sean, didn't matter. All that mattered was finding evidence.

"Ma!" Sean called to Maureen. "I'll take care of this. Go to Da."

Deedee watched Maureen disappear back into the house and felt suddenly very unsafe.

"Did you know?" She hoped her fear didn't show.

"There's nothing *to* know!" Sean was in her face, his finger jabbing her chest. "Caitlin's fed you some total bullshit because she's nuts— you've seen her talk to ghosts, haven't you? And you, you're so stupid that you believed her!"

"I do believe her," said Deedee. "I've seen—"

"You've betrayed us!" Sean's whole head was puce, his eyes bulging.

"You betrayed me," Deedee said. "You slept with Caitlin. You're sleeping with Lucy too, aren't you? She's barely twenty!"

Sean scoffed and walked back to his mallet. He resumed swinging, and this time the mallet punched through the wall.

"That's what this is about? You're mad because maybe I had the odd indiscretion?" He pulled the mallet back out and kicked the wall. "We should have broken up a long time ago."

It felt unreal to Deedee that they would be having this long over-due conversation only now and only under these circumstances.

"Just like your da's indiscretions?" She used his term.

"There's no need to make a big production of these things." Sean swung the mallet again. The roof of the darkroom juddered and slid forward very slightly. "You know how Michelle was." He aimed the mallet at the top corner of the wall. "She did exactly what she wanted to. You saw how she acted, how she dressed."

Deedee had; she had seen it all. She had said these very words herself. She had aligned herself with the worst possible offenders.

"When did you find out?"

"It's not a big deal."

"He was so respected."

"For good reason." Sean paused before he smashed the mallet back into the wood. "He's done more for Bannakilduff than anyone else! So, what if every now and then something happened?" He put the mallet down and leaned against the darkroom. "You'd have nothing without us. You are going to lose everything if you keep harping on this, Deirdre. You are going to be destroyed, do you get that?"

He didn't even know how Deedee had ruined her own career first. Small comfort to at least have that one be by her own doing.

She saw a glimpse of something through the hole Sean had knocked into the darkroom that he didn't seem to have noticed. The back view of shelves lining one wall had been revealed. A manila envelope had fallen down behind these shelves and stuck out of the hole.

It could be nothing, she thought. But then why was it hidden?

"You have to understand, this is my sister."

"I'm so sick!" Another swing of the mallet. "Of hearing! About Roisin!"

"Look," Deedee bargained, "we can live separate lives, OK? But I can help you."

"Help me how? What do you have that I would need?"

"Well, what are you going to do? Stay some old bachelor, hanging over twenty-year-olds? Colm had Maureen, he had a cover story. You could have me."

"And why would you do that?"

"I don't have anything without you!" It was part of her ploy, yes, but the desperate truth in her words rang out in her ears. She could tell that Sean caught it.

He laughed and swung the mallet so that one hand held the handle and the other the head. He had transformed over the last few weeks, Deedee thought. Or had it been longer? Had she just stopped looking at him at some point over the years? The sweet-faced boy she had fallen in love with had morphed into the sneering, glowering man before her. She had thought he couldn't get any more horrible, and then he spoke.

"Are you proposing to me, Deirdre O'Halloran?"

The manila envelope was still sticking out of the hole, its edge flipping back and forth in the wind that had picked up as they spoke. Deedee focused totally on Sean to avoid glancing at it and drawing his attention.

"Yes," she said. She only needed him to drop the mallet, to walk away from the darkroom. Then she could snatch the envelope and hope she was faster than him.

"Howya, lads," called a cheerful voice from the front of the property.

"I don't know who that is." Deedee spoke quickly, anticipating the trouble of Sean finding out she'd called someone.

"Come on around back!" Sean called out. To Deedee, he hissed, "It'll be your fault if anything happens now."

Jo appeared, one arm raised in greeting. "I popped by when I didn't hear back from you, Dee, and saw an ambulance heading away. Got a bit concerned, so I thought I'd come up, say hello."

"Hi!" Sean dropped the mallet. He hunched his shoulders and pushed his glasses up with his index finger. "That was my da, he's had a bit of an incident. Deedee might be able to tell you more about it."

Deedee couldn't resist looking at the manila envelope. She was so close, and now that Jo was here . . . Sean followed her glance. Deedee saw the shadow of that angry man pass over his face once more. She hoped Jo had seen it too.

"He's . . . sick. Colm. Sean's dad." Deedee couldn't begin to consider how to adequately lie about this.

"Colm Branagh! I've heard of him. And this is your feller, Dee?" Jo stepped forward to shake Sean's hand. She wore casual clothes: woolly hat and duffel coat. It was possible that Sean wouldn't know she was a guard. But then she said, "Dee and I met at work. I'm new here."

Deedee noticed Sean's posture stiffen.

"We're just doing some DIY, Jo," she said. "Sorry, my phone ran out of battery. We'll have to catch up another time."

"What did you have to tell her, Dee?" Sean asked. He positioned himself behind Jo.

He wouldn't, Deedee thought. He wouldn't do anything, surely; he wouldn't be that reckless. It would be insanity, there would be no way he'd get away with. But panic still pulsed through her. She'd been so wrong about him up until now as it was.

"Just Flo—he's taken a shine to Caitlin." She inspected the nails of her good hand as she spoke. If she looked up, if she caught either of their eyes, the whole thing would be blown.

"Would ye both not like to come to the solstice party?" Jo asked. "Everyone's down there, Flo himself and all. You could grab Caitlin, we could do some matchmaking."

Deedee held her breath. Jo had caught her lie and run with it wonderfully.

The smell of bonfire drifted over to her.

"I don't think we will." Sean picked up the mallet again. "But thank you for the invitation."

"Dee could come, couldn't she?" Jo tried.

Deedee tried to signal her to shut up.

"What do you think, Deedee?" Sean asked. "Do you want to go?"

Jo had tipped her hand. Sean was suspicious.

"No," Deedee said. "No, that's all right. Sean's right, I should stay here and . . . help."

"Are you sure?" he asked.

"Yes, maybe later. Thanks, Jo!" Deedee turned away from her and hoped she would take the hint.

"It's just a shame," Jo said. Her tone was off, too bright, too casual.

Sean swung the mallet as though testing its weight. She felt him watching her, even as she looked away.

He could kill me, Deedee thought. The sway the Branaghs still held, her own insignificance, no one to advocate for her . . . Things could happen in small towns.

Jo looked back at her calmly, confidently. Deedee could understand what she was thinking: *There are two of us and one of him. We are guards, we have the power. Give me the signal and I'll arrest him right now.*

But Deedee didn't feel powerful.

Sean swung the mallet once more, this time at one of the walls he hadn't yet hit. It was symbolic. Deedee felt his reluctance to risk anything coming out of the darkroom while Jo was there, but knew that he still wanted to remind them both exactly who was in charge at this point.

"Dee's a bit of a liability, you know," he said. "Did she tell you about her special relationship with the superintendent? Very well connected. And of course, Colm has helped her too. But Deirdre O'Halloran herself? She's just a messed-up cook with a drinking problem."

She heard a ring of truth in the words and it inflamed her. What he was saying, that was his opinion. That was how everyone here treated her. It didn't have to be who she was.

Deedee had saved Caitlin's life.

Deedee could be a hero.

She waited for Sean to drop the mallet low, the head of it below his knees, and then she sprang at him, spearing him in his abdomen with her shoulder and bringing him down. Jo immediately mobilized after her, joining her in restraining him.

"The envelope!" Deedee gasped. She reached up with her bad hand and her fingers only barely grazed the edge of it.

Sean capitalized on her distraction to throw Jo off him.

"Get the envelope!" Deedee yelled at her. Sean crushed her beneath his body.

"She's mad, Jo! She's just talking nonsense!"

"Get off her." Jo grabbed the envelope.

"I'm a Branagh! I'm Colm's son!"

Jo held the envelope, her thumb positioned to open it.

"No!" Sean leapt up and dived for her. Deedee scrambled after him, jumping onto his back from behind, throwing her arms over his head. Her Garda training left her, and she simply fought to bring him down. She clasped her hands together against his throat and threw all her weight onto them, hoping to drag him backward. He turned and rammed her against the side of the house, winding her. Still, she hung on to him.

"Sean Branagh, stop resisting." Jo was in front of them. Neither she nor Deedee had their handcuffs. "You must know that it's over."

"This is absurd!" Sean spat through clenched teeth. "You're watching me be assaulted!"

Jo stepped forward to grasp his wrists just as Deedee's own car pulled up and Doyle jumped out to join the fray. Between them, they had Sean cuffed quickly. Only once he was cuffed did Caitlin leave the car.

Deedee ripped open the envelope, and they all watched as photographs slipped out and flew to the ground around them. She heard Doyle's sharp intake of breath. She heard Caitlin's smothered sob.

"Mother of God," Jo exclaimed next to her.

The pictures were older. Deedee didn't recognize the children in them, but there was no doubt about what they depicted.

These ones Colm Branagh had developed himself. They wouldn't fade away into nothing. This was the evidence they needed.

59

CAITLIN

Doyle and Jo took Sean, leaving Deedee and Caitlin together outside the Big House, looking into an empty road. Music carried over to them from the solstice party, thudding bass lines, a bright spot of light and activity out in the fields. Strings of colored bulbs lit a path through the fields toward it from the crossroads to town.

"I've done so much for them." Deedee braced herself on the wall outside the property.

Together they had pieced it together, filling in the gaps in each other's knowledge. Roisin had been injured but alive when Maureen found her in the Hanging Woods. Innocently, she had told Maureen everything and expected help. Oisinn Quinn had spotted Colm leaving the celebration and run him over while Maureen strangled Roisin. Caitlin and Kathleen arrived into the mess and Kathleen, having no other support, called Doyle for help, believing she was saving her traumatized daughter. Doyle, still fond of Caitlin and unable to turn away when asked for help, had colluded. Quinn had been able to fix the car himself in his own mechanic's garage.

"They let us think we were the problem." Caitlin was realizing that it had never been her burden, that the guilt she carried had never been hers.

She thought of Roisin, finally resting in peace now. She wondered how Deedee could possibly stay here, knowing that the community found smothering Colm's crimes easier than facing them, than considering what they meant for them, about them; that they tolerated them.

"There's no one else," Deedee said. She was doubled with the grief of it, almost hyperventilating. "I have no one else."

"You're free then. You owe no one anything," Caitlin said, stopping short of saying, *You have me.* It mightn't be true. "What did you want to do, before? Roisin wanted to travel. Sean wanted to be just like his father, Maureen wanted to be a good wife, Colm wanted respect. What did you want?"

Deedee was quiet for a long time before she said, "It's almost frightening to think of. What do *you* want?"

Caitlin had hoped that Deedee would have some secret desire that she recognized in herself too, that triggered her own wants. She thought of everything she'd done, everything she'd thought she knew about herself. It all felt like a reaction to not knowing the answer to this question.

From across the fields, the whoosh of a roller coaster swooping by in time with the thrilled screams of joy. The lights so bright.

"I think I want to go to the solstice party," she said.

Deedee laughed. A big, deep belly laugh that rumbled on long enough that Caitlin bristled a little. It wasn't such a ridiculous thing to want, was it?

"Sorry." Deedee wiped tears from the corners of her eyes. "Just, yeah. Anything in the world and you want to go there?"

Anything in the world.

It was true for both of them.

"You don't even know what you want," Caitlin said, but she smiled. "At least I've got something."

"I wanted to be Mrs. Branagh just this morning." Deedee shrugged. "Maybe I should give up on wanting things."

"Nah," Caitlin said. "Better to just kick the Branagh habit."

"Actually, I do know. I want Colm to be dead. I want Maureen to be devastated." Deedee's desires were savage, blood on their teeth; she wanted everyone to suffer forever.

"Do you want to see him one last time?" Caitlin asked.

60

DEEDEE

Deedee had been born in this hospital; she'd visited her parents here after their fatal car crash. Every time she'd been here, she'd felt the mingling of hope and despair, but now she only felt hope.

The Branaghs had underestimated her so badly that she'd underestimated herself, but she had rescued Caitlin, she had found support in Jo, she had done hard things and brave things.

A gurney crashed past them, doctors and nurses lining either side of a prone, convulsing man. Deedee and Caitlin stepped back, pushing themselves to the wall. The man had a mane of hair shot through with white, and when his arm flung out, Deedee saw a tribal sun tattoo. She also saw the fresh track marks.

"Lee Casey," she whispered. An overdose.

It had been too much for him, being back, seeing Caitlin, the way the town was. Or maybe it was just that Bannakilduff could crush a sensitive person, if they weren't careful.

Caitlin walked beside her as they passed through to Colm's hospital room.

Maureen looked up hopefully as they entered, and they watched that hope curdle into disgust. Deedee shuddered with revulsion knowing that the figure on the bed was Colm. She had been wrong; she didn't want to see this monster ever again.

"What are you doing here?" Maureen spat.

"It's over." Deedee didn't want to draw things out. "The guards know everything, including what you've done."

"The guards!" Maureen laughed. "I'm not afraid of Mick Doyle. And I'm not afraid of you two damaged little girls, so desperate for attention you'd sink to any low."

"That's how you saw yourself," Caitlin said. "Damaged."

"I am a Branagh," Maureen snapped. "That means something around here."

"So, you couldn't have the truth come out, even if it meant killing a child." Deedee had never hated like this before, didn't know she had this much hatred in her.

"I've kept him under control since then; it has never happened again." Maureen sounded level, reasonable. As though she was discussing a news item.

"Was it worth it?" Deedee asked. "Was it worth murdering her to save a pedophile?"

"Don't call him that," Maureen snarled. "And it was an accident!"

"It was murder. They know everything now, Maureen. If he survives, he'll have to answer for this. There's no protection left for him now."

Deedee opened the door and two guards stepped in.

"They're making it up!" Maureen protested. "You can't arrest him, look at him!"

But the guards were not there only for Colm.

Maureen finally needed to answer for what she'd done too.

61

CAITLIN

They followed the brightly colored light bulbs toward the scent of the bonfire, the sound of laughter and yelling, thundering rides, and pop songs. A misting rain fell, blurring everything outside of the lighted fairground.

"I think I knew," Deedee said. She had been talking a lot, more than Caitlin had heard her before. It was all coming out in a rush, everything she'd ever thought. "All these years, I knew but I didn't."

"Doyle tried to look out for you," Caitlin said. The corrosive effects of Colm's crimes had managed to ruin the closest thing she'd had to family too: the three of them, Kathleen, Michael and Caitlin. "For both of us."

"Him and Kathleen, I can picture it."

"It worked, for a while."

"Do you feel differently about her now?" Deedee asked.

Caitlin hadn't forgotten the voicemail from her mother, but she had pushed it from her mind. "She left me a message that night."

"Saying?"

Caitlin shrugged.

"Christ, Caitlin!" The old Deedee was still there, exasperated and emotional. Now Caitlin appreciated that her strength of feeling came from wanting to do the right thing. "Listen to your dead mother's last message!"

Caitlin stepped aside and pushed her earbuds in.

"I know that you're a champion grudge holder . . ." Her mother's voice was tired, but clear as a bell. The way she just launched into what she needed to say, rarely bothering with pleasantries. The way she made such bold declarations, because everything was bold in Kathleen's world, everything was extremes. ". . . and I know that I did everything wrong. I could never do right with you, but guess what? Every daughter hates her mother. All of us! My mother, now she was a bitch. She was too much, a smotherer. I got you away from her, but when you leave, you can't go back. Some places you can't get back from. Dead to her, dead to you, and no one loves their mother but no one tells you how . . . how thankless it is to *be* a mother. Everything you do is wrong, too much, too little. My mother was too much. I rebelled, then what? I was seventeen and pregnant—and God only knows what I would have given to make that go away—but then it was you. I made you, you came from my body and I had to just let you figure out the world. I didn't shame you, Caitlin, I never smothered you. I have done things you don't even know about—can never know about. Terrible things. But it was for you. You hate me. I don't blame you. Pick up, Caitlin. Please."

Caitlin's whole life she'd wanted her mother's attention and had come second to the boyfriends, the drink, the partying. Until the end of it all, she'd never even realized her mother truly wanted her in her life. This was how Kathleen loved; by centering herself. By telling her own story but finding a niche for her daughter in a supporting role. It wasn't perfect. It wasn't what Caitlin would have chosen, but it was what she'd had.

"You OK?" Deedee asked.

"No," said Caitlin. "But I want to be."

"You know," Deedee said, in the kind of faux-casual tone that suggested what she was about to say was very considered, "I reckon I might go to New Zealand."

"Won't you miss this gorgeous weather?" Caitlin gestured at the general gloom that lurked outside of the celebration's lights. "I feel like I haven't seen sunlight since I landed."

"I think I could get used to a bit of sun quicker than you'd think." Deedee grinned.

They passed stalls selling hot dogs, candy floss, hot chocolate. Soon everyone would know what had happened and they would all have their own opinions, their own judgments. Soon the whole place would be full of whispers about them, but for now they were just two more Bannakilduff residents at a party.

"I love that smell of bonfires," Deedee said. "Festive. Makes me think of the holidays—Christmas and summer. Days without responsibility."

"The solstice bonfires," Caitlin said. There were no shadows on her vision. She was not seeing anything that she should not be seeing. This was real. For years, she had still been there, running from the monster, fighting with Roisin, hating herself. And now it was over.

"Wanta go on that?" Deedee pointed at the roller coaster. It was rickety, but everyone on it was screaming and laughing and as joyful as they were scared.

"Yes," Caitlin said. "Though it might be the last thing we do."

As they approached it, the speakers overhead began to blare out a familiar bouncy synth guitar bass line.

I come home in the morning light, Cyndi Lauper began.

Deedee looked at Caitlin, and grinned.

Together, they sang along.

62

ROISIN

O K, OK, you don't know this one."

It's one of those days where Roisin feels like she has so much energy she could burst. Like whatever she is on the inside is way too big for her puny human body. She karate-chops the air as she trails Deedee around.

"Antarctica!" Deedee says, exasperated. "It's always Antarctica with that guy. Get better questions!"

"You're not listening! You have to listen!" Roisin is small and very keen to not be overlooked. It is a crime worse than any other to not listen to her, to ignore her.

"Fine." Deedee rolls her eyes and slumps against the door. The action is phony, and Roisin doesn't respect it. Deedee is playing "annoyed big sister," and she knows she herself is playing "annoying little sister" but she doesn't know how to stop it.

"The hint is *last expedition*. The last one. Think about it. Shackleton's last—"

"Last one, yeah, I get it, so? What is it, then?"

"South Georgia!"

"Where's that?"

"In South America. His last expedition, it's where he was buried!" Roisin is gleeful, overjoyed at having outsmarted her big sister.

"That's gross. And it doesn't count. It's a cheat," Deedee scoffs.

"You're only saying that because you couldn't get it." Roisin punches the air in triumph. No one beats Roisin! "Watch this, I'm gonna do a flying kick!" She aims herself down the length of the hallway.

"Roisin, no. Stop it, you're going to break something, you'll get us in trouble."

Roisin can tell that Deedee isn't just playing annoyed now, but also, she hasn't seen a flying kick before, so really Roisin is about to do her a favor.

"Hiiii-YAH!" She launches herself into the air, flinging her right leg out and then tucking the left one under it. Flying kicks are pretty hard if you don't know what you're doing, but Roisin feels she has a natural talent. Unfortunately, that natural talent meets a framed picture of her parents' wedding day and knocks it to the floor. The frame comes apart at the edges. The glass shatters. Roisin lands heavily on her hip next to the mess and rolls quickly away from it. She springs back up to her feet, her legs locked together, arms flung wide, chest to the sky, gymnast style.

"Look what you did!" Deedee cries, and she almost is crying, which is weird.

"I didn't mean to," Roisin says, but Deedee has removed the photo from the wreckage of its frame and is running her fingertips over it. Over the faces of their parents. Roisin is angry; this feels like another phony action. Deedee is playing "sad orphan" and Roisin does not want to be part of that play. "It's fine," she says. "I'll save up and get a new frame. Don't tell Granny."

"It's not fine! There was glass all over it, you could have ruined it, ripped it, anything! You're so selfish, Roisin! And stupid; how could you get a new frame anyway? With what money? You're a stupid, selfish, never-thinking baby!"

"No, you are!" Roisin shoves Deedee, who is still crouching. Deedee falls backward. Roisin is mad, but she can't help but giggle at the sight of her sister rolling around on her butt like a turtle on its shell. Surely Deedee will laugh too? "You turtle!"

"It's not funny! You're not funny! I hate you!" Deedee is back on her feet and yelling now, pushing Roisin by the shoulders, lots of small pushes leading her up to the front door, and then Roisin is outside.

"Dee!" Roisin beats on the door. "Let me in! I'm not even wearing shoes!"

In answer, Deedee throws Roisin's runners out of the living room window.

"Never come back!" she shouts.

"I won't!"

It's a beautiful day. Roisin pulls on her runners and practices her karate kick, one on each side, for each shoe. Granny finishes her shift at the hospital soon. Roisin wonders if she will be mad about the photograph, but decides quickly that she won't be. No one is ever that mad at Roisin anymore. Granny will be mad at Deedee if she gets home and Roisin is gone, though. She'll get mad and ask Deedee where she is, and then Deedee will get in trouble, and that'll show her.

"I'll stay out then!" Roisin yells to the house. She sticks her middle finger up at it and then quickly shoves the offending hand in her pocket. Hopes the neighbors didn't see.

It's warm already, a real scorcher of a day, as Dad would say. The thought of him makes her smile, even though it also makes her feel sad. *Cheer up, rosebud*, her mam would say. Yes, thinking of them is a kind of horrible nice thing, because they're gone but she still has these memories. Today the thoughts are nice more than horrible, maybe because she has all that karate energy.

She meanders down the road. The solstice celebration is this afternoon, but even if it wasn't, she would still wander over toward the Hanging Woods, toward Caitlin. Over the summer, they've become friends. Well, in the way that they do most stuff together, even though

Caitlin is kind of boring and stuck-up, and Roisin knows that Caitlin doesn't like her that much either. Still, there's mutual respect there.

She scuffs her trainers on the dusty pavement as she walks.

At least now that she knows how dangerous they are, Caitlin won't want to just stick to the Hanging Woods. The thought makes her feel a bit chilly, even though it's still sunny. She walks faster. Tomorrow she'll tell Caitlin that a real expert needs to compare her surroundings to something different. There's another, smaller copse of trees on the other side of town. It'll be an adventure, and they'll never have to go back into the Hanging Woods again.

Roisin begins to run, the thought propelling her. She runs so fast, with so much joy, that her feet barely touch the ground—she's flying! She tips her face to the warm sun. The whole day lies ahead of her.

ACKNOWLEDGMENTS

Darkrooms was written while I was on the UEA Creative Writing (Crime) MA, so thank you to Henry Sutton, Jacob Huntley, Tom Benn, and Nathan Ashman for all your tutelage. My cohort are the kindest and most talented folks you could hope to spend two years working with: Samantha De Bendern, Sasha Wilson, Debbie Mills, Alex Edwards, Sarah Edmonds, Gina Hollands, and C. M. Orson. Please write down their names, and remember I told you about them first when they become literary superstars. Special mention to Rebecca Philipson, my fellow 2026 debut author and fountain of calm.

Ed Wood and everyone at Sphere. The enthusiasm Ed had for *Darkrooms* based on a snippet carried me through the end of the process. Nithya Rae, thanks for your keen eye and patience with my anxieties!

Cal Kenny and Danielle Dieterich, editors of dreams, who totally got it from day one and were wonderful to work with.

Everyone at William Morrow for receiving this manuscript so enthusiastically and believing in it.

Cathryn Summerhayes, the most passionate and enthusiastic force-of-nature personality.

Annabel White and Jess Molloy, for that first edit and everything that followed.

Gráinne Fox, superstar US agent and the only person I'm delighted to receive a call from at ten p.m. UK time, and Maddy Hernick.

Georgie Mellor and Aoife MacIntyre, for bringing my horrible characters into translation.

Everyone at Curtis Brown, thanks also for receiving my often foolish email questions with so much patience!

Everyone at WLAG, but especially Kerry Ryan, whose kind voice lives in my head whenever I feel discouraged.

Nicolás Obregón, who has spent the best part of a decade cheerleading for me and asking, "You finished your novel yet?" Thank you for your unerring faith and belief, and for being Bad Cop when I need it.

Ruairi O'Connor, the most stalwart friend I could ask for, first reader, and overall beautiful person. Thank you. Lucy Rose, knower of all things publishing and megatalent in so many ways, thank you for being a dream friend and the greatest moral support! The McXavs, Phil and Amy, biggest love all the time. Thanks for reading early extracts and all the Squid. Nat Littlewood and Helen Webb, early readers and extract proofers, and the best brunch companions ever. It was worth the rubbish job to meet you two!

The invented place name of Bannakilduff came from Katherine Nolan of dochara.com, and I mangled her other suggestion into Kinafallia. Thank you for sharing your knowledge so generously.

Shout-out to everyone who was contractually obliged to be around me for forty hours a week in an office for the last decade while I swung on my chair and did my best to distract you, especially several of my very supportive managers: Magnus, Christian, Elisabeth, Emma.

I drew a lot on (happy! Not traumatic!) memories of being a kid running around with my siblings, cousins, and aunts and uncles in West Cork, so a gigantic thank-you must go to all of them.

My mum, who said, "Yeah, obviously," when I told her I was going to write a book. Thanks for putting up with my shit. I love you.

Joni, who cannot read because she is only a tiny cat, but who brings me so much joy daily and demands so little in return.

James, my husband, Good Cop, and best friend, who never doubted me once. "All I've done and all I will do, all I know and all I want to."

Thanks to you, for reading and spending a few hours with my awful women and me.